LITTLE GOLD

ALLIE ROGERS

Legend Press
Independent Book Publisher

Legend Press Ltd, 107–111 Fleet Street, London, EC4A 2AB
info@legend-paperbooks.co.uk | www.legendpress.co.uk

Print ISBN 978-1-7871999-5-8
Ebook ISBN 978-1-7871999-4-1
Set in Times. Printed in Bulgaria by Multiprint.
Cover design by Anna Morrison www.annamorrison.com

Allie Rogers was born and raised in Brighton. Her short fiction has been published in several magazines and anthologies including *Bare Fiction*, *Queer in Brighton* and *The Salt Anthology of New Writing*. She has performed at local live literature events including the Charleston Small Wonder Flash Fiction Slam, which she won in 2014.

Little Gold, Allie's first novel, draws on her memories of the Brighton of her childhood.

Visit Allie at
allierogers.com
or on Twitter
@Alliewhowrites

For Mim, a fabulous, fierce big sister who left me shelves of books. Wish you were here to read this one.

PROLOGUE

OCTOBER 1983

There's a herring gull on the roof of the church. It dips its beak then throws back its head in an open-throated cry. Fictional gulls live only on cliffs and fly only over open sea but the truth is rather different. In a seaside town the gulls are there wherever you go. They sit, like that one, on the slates of lichen-splattered roofs, on buildings far inland. They are pegged in every sky like paper cut-outs; they speckle the playing fields at school on grey autumn days. They live alongside you, close sometimes, but ready, ready always, to rise and stretch, to let the wind sweep under their wings and lift them away.

This one's tugging a clump of moss from the church guttering, jabbing at whatever scuttles out from underneath. She watches its determination, its stripping, persistent beak, and then, after a few minutes more, the head-thrown abandon of another cry. The gull is announcing its ownership of the roof, its belonging here in the grey-green churchyard. She's glad of its certainty, feels herself catch hold of the trailing end of the cry. It's a rope made of sound, thrown down from the sky. She can use it to haul herself from the prison of school and skirt, bowed head and bitten lip, and back into the sanctuary of her liberated mind.

She stoops and sweeps grit and a few dry, bronze beech leaves, from the flat gravestone. Her cupped hand is small but confident in the touching.

There is no lichen on the marble yet and no mottling of age. It gleams still, as perfect and startling as the gull's china breast and she would like to keep it that way. Slipping her hand inside the sleeve of her school jumper, she crouches and, with one wool-covered finger, buffs the metal letters embedded in the marble. Silver set into white like amalgam fillings in a child's perfect tooth. Necessary. Painful. She works methodically, rubbing each line and curve until the whole thing is done.

The white stone is stark in the muted churchyard – a single bed with clean sheets made of two slabs of marble. On the vertical slab, the name and simple numeric dates are marooned in too much space. No sorrowing spouse. No grieving children. The stones around seem dense in comparison, heavy with flowery text.

This stone is incongruous. Dictionary definition:

strange because of not agreeing with what is usual or expected.

Vocabulary tests are weekly for the more able children. She knows she is both able and incongruous, though demonstrating incongruity rather more than ability here, crouched on the grave stone, her skirt pushed up above her knees. When she sits, the cold of the marble burns her bare legs but, after a while, the exposed skin will numb until it's pinchable and rubbery and hardly hers at all.

Her voice isn't a whisper but the softness of someone who knows the listener is close. And the words are all the words – happenings, perceptions and desperate questions, disjointed and repeated – that she says nowhere else. She pauses for replies.

The visitor stays until the light starts to fail and the grave to glow in the deepening dusk. Then she stands and slings her school bag like a sash across her body. A small and decorated soldier, she puts her palm once more to the name and turns away.

Tonight the gull has come down to the gatepost. Sulphur-eyed, it watches her go.

This scene will play again. Over months and years the elements will weather the grave and its visitor and she will learn that nothing is static, not even death. Change will come, barely perceptible shifts in her understanding that she will be too observant to miss and too honest to deny. But she will never stop coming here, because some connections are never broken.

CHAPTER ONE

MAY 1982

Little Gold is pacing fast along the road, eyes on the patchwork of paving stones, stepping on every pink one she can reach without breaking stride too much. In her head she's reciting the words to the Lord's Prayer. She doesn't believe in God any more than she believes in Father Christmas but it's a luck thing, like the paving stones. Bad days can get better and bad days can get worse and she reckons it doesn't cost anything to try to tip this one onto a better trajectory.

Still, in spite of the need to pick her path, and the distraction of the looping prayer, she can't stop her mind from offering up scenarios of the evening ahead and none of them are welcome. She misjudges a leap to the left and lands squarely on a grey paving slab scarred with the crusted remains of pale dog shit and a grey fleck of gum. Lousy luck.

Start again, LG, and it doesn't count… Our father…

She notices the shoes first – crinkled brown leather over yellow crepe soles. They're anonymous from this far along the road. Anonymous, androgynous shoes that look like they've been abandoned there at the bottom of someone's steps. But, as she gets nearer, legs in bottle green corduroy grow out of them, followed by a strange draping of something like a pale skirt over the knees. As the whole body appears, the skirt explains itself, suddenly, as a newspaper – a broadsheet, spread open there, with a head bowed over it.

She slows slightly as she passes and glances at the newspaper. There's an upside down, grey-scale image of a building that looks rather like The Pavilion in town. Floating over it is a head of soft, white hair. As if sensing her gaze, the head jerks up and pale blue eyes lock into her own.

'I'd like to see the Taj Mahal, wouldn't you?'

The voice is precise, each word delivered whole and perfect, as if she had the question ready for whoever came along. It just happened to be her, Little Gold supposes, but she feels somehow chosen nonetheless, and stuck for words.

Her failure to answer doesn't seem to matter to the old woman. The pale eyes continue to hold her own and Little Gold finds she's stopped, the toes of her trainers on the mossy line between a pink slab and a grey.

Forgive us our trespasses…

The words of the prayer spiral away into nothing and now there's just the sound of her own breath.

The old woman smiles and fans of deep lines spring open from the outer corner of each eye. She takes a drag on a cigarette held loosely in her right hand and then starts to rotate the newspaper, spinning the Taj Mahal until it's the right way up for Little Gold to see properly. There's the dome, the pillars she thinks might be called minarets, the strips of water. The whole thing is distorted though by the shape of the bony legs over which it's lying. The woman sweeps away a scattering of cigarette ash with the back of her hand.

'I believe it's wonderful.'

She might, possibly, be mad. There are two mad old people already round Fiveways – the lady who wears a powder blue mac, filthy down the front, who everyone says is naked underneath; and the man they call The Major, who strides down the road with a cane under his arm, talking to someone who isn't there.

But she *is* here, after all, and this old woman isn't dirty, she doesn't even have the old person smell.

'Is it in India?'

'It is. So I don't suppose I shall. Perhaps you will.'

It's not something she's ever considered, going to India, and for a moment she pictures herself there, standing alongside the water, looking up at the dome against a sky that would surely be a deep, deep blue. It would be hot, a heat far fiercer than this late May day. There would be smells she can't imagine, curls of unknown language around her head. The woman's voice brings her back.

'You're from 167, aren't you?'

She sucks on the cigarette again and Little Gold lifts her eyes from the newspaper and watches the fat snake of ash lengthen. It seems that the old woman won't ever exhale, so hard and so deep she holds the smoke inside, but, at last, it pours from her flared nostrils. Little Gold replies through the stream of blue.

'Yes.'

'I'm Peggy Baxter. I don't think we've ever been introduced.'

She grinds the stub of her cigarette onto the step, tosses it across the pavement into the gutter and holds out her hand.

Little Gold takes it. The palm is warm and dry and the long fingers enfold her own with a gentle firmness that feels somehow familiar. But it's over in a moment, the handshake, and then the old woman stands.

'Time for my cat to have his tea and for you to have yours, no doubt. Goodbye.'

'Goodbye.'

She uses the garden wall to steady herself, the newspaper folded in her other hand, and Little Gold watches her ascent – not ancient and doddery but careful, considered. When she reaches her front door she turns and raises a hand before disappearing inside. The sun winks from the letterbox, biting Little Gold's eye, and she has to look away.

There are plenty of pink slabs on this stretch so she can run and she abandons the prayer, freeing her mind to replay the moments before. She pictures again the slowly rotating palace, draped across the old woman's corduroy-clad legs.

I believe it's wonderful.

She feels the press of the heavy, loose-skinned palm against her own.

I'm Peggy Baxter.

The whole thing was odd – finding her there where she'd never been before, the way she'd spoken, the fact that she wanted to shake hands. But there's something else nagging in Little Gold's mind – some faux pas of her own that she senses but can't pin down.

It takes her until she reaches her front steps to work it out. And, as she sprints up them, panting now, it comes to her. She didn't say her name back. She was supposed to say her name. She flushes with embarrassment. What a div to just stand there. Still, Peggy Baxter didn't ask. She didn't say,

'And what's *your* name?'

in the sing-song way she might have done.

The key's still under the brick so she knows she's the first one home but still she calls into the house as the door swings open,

'Hello?'

Because he might be here. It's not impossible. He might be here because he has a key. He has a key on his blue leather keyring, stamped in gold, Carisbrooke Castle, that Malcy bought him for his birthday last year.

So, he could open the door, walk in and be here, waiting here when they got back, one day.

There's no reply, just the hum of the fridge. She closes the door behind her but slips the catch so that the others won't need the key.

The smell is overpowering. It's a combination of the riotous, rotten scent of the kitchen bin, with the usual sticky undertone that is the smell of home now. The south-facing house, sealed all through the hot day, has been simmering, building up its stench, and she runs through the kitchen to fling open the back door.

For a moment she stops and looks back into the room. Beside the overflowing swing-bin, the sink is a fortress of piled crockery, cutlery protruding at angles like the weapons of snipers. A fat, black fly is circling, soundlessly, above it.

Alongside the sink, a heap of used tea bags are a small, damp hill, behind which the enemy might be lurking. She remembers Malcy's soldiers, camouflage green, plastic men they used to set up against each other in lines across the front room carpet. He'd always sneak some behind the curtain to ambush her. Back when she was too little to know how devious people can be.

Turning away, she crosses a shady little yard and climbs the steps to a ragged square of grass. Wedged in the corner of the lawn, grown tight there with the thickening of its trunk, is an aged pear tree, rising to about twelve feet at its crown and spreading gently over the gardens to the right and behind. The bark is a chequerboard of nubby softness, dense and spongy against the sole of her foot as she braces it on the trunk. She hauls herself up and into the sitting branch.

He'd said to her, when she was first able to climb it, that it was a rotten old tree, that maybe one day he'd take it out and give the lawn a bit more light. But he didn't. He never got round to that. He took himself away instead.

The sitting branch is worn smooth as glass from generations of children's bums. But for now it's hers, passed on by Ali and Malcy, and hers alone. Letting her body find its place, she relaxes into the curve of the branch. She's wearing her blue cotton dungarees, tough and containing, the bib locked in place like a breastplate of armour.

The tree has not long lost its blossom and the leaves are still young. Little Gold pinches one between forefinger and thumb and feels its spring, the slight stickiness of something fresh from the bud. A rotten old tree, he'd said. But no rotten tree could do this every year, make all this from its ancient, brittle body.

She closes her eyes. It's a trick to amplify every other sense and it never fails. She can feel the cradle of the branch against her spine; smell cut grass suddenly, drifting from a garden down the road; hear the faint shouts of the boys over in the park. One of them will be Malcy, holding up his hand,

Pass!

No-one will.

Close beside her there's a wing-beat – feathers rippling the air. The rippling stills and she imagines, surely it can only be that she imagines, the tiny tick of a bird's blinking eyelid.

She opens her own eyes. Oblique, to her left, there is a blackbird, splitting his yellow beak and starting to sing. It's the song of a summer evening, pouring out, seasoning the air with its rolls and trills.

How lucky must this be? How lucky? Uninvited, with no wishes, it's surely as good as a four leaf clover or a solid chocolate Kit Kat with no wafer inside. And she keeps still, still, to preserve the blessing.

'LG! Little Gold! Are you up the tree?'

The bird flies.

'LG!'

She looks through the leaves. Ali's leaning out of her bedroom window, her hands on the sill, white arms braced and long hair framing her face. She's peering at the tree but not seeing her here, so close and so hidden.

'LG!'

A wash of anger over it now; she has to reply.

'Yeah! I'm here.'

'Bring the washing in!'

'Can't you?'

'I'm working for my bloody A levels, in case you've forgotten, and you're sitting in a tree. I put it out this morning. Just do it.'

Her head disappears and there's a squeal and thud as she lowers the sash. Little Gold climbs down and picks up the overturned laundry basket.

The washing is a mess of lights and darks, odd socks, everything bunched and twisted. There's one of Mum's skirts hanging in wonky, concertina pleats; Ali's best jeans; some of Malcy's pants and just one of her own, favourite orange socks.

The bra is one of Ali's. At its centre there's the body of a butterfly, spreading its wings across the shiny cups. As she yanks it from the line it catches on the strap of Little Gold's watch, fixing itself to her wrist like a lingerie viper. She shakes it off violently and it curls atop the pile waiting its moment to strike again.

Hefting the chaotic basket of clothes, sleeves and legs trailing, onto her skinny hip, Little Gold picks her way down the back steps and into the stinking kitchen.

CHAPTER TWO

Peggy's appointment is the last of the afternoon and the young man jangling keys is clearly keen for her to be on her way. As the door swings closed, he steps in to lock it behind her, glancing through the wire-meshed panel of glass. She catches the youthful, brown eyes but he ducks his head and concentrates on the lock.

Best not to encourage an old lady to interact, especially one who comes here alone.

But perhaps that's ungenerous of her. Perhaps he just wants to get home, out of the garrotte of collar and tie and into what's left of this glorious day.

She turns into a side-street that runs down towards the sea, away from the roar of a double decker bus belching exhaust that she feels in her chest. The intense heat of the day has faded but it's echoing in the bricks of the low wall on which she sits to light up. She stretches her legs across the sun-soaked pavement, flicks her lighter, inhales. She smokes with her customary dedication, letting the rattle of the cough roll up and out with the first exhalation, holding the passing moment steady with the drawing in of the glowing tip.

The street runs away towards the sea and, as Peggy sucks in the last of her smoke, her eyes are fixed on the spangled water. The cig has done its job and she feels revived, soothed, and surprisingly tempted by the beach. It's not sensible when she should probably get home and have a rest. Crossing the coast road, she takes a flight of steep steps that lead down to a lower prom, beyond which the pebble beach descends to the sea. It's calm today and she hears her mother's voice in her mind,

It's like a mill pond.

It was always that on a calm day and, on the days when, whipped by wind, it brought breakers up to fling shingle over the prom, Mum would declare it *a bit choppy*. A lifetime living beside the sea and she'd applied just those two categories. But then, the sea was a backdrop for Mum, the scenery past which she rushed to the market or the chemist, not something to sit beside, not something to watch.

What are you mooning at, Margaret? Come along, we've got things to do.

There are a few folk dotted across the beach today. The trippers' world of lollipop lights and slot machines doesn't reach far and then the people of Brighton stake their claims – loosening work clothes, kicking off sticky shoes, smoking, chatting. Peggy takes her place, her back against the pebble bank, her face turned to the glitter of the sea. No-one will speak to her and she need speak to no-one. Thank God.

The appointment, the need to find words to satisfy someone else, has been an effort and it's a relief now to be alone again, with just the regular thump of wave onto shingle and the tumbling drag of stone over stone as the water retreats.

The sea repeats its natural litany. If the tumble of questions never ceases, no more does the unchanging answer of wave on beach and that's a comfort. Peggy isn't a tranquil woman, not at the best of times, but she knows how to sit with her restless mind. Here the stones rattle their panic and turmoil but every time the wave answers. And that's enough.

Looking through the racks of leaflets in the waiting room, she'd passed over every one that smacked of religion. Line drawings of daffodils and crosses, offers of sponge cake and fellowship, none of them had tempted Peggy. She leaves church to other people. Nothing has ever appealed in the promise of everlasting life or the all-seeing eyes of a deity and there's always the obvious problem too. Even now, when the local Methodists are determined that any single old lady must be in need of coffee mornings or friendship visits, Peggy steers well clear. This is her church, she thinks, and she's given it a life-time of attendance.

But if Peggy has come for memories, she's not finding them

today. Somehow the beach is demanding that she be right here with it, now, on *this* May day. There are three youngsters at the water's edge, their spiked hair and t-shirts splashed with sea-water and the scrawled names of rock bands she doesn't recognise. They're larking about, catching each other's wrists and shrieking as the water rushes around their ankles, and she watches them for a while. They seem oblivious to her stares. She's just an old woman. Just an old woman watching.

An old woman who won't be able to sit here very much longer. The low sun is weak now and already the breeze is cooling the skin of her chest through her cotton shirt and numbing her fingers. The nail beds are lilac, bright as petals as she trails her palms over the stones. The blankest, blue-grey flints are her particular favourites but today the fates bring her a piece of pink quartz. It's the sort of pebble you never find on Brighton beach if you go looking for it. She slides it into her pocket and clambers to her feet, aware, suddenly, of the growl in her stomach.

In the arches on the prom there's a chippy, with a blackboard out offering tea and coffee, and Peggy counts coins into the pink palm of a youngster at the till. The girl wipes her hands on a greasy apron and starts to shovel the steaming chips onto their bed of paper.

'Open or wrapped?'

'Open.'

Taking the warm pouch across the counter, she adds too much vinegar, a thick crust of salt, and eats them from her fingers as she walks west, towards the Palace Pier, the vinegar singing in her nostrils. This is unexpected appetite, both for the exercise and the food, and she eats the lot, even picking out the treasure from the bottom of the paper – the crispy bits and the puffs of golden batter that swam free in the fryer.

Crossing the coast road, Peggy stands at the entrance to the Dolphinarium, closed now for the day. She thinks of the creatures inside, circling in the pool of blue water, blinking their round eyes at the never-changing horizon of tiered seating and strip lights. And as she chucks her chip paper into a bin, she takes a last look at the sea and imagines the captive dolphins set free, thrashing their tails as they swim the length of the pier and out into the open water.

The bus stop at the Old Steine is deserted and, checking her watch and the timetable, Peggy realises she's got a half hour wait until the next one. A yawn takes her by surprise, forcing her mouth wide and bringing in its wake a shudder of exhaustion. She's got money in her purse. She can splash out on a taxi. It's reason enough.

There's one at the rank nearby and she gives the address to the driver before sliding into the back. Letting her head rest against the car seat, she watches the town roll by. The Pavilion, ridiculous meringue of a thing that has somehow succeeded in making itself unremarkable here; the bays and railings of the tall Regency buildings and then the flints of garden walls fronting Edwardian terraces as they get further out of town. She blinks slowly, drinking down the evening, the softness of the air from the driver's lowered window and the patches of sunshine clinging still to privet hedges and front doorsteps. Her whispered words are turned away from the driver, not meant to be heard but needing to be said.

'Not a bad home town, Peggy Baxter.'

The taxi turns a corner and ploughs up the final stretch of hill, alongside the park opposite her house. Staring out, through the flickering trees and bushes, past the deserted tennis court, she sees a child on the swing in the playground. Her heart lifts at the soaring arc of movement, the blonde hair streaming from the head, as the child hangs back from the chains and lifts its face to the sky. It's her again. That same child. The one from 167. The one they call Little Gold.

CHAPTER THREE

Ali bangs down each plate in turn. She slams a handful of cutlery into the middle of the table and falls into the chair next to Malcy with a sigh.

The beef burgers are grey and shrunken, curled at the edges like upturned frisbees marooned in the centre of their plates. Little Gold pokes hers with a fork but it repels the attack without admitting even the tip of a tine.

Malcy digs, avidly, at the rubbery meat, stabbing and tearing until he manages to rip off a battered lump. His chewing is a sticky, open-mouthed business, accompanied by noisy huffs through his nose. After swallowing, he drops his cutlery with a clatter and scratches at the rings of livid eczema that run around his neck.

Little Gold glances at her sister. Ali's looking steadfastly away from the table, into the far corner of the room, her bloodless fingers gripping the seat of her chair.

Malcy takes a swig of squash, wipes his mouth on the back of his hand and shakes his blonde fringe from his eyes.

'Ali, have you got any money for my football subs?'

He picks up his cutlery and resumes his assault on his burger. Little Gold notices marks on his inner forearm – regular dark smudges, the bruises made by fingertips. She pictures the gripping paw of one of the park lads, Wayne Whittaker maybe, each finger sunk deep into her brother's arm, the nails cutting into the soft, pale skin.

Ali lets out a snort of derision.

'Erm, let me think…'

She holds her index finger to her forehead as if pondering some great mathematical puzzle.

'No.'

Her voice is dripping with snide, green and bitter as bile from an empty stomach. She tucks a strand of hair behind her ear and, pushing back her chair, goes to the sink to re-fill her glass with water. Malcy's reply is barely audible.

'I jus' wondered.'

Little Gold considers her plate again. She wishes for something to sit alongside the damp lump of grey meat – peas maybe, mash or chips or Green Giant sweetcorn with a melting blob of marg. But there's nothing else on their plates tonight, just the bread packet lying, slouched and gaping, in the middle of the table. Malcy reaches across to take a slice, slaps the ketchup bottle to deposit a large puddle in the centre, stuffs the mangled remains of his burger into the folded bread and licks his fingers. Little Gold considers doing the same but it looks even less appetising wrapped in the pasty slice of Sunblest so she contents herself with adding ketchup to her plate and, after extensive sawing with her knife, succeeds in rendering the burger into manageable pieces.

Malcy pushes back his chair.

'I need to find my shin pads.'

He runs down the hall and clumps up the stairs to their bedroom. Little Gold calls after him.

'I think I saw one under your bed, Malc!'

There follows, from overhead, a sequence of thuds, followed by the crash of Malcy jumping off a bed onto the floor. His style of looking for things is always noisier than it has to be. Ali winces at the crash and grips her chair again. Everything Malcy does these days, whether close to her or at the other end of the house, seems to cause her physical pain. She turns her gaze back to the table and to her own plate.

She hasn't got a burger, of course she hasn't, and her solitary slice of bread is cut into triangles, each one topped with a small sticky mound of cottage cheese. She picks up the left-hand triangle and takes a delicate bite, tucking her hair behind her ear again. Little Gold lays her cutlery gently on her plate and keeps her voice low.

'When's Mum back?'

Ali is still chewing, on and on, surely reducing the mouthful of bread to just a slimy pulp. At last she swallows and places the triangle carefully back into its place with one small crescent missing.

'Probably by eight. Dunno. Clive said she needed to make up the time from her headache last week.'

She lifts the piece of bread again, rigid as a Thunderbird puppet, and takes another mouse-bite. Little Gold coughs, fighting the urge to scream.

There's a knock at the door and Malcy scrambles down the stairs to answer it.

'Hi, Kev, I've lost a shin pad. Hang on a minute, yeah?'

He scrambles back upstairs and resumes the noisy search.

Malcy's best mate Kev is shuffling on the front step. Like Malcy, he's wearing the latest Albion shirt but, unlike Malcy, he has the whole, perfect kit – from socks to towelling sweatbands on his wrists. As he shifts about, there's the scrape of studs on concrete. Little Gold swallows the last mouthful of her miserable meat and waves down the hall.

'Hiya, Kev!'

'Hi, LG.'

He's got a good six inches on Malcy even though they're in the same year at Parklands. His shoulders are broader too and his voice is gruff when he speaks. Little Gold abandons her plate and goes to the front door, peering around Kev's legs to the path and steps beyond.

'You got Jake with you?'

'Nah, Dad says he can't be trusted at training after last week.'

Kev has a puppy, something black and white, soft around the edges still, with over-sized paws, which he brought to the park a few days ago. Malcy says it's a collie-cross. Little Gold longs for it, suddenly; longs to push her fingers into its fur and hang on tight. She shoves the ache away and finds a smile.

'Was he trouble?'

'Yeah! Got on the pitch, pissed on the half-time fruit bag…'

She laughs. A car horn toots from the bottom of the steps and Kev's head jerks towards the noise.

Little Gold cranes her neck and there, at the bottom of the steps is a silver estate car with the engine running. She can see the back of a man's head in the driving seat – Kev's dad, Roy. He's the coach, not that they're a proper team yet. Malcy says it's 'the early stages' and Roy's going to set it all up properly for next season and get them in the local league. She sees the head turn and Roy's face peering up the front steps. What's Malcy bloody playing at?

'I'll get him, Kev, hang on.'

Their bedroom is a fug of warm air and chaos. They haven't drawn the curtains all day and the light, through the thin, orange polyester, is bright as Fanta. Malcy's hurling stuff out from underneath his bed – clothes, comics, towels and bits of board games are raining down around him.

'Malcy, calm down. Look, over there!'

She reaches past her brother and tugs the corner of his shin pad clear from underneath a buckled copy of the *Radio Times*. It's the one she'd brought up here after Christmas, the one with a swirl of multi-coloured birds over a Christmas bell. She'd been planning to cut that out, to make a card for Mum and Dad for next year, to be super-prepared.

Malcy grabs at the shin pad and leaps up.

'Thanks, LG...'

'You got your inhaler?'

'Yeah!'

She follows him as he gallops down the stairs and comes to an abrupt halt at the bottom. There's a taller figure on the doorstep beside Kev, blocking the light from the front path.

'Ah, what kept you, Malcolm? Trying to get out of warm-up laps?'

Roy's wearing a bright blue Adidas tracksuit. The white stripes bulge at his upper arms and thighs and around his neck there's a whistle strung on a white bootlace. He exudes the same clean, pressed perfection as Kev, just more of it, and Little Gold's aware, painfully, of her brother's odd socks and the tangle of his hair at the back where he hasn't brushed it properly for a while. She steps through the door and pulls it gently closed to obscure the view into the house.

Malcy's still trying to get the missing shin pad jammed into his Co-op bag. She watches it twisting and pressing, distorting the plastic until it pearls and threatens to tear. She wants to take it from him, calm him down, show him how he could just slide in the shin pad alongside its pair, with no damage done. He's stammering out a reply to Roy as he struggles.

'Sorry, Roy, I was, I lost one of my shin pads.'

Roy pushes up the cuff of his tracksuit and checks the time on a chunky, digital watch. His wrist is splattered with thick, dark hairs.

'We'll be fine as long as there's no traffic in Patcham.'

Malcy finally succeeds in getting the shin pad into the bag and Roy laughs.

'Right then, lads, last one to the car's a pansy...'

Kev shoves Malcy in the chest and leaps down the steps two at a time ahead of him. Roy strides after them and Little Gold is just backing through the door when he glances over his shoulder at her.

'Goodbye, young lady.'

She feels the crawl of the words across her chest like a black beetle and steps swiftly inside, closing the door behind her. Adults don't know, of course they don't know, how much she hates it. How could they? It's just a thing people say and, after all, Malcy's 'young man' as often as she's 'young lady' and he doesn't mind. He doesn't care. Given his life among the boys in the park, his usual title of 'Malcy Woofter', it's probably a relief. It's just her that hates it. Properly hates it.

She hears the faint slams of the car doors and the rev of the engine as they drive away. He'll be gone until half eight. She glances into the kitchen, where Ali's still sitting at the table, before plodding up the stairs and back to their room.

Lying on the floor, just inside the door, is Malcy's inhaler. It must have fallen out of his bag. She slides the small grey cylinder onto his bedside table and then crosses the fingers on both hands for a moment, just as a precaution.

The room's stifling so she tugs open the curtains and heaves the heavy sash window up a couple of inches. It jams in the frame and won't go any higher but cooler air streams in and washes over her body. It's a huge relief because she's been too hot all day in this old sweatshirt of Malcy's. She crosses her arms and hauls it over her head. The t-shirt underneath, puckered, horribly revealing, is damp in the armpits. Better have a bath.

Radio One is floating up the stairs as Little Gold shouts over the banister.

'Ali! I'm having a bath!'

There's no reply.

Wedged among the clutter on the window sill is a sticky plastic bottle holding the dregs of some green bubble bath. It looks ancient but there's only a sliver of soap left, so she tips the bottle into the stream of water from the hot tap and chucks it into the bath, where it bounces like a listing ship. Dropping her clothes onto the floor, she steps quickly into the water, averting her eyes from her naked reflection in the mirror over the sink.

The water's tepid, piney and good. Closing her eyes, Little Gold feels it more – cooler, sweeter, fresher. Outside there's the noise of a mower, stopping suddenly, a ball being kicked against a backyard wall. She lets out a slow breath and floats, her toes nudging the end of the bath, toying with the plug chain. The house, its smell masked by the pine scent, its chaos blanked out for a moment, recedes and Little Gold feels her shoulders relax.

'Dad!'

The shout is from somewhere over the back. It's just the one word and she doesn't hear the summoned dad reply, but it's enough to break the moment and she opens her eyes, fixes their swimming gaze on the bath taps, and can't help but remember.

She remembers the morning he told them he was going. How Ali had woken early and found him and Mum together at the kitchen table making plans for him to leave, how she'd made them come upstairs to her and Malcy's room and tell them too.

'So I won't be living here any more.'

The street lights had still been on, heavy January rain turning to sleet as he'd spoken, hunched at the end of Malcy's bed in his black dressing gown.

'... met a lady called Sally. She has two children, Simon and Olivia. Simon's a bit older than Alison and Olivia a year older than you, Malcy.'

She can remember Malcy's sobs, sobs from deep down in his wheezy chest, Ali storming from the room, and her own silence. And the sleet had started to slide down the windows, making piles of ice, lit by the street lamps, in the corner of each pane.

Once Mum had wrapped Malcy's wailing head in her arms, he'd turned to her. She remembers his exact words, so unusual was it for him to address her by name.

'Are you okay, Little Gold?'

And her reply.

'I'm fine.'

And if it hadn't been true, which it hadn't, she'd somehow believed that it would be. Being the youngest wasn't the same as being the weakest, after all.

Three days later he'd left for Hemel Hempstead and his new job for a company selling Roneo Duplicators. She thinks now of his duplicator family – Sally, Simon and Olivia. A wife, a boy and a girl. That's right. That's enough, isn't it? No strange Little Gold to explain to anyone. He's trimmed away the excess, started again with a family probably better, probably so much better, than them.

And now they have just a scrappy note, his new address, stuck to the fridge with a magnet from last year's summer holiday. The magnet's shaped like an ice cream cone and across the cornet it says *Shanklin* in curled turquoise letters. Mum had bought it for shopping lists and letters home about school trips and dentist appointments and all the other things that used to happen in their old life. It holds just his address, the address where they could, she supposes, write to him.

Is that what he's imagining will happen? It hasn't happened, not so far as she knows. The thought of Malcy voluntarily putting a pen to paper is ridiculous. And Ali? In her mind she hears the spongy thud of the fridge door and her sister's hissed words.

'It'll be a cold day in hell before I get in touch with that bastard.'

And Mum had cried. And gone to lie down. And now, now she isn't even sure if Mum has been in touch with him and she can never find the words to ask. They catch and twist in her throat. And each week that passes solidifies the change around them all – crusted, caked, like the filth of the kitchen, this new form of family has emerged. Ugly and misshapen, scaled and hardened, held in the sealed house, they are this. Whatever was here before has gone.

Little Gold sniffs and pinches away a snake of snot from her upper lip, letting it slip from her fingers into the bath water.

Enough, LG.

There's no shampoo so she scoops up a handful of foam and dollops it on her head. Then she takes more and uses it to wash under her arms. There's still one hair, alone, on the right. She tugs it until it burns but it doesn't budge.

This has happened too, this swift and ugly unpeeling and erupting of her body. Nothing in it is right and yet it calls her, nudges her into hot sensation and demands that she notice. Scooting her finger tips through the hair between her legs, she rubs into the curling folds and lingers for a minute, body drifting in the soft water and mind blanking to just the press and hum and want of it.

'LG! Hurry up! I need the toilet!'

Her head emerges with a jerk, the peace fractured and anxiety rushing her. She feels filthy and caught, clambering quickly out of the bath, sloshing water onto the already damp mat. Rubbing her hair just a couple of times she pulls her pyjamas over skin still running wet.

'Come on!'

Ali's voice has the edge of panic in it and as soon as Little Gold looses the bolt, she bursts in, bundling her out with spiky fingers. There's too much white in her eyes.

'God, talk about slow!'

The door slams.

In the kitchen, two of Ali's triangles are still on her plate but beside the kettle, under the biscuit cupboard, there's a scattering of crumbs, raisins and sugar crystals. Little Gold opens the cupboard. Where there had been a full packet of fruit shortcake there is now just a twist of wrapper holding no more than three biscuits.

She goes into the front room and puts the telly on. It's *Are You Being Served?* Captain Peacock is raising his eyebrows as Mrs Slocombe talks about her pussy. The audience laughs but not quite loud enough so she turns up the volume. Miss Brahms adjusts her stocking and Mr Grainger grimaces. The audience laughs again. Little Gold laughs too, to make some more noise in her head. And again, without the audience, in some quiet moment that isn't even funny. And again, again, until the titles are rolling over the clink and ching of the music and there's the ticking clock and the announcer saying it's time for *Odd One Out*.

After a few minutes she hears the bolt shoot back on the bathroom door and the toilet flushing. Then the smell of Dettol slides down the stairs – caustic and violent but not quite strong enough to cover the tang it's there to mask.

CHAPTER FOUR

Peggy's sitting in her front room, a cooling mug of tea on the small table beside her and a cigarette burned out in the ashtray, when she becomes aware of the sound of claws shredding fabric beside her ankles.

'Stop it!'

She leans down and swipes with a rolled newspaper at the cat's wavering tail but he twists sideways and darts out of the room.

The velour of the settee is ragged. She tugs away a few of the longer strands and deposits them in the ashtray. It's a losing battle but it hardly matters. He isn't the first beast to have used that spot as a chosen scratching post and the thing's far beyond repair.

Startled by the phone, Peggy gets up and hurries into the hall. She lifts it from the cradle praying for a wrong number.

'502-494?'

'Hello, Peg.'

'Vern! How's tricks?'

'Fine, darling!'

Could he ever say anything else? It's a knee-jerk, an unchosen, sing-song response that she knows better than to trust. Sure enough, his voice drops to a whisper, the words forced through teeth she imagines gritted, lips held close to the honeycomb mouthpiece of the phone.

'Well, diabolical actually. If this man says one more word to me today I swear there'll be murder. It'll be in the *Argus* tomorrow, I promise you. Horror at Hove Park Homosexual Hellhole.'

She pictures him hunched on the Lloyd Loom chair they have beside the telephone table, his bony shoulders rounded, and wonders how long he's put it off, the urge to phone her and let rip. She can't have it, not this evening, so she diverts him, takes his words and repeats them, gently mocking, letting him know she's not keen on a stream of bitterness.

'Hellhole? With Dick's choice in objets d'art? I hardly think that applies.'

He laughs and his voice returns to its usual, musical warmth. Put-on or genuine, she can't bring herself to care tonight as long as there's no need for her to indulge drama.

'Yes, well, maybe that's why you're not a sub at the *Argus*. But, honestly, Peg, he's driving me dotty today and I'm desperate for a break. Can I come round this evening? Gin rummy? I'll provide the gin?'

'Can't tonight, Vern love. Sorry. I'm out.'

'Oh no… Well, just remember it's on your head when I'm hauled away in chains tomorrow for decking him with his best bloody Clarice Cliff.'

'Ah, now, don't do that, I love that jug!'

'Hmm, well, needs must.'

'What's he doing that's irritating you so badly anyway?'

'Oh, every little thing he can. Honestly, darling! But it's too tedious to drag it all out over the phone… What've you been up to?'

Peggy twists her finger in the coiled flex of the receiver, blinks, sees the beach in her mind, and then the child, the blonde child.

'Absolutely nothing and a lot of it.'

'Well that sounds like Peggy Heaven.'

'Yes.'

'Shame about tonight though.'

'Yes. Now you go and make that man a drink and suggest he takes you out for dinner, eh? Al Forno or somewhere? And then make him laugh all bloody evening.'

'Huh.'

'You know you can.'

'I know.'

'And let's get together soon. How about a meet in town one of these sunny days?'

'Well, when you can spare the time…'

'Vern, stop it. You'll get me fretting you're really cross.'

'Sorry, darling, of course I'm not. Be sunk without you, HMS Peg!'

'Ditto, HMS Vern!'

'Let's speak soon, darling.'

'Of course.'

''Bye!'

''Bye!'

She puts down the phone and leans back against the wall, feeling the trembling thump of her heart receding from her throat and the gentle fizz of adrenalin in her limbs. From the front room she can hear the cat at the settee again.

'Shaw! Shaw-aw! Tea time!'

She goes into the kitchen, followed by the galloping of heavy cat on lino.

'Rabbit flavour tonight, Mr Puss?'

He's been a good cat, this one. Fond of laps and a hopeless hunter, just what she needs these days. Vi was the one who could deal with dismembered sparrows and maimed mice. Peggy is, in spite of her firm assurances to the contrary, both squeamish and sentimental about the fate of small creatures in a house with a cat and she has always been so.

It was a shock to learn the brutal reality of carnivore as pet. Aged eight, with her first one, Daisy, young Margaret Baxter had faced the truth that a domestic cat is a small tiger. The memory comes whole and stark with white fur and needle teeth.

A flash of white across the yard and through the kitchen door. There's something wrong with the look of her, something distorted and alarming. Daisy Cat, a proud killer, raised fur running down her spine in peaks and her jaws gaped around the brown feathered corpse of a sparrow.

It had taken a week until she'd wanted to stroke her again. But she did, of course. And when Daisy had met her own bloody end, under the wheels of Moses Benezra's motorbike, she'd cried herself to sleep.

We're hardly consistent creatures, of course we're not. So many attractions are laced with revulsion, or, if not quite that, a certain disquiet. Shaw has turned his head to one side and is chewing hard on the sticky meat, his tail raised and fluttering.

Peggy sits in the back garden for the last hour of daylight, with a book, a cig and a satiated Shaw, all soft-pawed moggy now. He flops onto his side, offering the long, brownish fur of his underside for her delectation.

Along the road, past garden walls and leggy hedges, she can see the top branches of the pear tree where she first noticed the child. It was early spring, a couple of years ago now, when she mistook her for the older brother who's small and blonde too. But she soon realised that the child in the tree was the youngest girl, Little Gold, and ever since she's looked out for her.

The particular curve of the branches means that Little Gold is never hidden when viewed from Peggy's garden. The tree opens up to present her, even in high summer, framed in green, reading her book or staring into the sky. It's an appealing sight, a child in a tree, and this one has become something of a talisman. Even now she feels it will be a good day when she sees Little Gold. But this evening the tree is empty, swaying in a rising breeze. It's probably too late now, she won't be out again this evening.

Peggy's no good at guessing the ages of children. Children are not her forté, not her territory. But this one is still at the middle school, so she must be no more than twelve. Twelve. Peggy reaches inside to find a perception, a sensation, something in herself that she has carried from her own twelve-year-old life. It's hard to be precise. The memories are layered and slippery. Gymslip. Sherbert lemons. *The Prisoner of Zenda*. Yes, twelve, about twelve, was when she'd started to read long books, for long hours, in the little back bedroom in Arundel Road.

But the memory fades and Margaret Baxter pops like a soap bubble. Instead, Peggy pictures the child again, just as she was the other day in the street, standing on the pink paving slab, looking into her eyes. She'd been using just the pinks as she came along the road, head bowed, making bandy-legged progress with the occasional leap necessary. And Peggy had noticed, noticed her coming and been ready with something to say. She'd been wearing dungarees like a little American hick. What they can wear now, it's so varied, so endless. It's a world with all the categories breaking open and blurring. Not her world. Not her world of dividing lines.

And there she'd stood, the child, her blonde hair all rats' tails and her fingernails not too clean.

Peggy rubs her palms together, conscious of the advancing shadows, of the darkening silhouette of the child's tree against the sky. They summon her out of the perch, call that strange name into the branches, and the child climbs down. Little Gold.

Back in her kitchen, Peggy waits beside the gas ring, warming her palms and watching the blue flames licking the kettle. When had she last climbed a tree? Maybe that time she and Vi had gone to the New Forest camping with Magsy and Jean? Yes. They'd had to leave the camp site when Jean couldn't take the staring any more and had followed paths deeper into the trees, until they were far from all the eyes. She and Mags had stripped a clearing free of bracken and they'd pitched their little canvas hideaways. It had been wild and glorious, huddling in their woollies in the real darkness and, yes, early one morning she'd met Magsy crawling out of their tent with a particular gleam about her.

'Up the tree, Peg, come on!' Hand over hand, a slow burn beginning in her thigh muscles, an ache in her hips as they climb. Ridiculously high they go, until the tree tops are a sea of greens around them and they sit, legs astride a branch, facing the rising sun. An unexpected urge to kiss then. Panting, catching eyes. But butches, best mates, friends, and they pull away, laughing. Beyond the edge of the woodland, above an open field, something small and dark is hanging in the sky. Magsy points, 'Kestrel!'

Peggy's aware, suddenly, of her own reflection in the convex kettle. Old. She closes her eyes and there's the child again, her earnest face, green eyes, brave stare. She wants to tell her, can't imagine how she'll ever find the opportunity, never to stop climbing trees.

CHAPTER FIVE

Little Gold starts running from the corner but they're close behind. All the way along Edburton Avenue she can hear them, their taunts on her tail, turning the heads of other kids and mums with little ones.

'Strip the willow with Damian! Strip the willow with Damian!'

She can feel their presence too, heavy, bearing down on her as she sprints away. They're one girl with many heads. They're the hydra from her book of Greek Myths. When she'd asked for that for her last birthday, Dad had said,

'What do you want that for? Wouldn't you rather have something a bit more modern?'

And that goes to show how little he knows, because here's a bloody hydra after her in the actual here and now.

At the last road before the park she manages to dart across in front of a laundry van. The girls are forced to stop at the kerb but they keep up the chant, shouting over the noise of the passing vehicle.

'Strip the willow with Damian!'

She's almost at the fence around the playground, the hoops of metal as high as her belly but there's a trick to getting over, a trick Malcy taught her.

Just reach up with your right hand. Push down. Push down and jump and believe you'll get over. Then you will.

It works. She stumbles slightly but doesn't fall and runs on, towards the swings, desperate to be airborne.

It's Miss Spastic Spatling's fault. Spastic Spatling has made her day impossible, dragging her out the front in country dancing to demonstrate, making her take Damian's hand and prance about. And the girls watched it killing her. It wasn't his fault. There's nothing wrong with him, Damian Peters, but there's everything, everything wrong with her, and they can see it.

Little Gold takes the middle swing and kicks off from the ground as the girls come through the gate. They have to stop. She has to stand it until they stop. She can't let them chase her all the way home or they'll have won and it'll be worse tomorrow.

They aren't chanting any more. They wander over to the swings as if they haven't even noticed she's there, their Hydra heads tucked low and close, whispering and giggling. She imagines their necks elongating and entwining as they blink up at their quarry.

'Hi ya!'

The Hydra is speaking through Chloe's prissy, pink-lipped mouth.

'You're not upset are you?'

Of course you mustn't speak to a beast like this. It will find a way to take your words and use them against you. Little Gold swings higher, imagining a sword, the slicing sweep of a sword removing each head in turn.

Chloe takes the swing next to her. Little Gold can feel her gaining height, until they're side by side and she can continue her speech – syncopated, treacle-dipped – at the moments their paths cross.

'We're not being bitchy… We think it's really sweet… You and Damian…'

The rest of the Hydra heads are chorusing their agreement from the ground. This isn't going to stop and the swing has failed her, she's more trapped than ever.

Little Gold drags her trainers across the concrete and comes to a juddering halt. Chloe stops beside her and all the girls crowd in tight before she can stand. With a delicate finger and thumb, Chloe takes a strand of her hair. It's hanging like yellow thread, unwashed for a few days, just touching the bottom of her ears.

'Why don't you grow your hair?'

The girls chorus approval out of all proportion, their words rolling over each other as they bind tighter, close in. One of the mouths smells of cherry flavour Tunes but she can't tell which.

'Yeah! Yeah, you should grow your hair! Yeah, you could be really pretty…'

Chloe is turning her finger gently, her hand curling closer and closer to Little Gold's face, until she must pull away and brave the burn in her scalp. Chloe flicks the few strands of torn-out hair from her fingertips.

Behind the beast, beyond the swings, nestled in the long grass by the fence, Little Gold can see a fat, caramel-coloured dog shit. Metallic flies are clustered on the top like silver balls on a fairy cake. She concentrates on it, on its perfect foulness, as Chloe goes on.

'And you could wear some nicer clothes, maybe? Did you get that t-shirt from your brother or something?'

The other heads are hushed, waiting for the next bite.

'Won't your mum buy you *girl's* clothes?'

Cherry Tunes, a bubbling sniff and a huge bluebottle lands on the dog shit, lifts its delicate feet to wipe at its face.

'Anyway, you could at least wash them. You know, Persil?'

Little Gold can feel the sensual pleasure of the beast wrapped around her, imagines each head licking its lips as Chloe's words pierce and tear. She must get away. She leaps up, shouldering her way through the girls, running hard for the gate, words thrown after her but failing to strike now. This is the right choice.

'Hey! Hey, we're not being funny or anything. There's no need to get all narky. We all think you could be really pretty.'

Joanne, the new girl from London, more brutal than the rest, or maybe just more desperate to be seen drawing blood, shrieks after her.

'Yeah! For a freak!'

When she gets to the space beyond the clock tower, Little Gold bends double and pants. A stitch is crippling her right side. Words fall from her mouth in whisper and spit, like a curse should.

'Piss off… Piss off… Little gits… Fuck them… Bugger them… Fuck them…'

But the words aren't enough, not black enough, not real enough, so she finds more, forcing them out as she rubs at the raging pain under her ribs.

'Should've rubbed your faces in the dog shit, every face down in the dog shit 'til you choked.'

That's better. The image of the Hydra, splayed on the ground, thrashing in the caramel shit, under her foot, that's better. But she sounds like a nutter. Maybe she's being a nutter. So she stops now and bends to re-tie her lace. An unexpected tear escapes and drops onto the gravel of the path but she scuffs it away with the toe of her trainer and jogs up the hill, only glancing behind her once. They aren't there.

As she reaches the top of the park, and the inevitable football game, she catches sight of Malcy standing at the edge of the match with his ball under his arm. There's a man beside him. A tall man with dark hair. It takes her a moment to realise it's Roy, watching as Wayne Whittaker makes a sliding tackle on Barry Barnes. He leans down to say something into Malcy's ear, and Malcy nods.

Roy has the universal look of a man who's come from work – suit trousers and polished shoes that reflect the late sun. He's in his shirt sleeves, rolling them slowly up his arms now as he continues to chat with Malcy, and Little Gold is flooded, suddenly, with memories of the scent of Dad after work – beer on his breath from a can on the train, and a day's sweat. Is he arriving home now in his Hemel Hempstead house? Is there a garden gate swinging closed behind him?

Someone shouts Malcy's name and she sees Kev running along the top of the park, his schoolbag bumping on his hip. He stops beside her brother, who is instantly smaller than he was, darting his head from side to side like a sparrow as he watches Kev and his Dad talk. Roy laughs, loud and deep, and walks away from the match, the boys trailing after him.

The silver car's parked at the kerb and Roy unlocks it and leans into the front. He's rooting about in the glove compartment as Malcy and Kev peer into the boot, tapping on the glass. There's frantic movement inside and she realises it must be the puppy, Jake. He's nothing but a blur of black and white and she wonders why they don't let him out, don't let him have a run on the grass. Maybe there's no time.

Roy emerges from the front and hands Malcy a white paper bag and then, yes, it seems they're going, Roy beckoning Kev to get into the car. She's close enough now to be noticed and Kev calls to her.

'Hi LG! And 'bye LG!'

'See ya! Hi, Malc.'

Malcy looks up, startled by her voice, and then away again, watching as the silver car drives off. He's distracted, uninterested in her.

'Hi, LG.'

As the car reaches the corner and turns up the hill towards Fiveways, Roy toots the horn. Malcy picks up his school bag and they wander up the hill towards home, not exactly together but chatting across the necessary gap between them. She's desperate to know what he got from Kev's dad, what's inside that fat, white paper bag.

'Kev's going to get the Liverpool shirt in town.'

'Yeah? Has he got Jake in the car?'

'Yeah, he's got to go to the vet for something, injections or something.'

She thinks about someone sticking a needle in the puppy. It seems like a betrayal.

'And then they're getting the shirt. He might get the shorts too, he reckoned.'

Malcy's lucky to have Kev. A friend like Kev's the best armour – loaded, good-looking, cool, tall…

'Oi, Woofter, lend us your ball!'

He's not here now though. Wayne Whittaker crashes into Malcy's shoulder as they clip the corner of the match. He stinks of B.O. and his hair is soaked in sweat.

'This one's shit.'

He boots the ball at his feet and Little Gold recognises the thunk of a football that's losing air.

'Nah, I've got to go.'

'Home for tea! Don't forget to wash your hands, Woofter Boy.'

It's just a passing jab, not the start of something, and he sprints off after the saggy football.

Their front door's ajar and Ali's music is drifting down the stairs as they head into the kitchen. It's much cooler in there, and dark, the tap dripping fast into the loaded sink. Little Gold rinses a mug, half-fills it with water and gulps it down, the fingers of her left hand crossed behind her back. If he's going to tell her, it'll be now.

'Hey, look at this, LG.'

Yes. Malcy's holding out his school bag, the white paper gaping inside it, revealing a mass of shiny red packets. Football stickers. Far more packets than she can count at a glance.

'Whoah! Where'd you get those?'

Feign ignorance, LG.

'Kev's dad, Roy.'

'What?'

'Roy gave them to me.'

'How come?'

'Just now. He just said he had something for me and he got them out the glove compartment.'

Malcy's ladling the packets out onto the kitchen table with two hands. He looks like Sinbad with a heap of gold coins or something. As he spreads them out, she does a rough calculation in her head.

'But that's got to be two quid's worth, Malc!'

'I know!'

Malcy takes them into the front room and sits on the floor with his horde. He lets her open a few packets.

'This is gonna get you miles on in your album, isn't it?'

'Yeah! I can't believe it.'

'They must be really loaded, Kev's family.'

'I know, and I'm going to his house for tea on Sunday.'

'Really?'

'Yeah, he said he'll pick me up before The Big Match and we'll watch it together and then get a Chinese from the takeaway at Fiveways.'

'Bloody hell you're jammy, Malc!'

Malcy grins. He lines up the top corners of Nigel Spink and smooths him into place.

'Do you even like Chinese though?'

'I dunno, do I? But how bloody loaded must they be?'

Malcy picks at the back of another sticker, presses it onto the page and then holds it up to show her that Aston Villa are complete.

*

The cupboard under the sink is gritty with spilled washing powder but Little Gold can see at a glance that the box is empty. She takes it out and peers behind it to see if there's another one but there isn't.

Ali leans over her to fill the kettle.

'What're you doing?'

'We're out of washing powder.'

She bends down and moves a few things around in the cupboard.

'Yeah, we are.'

'Shall I go to the Co-op and get some?'

Her sister tugs open the small green tin that's standing on the work-surface next to the cooker.

'Nope. Not today, LG. It'll have to be Saturday, when I've got the Family Allowance.'

'Okay.'

So much for that then. Ali opens the fridge, dislodging the magnet pinning Dad's address to the front. It hangs by one corner and flaps as she lets the door slam.

'Ali?'

'Yeah?'

Her sister yawns, rakes her fingers through her long hair. It's dry and thin. Little Gold watches the magnet sliding down the fridge, the scrap of paper falling, floating out across the kitchen floor until it comes to rest face down, close to her foot. Ali hasn't noticed, she's stirring her tea, lifting the dripping tea bag out with a spoon and lobbing it into the sink.

Little Gold picks up the paper, folds it and slides it into her pocket. She'd better keep this safe. It might so easily be lost in the deepening mess of the house – drowned in a spillage or swept, sticky and crumpled, into the dark nest of cobwebs between the fridge and the wall. Mum might have another copy, maybe. Mum might even have a phone number but there's no way to ask that.

'Nothing.'

Up in the bathroom, crouching on the edge of the bath, she pulls down the top sash and leans out of the open window. A brown speckled gull, one of last year's chicks, is stalking across next door's roof, pecking around like it's lost something. Young gulls are cheeky. It looks right at her but doesn't fly.

Little Gold ducks her head into her armpit and sniffs. Not good. Not Wayne Whittaker-bad but not good and it's not her body, it's the clothes. Climbing down, she strips off and picks up her blue velour pyjamas that are lying under the sink. They're a bit damp from getting splashed and stuff and there's one of Malcy's trainer prints on the top, but they'll do.

There's a slim bar of *Shield* soap on the corner of the wash basin. It's meant to stop you getting B.O. She doesn't know if it'll work on clothes, but maybe. It's worth a try. Rubbing a slimy lather over the front of her t-shirt, she scrubs into the armpits with her hands inside her socks. Then she looks at her knickers. These days there's white, wet stuff there. She sniffs. It's a weird smell, like damp grass. She uses her sock gloves to scrub at that too and then she rinses it all under the cold tap, twisting and wringing the fabric so the milky water runs down her forearms.

Her jeans are filthy but there's no way she can get the water out once they're wet. They'll just be soaked and heavy and won't dry for days. They'll have to wait 'til they've got washing powder again and she can use the machine. Retrieving the slip of paper from her back pocket, she drops them on the bathroom floor under the sink.

Her bird book is the only thing she never loses in the mess of their room. It has one place, top left of the top bookshelf. Malcy never touches the bookshelves, preferring comics and annuals that he keeps in a stack beside his bed.

Easing the book from its place, she sits cross-legged on her bed and opens it to Birds of Prey. Golden Eagle, the biggest bird of the British Isles, she reckons it can keep this safe. She smooths the crumpled paper and slides its edge into the spine. Then, holding the book flat on her two palms, she closes her eyes and says the Lord's Prayer all through before putting it back. It's as safe as she can make it in this house and maybe she's going to have to be the one who does it, the one who writes.

CHAPTER SIX

In the Co-op, Peggy rests the shopping basket against her hip and prays for a swift resolution to the argument holding up the queue. A man is proffering a book of stamps that's either been through the washing machine or a monsoon season. It's not welcome. A dart of pain in her hip forces her to shift the basket again, swapping hands and leaning it on a shelf stacked with boxes of Daz. She issues a silent plea to the man to give up or the checkout woman to give in but neither seems likely as the man's voice is raised and the woman leans under the till to press the bell that will summon authority.

Authority arrives in the form of a lad barely out of his teens with a badge proclaiming him Assistant Manager. With luck, he'll give in quickly and spare them all any more of this pantomime. She looks down and realises that the child is standing close behind her, a loaf of white sliced pressed under her arm.

Her eye follows the parting of the fine, blonde hair. It's messy, kinking this way and that. It could do with a wash too. She looks up and meets Peggy's eyes.

'Hello there.'

'Hello.'

The loaf is getting a fierce pinching in the child's armpit as she fiddles with a coin, passing it from hand to hand, turning it, peering at it. She holds it out.

'Look, it's one of those 50ps with the hands on.'

'So it is.'

It seems the ice is broken. The chat the other day was enough to make her approachable.

'Now, have you ever spotted that one of those hands is a woman's?'

'Oh, yes.'

The child wedges the loaf even harder into her armpit and holding the coin on one outstretched palm, she points to the female hand in the circle of male ones.

'That's the one. Not much gets past you then?'

The small mouth curls but she doesn't confirm or deny.

The Assistant Manager has, indeed, resolved the issue at the till by giving in at last and Peggy inches forward in anticipation. The customer in front, fairly bloated with smugness, is standing with his arms folded as his tuna fish and macaroons are shoved into a bag by the angry cashier. She's jabbing at the buttons of her till as if she'd like to kill it but making no attempt at speed. Peggy leans close to the child's ear, cupping her cheek, startled at the smoothness and warmth. Touch is a rarity. She whispers,

'I should think we might get home by Christmas!'

The child lets out another half-smile, trying to hide it by looking down at her feet.

'Can I help you?'

It's an admonishment not an invitation and Peggy straightens up and hurries forward with her basket. As the cashier rings up the items, Peggy reaches for a packet of Polo's from the adjacent display and drops them in alongside her shopping. The woman's tut is audible and only just on the verge of rude. She's going to have to calm down or Assistant Manager will be needed again.

'And will *that* be all?'

'Yes, thank you. Thank you so much.'

The frosty exterior thaws slightly as she recognises Peggy as a regular and usually no trouble, apart from liking her bacon sliced from the joint.

'That'll be one pound and twenty-seven pence, please, madam. And I'm sorry to have kept you.'

'Not at all. Thank you.'

Peggy waits on the slope outside the Co-op without fully admitting it to herself, pretending that she needs to re-pack her purchases. A wheezing pug is tied to the railing with a loose loop of lead and two girls are roller skating outside the hardware shop, closed now for the evening. Each is wearing one skate, clunky things like boots, with bright rainbow laces. The girls have their arms around each other's shoulders as they giggle and stagger.

The child appears and Peggy realises that the battered bicycle leaning against the wall must belong to her. She pockets her change and, with the loaf wedged clumsily in her armpit again, turns the bike in a tight circle.

Peggy hesitates before calling to her.

'Um, would you like to pop your loaf in my bag, if you haven't got an easy way to carry it?'

Little Gold looks up.

'Oh, if you don't mind. I forgot to get a carrier... I could hang your bag off my handlebars if you want, though? I won't ride, I'll just push it.'

Peggy hands over her bag and Little Gold arranges it on the bike. It's an ancient steed, rusty in patches on the frame and the tyres worryingly bald. They make their way along the road, the bike between them and the bag swaying gently.

'So, have you seen the dandelions in my front garden?'

She looks up. Green eyes with a slightly anxious tinge, as if Peggy's setting a test. She hadn't meant it as a test. There's an art here that she isn't sure she can master. Still she tries again, startled at her courage and the words she hadn't known she was going to say.

'I wondered if you'd like to come round and give me a hand grubbing them out at the weekend? If you're not busy?'

That's better though, a straightforward request, and the child nods.

'Yes, I'd like that.'

'Can you come on Sunday?'

She nods again.

Several of the garden walls are topped with purple campanula flowers and some dotted with cavities where the flints have come out. Each is different and Peggy realises she knows them all rather too well. It's not just touch that's a rarity, even company, someone to walk beside her, has become an unusual thing. The bike is ticking quietly. Peggy glances at the small hands gripping the handlebars, steering carefully around a lump of tree root bursting up through the pavement.

As they reach Peggy's house, the child brings the bike gently to a halt and Peggy reaches out to take her shopping. She hands over Little Gold's loaf and dips deeper into the bag, her fingers searching for the roll of sweets.

'The other thing I wondered was if you like Polo mints?'

The delight is out of all proportion, she thinks – the child gazing at the sweets with a look of rapture. Then she grins at Peggy. It's slightly lop-sided and open as a book. Bingo.

'If you take these up that pear tree in your garden then I guess you won't have to share them with your brother or your sister.'

I see you up your tree. I know you have a brother and sister. I think things might be hard these days.

'Thank you.'

'You're welcome. Thanks for carrying my bag. I'll expect you about two on Sunday then?'

'Yeah.'

Little Gold's head is bowed over the packet, her mucky fingernails already picking at the foil.

'Goodbye.'

The child looks up and smiles again.

''Bye.'

She slips a mint into her mouth and wheels her bike away, the loaf limp and defeated in her armpit once again.

*

Peggy slides the olive oil into the cupboard and places the bacon and cheese into the white-lit cavern of the fridge.

It's a mission. She appears, after very many years of not seeking out other people, to be on a mission to befriend the child. This is somewhat unexpected, somewhat beyond comprehension, and she thumps the fridge door closed.

Peggy Baxter does not do things like this.

Vi's laugh rings out as if she is behind her still, sitting at the kitchen table with a cig and a coffee.

'Peg, will you stop telling yourself what you don't do and just *do* what you *do*?'

She answers imaginary Vi out loud because she may as well.

'Well, that was rather your speciality, no?'

Life with Vi had been peppered with 'doing', with some incidents rather more successful than others.

Some were undoubted triumphs though, she had to admit that. Like the time she'd got in from work and found Vi emerging from the middle bedroom, her black hair full of dust and grit, the chisel in her hand, a twinkle in her eye.

'What in God's name are you doing in there?'

'Uncovering the lovely Edwardian fireplace some idiot had boarded over, come and see.'

And, yes, there was the fireplace – delicate pink roses rambling up the tiles and birds, their wingtips touching, in the wrought iron of the grate. Exquisite. Vi had cleaned it. Polished the black to a bottomless ebony, washed the tiles with a soft cloth.

'You see, Peg? Sometimes you've just got to stick the chisel into life to find the buried treasure!'

'And if you'd just gouged a bloody great hole and there'd been nothing under there?'

'Ah, but there was.'

Vi has the art of finding treasure. But then Vi is something of a pirate, even now.

Peggy reaches under the counter for an onion. She dices it into regular pieces as she heats oil in a pan. The oil ripples, the onion softens, becoming slowly translucent and releasing its scent into the air. She beats two eggs, adds a shake of dried basil and pours the mixture over the onion. The yellow and white swims gently into solidity and Peggy waits. She wants it perfect and she'll get it near as damn it.

As she walks to the table with her pan, Shaw twines himself around her ankles.

'We're having company at the weekend, beast! You'll have to behave.'

She's a particularly lovely child. That's what it is. Outside a lot, racketing around on that old bike and reading in her tree. Bit of a tomboy. The sort of child…

And, she supposes, there really are no rules about how she should live this part of life. There's nothing to lose and perhaps something to give, even if it's just the odd packet of Polo's. The family don't have much, it's clear, and it was Mrs Theaker in the newsagent who enlightened her as to why. She'd leaned over the counter towards Peggy, her vast bust resting on the *Radio Times*, and murmured,

'That poor woman at 167... You know her husband did the dirty on her? Away on his toes to Hemel Hempstead and her left with the three kids. Got herself a job but I'm not sure she's coping too well, if you know what I mean.'

Peggy tries to bring the father to mind. A thin chap in short-sleeves, his suit jacket over his arm, walking up the hill from the station of an evening? Yes, she'd seen him sometimes but the face swims in her memory, refusing to be fixed. Brown hair? Glasses? It's been some months since she saw him last.

The mother's small and harried with an air of being chased. Even before the husband went she'd always seemed on the edge of something, glancing behind as she hurried down the road with the shopping, almost as if she expected something to pounce. The older girl she sees quite often, head down, purposeful, with a bag that looks heavy on the bony shoulder. The boy is one of the gang who play football in the park. And then there's her.

Peggy reaches across the table and flicks the wheel on the radio. The kitchen is instantly filled with urgency, a voice telling of fighting, of losses. Young lives in jeopardy in a place far away. She doesn't think she'd ever heard of the Falkland Islands before all this happened. The place names – South Georgia, Port Stanley – might have belonged in the American Civil War. How quickly the world snatches up its next battle and how swiftly the names drop into history books. What's happening in Saigon now, she wonders? What's happening in Inchon? What about Malaya? All these faraway places that were once shorthand for death and are now never mentioned. All that wasted life. All that broken youth.

She turns off the radio and pushes away her half-eaten omelette.

Vi wouldn't have had it, her running away from reality. Vi had demanded to know it all – every strike, war, murder or injustice. And yet it had never seemed to bring her low. She could watch horror, read an account of suffering and pain, and then touch up her lipstick, squirt a bit of Chanel and declare her intention to go out dancing. And she was firmly of the opinion that everyone else should do the same.

But Vi doesn't live here now, hasn't lived here in almost nine years, and if Peggy wants peace in the evening, she'll have it.

She slips the silver paper from the top of a new pack. Players No. 6, her smoke for decades. You don't need to say tipped any more but she always does, afraid that to vary the words would vary the commitment. As she speaks, Mrs Theaker will already be reaching for them from the racks behind her; it's their shared afternoon ritual. Her *Evening Argus*, her pack of twenty and the occasional bar of Whole Nut. Mrs Theaker will rarely accept a penny for the chocolate. Vi speaks again, this time calling through from the front room, one grey Saturday years ago.

'Darling, with your Players and my Bensons, she's probably taking her summer break in Cannes on us already! I think she can spare a bar of chocolate.'

The thought of Mrs Theaker in Cannes had kept them laughing for weeks. Mrs Theaker at premieres with her hair net on. Mrs Theaker on the beach in her forty denier stockings.

Mrs Theaker had asked just once about Vi, about three months after she'd left and when Peggy was at her thinnest, her most drained.

'Your friend hasn't been in for a long while.'

'No, she's moved to Bath. Got a new job there.'

'Ah well, you have to go where the opportunities take you. That's what I said to Mr Theaker all those years ago when he was reluctant to make the move from Barnes. I said we had to bite the bullet and knuckle down to Brighton.'

Mrs Theaker's endless supply of misapplied sayings were a source of some delight for Vi. Peggy had made a mental note of that one to include in her next letter.

Shaw struts into the room looking tetchy, his tail twitching.

'What's the matter, puss cat? You still sulking that it's Kit-e-Kat and not Whiskas? 3p cheaper per can, I'll have you know!'

He sits at her feet and starts to wash his paws.

'Ah, no doubt I'll cave in next week and put you back on the posh stuff.'

Peggy gets up, draws the curtains and switches on the standard lamp. She's got a new book, *Union Street* by Pat Barker.

'You must read it, Peg,' Vi's letter had said. 'It's gritty, urban, and all about women.'

But one page in, Peggy starts to weaken. This will have to wait. Tonight she needs to pursue her goal of escaping the painful. She reaches up to the top shelf of her bookcase and takes down her favourite Margery Allingham book, *Death of a Ghost*. Albert Campion, debonair sleuth, companion of some of the hardest years in her life. The cloth-bound copies take up a whole row. Inside each is the curl of her own teenage handwriting:

Margaret Baxter, 24 Arundel Road, Brighton

Peggy is just starting chapter two when Shaw decides she looks settled for the evening and, leaping onto the settee in a rare display of agility, he drops his warm bulk into her lap.

CHAPTER SEVEN

Malcy's draped sideways across the chair, bouncing his feet in time to the theme music of *A Question of Sport*. The feet have a particular smell, a mixture of warm cheese and dog biscuit and tonight it's overwhelming. Little Gold shuffles across the carpet away from them.

'Malc?'

'Mmm…'

'Do you reckon I should write to Dad?'

His gaze doesn't move from the telly, where David Coleman's asking a question about who scored a winning goal in an FA cup semi-final.

'Ian Rush! No, no, um… Aaargh! I knew that…'

'Malc?'

Malcy holds up a hand to silence her while he listens to the next question.

'Steve Cram. No, Steve Ovett!'

The little bloke, the jockey, makes a joke and the studio audience laugh.

'Malcy, do you?'

'What?'

The word's hard-edged and she's startled by the anger in his glance. But he looks back to the telly in a moment, his voice softening.

'I dunno, LG. If you want, I suppose.'

It's the round where sports people wear a disguise and do some ordinary thing, like filling their car with petrol or mowing their lawn. The teams have to guess who it is. She doesn't know enough names to guess and, anyway, she doesn't really care. Some bloke takes off dark glasses and a Sherlock Holmes hat and there's a chorus of surprise and laughter. Malcy's face is blank, he obviously didn't know that one either.

Three sharp knocks on the front door make them both jump. It's getting dark outside and they aren't expecting anyone. Little Gold stands up.

'Shall I go?'

Before Malcy can answer there are three more raps and then a voice booms through the letterbox into the dark front hall.

'Hello?'

Little Gold drops into a crouch and scuttles across the carpet to the telly, sliding the volume control down until David Coleman's mouthing silently into the room. The letterbox slams and they hear a sequence of muffled sounds from outside the window – grunting and scrabbling and then the noise of a plant pot smashing and a shout.

'Jesus Christ!'

It's someone climbing over the wall into the front garden, she's sure that's what it is but still the knock on the window makes her squeak. She's instantly embarrassed but Malcy doesn't seem to have noticed. He's frozen in his chair, biting at his thumb, his teeth sunk into the knuckle of it and his stinking feet held still. She tries to catch his eye but fails.

'Open the door! I know you're in there. I can see your light through the curtain. I'm not going away. Come on!'

He knocks again on the glass and Little Gold leaps up. She takes the stairs two at a time and bursts into Ali's bedroom.

'Ali! Ali! Clive's at the door!'

Ali's sitting in the puddle of light from her angle-poise lamp, a fat book propped open in front of her sheet of lined paper and four long Twiglets lined up beside her pens. Tea. Her head jerks up. Her face, in the stark light, is paper-white too and her hollow temples create an illusion of huge, bush-baby eyes.

'You didn't answer it?'

'No, but he knocked on the window. He's shouting that he knows we're in here.'

'Ah, shit.'

She drops her pen and hurries down the stairs. A blurry Clive is back on the doorstep now, a bulky, shifting shape on the other side of the patterned glass.

Little Gold hangs back as Ali opens the door a crack and angry words pour into the hall, as if loosed from a stoppered bottle.

'Oh, well thank you! Thank you very much for having the courtesy to answer at long last! I want to speak to your mother.'

Ali opens the door slightly more and Little Gold can see him – red-faced and sweating in a shiny shirt printed with small brown anchors. His car keys are dangling from his fat hand as he pushes a strand of lank hair back across his balding head. His face is red, rough as sandpaper, with a bulbous nose like a walnut. She'd liked him. When he was one of Dad's friends who used to come for beer in the garden in the summer, he'd been one of the ones who bothered to talk to her, seemed not to notice her failure to be a proper girl, or maybe just hadn't cared.

Ali's hand is all knuckles, gripping the edge of the door like a claw.

'Mum's not well. She's in bed.'

'Yeah? So I'm to assume that's why she didn't turn up at work today then?'

'Didn't she phone?'

'No, she didn't bloody phone and the first I knew of the office being closed was when a client called to tell me he'd gone to drop off some property details and the place was locked up.'

A fleck of frothy spit sails from his mouth and lands on Ali's chest. She steps back, closing the door a fraction of an inch. Little Gold feels sorry for him, spitting and sweating and making a fuss. There's no point.

'She would've meant to phone you, Clive, I'm sure she would. She must've just been so ill she couldn't.'

Clive pushes back his wayward hair again and huffs.

'Can you fetch her now, please?'

Ali glances round at Little Gold and then looks back to Clive.

'She's asleep. She's taken one of her migraine pills and they knock her right out.'

'Yes, I bet... Look, Alison, I want you to give your mother a message. I want you to tell her I will expect to see her in the office at 8.30 tomorrow morning with a full explanation of what happened today. Have you got that?'

'Yes. I'll tell her. Thank you for being understanding, Clive. I'm sure Mum wouldn't have meant to let you down.'

Clive deflates slightly. He wipes his great paw across his sweaty face and sighs. Little Gold wants to get him a tissue to wipe his face properly, and a drink of water. Instead she tries to watch with kindness as he blusters away.

'Look, I understand how hard it's been since your dad left. I wanted to give your mum a chance with this job. But I'm not a charity. I can't go on and on. It's costing me money. You're a big girl now, Alison, you must see the position I'm in. Can you not speak to your dad about things?'

Ali recoils from the door as if he's hit her and Clive leans to one side and catches Little Gold's eye.

'You alright there, little'un?'

She nods. Ali recovers herself and steps across to block Clive's view into the house.

'I'll make sure she's there in the morning, Clive.'

'Yeah, well, you do that.'

He shuffles awkwardly away down the path, hitching his trousers around his pendulous belly.

Ali closes the door and leans against it for a moment. As she passes Little Gold she ducks in close and hisses into her ear.

'Don't say a bloody word to him, ever. Do you understand?'

Little Gold nods.

Malcy's standing just inside the living room door, scratching frantically at his neck. Tiny beads of ruby are erupting from the pink skin as he tears at it.

'Malc, stop!'

She catches his wrists like Mum used to.

'Get off, LG!'

He jerks his hands away but stops scratching, rubbing instead with his palms, smearing streaks of blood around his throat.

'You'll get really sore. Where's your Betnovate?'

'It ran out.'

'Well, hang on. I'll see if we've got any of that pink cream Mum puts on bites and things.'

Little Gold finds a curled tube, a bit cracked, in the bathroom cabinet and runs back downstairs. Malcy takes the cream, squeezes a pink blob onto his fingers and tries to rub it into his neck.

'You're missing the worst bits! Let me do it...'

She scoops the cream from his hand and dabs it onto the angry skin. Malcy flinches.

'Ah, shit, it stings!'

'Sorry. There, that'll do. Leave it now, eh?'

Little Gold turns up the volume on the telly and flops back against the settee. She can feel her heart beating too fast, too high in her chest, like it needs to get out. She tries to slow her breathing.

'...avratilova... Originally from Czechoslovakia, of course, now residing in the United States.'

Something about the tennis player reminds Little Gold of Peggy Baxter. Something about the way she's standing, or the way her smile lies on her face.

'Malcy? Do you think Peggy Baxter used to play tennis?'

'Who?'

'Peggy Baxter up the road.'

'That old lady who lives by herself?'

'Yeah.'

He laughs, a proper Malcy laugh, not flinty like Ali's, and grinds his palm against his flaming neck again.

'I dunno. Blimey you're a weirdo, LG. Why do you think that?'

She shrugs. She's got no idea why she thinks that.

*

In Little Gold's dream, something is growing through the house. Some sort of vine, bristle-stemmed and thick, is coiled in every room, running down the landing and through the hall to the kitchen. She's struggling, clambering over the growth to reach the front door. Beyond the patterned glass there's someone waiting, knocking and knocking again and she wants, wants with a deep and hungry desperation, to reach them. But it's taking her too long. She shouts and it's muffled, muffled and choked and the person beyond the door will never hear her. As she fights on, the figure behind the glass melts away. Little Gold opens her eyes.

Malcy's beside her bed, a darker shape in the darkness. His breath has the high, dry wheeze of an attack already well underway and she reaches for her lamp switch. It shoots home with a definite click but there's no light. Her hand catches a cup and she feels it tip and fall to the floor as Malcy starts to grab at her, yanking at whatever he can find in the dark – her duvet, her sleeve and then her arm.

'Let go, Malcy! Let me go and put the light on. Let go!'

She rips her wrist from his grip and scoots across the bed, catching her leg on the bedframe.

'Shit! Ow!'

The bright yellow light reveals Malcy, wearing nothing but red y-fronts, hunched over her bedside table like an old man. The pants are baggy, slack across his trembling, concave belly. His eyes are pleading. This is a bad one.

'Hang on, Malc!'

She doesn't hesitate, for the first time in weeks she doesn't hesitate outside Mum's bedroom door, but runs straight in and turns on the light.

Mum's a hummock on the far side of her bed, her back curled towards Little Gold and her head invisible in the duvet. Little Gold scrambles across the empty expanse of Dad's side and shakes her shoulder. Mum rolls heavily, like a whale in the sea, but doesn't stir.

'Mum! Mum! Malcy's wheezing.'

She rocks the body again but still Mum doesn't wake and, with each rock, a wave of booze-laden air washes over her.

'Mum!'

Mum grunts and shrugs, burrowing into her pillow. There's a keening cry from their room, high, wild and full of fear.

'It's okay, Malc! It's okay! Hang on.'

Abandoning her efforts to wake Mum, Little Gold runs to her sister's room. Ali's already getting out of bed as Little Gold switches on her light.

'Ali! Ali! Malcy!'

Ali stumbles from the room, shoving Little Gold ahead of her.

'Get Mum!'

Little Gold spins round, anger clipping her words.

'I tried, I can't wake her!'

They arrive together, shoulder to shoulder in the narrow bedroom doorway. Malcy is framed there, a picture of panic and distress, the struggle to breathe making a birdcage of his skinny torso.

'Find his inhaler! I'll get her up…'

Ali's gone again and Little Gold starts to lift things from Malcy's bedside table, trying not to look at him, pretending he isn't drowning in the bedroom beside her.

'Where's your inhaler, Malc?'

He's flapping, she can see from the corner of her eye that he's flapping his hands like a weirdo kid, like some kid who can't even talk.

She rifles through his stuff – sticker backs, pens, badges, exercise books – and it rains onto the carpet at her feet. It's not here. But wrenching open the top drawer she scans the mass inside and there, wedged into the front right-hand corner, is the inhaler.

She grabs it and, jumping across her bed, thrusts it towards Malcy. He fumbles and the small object slips between them, falling into the dark crack between the head of her bed and the wall.

'Ali! Ali!'

She thrusts her arm into the gap, clawing into the mess there, yanking out dirty knickers, comics, used tissues thick with grey fluff.

Malcy whines again, the high, fearful cry and she's furious suddenly, wants to lean over and slap his wide-eyed face. Instead she directs the anger into her body and wrenches a jumper sleeve stuck in the mass of junk. The inhaler leaps like a fish out of the sea and lands on the mattress. This time she holds it with care, offers it to Malcy like a communion cup, guiding his thrashing hands. Together they shake it a couple of times and then, her palms still around his knuckles, he squeezes and inhales. Squeezes and inhales again and she doesn't let go.

It doesn't take long for the drug to do whatever it does in the tight hive of Malcy's chest. Little Gold guides him onto her bed, helps him sit back against her grubby pillows.

'You're okay Malc, yeah?'

He can't speak yet but he meets her eye, curls his soft mouth into a hint of smile.

'Fuck you! Get up!'

Ali's shout startles them both. There's a thud from the back of the house and her voice again.

'Get up!'

The fear, only just receding from Malcy's eyes, surges back and she puts her hand on his shoulder.

'It's okay. It's just Ali being Ali. I'll go. I'll get you some water too, yeah?'

Malcy closes his eyes. She doesn't want to leave him, can feel the trembling fragility of him against her palm, but the shout comes yet again.

'For Christ's sake, Mum!'

Little Gold runs down the landing, back to Mum's room. Ali has managed to get her sitting up, her feet on the floor, but she's not attempting to stand, just swaying there gently like the jingly clown they had when they were small – a pin-head and a wide base, it spun and rocked and grinned. Mum isn't grinning though and Ali's tugging ferociously on one of her limp hands.

'Come on!'

She yanks again and Mum sways dangerously. Little Gold pictures Mum's head in contact with the glass top of her bedside table and tries to get between them.

'He's okay, Ali. It's okay. I found his inhaler.'

'Fuck it, LG! Look at her! Look at her… Get UP!'

Ali shouts right into Mum's face and suddenly, as if she's just woken, Mum rises up and weaves an unsteady path to the bathroom. She doesn't close the door fully and they can see a slice of her hoicking up her nightie and staggering back onto the toilet. She calls through the gap.

'There's noneedta shout a' me, Alison. Go an' be with your brother an' I'll be there in a minute.'

Little Gold runs to the kitchen, fetches Malcy a glass of water and returns to their room to find Ali sitting on her bed. Malcy takes the glass from her.

'I'm alright, LG. I'll be okay now.'

The words are punctuated with small gasps. She looks at the damp fingers of hair, darkened and stuck to his forehead. It was a really bad one.

'Yeah, you'll be alright.'

The burn in her bladder's a surprise, she must have been needing to go all this time and it's suddenly urgent. As she heads to the bathroom she crosses paths with Mum, pin-balling her way along the landing, calling to Malcy.

'S'okay Malcy, I'm on my way.'

There's a broad, warm puddle of piss around the base of the toilet. She walks right into it before she realises and it's too late to back out. Instead she sits down, lets go of her own hot gush and lifts her dripping toes from the floor. She does her best to mop it up with loo roll but it runs out before she's really finished the job.

Her toes are cringing, tacky on the floor as she stands. This pungent stuff, this ripe liquor distilled in Mum's body, she wants it off her skin. Little Gold lifts one foot at a time into the wash basin, letting the warm water flow hotter and hotter, rubbing between her toes with the fragile remains of the soap. Hunched on the bath mat, she dries carefully, systematically, whispering the rhyme.

'This little piggy went to market…'

CHAPTER EIGHT

Peggy Baxter is on her front lawn, kneeling on a red velvet cushion that looks too good for gardening, looks more like something you might use to pray. But she isn't praying, she's driving the prongs of a small garden fork into the dry ground and breathing heavily.

'Hello.'

'Ah, my under-gardener! A timely arrival. Take a turn with this fork while I have a cigarette.'

The old lady levers herself to her feet, using her own bony knee for support, as Little Gold hops over the wall and settles herself on the cushion. It's actually very tatty close-up, the fringe hanging off and a distinct bald patch in the middle.

Little Gold pushes the fork into the grass alongside the waxy leaves of a hearty dandelion and waggles it in small circles to loosen the earth. She drags the plant from the ground, trailing its long, dusty tap root, and tosses it onto a pile of weeds.

The old lady is rolling the tip of her cigarette gently on the rough edge of the wall and a trickle of ash tumbles down.

'I can see you've done that before.'

'My grandad showed me.'

'Ah.'

She starts on the next plant, wheedling the fork in, twisting and grinding it. It takes more effort than she remembers from before. Maybe the ground wasn't so hard then, or maybe she hadn't really bothered, just got it started and let Grandad finish it.

'Well, you've got the knack. Does he like gardening, your grandad?'

She hasn't seen him since Christmas Eve. She remembers being wedged with Malcy on Grandad's tiny settee, shop-bought mince pies on their knees, as Mum said nice things about all his Christmas cards and Dad stared out the window. Ali had disappeared to the loo.

'He has a sort of greenhouse on the back of his kitchen with tomato plants and things.'

The old lady takes another drag on her cigarette. She tilts her head to one side, like a magpie considering whether something's worthy of interest, and Little Gold can feel herself blushing. There's a word for that sort of greenhouse but she can't remember it.

'Ah, my tomatoes are awful this year. Has he got any good ones on the go?'

Little Gold shifts the cushion to her left and attacks another dandelion. This one is lifting more easily and she pulls it free with one tug.

'I haven't seen him for a while. My dad used to take us but he's moved to Hemel Hempstead.'

Peggy stubs out her cigarette, reaches down beside her coal bunker and holds up a pair of ancient garden shears.

'You're making short work of those. Reckon you'll be able to chop the grass back a bit too?'

The shears are heavy, the blades rusty at the tips and dark and thick with grease where they hinge. They tremble as Little Gold closes them on a fringe of grass and it falls like hair. If she can do this for Peggy Baxter then she can do their front garden too. Maybe she should. Sweat is trickling from her armpits down the sides of her body but this feels powerful and satisfying.

'Time for a break. We'll have another go later. Come and get a drink.'

Little Gold wipes her grassy trainers on the doormat and blinks into the front hall, her eyes struggling to adjust to the dim interior of the house after the blinding sunshine outside.

'Come through to the kitchen.'

The house is the same layout as her own, of course, but it seems huge – the shining expanse of the kitchen floor inviting her to dance across it. She doesn't. Instead she sits at a ladder-backed chair at the broad kitchen table. The house smells so good – furniture polish, old cigarettes, toast.

Peggy hands her a glass of water, grey cubes of ice bobbing at the surface and Little Gold gulps it, teasing at the ice with her tongue.

Lighting the gas ring with a square, silver cigarette lighter, Peggy sets a kettle on the hob and turns to face her.

'Are you hungry?'

She is. For some reason, the Family Allowance didn't fill the cupboards yesterday and Ali wasn't up this morning to ask about it. But she doesn't reply. Instead she takes another gulp of water, opening her jaws wide and clamping her teeth around a squeaky ice cube.

'Well, hungry or not I think these slip down don't they?'

Peggy rips open a box of Jaffa Cakes. She pours them in a crescent onto a plate and places it in front of Little Gold, before turning away to the kettle again. The whole packet. Twelve. She nibbles at the sponge-edge of number one but the first burst of sweetness breaks her resolve and she crams in the rest of it, chewing and swallowing quickly. She takes two and three together and finishes them in four bites.

The old lady is stirring a squat, brown teapot with a teaspoon, moving it in slow circles.

'I think they call you Little Gold, don't they? I've heard them shouting to you when you're up the tree out there. Would you rather I used your proper name?'

The last mouthful of Jaffa Cake slips down and she is about to reach for the next but she stills her hand and slides it underneath her thigh.

'I'd rather you called me Little Gold. I, I don't like my proper name.'

Peggy Baxter nods. She's concentrating on pouring their tea, a bright stream of amber, through a strainer into mugs.

Little Gold's a bit dizzy. It's probably the heat and being so hungry and now all this sugar at once, running riot through her bloodstream. She takes a sip of her water and finds that she's speaking again.

'You see, people always say it's a pretty name and I think it's horrible to have a pretty name when you're not a pretty girl. I wish they'd called me something that can be a boy's name. Alex or Sasha or something.'

Peggy places the two mugs on the table and gestures to the sugar bowl.

'Help yourself if you want sugar.'

She opens her cigarette packet, takes one out and taps the end gently on the table top.

'Names are important. There's no point answering to something if it isn't who you are.'

She's still dizzy and, for some reason, she can feel tears in her chest, tight and threatening. Peggy holds out the plate.

'Go on, have another one, Little Gold. They're mostly air anyway.'

Little Gold waits while the tears drift away and she can trust herself to speak without sounding weird. Then she takes another Jaffa Cake and a sip of her tea.

'Thank you, Peggy Baxter.'

Peggy Baxter laughs, a bark like a sea lion at the aquarium, and lights her cigarette.

*

Little Gold has her ear flat against the panel of the kitchen door, listening to the hum of Mum's phone conversation but it's competing with the growling of her stomach. A smattering of clear words leap through the wood.

'No, I'm not going to. Because I'm not. If I'd had...'

Is that the way she used to argue with him? Is that him on the other end of the phone? She leans harder, until her ear is as sore as her stomach, but Mum's gone back to murmuring. Little Gold lets her chin fall onto her chest.

The front door opens and there's Ali, dropping her bag to the floor at her ankles. It's green, graffitied all over with CND symbols and band names and stuff. Badges are clustered like acne over the left-hand side.

'You ear-wigging LG?'

'No, I just wondered what's for tea.'

'I don't 'spose Mum's going to tell whoever that is on the phone.'

'Do you think it's… '

The kitchen door swings open and Mum appears, holding a tall glass half-full with bubbling golden liquid. She speaks as if she's been looking for them, rather than arguing with someone on the phone.

'Ah, there you are, where's your brother?'

The flush of red down her neck looks like a spillage. She takes another gulp of her drink. Apple tang on her breath. Cider.

'He's gone to Kev's for tea, remember?'

'Ah, yes, that's right. What shall we have to eat then, girls?'

Little Gold and Ali trail behind her as she walks back into the kitchen, holding her glass aloft like a lantern lighting their way.

'Foie gras and champagne?'

She starts to open the cupboards, one after another, each with a flourish. She has the air of a magician revealing a vanished lady and her voice is loud and theatrical.

'Caviar and steak?'

Finally she swings open the low cupboards under the sink, presenting the jumbled stack of pans, the Tupperware boxes and grotty old flower vases. Then she turns away from them and drains her glass.

Ali mutters,

'Christ's sake, here we go…'

'Did you say something, Alison?'

'No.'

The stream of cider refilling the glass is like liquid sunshine, fizzing and alive, and Little Gold wonders if it tastes as good as it looks.

Mum roots in the back of the cupboard where they keep the tins, bringing out a dusty jar of Bisto and a small can of mandarin oranges. Little Gold glances at her sister, who's leaning in the doorway, her head hanging.

'Ta-da! Would you believe it? Dinner is served!'

Mum's found two tins of ravioli, way in the back somewhere. One of them is dented.

Ali's head jerks up and she hisses.

'Tschh! Jesus!'

'Not t'your taste, dear?'

Mum drains her glass again.

'You know I can't eat that muck.'

Face to face, the difference in their height is much more noticeable, Ali looking down her nose, scowling. But Mum's new persona, this sinister showman, won't be quelled by a few inches of height.

'Sorry? You're turning up your nose at this feast? At this wondrous bounty?'

Ali backs away slightly, disconcerted. But she won't back down and Little Gold knows it.

'I said you know I can't eat that muck. It's about a thousand calories a greasy little pillow.'

The showman bows out, dying in her face, and Mum's voice drops to the plodding, resigned tone they're more familiar with.

'It's what we've got, Alison, so it's what we're having.'

'I'll make myself a sandwich or something then.'

She strides over to the counter and opens the bread bin.

'We're out of bread until I can get to the shop tomorrow.'

There's a derisive snort and Ali spins round and spits her words across the room.

'And you'll pay with…'

The slam of the bread bin is hollow and Mum says nothing in reply, just stares, blank and unreadable.

In the silence, Little Gold feels the pull of knowledge, the dark tug of awareness. She knows what's happening. The inevitable crisis, the moment at which his absence, or more particularly, the absence of his pay packet, will bring all it all down around them. Still, it seems they need her to be a kid, to ask a stupid question, to make them talk.

'What's… what's going on? Why didn't anyone get the shop yesterday?'

Mum sighs.

'We owed them a bit at the VG shop, love, and they wouldn't let us have any more credit.'

'What do you mean?'

Suddenly Ali stumbles towards one of the kitchen chairs. She sits heavily, her mottled hands shaking as she rubs at her bare arms. The legs of her jeans, drainpipes, are ruched like curtains on her thighs.

'Don't be thick, LG. The VG shop bloke's been letting us get more stuff than we could afford. That's called credit… tick, you know? When I went in yesterday his brother was on the till and he said I couldn't have any more and we needed to pay up what we owed. He saw that I had the Family Allowance in the purse and he took it.'

'Took it?'

Ali looks up and her eyes are swimming with tears.

'Well, he said, in a loud voice, what we owed and that he could see I had the money. There were all sorts of people in there. I had to pay.'

Mum sighs again.

'Yes, well, I can't help thinking there might've been a way to come to some sor' of arrangement…'

Her words trail away into her glass.

'Oh, right! Well you go down there in the morning Mum and make a bloody arrangement with him, eh? You weren't there. You don't know what it was like.'

Ali's voice is liquid, tremulous and weak. Little Gold takes a step towards her.

'Look, come on, let's eat, yeah? We'll maybe all feel a bit better if we…'

'Bloody hell!'

She jerks to her feet and runs down the hall, a single sob audible before she stamps up the stairs and slams into her bedroom.

Mum shrugs and reaches for the tin opener.

'All the more for us, eh?'

Little Gold watches as she stirs the ravioli in the pan and wordlessly ladles it into two bowls plucked from the stack of dirty crockery and rinsed. She holds one out to Little Gold, who pads after her into the front room.

She tries not to wolf it but it's difficult. The dense greasiness is so good – rich with sweetness and salt. She feels it falling, warm and heavy, into her stomach as she concentrates on each forkful, scrapes up the remains of the sauce and then wipes the bowl around with a licked finger.

Mum's curled her legs onto the other end of the settee and she's watching *Antiques Roadshow* with glazed eyes, her half-eaten ravioli abandoned on the floor.

'Mum, don't you want that?'

She shakes her head and Little Gold falls on the bowl, stabbing and devouring the remaining parcels in swift succession until her stomach hurts with a pleasing, slightly sickened, pain. Then she curls her legs up too and tries to concentrate on some stupid woman gawping at Hugh Scully because her vase is worth two thousand pounds.

Do they do credit at the Co-op? She imagines the young man with his clipboard and doubts it somehow. Imagines herself standing there as he shakes his head and people all around stare and tut.

Mum's feet are bare, calloused and ugly from shoes that don't really fit. They stink almost as much as Malcy's and Little Gold tries turning her head away and breathing through her mouth but it's no good. She clambers over the arm of the sofa.

'Gonna go and read for a bit, Mum.'

'Alright, love.'

Her eyes are closed now and her head lolling back against the settee. The people on the telly haven't noticed though, they're still enthusing about the rare and ugly vase as Little Gold leaves the room.

The golden eagle has a lamb in its talons and the dark green of Christmas spruce around it. The feathers are more fuzzy than they should be but she can see that the person who drew it was trying their best to show quite how fierce, how surprisingly big, the bird is. She peers into its murderous eye and strokes the torn wool of the lamb. Needs must.

Sliding the slip of paper, carefully, from between the pages, she lays it on her pillow. Dad wrote this, pressing the blue biro into the paper, meaning something more than just the numbers and letters of it, surely? Surely he left them something more than that?

Words circle in her head, dancing with each other in surges of anger, helpless fury, turns of small, pathetic fear.

Dear Dad

There's nothing for tea tomorrow

Dear Dad
Ali throws up whatever there is anyway
Dear Dad
Mum isn't like Mum anymore. What have you done?
Dear Dad
I don't know if there's any stuff left in Malcy's inhaler

Well, that's one she can solve, isn't it? It's still where it was on the night of his last attack. She shakes it. There's the comforting rattle. She presses the top and a fine mist of droplets bursts into the still air of their bedroom. There's that anyway. There's the stuff that calms Malcy's raging chest.

Little Gold curls up on her bed, watching the white sky. A noisy tumble of starlings, maybe ten or twelve of them, flit across the pane and settle on one of the roofs opposite. In the autumn there are big flocks. Mum takes her, took her, to see them turning in the sky over the sea, covering the old West Pier with their dark braiding. Then they'd lift. They'd all lift together and ball, spin, churn in the air like someone stirring the sky. All together. All communicating somehow. All understanding.

Little Gold closes her eyes and, when Malcy gets home later, she's fast asleep on top of her duvet, wearing all her clothes.

CHAPTER NINE

Peggy's sitting very still in the twilight, waiting for the tablets to work. Cars pass on the road outside and her bedroom clock ticks its sweet, familiar heartbeat. She's holding tight to the ribbon that binds the edge of her powder blue blanket. Heals in the Tottenham Court Road, 1957. Her fingers stroke the satin, grip the springing wool. It's still in good nick because you get what you pay for.

Roll, swell and breath-stealing peak of pain.

She waits, eyes closed.

Peggy knows well how to acknowledge pain and let it be a companion rather than an adversary. Pain acknowledged is pain borne. Pain fought will always defeat you.

But it's not a companion she seeks. Peggy is no masochist. Hence the tablets.

As the surge recedes, there's a pleasing picture behind her eyes – the child at her table, swinging her feet and munching the cake. Her blonde head bowed. Little Gold, something small and precious and formless still. Peggy feels her breath evening out again but, soon, too soon, there's another surge.

Grinding pressure inside somewhere like the twist of a broom handle to her back, something driven through her pillows into her body. It builds and, at its peak, seems to echo, pulsing in her shoulder, her forearm, her gut.

Sleep isn't possible with this much pain and neither is ordered, sequential thought, but bubbling memories are frothing, lapping at the exhausted edge of her mind. Memories of time spent with this companion before – in migraine-afflicted middle years, in the first flush of her arthritic hips or the raw agony of a scald on her arm.

She's known pain in a thousand guises, from broken skin to broken heart and, stripped down, it's always the same companion. The months she spent closest to its cold, blank centre were the ones at the cusp of girl and woman and, though she tries ineffectually to bat them away, the memories come spooling out.

Under her sheet, curled tight in the ivory light, Margaret can smell herself. She picks the scents apart – armpits rich, crotch yeasty and tinged with stale urine. The musty scent of her hair glued to her sweating scalp. The bad air crawls in, stripping her nostrils, corroding inside, keeping her alive in spite of herself. Each moment is stitched to the next – day becoming night becoming day again and still she is lying here, her body transforming into something hollow, a broken dog-whelk shell, perhaps, exposed on the peak of a pebble bank. The wind whistles through the shiny, calcified structures of her.

Peggy blinks. It's been a long time since she ventured back underneath that sheet. She opens her eyes wide, peers at her liver-spotted hands, knows that memory, that perception of herself as a broken shell, that was real, that happened. And somehow it was that, turning herself into a metaphor, that had enabled survival. She was something other than herself when herself was simply too hard to be.

Up, like Lazarus, to empty her bladder. Her bare feet on the back step. Waiting for the lav in the startling light of outside. She hears the snap of his braces, the clank of chain and then he's there. She meets his grey eyes and drops her gaze to the Picture Post *rolled in his fist. She steps aside. In the lav is the smell of his bowels, fruit and dark, and the seat is still warm from his skin. She manages a trickle of hot pee that burns before shuffling back to her room. Mum comes with the nightly mug of Bovril, the* Evening Argus *opened to situations vacant and a stub of fat pencil. She lays them beside the bed like offerings to a deity. 'Come on, Margaret, you have to try.'*

But Mum had been wrong about the trying, of course. Sometimes there is no trying to be done, just waiting. Margaret had known that if she were a broken whelk shell she would, in time, be something else. And so it had proved, in time. Peggy looks at her bedside clock. It has been four minutes since she swallowed the tablets, which is no time at all. No time.

Breathe. Close your eyes. Wait.

Mum's mystified face floats against the flashes and bursts of Peggy's sealed lids.

If the war hadn't come? What then? Committal? St Francis'? Cropped hair, straightjacket, funnel in her throat? Paddles applied to her to her pale, white temples? Fire in her cortex to burn the madness out? It happened to others, more than rarely, to girls like her, to girls who lay like shells on mattresses.

But the war came and changed it all. The war came and changed her.

Allen West, Munitions. Women in overalls with pursed lips, their fingers fast and precise. Jokes to turn the air blue. 'Not in front of Margaret!' 'Don't listen to 'em love!' 'No better than they ought to be.' Songs rippling the length of the bench as they work their chain of metal pieces. They twist, connect, conduct. Transmitters. Receivers. A bite of something sneaky slipped underneath the table to her palm. A smile. A nod and a yawn. Margaret assembled, re-assembled. A woman out of a girl.

The drug is doing its work in her body and gifting her the sweet, sweet lessening of pain at last. Nothing is so sweet as that lightness, that lifting. Always true. The reward. She whispers a quiet mantra.

'The reward for staying alive is being alive, Peggy Baxter.'

She closes her eyes and lets the story roll on.

Fire watching. A night on the hill looking East across town. Watching for flames in the velvet of the blackout. Someone leans across with a cigarette. 'If Hitler comes there's no point running, and I've always made my home by the sea. Do you smoke? Here, go on... It's Margaret, isn't it?'

'Peggy, Peggy Baxter.'

Peggy's eyes fall on the packet beside her bed. She picks it up, shakes it and lays it down again. Three or four at least. Enough for now.

Re-christened, Peggy walks home in the grey dawn light, splashed silver across the sea. The barbed wire beach and nameless streets leave her aching for change, for escape. And, at home, there's Mum.

'I'm going in with a couple of the girls. Digs near the factory so it's not so far to come.'

Sleep's washing over her now, memory melding to vivid dream. Assisted by the tablets, surely, but, for all that, no less her own unconscious, no less the loosing of her own mind.

Mum and Dad at a timeless tea-table, spread as a picnic on the grass of the crem. Stale digestives. Potted meat sandwiches. Dad knocks out his pipe on his heel, clears his throat but doesn't speak. Mum has a bowl of water there, her wrists blunted in the suds. Washing her nets on the grass by the teapot.

'Shameful these are. The filth of them…'

Somehow she hangs them in the crystal Downland air, layer on layer of drapery until Peggy must force her way through. Then she's running, pelting down the chalk-splattered hill, feeling the bite of flints through the thin soles of her shoes. Full-pelt. Out of control. There, beyond the iron gates, the child is waiting.

CHAPTER TEN

Little Gold is sitting behind the privet hedge that runs around the tennis courts in the park. It's at its most dense now – the dark full-green of summer, each leaf dusted white. She's close to the playground, can hear clearly the shrieks and shouts of kids on the swings and the roundabout, but she can't be seen.

She's digging into the dry, grey earth with the folded corner of a small rectangle of card, her invitation to the end of year Leavers' Party. Her first thought, as she picked it up from where Miss Hawkhurst had laid it on her desk, was that she didn't have to go. They can't make you go to a party, surely? Still, she's weighing up the cost. Go and there's a list of problems, not the least of which is clothes. But don't go and they've got one more blow in. Next year, at Parklands, she'll arrive as the girl who was too scared to show her face at the Leavers' Party.

Malcy's voice surprises her. He doesn't come down to this end of the park much and, if he does, he's usually on his own, having been sent to fetch the ball back. But now he's just the other side of the hedge, probably on the bench there, talking to someone.

'Half four?'

'Yeah, about then. Dad'll be here in a minute, you can check with him.'

'Sounds really good. Who's gonna be there?'

'Just some friends of Mum and Dad's – Don and Elaine. Elaine's got incredible tits and she never wears a bra.'

Little Gold freezes. Boy Talk in Boy Land and she's listening in. The heat in her cheeks infuriates her. There's nothing they can say that will embarrass her, so why is she blushing? Malcy's laugh is a stilted see-saw covering the need to speak, so at least she knows he's feeling awkward too.

'And there's a kid called Peter who might be there if Keith brings him.'

'Who's he?'

'Oh he's from a children's home in Croydon. He's alright. He's a coloured kid. Okay though.'

'Will he be staying over too?'

'Dunno. Depends… There's Dad!'

There's a scuffling noise of Malcy and Kev leaving the bench and running up the steep bank towards the road. A car door slams and there's his voice. It rings out, a bit too loud, like a newsman from the telly, or a DJ on *Top of the Pops*.

'Hello boys! Malcolm, I believe Kevin has invited you along to our place on Friday?'

Malcy's reply is too quiet to catch. She crouches at the edge of the hedge. The simplest thing would be to just go over if she wants to know what they're saying but if she stands up she'll be revealed as the earwigger she obviously is.

'Yes! I'll swing by in the Sierra and pick you up…'

It's infuriating, this half-heard conversation, and Little Gold leans slowly out from the hedge. Malcy and Kev have their backs to her but Roy is facing into the park. Squatting beside the privet, her knees cramping and calf muscles burning, she shifts and shuffles and Roy's eyes dart into hers.

'Hello, young lady, I didn't see you down there.'

Malcy spins round as if he's been slapped and Little Gold looks away.

'Right then, Kevin, we'd better be making tracks. I'll see you on Friday, Malcy.'

As the car reaches the corner, Malcy lifts a hand to wave.

'Were you spying on us?'

He's stamping down the slope, his bag bouncing on his back.

'What? No!'

'Yes, you bloody were, LG. Hiding down here listening to us.'

'I was here before you arrived. I didn't know you were gonna sit down so close, did I?'

Malcy turns away and sets off towards home. She jogs after

him, calling out to her brother, in spite of his hunched shoulders and stamping feet.

'I wasn't spying, Malcy. Honest I wasn't.'

Her tone is a measured blend of aggrieved and apologetic and it does nothing to appease him. He shouts back.

'Yeah, well, you should mind your own business.'

He's panting, lengthening his stride to out-pace her, but Little Gold just starts running, until they're shoulder to shoulder again.

'You going to a party at Kev's then?'

'What did I just say?'

He's trying to keep hold of it but his anger's fading with the energy expended to get up the hill so fast. She chips away, needling him to let her in.

'Yeah, but, are you?'

'You know I am. You just heard. Friday night. I'm staying over.'

'That sounds brill.'

Malcy stops to pant and Little Gold stands alongside him, panting too.

'Really brill.'

Malcy's like her – temper up and temper down, not a patch on Ali's boiling rages that can simmer on for weeks. The last spark of anger dies in his eyes.

'I've got to go down the doctors, LG. Mum said I have to ask for a repeat prescription for my inhaler. I'll see you later, okay?'

He could have invited her to come along but there has to be some sort of punishment and it doesn't matter really, not if he's forgiven her. She watches him jogging away. His hair's well past his collar now and hours of sunshine have bleached it pale and bright.

Little Gold wanders on up the path, head down, kicking a stone and trying to imagine herself at the Leavers' Party. It's proving difficult. She can picture the hall, everyone in their best stuff – girls in ra-ra skirts and legwarmers…

'Oi, watch it, mongy!'

She's almost walked into Wayne Whittaker, broad and red-faced, blocking the path in front of her. She averts her eyes, swiftly, from his face. His trainers are black with yellow stripes, bulging, struggling to contain the hefty feet inside them. At the toe, a curl of rubber is coming away like orange peel.

She takes a step to one side and so does he, blocking her path again.

'I said, watch it, spaz...'

She glances to her left. Malcy's long gone. The park's emptying and she realises the football game's broken up for the day.

Wayne takes a step closer and she can't help but step back. His smell is layered, deep tones of the grimy clothes and a wash of today's ripe sweat.

'Got a message for your brother, the bender. Malcy Woofter. Tell him the blokes in the toilet want him for a gang bang.'

It's idle, this sort of insult. He just hasn't got anything better to do and she waits for him to be satisfied, to say whatever he thinks will hit hardest and then let her go.

'Know what I'm talking about, little spaz? In the toilets, yeah? The poofs, the benders? They want your brother. They've all heard about him.'

She does know what he's talking about. She's not sure exactly what they do in the park toilets but she knows it's dirty stuff. The boys are all warned off by parents, older brothers, each other. They piss in the bushes at the opposite corner of the park and jeer at men making their way to the toilet block.

She lifts her head and looks into his face. There's a crust of something bright orange in the down on his upper lip and the smell is sickening on his breath – Wotsits. He notices her looking and wipes a fat, pink hand across his mouth. That's unsettled him, her noticing. Just the flick of her eyes was enough to drive him away for a moment. But he rallies quickly and resumes his assault with relish.

'They all know he's a Little Bummer Boy. That's what you need to tell him, okay? Tell him Wayne says they all want their Little Bummer Boy. Got that?'

She isn't quick enough. Her decision to run translates itself into just a hesitant step forward and then there's his hand on her shoulder, heavy and hot through her t-shirt. She can feel the damp of his palm, seeping through the cotton onto her skin and she imagines it marking her like black, squid ink.

She's handed him control and as he leans in for the kill, she flinches with each word.

'He's a Little Bummer Boy in a family of freaks. Your dad

fucked off with a tart because your mum's a piss artist and everyone knows she's shagging that old tosser she works for.'

Those are his best shots and each insult is cumulative, like a volley of slaps to her head. Little Gold's reeling, stunned that he seems to have this speech prepared and that, wrapped in the idle insults, there's some filthy kernel of truth.

In one movement she ducks, twists and runs, crossing the road with swift glances right and left. As she streaks along, she passes Peggy Baxter on her bottom step, holding onto the wall, her foot hovering over the pavement.

'Hey! Little Gold!'

Little Gold slows but can't make herself stop. Instead she dances lightly on her toes as Peggy finishes her careful descent.

'Where's the fire?'

He's still there, just across the road.

'I've been hoping to bump into you, but it seems you almost bumped into me.'

She tries to acknowledge Peggy's weak joke with a laugh but it comes out in an unconvincing blurt. He's at the kerb now but he won't cross, surely? He won't say any more in front of Peggy Baxter.

'Anyway, here's the thing. I wondered if you could spare some time on Sunday to help me with my books?'

Her eyes are such a light blue, it's almost white, and Little Gold feels herself held in their gaze. Peggy Baxter's gaze might be a force-field. Like a *Star Trek* trick of invisible protection, these eyes are shielding her from the looming boy.

'I think you'd like that, wouldn't you?'

Still it's hard to reply.

'Y…'

She glances across the road and Peggy Baxter looks too. Wayne Whittaker turns and walks into the park. Better than a force-field. Weapons in her eyes. She turns them back to Little Gold and they dance with her smile.

'Yes?'

Little Gold nods.

'Same time as before?'

'Yes. Thank you.'

And then she runs.

CHAPTER ELEVEN

On Friday, after school, Little Gold finds Ali sitting on the front steps drinking a can of Diet Pepsi. The radio beside her is spilling out a news bulletin into the sunny air and Ali's book is splayed, fat spine up, on the step beside her. Little Gold sits down next to her sister.

'What are you reading, Ali?'

Ali holds up a hand to silence her, her head tilted to the voice on the radio talking about Argentine surrender. The book's black cover is split by a bright green stem topped with a red rose bud and the raised words of the title, *If There Be Thorns*. She starts to read the back but her sister reaches across and plucks the book from her hand.

'It's pure escapism, LG, and not for you.'

The news bulletin ends and there's the jazzy, over-excited voice of the DJ introducing the next record. Ali turns down the radio and sips her Pepsi. Little Gold imagines the fizz on her own tongue.

'Are all your exams done now then?'

'Yep, that's it. Now I'm going to do shifts at Woolies and wait for the results.'

Results will mean university. Results will mean Ali gone. But that's ages away, weeks and weeks, and in the meantime she's here and finally free from the endless revision. Little Gold watches a wasp circling the radio, each loop bringing it closer to the sticky attraction of the Pepsi can.

'Now we've won the war with the Argentinians is that just it? All over?'

'Nobody wins in wars, LG. Anyway, that whole thing was just some last gasp of imperialism or a way for Thatcher to boost her popularity by murdering conscripts. God knows.'

Little Gold doesn't know what imperialism means. There are mint imperials – hard, white mints like tiny beach pebbles. But last gasp means something dying. The soldiers have been dying, burned and drowning too, she's seen it on telly. Maybe the next war will come soon.

'What about Russia and the nuclear weapons? Do you still think we'll all be killed by them and the radiation sickness and all that?'

She *is* interested in what Ali will say but she's distracted too, her eyes drawn back to the damp can tucked close beside her sister's hip.

'Oh, yeah. This doesn't change any of that. Most likely scenario is we'll all be annihilated, I'm afraid.'

'Oh.'

'Don't worry about it though, there's no point.'

A bead of wetness slides down the side of the can, bisecting the logo.

'Can I have a swig?'

'No. Get your own.'

'I haven't been getting pocket money.'

Ali sighs and passes her the can.

'A sip. A sip, not a gulp.'

Little Gold tilts her head and slurps at the Pepsi, squinting into the sun.

'Hello, girls.'

She's standing at the bottom of the steps, her corduroy jacket draped over her arm and her bag sliding from her shoulder. Her blouse has popped open on the swell of her bust and Ali gestures at the revealing little gape.

'Mum!'

'Oh…'

Her fingers scrabble, hopelessly, at the small pearl button.

Little Gold sips gently at the tilted can again, but Ali's hand swoops in like a hawk and whips it away. She tucks the drink back onto the step and looks down at Mum.

'You're early.'

'Well, yes.'

Her ascent towards them is erratic, each step angled slightly differently as if each is a separate challenge. She smells of armpits and, worse, there's a rich hum composed of fish and old wee drifting out from under her polyester skirt. Little Gold locks her eyes on the ground. It's what they call 'letting yourself go'. God knows where Mum has gone these days.

Mum pauses in her climb and looks down as if she's forgotten they were there even though she spoke to them barely a minute ago.

'Ah, girls, come inside now. Where's your brother?'

Little Gold answers without looking up.

'He's gone to stay over at Kev's, remember?'

'What, again?'

Mum coughs and scratches her armpit.

'Oh, yes.'

She clearly doesn't remember any such thing.

They trail into the kitchen, a miserable caravan, and Mum attempts to fill the kettle but the stack of crockery in the sink is too high. There's a dangerous shifting as she rams and twists it to get it under the tap. Little Gold hovers at her shoulder imagining the damage happening deep inside the mountain of china and glass. Eventually Mum gives up.

'Damn it! Don't any of you know how to wash a plate?'

Slamming the kettle down onto the counter she reaches up and takes a small glass from the highest cupboard. The half bottle of vodka is a new departure. Little Gold looks at its apparently innocuous clarity and shudders. Something about the flatness of the bottle, small and medicinal, made to be slipped into a pocket or a bag, seems to whisper secrecy, solitude, illness.

'Sit down. I need to talk to you.'

Her drink is gone in a gulp and she pours another.

'It's not good news.'

Little Gold's shoulders are tight and high and she senses something in the tingling tension, something like the peeling of wings from her back. She's a sparrow suddenly, poised on the edge of her chair, ready to fly.

'He's sacked me. Clive's sacked me.'

'What? No!'

Ali's shrill voice does it. Little Gold finds that she's flitted up onto the top of the kitchen cupboards and is looking down at the miserable tableau of their filthy kitchen below. Her beady eye takes it all in – the grit and stick of the floor, the cheesy patch on the counter next to the fridge where spilled milk has hardened into a yellow crust, the thick black of the cooker top. And there's Mum, re-filling again, and Ali leaning across the table with veins bulging on her thin neck.

'Well, what the hell are we supposed to do now then?'

Mum's reply is stone-weary and slightly blurred.

'You can stop bloody screaming, Alison. That's what you can do. Stop the bloody screaming and drama.'

'Because it'll all be fine, yeah? Is that it, Mum? It'll all be fine somehow. By bloody magic?'

Mum's answer is a shrug and her palms raised to cradle her forehead.

'Well, there's no point talking to you. This is pathetic.'

Ali leaves the room, stamps up the stairs and slams her bedroom door.

Little Gold blinks, considers the crack of the kitchen window propped open above the sink. How many wing-beats to Peggy Baxter's house? It's not far to that glowing kitchen with the open back door and Jaffa Cakes on clean plates. Mum's voice, muted and dull, tugs her back.

'I'll take a couple of Codis and have a lie down.'

It's a new box. Splitting the foil with trembling hands, she drops the pills into her glass where they froth immediately in the dregs of vodka. She tops the glass with water and pads off along the hall in a foggy cloud of unwashed defeat. Little Gold, still a bird, blinking from the top of the kitchen cupboard, watches her go.

Then she plummets, folds her wings and becomes human again, human and determined, suddenly, to do something. The gluey hopelessness of Mum, the brittle fury of Ali, they aren't the only choices. She needs to find a problem she can solve.

The silken drape of the shirt, hanging on the rail in their bedroom, is somewhere to start. It was Malcy's big mistake.

He'd worn it just once. A cream, double-breasted shirt might be the epitome of style if you're in Duran Duran but it can still make you a total poof if you're fourteen and wear it to a Christmas party. It's beautiful though. She fingers the sheen of the cotton and slips the shirt from the hanger.

Struggling out of her t-shirt, she slides her arms into the sleeves. The fabric is cool. It takes her a couple of minutes to figure out the buttons, the placket of the front, and she has to turn back the cuffs. But it's good. It's light and bright, a fragment of something clean and un-stained by the chaos of the house. She lifts the collar around her neck and feels transformed, instantly more powerful, and she thinks this might make it possible. If she can wear this to the Leavers' Party, then it might just be okay. But what else? What can she wear with it?

She twists the wheel on the radio and Adam Ant fills the room. Little Gold clambers onto Malcy's bed and starts to bounce, trouserless, her skinny legs scissoring in the air as she sings.

'You don't drink, don't smoke, what do ya do ya don't drink, don't smoke…'

Black trousers. She needs black trousers and sticking out from under the bed is a mud-crusted leg of just that. It's one of Malcy's two, school uniform, pairs – evidently the one he's currently calling dirty. She jumps down and tugs them out of the mess. Five minutes scraping with her fingernail and she's shifted the worst of it. The rest will come away with a damp cloth.

Nik Kershaw was on *Top of The Pops* with his trousers rolled up, so that's okay, and it only takes three turns to make them wearable. The gape at the waist is too much though and she digs into Malcy's drawer for a belt. The trousers bunch on her hips but that'll be okay because the shirt will hang down. Footwear's a problem. It'll have to be her trainers because that's all she's got but in her mind she's wearing black boots, silver buckled and tight to her knee. Dandy Highwayman. She sweeps two fingers across the bridge of her nose, adding an imaginary stripe of white.

Drawing two curled pistols from the air at her hips, she fixes one of Malcy's sticker footballers, stuck wonky on the chest of drawers, with a gimlet eye.

'Your money or your life!'

He stares back from his little frame, oblivious to the hold-up.

She runs to the bathroom and considers her reflection in the toothpaste-splattered mirror. This will be okay. This is the best she can do anyway, so it'll have to be. She'll add a white t-shirt underneath the shirt. It'll be too hot, of course it will, but better safe than sorry.

The sense of having a plan, of being prepared for something, is a welcome relief. She can hear Mum snoring from her bedroom, a gurgling roll and then a grunt, but she doesn't need her, she's solved this herself and now she's going to tackle something else she's been putting off.

Lying on her bed in her pyjamas, Little Gold smooths the sheet of crumpled paper over the back of an annual. She's torn it from a pad and it's got a ragged edge. The ghost of Roy of the Rovers is coming through from underneath. She can't find a pen, but there's a pencil lying on the floor, a bit blunt but useable.

Dear Dad,

I hope you are well. I am well and so are Malcy, Ali and Mum. Ali has done her exams. I am going to the Leavers' Party at school. Malcy has got lots of stickers in his album now because Kev's dad bought them for him. Mum

She looks at the slanting lines of writing, too fat and silvery in the blunt pencil. It's a mess, the mess made by someone who didn't have decent paper, who couldn't even find a pen. She screws it up and hurls it across the room. So much for plans, so much for sorting things out.

It's getting dark now and Little Gold slips under the covers, suddenly heavy with weariness. She wanted to wait up for Malcy, to hear about the party and the people there. But perhaps he's not coming home – she doesn't know, can't remember. She hears Kev's voice in her mind,

Incredible tits and she never wears a bra…

There's a buzz, a fizz between Little Gold's legs, and the startling image of nipples, peaked and visible through clothing. She slides her hand into the warmth of her pyjama bottoms and closes her eyes.

CHAPTER TWELVE

Shaw hauls the slice of lamb's liver from his bowl and across the lino, gnawing with his side teeth as Peggy watches the lengthening, bloody trail of what should have been her dinner. There's something pleasing in his gory, ruby pleasure; the slick noises of his teeth and tongue and ecstatic purr. He's the essence of himself.

When he's finished eating, the cat leaps onto the table, washes his face and paws and settles across her open newspaper. Accepting the inevitable, Peggy gives up on the article she's trying to read about youth unemployment and devotes herself to his demands. Her hands pour in smooth sequence over his black silk head, down his spine. They're good hands, and she's vain about them still, the long fingers and broad palms.

'There we are then, my sleek Prince. There we are.'

He rolls and arches his back – the blackberry pads of his paws stroking at the newspaper, caressing the face of the Pope.

'Ha! You leave the Pontiff alone you old atheist. There's nothing for you there.'

The cat nuzzles at her fingers, her knuckles, lavishing her with feline adoration.

'Cupboard love, my darling, cupboard love and I know it.'

And isn't that a comfort? There's nothing this cat needs beyond a slab of something bloody and a warm hand on his spine. Simple needs she understands.

Peggy takes a sip of her gin and tonic and eases open the button on her trousers. The cool juniper's blurring the edge of the evening, just enough, just enough for now. Blurred edges seem unavoidable these days. Sleep, like eating, is abandoning its patterns, sliding through cracks and claiming her when she stops for a moment's rest in the armchair, then staying just out of reach in the small, dark hours. Dawn can be nightfall and nightfall dawn and one bite of toast can be breakfast or supper. Even she herself, her orderly self, so comforted by patterns, by delineated times and spaces and people, is fuzzing at the edges. She can feel herself blurring, like watercolours bleeding out over the permanent ink of her boundaries.

She's invited the child again. She's invited her to come close, to slip a small hand around the spine of a book and read the title. Perhaps to look at her and ask,

'What's this about?'

Admittance. Admission. Some sort of... It's ridiculous to be nervous but she is. The thought of the sharp eyes scanning her titles is making her heart knock at her chest. There's an intimacy in it. An undoubted intimacy.

Where's the mother? It's been weeks at least since she's seen her. And the child seems hungry. Are they always that hungry? A mess too. A beautiful, raw-edged little mess. And the other day she was running, running from that big lad in the park, perhaps? What does any of that mean? What does anything signify? She doesn't know. She doesn't know and she's tired now. She swallows the last mouthful of her drink and closes her eyes.

Here's Mum with the flat iron hissing on the steaming collar of her blouse, pressing sharp the gymslip pleats as Dad buffs her conker shoes. She's their little ambassador in the world across the doormat. She's untrammelled still, believing she's all the sorts of clever the teachers say she is. Plaits bouncing. Macbeth in her satchel.

'What's that you've got, Margaret?'

'Miss Fitch lent it to me.'

Tragedy. Inevitability. It's one of the stories of Margaret Baxter anyway, well-turned out on her way to school. She was decent. She was beyond reproach.

Peggy takes her glass to the sink and rinses it, then rinses it again, running her fingers around and around the rim.

She wants one last cigarette before bed and she smokes it in the living room, in the yellow glow of the standard lamp, running her eye along the bookshelves. If she trips and stumbles on the third row, where Radclyffe Hall sits between a Dickens and *Mrs Dalloway*, Little Gold won't. She's just a child, a child coming into her home to sort books, to eat biscuits and chat. Chit chat. That's all. Company. Peggy grinds her cigarette stub into the glass ashtray and turns off the lamp.

CHAPTER THIRTEEN

The old lady's veined hand draws a book from the shelf and passes it down. Little Gold wipes it over with a duster and adds it to the cardboard box beside her.

'I think, Little Gold, that I should not be allowed into second-hand bookshops.'

It's a stretch to the next shelf up and there's the sound of strain, of effort, in her voice.

'They're my downfall, my absolute downfall. It's so hard to resist.'

She turns a few pages of the book in her hand, lapsing into silence, and Little Gold waits, crouched beside the box of rejects, holding the soft yellow duster in her hands.

The bookcase, viewed from this angle, looks like a cliff face, with the new, dark spaces being caves and niches in the rock where a small sea-bird might nest. Tiny, light as a hummingbird but fierce as a gannet, flitting about Peggy Baxter's house, she could be that. She pictures her abandoned trainers and shucked clothes in a heap on the floor and Peggy Baxter explaining to them all.

'She's living in my bookshelf. I don't think there's any cause for alarm.'

But then she remembers Shaw. She wouldn't last long.

From nowhere, the thought of the Leavers' Party pushes to the front of her mind. The Adam Ant clothes, folded and ready in her drawer, seem ridiculous suddenly. Perhaps it's impossible, un-survivable. Maybe she won't go.

Peggy sighs and relinquishes the book.

'Here we are. I think this one's had its day too.'

The book is hard-backed, with a plain, anonymous cover and the title stamped on the spine. Little Gold opens it, admiring the purple-tipped pages. There's a smell, comforting and dry.

'Why do you like second-hand books so much?'

'Lots of reasons. You get more for your money than buying new ones. And there's so many books I haven't read, why limit myself to new publications? Oh, and I'm very keen on hand-written dedications.'

'What do you mean?'

'You know, where people have given them as presents... Like this.'

She's holding out an open book and, on the faintly spotted title page, there are words written in pale blue ink.

To Tabitha, I don't suppose I ever shall. J.

Little Gold takes a moment to work out the handwriting, the elaborate curls of the script and the large, sure-of-itself, J. J must have been certain that, no matter how many years passed, Tabitha would remember and understand the message.

Peggy sits for a moment on a low rush stool and leans over Little Gold's shoulder.

'That's an excellent one. It adds a whole other story to the book, doesn't it?'

'Yes, I suppose it does.'

Little Gold looks more closely at the J. John, Janice, Jeremy, Joan...

'Now, coffee, I think. Would you like to try milk with a dash? A little bit of coffee in hot milk?'

Little Gold's wary. The old lady doesn't have normal coffee – hers gets brewed in a glass domed pot on the stove, hubbling and spitting like a witch's brew. It smells good though.

'Um, can I have a small cup?'

'Of course. I'll do you plenty of sugar in it. I couldn't get Jaffa Cakes, I'm afraid. Do you like Wagon Wheels?'

'Oh, yeah! Thank you!'

When Peggy's gone, Little Gold wanders around the room, stroking the surfaces and peering more closely at the decimated bookshelves. Catching sight of herself in the large mirror she stops, stretches out her arms to span its width and then starts to turn, slowly. There, in the mirror world, its corner sparking with reflected sun, its surface misted with dust motes, she's entirely safe, untouchable and warm. She can hear her breath, lets her fingertips stretch and when Peggy returns, their eyes meet in the glass.

'Here we are then.'

Peggy puts down a tray and hands a mug to Little Gold. The drink is milk-soft with just a hint of the fierce coffee underneath. Peggy holds out a Wagon Wheel.

'Tuck in! Now, there's plenty more books up here that can go... If you can just put the photos on the table out of the way, then I can see what's what...'

She takes a gulp of her own coffee, black and steaming, and starts to lift photographs down from the highest shelf.

She passes two to Little Gold, both in frames made of wood so dark that it's almost black.

Little Gold wipes her fingers hurriedly on her jeans and arranges the photographs on the small table in the bay window. They stand in rings, like the audience in an amphitheatre, the largest at the back and smaller ones in the front row.

Most of them are posed, formal groups of people in close up but one is a figure, blurred and windswept, standing next to a motorbike on a stretch of empty road.

'Not much of a picture, I know. It was taken by some chap I asked in the pub car park, at Kingston, near Lewes. It was our first trip out together.'

Little Gold looks more closely, peering into the fuzzy features.

'Me and my Triumph, I mean, not me and the chap!'

'This is you, with the motorbike?'

The shock in her voice is embarrassing and Little Gold feels herself blush. But Peggy seems quite unconcerned. She reaches up for another photograph.

'Me, 1959. I loved her. Here's another one, look.'

In the next picture, Peggy's standing beside her bike with two other people. Little Gold recognises the Dolphinarium on the seafront with the railings that are still there today. The bike is black but gleaming white down one side in the sun coming off the sea.

'Who are they?'

'My friends, Magsy and Jean.'

She looks more closely, making out the curve of breasts under the jumper of the one she'd thought was a man. She's wearing trousers with pleats at the front and her hair is dark and slicked like Elvis. Peggy leans closer and points at each figure in turn.

'Me, Magsy, Jean. Vi took the photo, I think.'

Magsy. She looks again at the quiff of hair, the sharp crease of her trouser legs, the pointed shoes. Jean's wearing a wide skirt like one of the girls in *Grease*. She's got a handbag on her arm and she's turned toward Peggy. They're both laughing.

'Here's one of Vi.'

It's a large close-up photo of a woman stroking a cat as it walks across a table in front of her. Little Gold realises that it's the table she's standing beside and that the room is this one.

'Is Vi your sister?'

'No. Vi used to live here with me.'

She has long dark hair, held back in a ponytail, and dark eyes. Her head is tilted to one side as though she's talking to the cat. The line of her chin is straight and the cream expanse of her cheek looks so soft that Little Gold wants to reach into the photograph and touch it.

'What's the cat called?'

'He was called Bumpkin. Can you give those a dust for me, do you think?'

Little Gold wipes the cloth gently over Vi and Bumpkin as Peggy starts to hum. It's a song that she recognises, 'You are my Sunshine'. But, as Peggy repeats the tune, she spins it off to other notes that carry it higher, lower, away and back.

As the shelves are thinned of books and the dusted photographs replaced, the song spins on. When the clock chimes five, Little Gold wants to reach out and take its slender hands in the tips of her fingers. She wants to pinch time here and hold it still so that she never has to leave. But she must.

As she opens the door for Little Gold to leave, Peggy pauses.

'Little Gold, is it okay, you coming to help me like this? Should I maybe talk to your mum about it, do you think?'

*Mum, hummock in her bed. Or shuffling through the kitchen –
ragged, greasy, trailing her smell.*

'No! No, it's fine. She's fine about it.'

'Well, in that case, would you like to come again and perhaps
help me with some of the boxes in my loft?'

'In the loft? Oh, yeah!'

She can't help the grin and Peggy chuckles.

'I suppose that suits your avian nature, eh?'

Little Gold remembers that word used in her book at home.
Avian: of, or related to, birds. It's why a bird enclosure is called
an aviary.

'Yep, I like all high places.'

'Thought so.'

Little Gold turns to leave.

'Hang on a minute… Take these, eh?'

She's holding out three more Wagon Wheels.

'They're a bit much for an old 'un like me.'

CHAPTER FOURTEEN

Little Gold shouldn't be this far from home on a school night. She's allowed over the park and up to Fiveways, but not down here to the cycle track, not without asking. Asking wasn't an option today though. Mum's afternoon rest stretched on past tea time and no-one else was about.

She's not sure why she's come here in particular, her feet just brought her, and she's sitting on one of the low wooden benches looking at the big circle of sky above the track, cut into segments by the vapour trails of planes.

'Right then.'

She takes the pad of writing paper from her shoulder bag and turns to a blank page. If she's going to do this then she's going to do it properly. She puts their address in the top-right corner and then the date and then pauses. Miss Hawkhurst says the best thing when you're writing a letter is to have a plan about what you're going to say. All day, all through singing and science and geography, Little Gold has been listing in her head, ordering her thoughts but now, faced with the blue-white sheen of Mum's best writing pad, none of it seems possible.

Why? Maybe because Dad left them in the other world, the one where clothes got washed and folded in her drawer, where tea was always on the table and Mum was in the kitchen with her hair brushed, not in bed in her thick, fishy stink. It doesn't seem possible, to make him understand and, more than that, she doesn't want to put the words there. Words written down make things more real, more true.

She closes the pad and wanders over to the fence surrounding the cycle track. The gate's locked but she can just get her toe into the mesh and she clambers over and drops onto the tarmac. Dad taught her to ride her bike here, running along behind shouting,

'Keep going! Keep going!'

And she'd been dead proud. Only six and good enough to ride figures of eight and race Malcy for whole circuits. Malcy always won though, unless he got wheezy.

She jogs a circuit of the track and runs through the list in her head again. What matters most? What should Dad know? Nothing, nothing, nothing. None of it. She runs faster, pumping her legs and sprinting flat-out until her chest is burning, her thighs are jelly and her mind a pleasing blank.

She stops at the gate and pants for a few minutes before climbing back over and wandering out into the street. An elderly couple, arm in arm, the man wearing a grey suit jacket like Grandad might, are crossing the road towards her. She steps to one side so the lady doesn't have to put her puffy foot into the drain.

'Thank you, young man.'

Little Gold replies with a smile, small and closed-mouth like a boy, and crosses towards the horse chestnut trees running in a leafy strip up the centre of Surrenden Road. She certainly shouldn't be heading this way, it's even further from home – a dual-carriageway that the traffic roars along. There's not much roaring this evening though, just the purr of an occasional car over the noise of the breeze in the heavy leaves.

It's way too early for conkers, the small spiky cases are just forming on the branches overhead, but she looks into the grass anyway. Before he left, when he was just a normal dad, coming home after work, taking Malcy to football, he was never the one they went to with problems. Not even Malcy would have told him anything that mattered. He'd have waited 'til Dad was at work and then gone to Mum, found her peeling the potatoes or ironing or something and asked her. They all did. Maybe not Ali. Maybe Ali had never talked to any of them.

She reaches a curve in the road where it branches off to Patcham and the fields of the Downs beyond. She's come further than she meant to and she realises, with a little dart of shock, that it's getting dark. It must be way past nine. Crossing from the tree-lined strip in the centre of the road, she reaches the pavement and starts to jog home. The large houses are mostly fronted by high walls, some with overhanging shrubs and trees, which the wind is stirring. Shadows are dancing on the pavement as the streetlights flicker into life. Her jog becomes a run.

'Hey! Hey! It's Malcy's sister, isn't it?'

The man is standing beside a large car, parked in a curved driveway. It takes her a moment to recognise him and it's really the gleam of the silver car bonnet that makes her sure.

'Where are you off to in such a hurry?'

Roy holds up his car keys.

'Can I give you a lift?'

She's panting slightly, her feet itching to run on.

'It's okay. I'm just going home.'

The light's on in the living room and a woman, tall and slim, wearing a cream dress like a Roman toga, is drawing the curtains. Kev's mum. Roy jangles the car keys.

'Come on. I'm just going up to the off-licence at Fiveways, anyway. I'll drop you off.'

Little Gold doesn't move.

'It's okay. I… I don't mind running. You don't have to.'

'No arguing, young lady, I don't think your mother would be very pleased to have you roaming the streets quite this late, would she? Come on.'

He unlocks the car and reaches across to the front passenger door. It swings open towards Little Gold.

'Hop in.'

It would be rude to run off, really rude. She climbs into the car, her heart hammering with shame. She's been caught out, too far from home, too late, and now this is the punishment. He slams his car door and she's overwhelmed by the smell of his aftershave in the small space.

'Seatbelt on please.'

Little Gold reaches over her shoulder, fumbling with the belt. The more she tugs, the more it catches. Roy twists sideways, looming hot and close beside her, his breath huffing and the scent of cigarette on his breath. Little Gold jerks the seatbelt frantically, but can't get it across her chest.

'Now then, aren't you getting in a pickle, eh?'

He takes the seatbelt from her and Little Gold drops her hands into her lap.

'Here we are then.'

It's taking him a few moments to draw the belt in a slow, smooth line across her. One hand clips it home and the other rests on her chest, his thick, hairy fingers splaying out now, containing the strip of seatbelt but pressing, cupping around her nipple.

She looks at the glove compartment, where he kept the stickers for Malcy. She looks at the dials on the dashboard. Petrol gauge, speedometer. Just her eyes can move. His fingers press and circle and it hurts.

Finally he takes his hands away, turns the key in the ignition and reverses out onto the road.

'What are you doing down here then?'

She can hear her voice replying, cracked and dry at first, but then clear. She sounds like herself. That's her voice, over the rush of blood in her ears, the thundering pulse of her heartbeat.

'I just went down the cycle track.'

'Uh huh, and…'

He pauses at the junction with Preston Drove, waiting for a car to turn and Little Gold hears laughter spilling through the open door of the pub beside them.

'And forgot your bike, I see.'

 No. I was just… I was just having a run.'

There's her voice again, doing its best to sound normal.

'I see.'

The car is humming up the hill and Little Gold fixes her gaze on the passing lampposts, counting the road junctions. Any minute now they'll be at her house. Roy pulls the car alongside the kerb and silences the engine.

'Here we are then, your royal highness. One princess delivered home and all before midnight.'

She's punching at the place where the seatbelt fixes to the car as his hand descends and covers hers.

'Allow me.'

There's the crush of his knuckles over her own and then the sudden give of the button and the freeing of the belt. She scrabbles at the door, flicking up the ashtray in a shower of dark specks. Roy chuckles and leans across her again, freeing the catch. Little Gold scrambles out of the car, stumbling up the kerb.

'Thank you.'

She's already running and he raises his voice to call after her.

'You're welcome, sweetheart. Come down with Malcy some time, eh?'

The wind is wild now – gusting and shaking the overgrown bushes of their front garden as she runs up the steps. As she slides the key into the front door, she hears the car driving away.

CHAPTER FIFTEEN

The park is heavy with the scent of mown grass. From down by the playground, mostly deserted because of the ferocity of the grid-iron heat, Little Gold can see that the football match has given way to a fight with the clippings. The shrieks and shouts, the laughter, are wild and edgy, clumps of grass bursting against retreating backs like snow. She wanders slowly up the hill watching the boys hurling, turning, leaping like dancers.

'Oi, Darren! Darren! Here ya go!'

'Ha! Spastic! Nice try!'

Malcy's there, mostly running away but getting in occasional, ineffectual handfuls. The air is thick with dusty specks. Then, by some fluke, Wayne Whittaker turns round and takes Malcy's latest missile full in the face. His anger erupts with a roar.

'Aaargh! Bastard! Want some, do you?'

In a moment he's on Malcy and she sees her brother crumble to the ground. The boys bundle in and he disappears under a tide of bodies. She starts to run but it's a steep uphill climb and she's aware that she's slow, far too slow. The boy-clump writhes and buckles and for a moment she sees one of Malcy's skinny legs and his kicking foot in its blue and yellow trainer. She runs harder, pushing through the burn in her chest, feeling the saliva thickening in her mouth.

She's close enough now to hear the words peppering the grunts and laughter and she can see her brother again, staked like a sacrifice on the shorn grass.

'Thinks it's a hard man, eh? Little poof…'

Darren Coles and Wayne Whittaker are each pinning one of

Malcy's shoulders to the ground as the other boys grab handfuls of the cut grass and shove it down his shorts.

'Here you go, Woofter!'

He's fighting, purple faced and covered in sweat, but he's hopelessly outnumbered. One of the boys grabs his kicking legs, pressing his shins down, and his trainers scuff wildly, sending clouds of grass and dust into the air.

'Piss off! Wayne, piss…'

And then Wayne's thick hand is over Malcy's mouth, cramming it with cut grass, and Little Gold leaps, launching herself over the backs of the crouching boys and slamming into Wayne's head and neck. She feels her kneecap strike him with a sickening bony clonk, just below his ear. Her small hands claw at his greasy hair as they both topple sideways onto the ground.

'Hey!'

He shoves her and she scrabbles away, crouching among the boys like a cornered cat. There's a sudden stillness and the only noise is the high whine of Malcy's wheezing breath. Hands are withdrawn from his prone body and he struggles to sit up. Little Gold is aware of a deep throb in her kneecap and Wayne is rubbing his head as Darren Coles speaks.

'It's his little sister! Malcy Woofter's likkle sister.'

It's a faltering, nervous attempt to regain the upper ground and the other boys don't respond. Little Gold feels fury erupting from her gut, astonishing her even as she spits out words, lashes her arms at the boys, clearing them away from Malcy as if they're a pack of wild dogs.

'You fucking get off him! You bastards! You fucking bastards! Can't you hear him? You could fucking kill him, you know?'

Malcy struggles to his feet, picking strands of grass from his wet lips, spitting, wheezing deep in his chest.

'You don't fucking touch him! Bastards.'

She's backing away from them, aware of Malcy stumbling alongside her but not daring to really look at him, keeping the boys her focus until they reach the road. Her knees are trembling and she braces them tight as they stand at the kerb, letting cars go by. Finally, she looks at him properly and Malcy's eyes are wide with fear. She blinks away an image of him darting into the traffic, getting struck and then rolling from a car bonnet. Grabbing his hand, she whispers sideways,

'It's okay, Malc. Hang on.'

The hand in hers is hot, damp and limp.

The cars swish on, too close to get between, too fast to risk running. And all the time she can feel it, his increasing struggle to breathe.

'Hold hands on the road like a good boy!'

There's a hesitant wave of laughter from behind them and Little Gold forces herself not to turn round, to keep her focus on the road.

'It's okay, Malc. I'll get your inhaler. Come on, Malc.'

Finally, there's a break in the traffic and she strides out, tugging Malcy's hand. The front steps are a mountain and he can climb only one at a time. Little Gold shoves open the door and shouts into the hall.

'Hello? Mum! Ali!'

There's no reply. Malcy's leaning on the wall now, his eyes closed, each whining intake of breath seemingly louder than the last and Little Gold can feel herself slipping into panic.

'Hello?'

Still there's no reply.

'S'alright, Malc, I'm getting it. I'm getting it. Hang on.'

She runs up the stairs into their room and wrenches open his bedside drawer. It's not there. There's a small, cylindrical space in the corner, like the cavity of a lost tooth, but no inhaler.

'Shit! Shit!'

She starts to pull stuff out, hurling it onto his bed, until the drawer is empty – just a grubby white panel staring up at her. She runs her hands over the mess of objects on the bed –pens, sticker-backs, gum wrappers, a broken yoyo – praying for something to transform under her touch, to become the thing they need.

'No… No…'

She is close to tears, the room starting to swim, when she spots a bag on the carpet by the bay window. It's stuffed fat, lying in a block of sunshine, the straining plastic dotted with droplets of condensation – his swimming bag from school. The warm plastic gives under her ripping fingers and there's the smell of chlorine, the thin dampness of the old yellow towel, Malcy's trunks and, yes, his inhaler. She snatches it up and hurtles down the stairs, stumbling and swinging around the banister post.

He grabs at her hands.

'Don't panic, Malcy! Don't panic!'

It's a stupid thing to say. As the words spill from her mouth, over and over, she's seized with a mad desire to laugh. She's Jonesie from *Dad's Army*, piss-weak with terror, pretending she knows what to do.

He's jetting the stuff now, struggling to calm himself enough to time it right, his hands shaking too much. He tries again. If it doesn't work she'll have to phone an ambulance, right? Yes. It'll be a woman and she'll say,

'Which service do you require?'

And she'll say, 'Ambulance please' and give their address and make sure not to sound like a kid mucking around because they won't come then. They won't come if they think she's a kid mucking around.

But as she rehearses the words, hovering in the kitchen doorway, her eyes flitting from the phone to her brother's face and back again, she sees the terror subsiding. There are droplets of sweat across his forehead and upper lip and his sea-green eyes look filmy and exhausted but the fear is seeping away. He sits down on the bottom stair and she slides alongside him, trying to match her breathing to his, willing the soothing air to slide down into his lungs the way it slides so effortlessly into hers.

As his breathing quietens she can hear the drip of the kitchen tap into the sink and the hum of the fridge. His upper arm is warm against hers and she looks down at their feet, four battered trainers lined up close. The croak of his voice startles her and she jumps.

'I'm going to have a bath. I'm knackered.'

'Okay.'

Following him up the stairs, she watches from the bathroom doorway as he turns on the taps. As he eases his t-shirt over his head, cut grass rains down around him. On the insides of his pale upper arms there are patches of bright rosy finger marks and scratches. He turns his back and she gasps. Each of his shoulder blades has a raw patch where it was ground against the hard earth and she's reminded of the body of a pigeon she once found on her way to school, its wings ripped off by whatever had found it in the dark.

'Jesus, Malc, they've really hurt you.'

He turns to her, frowns and gestures for her to step away. Then, without a word, he closes the door in her face.

Mum's bedroom is dim and quiet but Little Gold hears a rustle and a muted snore from inside. There, curled on her bed as usual, is Mum, wearing her blue skirt and apricot blouse as if she'd got up for work and then realised there was no point. Her face is smooth, calm and peaceful and Little Gold flounders for a moment, a sob pushing up from her chest. There's a flash of anger too, sharp as a firecracker, but it dies away, leaving nothing but the strange fizz of relief. They're here and safe, and soon Ali will be home from work.

She hesitates, for a moment, outside the bathroom door, listening to the sloshing inside, and then goes to their room. Lying face down on her bed, relishing the cool of the cotton against her cheek, Little Gold feels her body vibrate with the receding wave of adrenalin and yawns burst from her mouth, one after another like a knotted chain of magician's scarves. She closes her eyes for a moment.

When she opens them, her eyes blur and then focus on Malcy's bed. There's something sticking out from the corner of the mattress. It looks like a magazine but it's been ages since Malcy had a *Smash Hits* – not since pocket money stopped. She gets up, crosses to her brother's bed and tugs it free.

What strikes her first is the shocking incongruity of the lady's make-up, her perfectly styled hair and the fact that she is topless. Of course, she's seen page three women before, but this is different, the colours so bright and shiny, the letters of the magazine title running across the top of the woman's halo of blonde curls: *Men Only*. The woman has glossed, parted lips and open legs fringed with a beaded skirt. Little Gold is sure that inside there will be something more.

She glances over her shoulder and down the length of the landing. The bathroom door's still shut.

'You okay, Malcy?'

'Yeah.'

She feels instantly guilty, calling out like the caring sister when she just wants to know if he's still in the bath, if she has a few minutes more to investigate this astonishing thing. Opening the magazine at random, using just the very tips of her fingers, like Malcy might dust it for prints, she gasps.

How could you do that? How could you look into a camera like that with your legs wide open? The woman is lying back in a wicker rocking chair, her eyes half-lidded and her tongue lapping at her own upper lip. With one hand she is lifting and cupping a breast as if she's offering it as a gift. She's naked but for a pair of red sandals with stiletto heels. Little Gold feels a tightening between her legs, a rush of heat and a fascination so intense that she turns the page without even glancing towards the bathroom.

This woman has her fingers there, parting and spreading the dark-fringed pinkness and looking down at it as if she's surprised at what she's found. Little Gold can feel her heartbeat in her throat and her hands shake as she turns the page again.

There are dense columns of text and she reads the first paragraph quickly. It's a story about a slave woman called Maisie and a cruel master called Mr Pearce. He has stripped her cotton shift from her ebony body and is preparing to whip her as Little Gold hears the sharp crack of the bolt being loosed on the bathroom door. In one swift movement she closes the magazine and thrusts it back under Malcy's mattress.

She gets up and steps aside to let her brother enter the bedroom. He has a towel wrapped around his waist and she tries not to stare, not to look at his damaged body.

'I'll let you get dressed. I'm gonna go and see if Ali's on her way down from the bus stop.'

'Okay, LG. Don't go over the park though, will you?'

''Course not.'

She hurries out of the house and into the relief of the cooling, evening air.

CHAPTER SIXTEEN

The bus swings around the curve of the Old Steine and judders to a halt. Peggy thanks the driver and steps down onto the pavement. There's a stiff sea breeze rippling her white hair and she stops for a moment and breathes in as deeply as she can. Mum's voice gusts into her mind.

Get some of that ozone into your lungs, Margaret! There's nothing like it.

Gulls are wheeling above her, their lusty cries overlapping each other and, down on the prom, trippers are packed tight. The entrance to the Palace Pier is a dark sea of bodies and, as she watches, two young people emerge from the crowd and run across the coast road shrieking. On a day as glorious as this one, Brighton never fails to show the trippers a good time.

She looks at her watch; he'll be waiting.

The Lorelei was a haunt right back in the fifties, somewhere they'd all felt comfortable, and it's here still, tucked into Union Street in the Lanes, its little glass panes gleaming. There's no sign of him and she is just easing herself into the window seat when she remembers the garden. And there he is, of course, Vern, sun-worshipper, sitting at one of the small wrought-iron tables smoking a cig, his eyes closed and his face tilted to the sky.

'Hello HMS Vern.'

He opens his eyes, smiles broadly and stands up.

'Darling.'

His kiss on her cheek is firm and she's immediately caught in the wave of expensive aftershave and Consulate cigarettes on which he sails through life.

'Sit you down.'

As he pulls out a chair for her, Peggy is aware of his gaze sweeping her up and down. Nothing gets past Vern.

The young waitress takes her coffee order and Peggy opens her cigarette packet. The flint's going in her lighter and, after a couple of failed attempts, Vern reaches into his jacket pocket and offers her his box of Swans. Never a lighter for Vern, always the little rattling box of pink-tipped matches, struck alight on walls or the sole of his shoe.

Late night, in a shelter on the front, Vern strikes match after match as each one is gulped down by gusts coming off the sea. They're giggling, half-cut, shivering. 'Darling, you're going to have to get closer.' Hutched into the wing of his open jacket she catches, at last, the little flame, sucks it into her cig. A bobby passes by, glancing at them, taking them for lovers.

'So, Peg, duck, how's things?'

'Pretty good. How about you?'

'Fair to hideous, darling, fair to hideous. Dick's been talking about moving to Eastbourne again.'

Dick's threat of Eastbourne is no more real than Vern's exaggerated response but it's a safe old battleground on which they can engage.

'Does he mean it this time, then?'

'Oh, I don't know. If he insists though, Peg, it will be the end of me. Can you see me there? Sitting out my final years in a piddle-warm armchair, eating Madeira cake?'

She smiles and looks sideways at her friend, her blue eyes twinkling and playful, enjoying his familiar vivacity, the way he attracts glances from people at the tables around them.

'I can't see it ever coming to that.'

'Well, so you say. But we're not all like you, a lady of independent means with a house of her own.'

Dick has the money in their partnership, partly because Vern had never been one to keep a job. He's far too easily bored and endlessly distracted. Still, they're comfortable together and Vern can look forward to a safe retirement in a beautiful home.

'I know, I know you're a kept man and how you hate it.'

'I hate *you*, Peg Baxter.'

She winks at him and Vern rolls his eyes.

Vern Henderson, her 1951 discovery. A dark-haired boy, painfully thin and almost impossibly beautiful. He stood at the bar of the Black Lion, his wallet open in his hands like a book, seemingly oblivious to the turned heads all around him.

'Gin and IT, please.'

He sipped his drink and caught her eye.

'Is this seat taken?'

'No, please.'

She was startled by the proffered hand.

'Vern.'

'Peggy.'

She has often wondered what life would have been like if she'd decided to go home ten minutes earlier that night or if he'd just walked by and sat with the paunchy, balding man at the next table who'd been all but salivating since he walked in.

But he'd come to her. Seven years her junior, brimming with unwarranted confidence and mystifying levels of trust. Peggy had watched him career through the town like a newly fledged gull chick.

With the help of Marguerite Patten, she'd ended his days of Spam and boiled potatoes. In return, he'd broadened her horizons in other directions, taking her on the train to London and shoving her at the door of The Gateways.

'Remember you're a catch, Peg Baxter.'

The waitress returns with her coffee and a plate for Vern – Welsh rarebit, bronzed in patches, with a sprinkling of cress and a sliver of tomato.

'You eating, Peg?'

'No, thanks, I'm fine with coffee.'

As the waitress turns away, the tray dangling from her hand, Vern reaches out and catches her wrist; holds her broad, blotched arm as if it's porcelain.

'That's a beautiful bracelet you've got there.'

The waitress, previously at the surly end of civil, melts in front of Peggy's eyes.

'Thank you!'

'Honestly, it's gorgeous, reminds me of one I saw in Chelsea recently. Suits you. Whoever gave you that, they're worth keeping.'

The waitress smiles her thanks to him again and there's a bounce in her walk as she goes to clear an adjacent table. Peggy exhales and peers at Vern as he unwraps his knife and fork from the paper serviette.

'Charmer.'

'But of course! You get nowhere without charm, which I think I've mentioned before.'

Vern never means to wound and when he goes too far she retreats to one of her scripted responses, something built of levity but a barrier between them still.

'I've done alright, thank you, Vern Henderson.'

He cuts a large triangle of rarebit and chews happily, tilting his face up to the sun again. He really is a man who finds joy everywhere he goes and her love for him is resilient. Whatever Vern says or does, the love springs up again, like a shaggy dandelion in the centre of the lawn of her life.

'You and Dick getting away this summer?'

He sips his coffee.

'No. He wants to get the lounge decorated and the back garden re-landscaped.'

Dick owns a beautiful house in Hove, near the cricket ground. Somewhat to her surprise, but also to her immense relief, Vern has been living there with him for more than fifteen years.

This one's special, Peg.

How she'd heard that before, for decades. Through all the handsome, dangerous men – the liars, the thieves, the ones more broken than wicked but none the less destructive for that, the ones too ready with their fists, the ones who'd taken so much she was sure Vern wouldn't get up again. And all the while he'd seemed oblivious to anyone kind, anyone gentle or warm. It was as if he'd been put on earth to seek the bad ones and to pay for it.

As Vern eats and drinks, Peggy watches his slim wrists, marked with silvery scars on the inside, where the skin is softest. So much paid and yet here he is still, chewing his rarebit and making her laugh as ever.

And this one, it seems, really is different. Dick is a man

more realistic about Vern than anyone else has ever been. He's indulgent without being stupid and he has something that Peggy recognised on their very first meeting: integrity. Still, that doesn't mean he never plays games.

'So the Eastbourne plan's nonsense as usual then? He wouldn't be doing the place up if he wanted to leave, would he?'

'Well, I don't know. He says it's to make the house more attractive to buyers.'

'But it's all to his exacting specifications, I imagine, Vern?'

'Oh yes.'

'Well then, he's just torturing you.'

'Terrible man. I don't know why I stay.'

She says nothing to that and he reaches across the table and takes her hand.

'Anyway, how about you, Peg? Any exciting summer plans?'

He knows better than to ask if she's going away.

'I'm getting my house in order too, Vern. Having a damn good clear out.'

'Oh, good plan. You've got God knows what old tat in the loft, haven't you? And all those books.'

Vern isn't much of a reader and she's long since given up trying to persuade him. He loves his *Coronation Street* and films of any and every sort. That's something he shared with Vi, trips to the cinema. As if on cue, Vern speaks,

'And will Her Majesty be gracing us with her presence this summer?'

Standing beside Vi at the door of his Brunswick bedsit, Peggy's aware it's been too long since she knocked. Inside she hears him moving around but still he doesn't answer.

'You look nervous, Peg.'

'I just want him to like you.'

Vern, taciturn, shoulders hunched, sloshing tea into a filthy mug as Peggy bites her lip. Vi meeting his eye as she knocks it back and then, as she drains the dregs, giving him a crooked little smile.

'I think you'll find that needs a go-round with a Brillo.'

They'd adored each other immediately, maintaining a terrifying level of banter over the following twenty years that often made

Peggy gasp. Each striving to outclass the other with ever-more-inventive offensive wordplay and yet never once, in all those years, falling out.

'I'm thinking of inviting her for a few days, if she's free.'

Vern tilts his box of Consulate in her direction and Peggy shakes her head.

'You know I have to be three sheets before I find those appealing!'

He strikes his match on the whitewashed wall beside them and Peggy is warmed by a dizzying surge of affection, not just for him but for the sunshine and the sweet safety of this little yard of a garden, a place where they fit. She orders another coffee and Vern asks if they have any shortbread.

*

He walks her to the bus stop, kisses her cheek and squeezes her elbow.

'You'll let me know when Her Majesty's due then?'

'I will.'

He waves as he turns the corner and she feels herself relax. It had been good to see him and to see him looking so well. That's one less thing to worry about anyway. Vern's safe and sound with his man, his Swan Vestas and his immortal, spotlight charm.

An old chap in a flat-cap holds out his hand to indicate that Peggy should board the bus ahead of him and she nods her thanks, pays her fare and heads upstairs. Upstairs is so she can have a cig, of course, but she doesn't. Instead she watches a family, three ginger children, one ginger mother and a bald father, traipsing along Grand Parade towards the sea. The sun's gone in and the wind picked up again and they look thoroughly miserable.

If Vern ever wonders what happened between her and Vi, he never lets on. For a while she'd waited for him to ask. For a while more she'd longed for it. And then she'd accepted that he never would. Sometimes Vern is too scared to look. A little boy with his fingers laced over his face, he waits for the bad thing to go away.

That's what he did when she and Vi fell apart. It *was* frightening, of course, what could happen between people who loved each other, people who had seemed, even to themselves, so securely attached. But sometimes bombs go off, don't they? Sometimes there's a doodlebug chugging overhead. Then its engine cuts out and in the moment of awful silence you suddenly realise it's far too late. Peggy closes her eyes.

A September morning, dew-soaked and autumn blue. Vi is approaching forty and Peggy far beyond it and all is well in her world that day. All is light and tranquil as she steps across the back step and into their kitchen.

'Look! Aren't these glorio… Darling, what is it?'

Vi's head is on the table, her forehead pressed against the surface and her shoulders heaving. For a moment Peggy thinks death, a phone call, a telegram, something… And then the words. Vi speaks the words and the bomb goes off.

'I want a baby, Peg. I want to hold my child.'

The kitchen tilts and the words keep spilling, over and over, from her lover's mouth.

'I want a baby. I want to hold my baby, Peg. Peg, it hurts. It hurts.'

Peggy lays her hand on Vi's shoulder. It's heavy and empty – a knight's gauntlet – and she's desperate to get away, desperate to leave the room.

'Give me a minute, Vi. I just need the lav.'

There were very few things Vi had wanted in life that she hadn't made happen, very little she had ever denied herself and many things she had achieved that other people had told her she could not.

'And it's not impossible, is it? I know it wouldn't be easy but it's not like you can't abide men. Think how you love Vern. If I found someone as sweet as Vern? And what if it were a girl, Peg? A little girl! I know you'd love her.'

But her cold stare had silenced Vi and they'd lain rigid in bed that night, back to back, unspeaking until, finally, at dawn, Peggy had slept. In her dream she'd been on the beach at low, low tide.

A small child is standing on the shingle bank. His face is tear-streaked and he's pointing at her. He's pointing in horror at Peggy Baxter, skulking in the shadow of the pier. Vi crouches beside him, her hair flying, her wide skirt fluttering. Peggy knows

*the words she's saying, as she clutches him close, lifts him, walks
away. She knows, even though she's far away now, out of earshot,
out of sight.*

'There, there my baby. There, there.'

And that was it, Vi's great baby hunger. It lasted for many
months. It persisted like illness, a fever, a cancer that ate
through their life together. Peggy felt herself weaken, shrink,
blacken, desiccate, until all she wanted was it to stop. All she
wanted was silence.

The bus is juddering at the lights. Peggy grips the metal of the
seat in front and tries, in vain, to halt her memories.

*Walking together in a summer downpour. They're on their way
to the library, pretending life is going on. Vi is crying steadily,
tears lost in the raindrops on her face. Her sobs are pitiful but
Peggy feels nothing, nothing but fury. She grabs the sleeve of Vi's
mac, spinning her on the wet paving slab, and hurls sharp words
into her astonished face.*

*'Stop being ridiculous! Stop being so bloody ridiculous! Why do
you think you can have everything, everything you bloody want?'*

*A bloody thing, a baby, a squalling, new-born baby, is lying
there between them on the pavement in the rain.*

The bus stops alongside the Open Market and Peggy watches
the stallholders packing up for the day. A woman tips a box, half-
full of peaches that look so perfect still, and they fall onto a heap
of rubbish – screwed-up paper, cauliflower leaves. She must
know they aren't saleable now – not good enough, no matter
how they look. The lights change and Peggy's bus starts the long
climb to Fiveways, growling its way up the hill. She rubs her
temples, realising she's bone-tired suddenly, but the memories
won't stop coming.

After that outburst at Vi, she'd got her silence. She'd got
silence to fill her boots, her life, her heart.

'You know I have to go, Peg.'

'I know you have to go.'

*'Don't think I don't love you but it's not enough to love you, not
if it feels like this. Not without the warmth.'*

*Peggy watches as the car sinks over the brow of the hill and
goes back into the house. It's her turn then to sit at the table and*

howl. She howls like an animal, all wound and fear. She curls on the ladder-backed chair, her knuckles in her mouth, waiting for the return of Margaret's awful dark.

It hadn't come, the darkness. Instead there was just the silence of regret. Every day was a little dimmer than it had to be and there was herself, and only herself, to blame.

The bus stops and Peggy steps carefully onto the pavement. The tarmac beside the kerb is sticky in the heat and caught in it there is a soft downy feather. Looking up she sees the gull chick, curled on the grid-iron roof. Its beak is twisted into its feathers and it has no option but to sit and wait there.

She calls into the newsagent for her cigs and her paper and, though she's exhausted, she finds civil words for Mrs Theaker.

'Lovely day, Mrs Theaker, just a bit gusty now.'

'You've had the best of it, I think, Miss Baxter. I think there might be rain on the way.'

CHAPTER SEVENTEEN

Little Gold is holding her breath as she watches Peggy climb. The fragile curve of her ribs is draped in a fine cheesecloth shirt that sways gently with each step up the ladder. With a last push she steps off the top rung and, for a moment, disappears into the darkness above. Then there's yellow light and her face looking down from the hatch.

'Up you come!'

Little Gold darts up the ladder and clambers into the still, hot air of the loft. It's a dense heat and there's the musty smell of things long undisturbed. Peggy picks her way through the piles of boxes, heading for the back of the roof where there's a small square window set into the slope.

She has to stretch to get her fingers to the catch and, even then, it's beyond her grasp.

'Damn thing…'

Little Gold looks around the heaps of cardboard boxes and random furniture. Wedged between a pile of cushions and a table top, she spots a tall stool.

'I bet I can reach if I climb on that!'

Peggy follows her pointing finger.

'Blimey, that old thing was never very stable at the best of times. I wouldn't want you to hurt yourself.'

'I'll be okay.'

Little Gold tugs the stool out and carries it over to the window. As she clambers up, Peggy grasps the seat to hold it steady.

'Easy does it. No rush. Can you reach? We can always postpone until a cooler day.'

'No! I can reach!'

She's alive with curiosity, her eyes roving hungrily over the gaping, bulging boxes, and she can't have Peggy giving up.

The window's resisting though, seeming to deny that it has ever opened, that it was ever anything more than a fixed square of light.

'I just need to give it a bit of a shove…'

The window crackles as the sticky casing rips away from the frame and the small pane of glass levers up into the sky. Little Gold lurches forward and Peggy's hand leaps, presses warm against her tummy to stop her falling.

'Oh! Mind how you go there.'

And then the hand is gone, back to the stool, holding it steady as Little Gold climbs down.

'Well done! I don't think I've had that window open in twenty years.'

Little Gold wipes her sticky palms on her jeans. The heat is still ferocious but cooler air is trickling in.

'Right! What next?'

Peggy Baxter holds out a cherry-red notebook with a springy spiral binding down the side.

'First things first. I think, if you don't mind, I'll give you this pad and pen and you can list things for me as I call them out. Okay?'

Little Gold sits cross-legged on the high stool and writes a heading at the top of a clean sheet of paper:

Contents of Peggy Baxter's loft – 7th July 1982

The window, north-facing and grubby, provides just a dim patch of grey light and most of the loft is illuminated by a weak bulb, dangling from a flex draped over a rafter.

As Peggy moves from box to box, tugging open flaps and shifting heaps of fabric, she hums quietly and emits occasional soft noises of surprise and appreciation. Her outline is indistinct among the clutter and from time to time she disappears completely. There's a silent pause lasting several minutes and Little Gold is about to climb down when the old lady's voice rings out, disembodied, from behind a tall mirror on a stand.

'Right! No more dilly-dallying! Item one!'

It's a strange sort of list. Little Gold recognises some of the things: stepladders, suitcases, Christmas decorations. But there's a lot of paper, stacks of magazines and piles of yet more books. Peggy lifts the lid of a shoe box and exclaims,

'Ah! One box of Kenric newsletters…'

She's silent again, leafing through the contents of the box.

'1967–1975ish…'

Little Gold's pen hesitates.

'Who's Ken Rick?'

Peggy barks out one of her sea lion laughs.

'Ha! No – K-E-N-R-I-C.'

'Okay.'

She's bending over to peer into the box, the ridges of her spine punctuating the curve of her long back.

She speaks again without looking up.

'It's a women's organisation, Kenric.'

'Oh.'

Little Gold has no idea what that might be but suddenly she remembers Avon. That's a women's organisation – a lady used to come to the door with make-up and creams for Mum and leave catalogues too. Maybe these are something like that, though it hardly seems likely.

Catalogues make her think of magazines and she shifts on the stool, feeling a blush rising in her already-pink cheeks. Peggy turns round, offering Little Gold a newsletter.

'Here, look.'

It's just a couple of typed sheets, stapled at the corner and dated August 1974. Little Gold's eyes flick down a list headed DIARY OF SOCIAL EVENTS.

September 25th. Bring your own choice of classical records to a music evening at Maureen's in South London. Refreshments 20p. To book please ring Maureen 698-2870.

Saturday October 9th. COACH TRIP TO BRIGHTON. 50p for members and 75p for guests. If there are any members in the Sussex area who would like to rendezvous with the coach party, would they please contact Rita.

Peggy's smoking now, leaning against a tall roll of carpet next to the window, blowing her smoke through the crack of the open pane. She catches Little Gold's eye and smiles, flicks her ash out onto the slates.

Little Gold flips the page and starts on a column headed ADVERTISEMENTS.

Sussex member late 40s (fem) seeks friends. Box no. 119/74

Feminine lady 38 would like to meet masculine person 40-55. Human and sincere – any area. Box 120/74

Underneath there's some large, bold, curvy type:

Gay Women Read SAPPHO. Vol. 2 available now. 35p

Her eyes lock onto the word and she reads the advertisement again. Gay women. Gay women read *Sappho*. She starts to read faster, darting her eyes down the columns, picking it out again and again. Gay. Gay women. Gay lady. Then her eyes fall on a section in a box on the bottom of the back page.

KENRIC 'PHONE A FRIEND' SCHEME

If you are feeling a little downhearted and would like to have a friendly chat you are invited to contact one of the following members:

Sussex: Magsy Sullivan. Brighton 32522

'Peggy Baxter?'

The old lady is reaching up to the lip of the open window and grinding out her cigarette on the flaky white of the metal frame. She tosses the butt out into the sky.

'Little Gold?'

'Is this your friend, Magsy? The one in the picture downstairs? It says Magsy Sullivan.'

Peggy reaches to take the newsletter back and looks to where Little Gold's grubby fingernail is picking out a name.

'Oh, yes, that was our Magsy.'

She laughs but not a sea lion one, more gentle, a chuckle.

'That was our Magsy alright.'

'Does she still live in Brighton?'

'Oh, no, she got very into the women's movement and moved to London. Travelled up to Leeds for a bit and then lived in a women's house in Islington. Became a real firebrand, rather unsuited to the polite ladies of Kenric.'

'What's a women's house?'

'Just a house where a lot of women live together. Sort of a

commune type of thing. Never my cup of tea, Little Gold. But Magsy was a fair bit younger than me and she'd had her head turned for a while by a woman called Ronnie, if I recall correctly. We lost touch a few years back.'

Peggy returns the newsletter to the box and tucks the lid into place.

Little Gold's head is throbbing and she can't decide whether it's the heat or the pressing of all the questions inside it. 'Women's movement' is something she's read before… She thinks it might have been in one of Ali's CND pamphlets, maybe about the women who've gone to Greenham Common. But what the hell's a firebrand? It makes her think of the *Phoenix and the Carpet*. Like a person hatched out in a flame.

She rubs her damp forehead and closes her eyes for a minute. More than anything, more than anything there's the word gay. Over and over on the soft yellowy paper. She can see it there behind her eyes. Of course she doesn't have to ask what it means. But there are other things to ask, so many other things.

'Come on Little Gold, I think that's enough for today. We're cooking up here. Let's go and have a cold drink in the garden. Can you magic that window closed again?'

As Little Gold reaches for the catch, her eye is caught by movement on the slates outside. There, very close, is a bird. She freezes. She doesn't know it. It's something she isn't sure of – bigger than a songbird and, though it's mostly pale brown, its wing is marked with black, white and a startling patch of blue.

Peggy's whisper makes her jump.

'A jay!'

The bird flies and she turns to the old lady.

'Jay? I've never seen one before, I don't think. Are they in the crow family?'

'I think they might be. I'm not sure. I've got a bird book somewhere. I'll dig it out…'

'Oh, it's okay, so have I. I'll check when I go home and let you know.'

Little Gold skitters down the ladder and waits while Peggy makes a more careful descent.

'I bought a bottle of Ribena, Little Gold. Do you fancy a glass?

It's nice with ice cubes on a hot day. And it goes well with a drop o' rum of an evening too.'

'Yo ho ho and a bottle o' rum!'

There's cold Ribena in the world. There are jays and newsletters full of words. There are boxes in lofts and places where no-one can reach you, no-one can touch. She gallops down Peggy's stairs and jumps the last four.

'That's a fine leap, shipmate!'

Little Gold turns and looks up at Peggy making slow progress down the stairs, her hand on the banister.

'I can jump from the sixth stair really – I do it all the time at home. And Malcy does eight. But I didn't want to scare you.'

Peggy smiles.

'That's kind. You go on out to the garden and I'll bring the drinks.'

Outside there's a wisp of chill in the air. It's probably a sea mist down in the town but it never covers them up here on the hill.

Peggy arrives with the drinks and Little Gold gulps eagerly, draining her glass and crunching her way through the ice cubes. Peggy lowers herself onto the grass.

'That met with your approval then?'

Little Gold nods, her mouth too full to speak. The old lady winks and turns her head away to blow a long stream of smoke through the branches of the forsythia bush.

She looks, sometimes, like someone not quite real, like someone in a black and white film on BBC2 on a Sunday afternoon. Maybe she is. Maybe that's what's going to happen next. Maybe she's going to wake tomorrow into a World War II epic where she's Peggy Baxter's evacuee in a village in the country, German bombers ploughing through the sky above to devastate London. Then she thinks of Mum, Malcy and Ali and fingers of guilt crawl around her heart. How wrong is it to dream yourself into another life?

A spectacularly fat bumblebee, its legs thick with clumps of pollen, is crawling around and around the sticky yellow inside of one of Peggy Baxter's white hollyhocks. Then it heaves its heavy body into the air and settles on the wall of the small blue shed.

'Are you going to sort out your shed too?'

'Do you think I should?'

'It might be a good idea. When we finish school next week, I'll have lots more time to help you. If you want.'

'That, Little Gold, would be lovely. Now, do you want another Munchmallow? They're in the cupboard above the kettle.'

When she gets back, Peggy's stretched out on the grass with her eyes closed. Little Gold settles herself quietly beside her, picking off the chocolate from the white marshmallow and breathing in the smell of the dusty ground and the ghost of the cigarette. Then she closes her eyes too and listens to the noise of the ambling bumblebee and someone's mower a few gardens away. When she opens her eyes again she realises the old lady's asleep – whistling gently on each out-breath.

She sits up and looks closely at the weathered face, at the deep wrinkles around the eyes, the thin purple skin of the lids. She has thick silver eyebrows a bit darker than her hair and the skin underneath her eyes is dark too, and deeply sunken. Her cheeks rise up like small, soft pillows, covered in a criss-cross of fine lines.

She curls up again on the grass, as close as she dares, but not touching – her eyes focussing and unfocussing on the cloth of Peggy's shirt, just inches from her nose. It's only a minute or two and then the old lady starts awake with a gasp.

'Oh, I do apologise, Little Gold, I must have nodded off for a minute.'

She looks down and Little Gold feels the smile burst over her like when they speed up film of flowers blooming. Like there's a big, fat daisy bursting open over her head.

'You look like some small mammal curled up on my lawn.'

And it isn't even embarrassing and she doesn't move. Little Gold smiles up at Peggy Baxter and they stay just where they are, just like that, for a few minutes more.

CHAPTER EIGHTEEN

'Six! Six! Go on…'

Chloe shoves Little Gold in the back to propel her into the space at the centre of the circle of children. She pulls on the thick woollen coat, loops the scarf around her neck and pushes her hands into the men's gloves. They're so large that she struggles to pick up the cutlery but she does and, stabbing at the soft chocolate bar with the fork, she hacks into it with the knife.

A chunk breaks from the corner and she rams it into her mouth. The slab of melting sweetness is almost too big and she struggles to keep from dribbling as she attacks the bar again. It's so hot in the room that the chocolate is tearing like clay under her fork and the noise of the children is full of heat too, a roaring heat bursting from their open mouths as they scream.

'Nah! Ah! Give it! Oh you div, it's there look!'

They're rolling the die in a frenzy of hope and it skitters under crossed legs, away across the parquet of the hall floor and even scoots under the hovering shoe of Mr Tabor as he supervises the bedlam. He laughs and boots it back. She's struck by the anarchy, the breakdown of all that is school.

At last Matthew Collins rolls the longed-for six and Little Gold can sit down. Her mouth and throat are thick with chocolate and she's desperate for a drink but she doesn't dare get up for fear of attracting the eyes again. Every moment in the ridiculous clothes, hacking clumsily at the chocolate, she'd felt them, the laughing eyes of the girls, mocking her.

'Finished!'

One of the other teams has managed to get the whole lot

eaten. The children around her fall on the leftovers, snatching and shoving. Little Gold hangs back, edging towards the wall, but Joanne and Chloe move in on either side.

'Suited you, that coat…'

'Yeah, went with your outfit…'

They snort with laughter.

Little Gold thinks about Malcy. She'd stood in front of him before she left for the party. She'd made him promise to be honest.

Really, though, Malc! Is it really okay?

Yeah it suits you much better than it did me.

And he'd meant it. Malcy hadn't thought she looked like a joke.

She starts at the sudden blast of the playground whistle and they laugh again. Mr Tabor's standing on the podium at the end of the hall holding up his hand for quiet. He doesn't get it but the noise level drops enough for him to shout over the top.

'Okay! Now, no scrum, please, ladies and gentlemen! Help yourselves to the food in a civilised manner!'

Little Gold hangs back from the surge, watching as polystyrene cups of lemonade and handfuls of iced gems rain down on the floor around the feet of the battling children. Mr Tabor adds a sharp edge to his voice as he shouts again.

'NO PUSHING!'

But the scrum goes on and he gives up and goes to chat with Miss Hawkhurst in the doorway of the hall. Little Gold is startled by the touch of someone's fingers, tapping gently on the back of her hand. She turns to find it's Jessica the Jehovah – a girl so shy that Little Gold has exchanged barely a dozen words with her in the four years they've been in the same class.

'What's next? Do you know?'

'I think it's the disco.'

Everyone knows Jehovahs aren't even allowed a birthday party, so how come it's okay for her to be here? She'd like to ask, like to know more about the rules that govern this girl's life and she wonders, suddenly, what's stopped her asking in all these years.

'Jessica, how come…'

She's cut off by the whistle, three blasts this time, and Mr

Tabor's back on the podium, holding both hands in the air. She can see sweat patches in his armpits darkening the beige and cream check of his shirt.

'All cups and plates on the table now! Then into the middle of the hall – boys to the left, girls to the right.'

As the children flow and split into the two groups, Little Gold stands immobile, feeling sweat prickling between her breasts and a renewed wave of nausea in her gut. There's the toilet. Surely, they'll let her go to the toilet? But she's too late. Mr Tabor's taken advantage of her stillness to catch her eye and he beckons her over.

'The idea is to get everyone dancing. You take this bag round the girls and they pull out a slip of paper with a number on it. They dance to the first song with the boy who has the corresponding number.'

She takes the dark blue cloth bag from him. It's the one they keep the quoits in for PE and the inside is giving off a dark, rubbery smell. Alan from 4H, a lanky kid whose nose is always lightly crusted with snot, is circulating around the boys' side of the hall with a similar bag. She edges towards the first group of girls, not looking at their faces, addressing her words to the floor.

'Take one. Find the boy with the same number.'

Word soon gets round and the girls arrange themselves into a loose queue in front of her, hands dipping in to retrieve the folded slips of paper. Joanne, Chloe, all of them come and take numbers but they say nothing to her, seemingly preoccupied with who is to be their dance partner.

Jessica doesn't come and finally Little Gold takes the bag over to where she's standing, close against the radiator.

'You have to take one of these and dance with the boy with the same number.'

She shakes her head. It's barely a movement at all but it's clear and she spins on her heel and slips out the door towards the cloakroom and toilets. Little Gold almost drops the bag and runs after her but she glances towards Mr Tabor and he's watching her, his eyes steady and firm. She pulls out a slip of paper for herself and takes the bag back to the teacher.

'Thank you.'

There's a triumphant look in his eye.

'Alright, ladies and gentlemen. Get partnered up and get dancing. I don't want to see any wallflowers. Let's have you all joining in.'

There's nothing for it but to find the boy who's number 53 and when she does it's Reuben, which could have been a lot worse. He nods at her as Depeche Mode starts to roll across the hall. She looks at the floor, at her own hesitant trainers edging from side to side and then across the room to where Joanne is advancing on Joel Barker. He's a cool kid, has a brand new Harrington jacket and is famous for his ability to shin up the ropes in gym faster than anyone else but he looks ridiculous, Joanne towering over him by more than a head. He's puce as he reaches out tentative hands and cups her waist. She tosses her hair and attempts to rest her cheek on his shoulder, which is a logistical impossibility given the difference in their height.

Mr Tabor slides down still further in her estimation as she watches him laughing with Miss Hawkhurst. This is a game for them. She and the other kids are their toys, paired up like amusing combinations of Muppets. Miss Hawkhurst leans back against the pink sugar paper on the noticeboard, looks down and then up at Mr Tabor through her eyelashes like she's in a photo story. Little Gold imagines the thought bubble over her head.

Maybe he really likes me!

Around her, more pairs are touching now – awkward, arms' length, embraces of waists, rigid palms resting on shoulders. Little Gold thinks suddenly of the sea, of running on the beach, of what wet sludgy sand feels like at the end of a hot day. She stops edging from side to side and shouts to Reuben.

'Need the toilet!'

She scoots through the children and slips out the door, not caring who has seen, not even caring if they come after her. Nothing is getting her back in the hall. Galloping down the stairs into the basement she almost slips, catches at the handrail and crashes through the double-doors into the cloakroom.

There's a small cry of shock and there, hunched on a bench with her feet up and her arms clasped tight around her knees, is Jessica.

'Sorry! It's just me. Didn't mean to scare you.'

Jessica shrugs, trying to regain some dignity in the face of her obvious fear. Little Gold sits down beside her.

'I didn't like that.'

Jessica shakes her bowed head and scuffs the toe of her black patent shoe up against the edge of the bench. Her outfit is hideous – a purple party dress with a white yoke that looks like her mum must have chosen it. As they sit there, Little Gold hears Depeche Mode fade away and Heaven 17 taking their place. Jessica's twisting one of her brown plaits around her finger, tighter and tighter. The bound finger reddens – blood-choked and ugly.

Little Gold glances at her watch. Half an hour more. They can't just sit here. The door to the bottom playground is ajar and she nods her head towards it.

'Come on!'

They've been told the rules for the evening. No-one is to go into any other room in the school than the hall and the toilets and *under no circumstances* is anyone to go outside. But she's going to, and she's going to take Jessica with her, under these circumstances. Right now.

The air outside is soft and cool and the low sun is hitting the end wall of the playground, making the bricks glow a deep orange and winking from the flints. Little Gold leans over the drinking fountain, closes her eyes and sips at the cold water, feeling it trickle over her chin. The relief of her thirst is delicious and she drinks on and on.

Finally she straightens up, wipes her mouth and smiles.

'God I was thirsty! I had to eat about half of one of those massive chocolate bars.'

There's no reply but a grave nod and they walk together the length of the deserted playground. Little Gold can feel the sweat drying on her body at last. Above the high playground walls, the tops of the elms are dancing in a light breeze.

If she doesn't ask her a question then she won't talk. But you can't just demand to know all about being a Jehovah, can you? It's not something anyone talks about.

They sit down on the gritty tarmac, Jessica curling her legs carefully to one side, tucking her skirt around her milk-white knees.

'Where you going next year?'

That's safe. There has to be an answer and there is, but Jessica's voice is so quiet that she has to strain to hear it.

'Parklands.'

'Yeah, me too.'

There's a pause and she hears an ice cream van somewhere, a few streets away, playing a wild and distorted version of *Greensleeves*.

'Is it true that they put people's heads in the toilets?'

Fear has driven the words from her reluctant lips. Little Gold can see it there, flickering in the amber eyes.

'Nah. That's just what people say. My brother's there and my sister went too and it's never happened to them. It's okay at Parklands. It's just big.'

'Oh.'

She can sense the relief, the lifting of some great block of terror, and Jessica leans over and strokes the silky cuff of Little Gold's shirt.

'I like your shirt.'

She's saying thank you. She's saying thank you for the next-to-nothing of just reassuring her that no-one sticks anyone's head down the bogs at Parklands. Everyone knows that. It's an old rumour that goes round every year and every year it's refuted too. Everyone knows it. But not if no-one talks to them. Not if all they hear is the tail end of conversations, the loudest snippets of stories and fights. Not if they're Jessica.

'It was my brother's.'

'I've got a little brother, Nathan, he's only three. He calls me Dessica 'cos he can't say his J's.'

Little Gold laughs and Jessica's pink lips twitch. Her skin is so pale, almost translucent, with a splash of light freckles across her nose. There's something fascinating about the way her face fits together, about the shapes of it, about the thoughts she can see behind her eyes that disappear without being spoken. But she's staring and Jessica's pale face flushes.

A new song is drifting out from the building.

'Hey, Jessica, this one's great!'

The rolling, rising opening bursts into the thumping chorus and Little Gold jumps up.

'Every little thing she does is magic…'

Dancing out here is nuts. But out here there's just the two of them. Out here on the edge, this pale, clear girl with amber eyes, with the ugliest dress in the world, can stare at her and it doesn't matter. Out here, she, in her New Romantic shirt and her brother's trousers, can stare back.

Little Gold knows all the words to this song. She dances wildly, kicking her feet and laughing at Jessica's wide eyes. As the piano slides fast and sudden down the scale, Little Gold collapses herself like a puppet with cut strings and then leaps straight back up again. Jessica bursts into giggles and Little Gold's beaming now, holding out her hand, certain that Jessica will take it.

'Girls! What are you doing there?'

Little Gold freezes and Jessica's laughter chokes to a halt. Miss Hawkhurst is leaning from the open door, the heads of girls darting in and out on either side of her – Joanne, Chloe, Rebecca, Kelly – the writhing heads of the hydra. Jessica scrambles awkwardly to her feet and they make their way back towards the building. Little Gold has the words ready.

'Jessica was feeling sick, Miss. She nearly *was* sick, by the coat pegs. I thought she should come out and get some fresh air.'

Miss Hawkhurst stands aside to allow them through the door. The other girls straighten into a line – chins lifted and uniform smirks.

Miss Hawkhurst's words drip with disbelief.

'And are you feeling better now, Jessica?'

'Yes, Miss Hawkhurst.'

Little Gold prays for her to embellish a bit, say she'd *so* nearly been sick, make up something about an allergy to iced gems. Anything. Instead, she bows her head and turns herself back into a drawing of a meek Victorian girl.

'Go back up to the hall and sit quietly until your mother comes then.'

She turns to Little Gold. Years of being a good girl, of ten out of ten for spelling and polite questions with her hand up, all of that must surely count for something?

'And you? You can go with these girls to fetch brooms from the cleaning cupboard. It's going to be quite a job to sweep that floor.'

Trapped. No telling-off, no punishment, but delivered into their hands with no opportunity of escape.

'Go on then, girls. Hurry up.'

They head for the walk-in cupboard where all the cleaning stuff's kept and, as they reach it, Little Gold glances over her shoulder, hoping the teacher's gone and she can just leg it again, hide in the coats, find a way back upstairs. But there's Miss Hawkhurst, hovering, waiting to see them go inside before she heads back to the hall.

'Hurry up, girls! Brooms, dustpans and brushes!'

Little Gold hangs back, trying to keep from entering the cupboard, but the girls curl into a semi-circle in the small space and she feels Miss Hawkhurst's eyes on her, driving her inside.

The air is heavy with chemicals: bleach and something else, something that might be toxic, probably is. She takes a broom from a hook on the wall and holds it across her body but Joanne catches her sleeve – her draped, Depeche Mode sleeve. She has no choice but to stand still as the fist twists in the soft cotton. Her first words are a direct hit.

'That's a boy's shirt, isn't it? And boys' trousers.'

The twist of the fist in the fabric tightens.

'You're a bit of a freak, aren't you?'

A foot slides between hers and the face looms closer. Fish-eye close. Little Gold can feel the heat of her breath.

'You look like a joke. You know that, right?'

Heads nod around her. There are vague affirming noises and odd words dance in the small space like erratic echoes.

'Freak… Joke…'

'And what's with you and Jessica the Jehovah? What did you say to her, '*Lesbe* friends?''

The hiss of laughter flows from head to head.

'Did you take her out there to feel her up?'

That's a cue for the beast to burst into a chorus of disgust. There's the hawk and gag of retching, the imitation of vomit on shoes.

'Disgusting… usting… sick… makes me sick.'

Little Gold tears herself free, her sleeve letting out a sequence of tiny pops at the shoulder as the seam gives way. The broom clatters to the floor between the girls, catching an ankle.

'Oi, bitch!'

But she's away and running, laughter and words bouncing off the tiled walls and floor, slapping her back as she flees up the stairs and through the swing door to the hall.

The noise-level in the hall makes her ear drums rattle. Some of the boys are running across the floor and dropping down to skid on their knees, while Miss Hawkhurst crouches by the piano, mopping up a big pool of liquid with green paper towels. There's no sign of Jessica.

Over in the corner, Mr Tabor's standing in the open doorway to the playground, where parents are arriving to pick people up. Her heart sinks as she visualises the line at the bottom of the invitation, added in Miss Hawkhurst's best italic writing.

As the party will not finish until 8.30pm, please ensure that all children are collected by a parent or guardian.

She forgot. Shit. She'll have to talk her way out and she'll have to do it quick.

She watches as one of the dads slaps Mr Tabor on the shoulder and then leads his wife and child away, one in each hand. Simon Snickett's mum steps up, ushering Simon in front of her to make him say something. God knows what.

Can she just slide past? If he stops her, what will she say? Can she make up something that will work to set her free?

And then, suddenly, there he is, no taller than many of the kids around him, bobbing like a robin in a hedge, looking for her. Malcy. He's remembered that she'd need collecting. He's come.

She runs through the crowd, twisting her shoulders, swerving and ducking to avoid collisions, and he waves to show he's seen her. As she gets closer, she hears what Mr Tabor's saying to him.

'Malcolm! How are you then? I hardly recognised you. You're such a strapping young man now.'

For Christs's sake, is the man blind? From this close, Little Gold's even more aware of Malcy's slight, fragile frame and lack of height. She stands shoulder to shoulder with her brother as he mutters his reply.

'Um, yeah, thanks. I've come for my sister 'cos my mum's not well.'

'Oh dear, nothing too serious, I hope.'

'No, she just, she just said could I come and pick her up.'

This needs a swift intervention, something to bring everything to a close. She sticks out her hand.

'Goodbye, Mr Tabor. Thank you for the party. We'd better get home now or my mum will be worrying.'

Mr Tabor's clearly startled by her outstretched hand but he shakes it.

'Goodbye. Best of luck at senior school though I'm sure a clever girl like you…'

'Goodbye!'

She waves and they sprint off together, across the playground, jostling past parents and kids at the gate and tumbling out onto the pavement.

The laughter bursts from them, wild and too loud as they tear up the road. An old lady in her front garden backs away towards her open door and Little Gold imagines what she's seeing – mad kids in the evening laughing like lunatics. Trouble.

They stop round the first corner they come to and Malcy bends over, moaning with pain.

'You… You only went and shook his hand! You wally! LG, you shook his bloody hand… Like a nutter!'

They collapse onto the pavement. The pink paving stones are still warm. Little Gold leans back against a front garden wall, feeling the familiar jut of a flint against her spine.

She can reply only in gasped snatches.

'I know I… I shook his hand like… like a businessman!'

The laughter rips out of her again – heaving and bursting from her chest. She feels tears pooling in her eyes and then streaming down her face. Wrapping her arms tight around her aching belly, she lets the tears flow, on and on.

CHAPTER NINETEEN

Peggy is stirring a spoonful of sugar into her steaming mug of tea. This taste for the sweet, for the treacly undertone, has re-emerged from some buried, youthful place. Like Margaret coming in from school, making the brew, ladling in heaped spoons of white, her hand returns again and again to the sugar bowl. It's pure energy, of course. It's a weapon to fend off the encroaching sleep that wants to take her this afternoon, to knock her spark out and eat her day away.

Nodding off in the garden, with the child here too, had been an astonishing lapse in control. To wake and find herself in the open air, with Little Gold so close, had felt strangely wild. Like something animal. She was an aged beast curled on the grass in the daylight with the young beast curled beside. And it was a shock to succumb to this old body's failings and so be laid bare to the child.

Peggy sits at her table, sipping the sweet tea. She slides her feet from her shoes and holds the mug to her brow for a moment.

Being watched as we sleep is an intimate act and it wasn't an intimacy she'd anticipated sharing. Laid out on display, unable to parry the small watching eyes, what had she revealed?

In the years with Vi, Peggy learned the art of waiting for her lover's slow, regular breaths before she let go. And in the mornings, ever an early riser, she'd lain and watched Vi, her eyelids flickering in dream and lips twittering on the edge of a smile. When Vi had opened her eyes, there was Peggy, usually sitting up with her book on her knee and a ready word. She was never the one exposed, she was always the one watching.

Hello, sweetheart.

Watched when asleep we are truly naked and that's a vulnerability not to Peggy's taste. It would need such a certainty, an assurance of unconditional benevolence. Something like the gaze of a parent on a child.

Her parents must surely have watched her as she slept? Her mother must have bent over the crib, touched the tiny chest rising and falling to certain herself that all was well. But if it were so, it ended long before Peggy can remember. Waking in childhood had been a solitary thing, returning to herself in the back bedroom with the yellow counterpane and daisy-patterned nets.

A beautiful room for a little girl.

No-one else there, not ever. An only child with no extended family so no top-and-tailing with a gaggle of cousins. Not a joiner-in so no Girls' Brigade or Guides. And even in the war years, when so many people had been forced into shelters and tube stations, lined up on benches and floors through the night, she'd mostly been in her own bedroom still, listening as the bombers flew over to London.

There was one night, later on, back-to-back in a single bed under a sparse utility blanket with a bus conductress called Yvonne. A choice made in a moment of drunken, lonely desperation. Peggy had allowed herself to doze but had mostly lain awake, watching the light slowly reveal the shapes around her – Vicks VapoRub on the windowsill, splayed paperback on the lino beside the gas fire. Just before the birds started, Yvonne had turned, flung her arm across Peggy's chest and muttered something into her neck – a name, someone's name and a grunt of fury. Her contorted features and uncensored words were enough to make Peggy certain that in sleep she was not safe. That would never be her, so unguarded.

Hence the care, the habits she cultivated in the long, loving years with Vi – learning to cradle her body as it softened and to know the exact moment when it was safe to let go. Then waking early, easing herself apart, to be covered and smiling when her woman woke.

And now she's alone again in bed each night, her only company the people who populate her dreams. And Shaw, of course, with his unjudging, feline nature.

Of all her dream companions there's one, a girl who returns

again and again – in theatres, on aeroplanes, laughing like she's never been away and pulling Peggy into a thousand beds in a thousand rooms. If she could have slept with her, with Enid Gallowglass, curled with her in dark nights, listened to her heartbeat, there might perhaps have been so much less care needed in the years that followed.

She's astride the wall with Enid Gallowglass in the shadow of the great gasometer. Fingers entwined and cotton skirts hitched, they swing over the top and drop down onto loose chippings, beside a buddleia covered in Monarch butterflies.

She'd been waiting for love. She'd believed it would come. Like Jane Eyre found Mr Rochester, there'd be a moment that she'd find him. Studying lads on the tram, in the shops, she'd assumed that one of them would make it happen. One of them would work that spell and she'd wake to a world lit with new light.

If she knew that a woman's scent, the nape of a neck and the swell of a breast, made her heart knock sometimes, she banished that knowledge to the gutter of her mind and held fast to the story of the lad and the fall. It was the universal story, surely? Why wouldn't it happen to her?

But then there's Enid Gallowglass. Enid, her parents and a van full of things from London. Her mother broad as a battleship, her father tubercular and tiny, and Peggy watches as they move their possessions into the house across the street. An ancient aspidistra, a dozen tea chests. Enid Gallowglass sitting on the front garden wall – long legs, honey pigtails and buck-teeth in her smile.

And that was love, or something like it, kicking away her fifteen-year-old-feet. Margaret, reeling, astonished and claimed, could do nothing but accept it. Her days became governed by what she could see from behind the nets of the front-room window.

Mr Gallowglass, a book across his spindly legs, is sitting in a deckchair on the pocket-hanky lawn. Enid Gallowglass brings him a cup of tea, leans on the front wall and makes Margaret gasp.

It hadn't taken much. One walk together to the corner shop for sago and the sharing of a liquorice stick and they were friends. From friends to something more was an unspoken step. But they took it nonetheless.

Peggy lets her eyes slip out of focus. She watches shadows dancing on the kitchen wall. She sees them, Margaret and Enid. Margaret and Enid on the undercliff walk.

Feet cold from the rock pools, they huddle against the white cliff. Something in the evening air is changing. A laugh becomes a spark and then they kiss. Margaret can't understand how right it feels but she knows she can't stop. It's a helter-skelter of a thing. There's no way to stop.

'See you tomorrow.'

Dad's in the hall when she opens the front door.

'And where have you been, madam, 'til this ungodly hour?'

'Sorry, Dad. I was with Enid, Dad. We got chatting and just lost track of time.'

That part was true, in a way, the losing track of time. There was nothing in that summer to hold time properly in check. It ran too fast or hiccupped into eternity and all that Margaret knew was she'd found the love of her life. She lay in bed at night imagining their digs in town, saved shillings for a trip abroad, a Christmas tree with silver bells. All of that imagining but no talking. How on earth, how on earth had she imagined that would ever work?

Peggy scoops Shaw from the kitchen table and he allows a brief nuzzle before struggling from her arms.

'You'd probably not be a Shaw if I hadn't met Mr Gallowglass.'

Mr Gallowglass is peering over his specs, offering her a battered copy of St Joan. 'Read, Margaret. Don't let life stop you and don't you ever go settling.'

She's sitting in their back room as Mr and Mrs Gallowglass talk. The conversation is punctuated by his small, hard coughs. Mrs Gallowglass gestures with a rolling pin, Mr Gallowglass thumps his slender fist on the table.

'Bloody fascists... Strike... Divide and rule... Who's for a scone?'

There are crumbs on Margaret's lap. She brushes them away and catches Enid's burning eye.

Mrs Gallowglass invited her to stay so many times that Mum was shamed.

'They'll think we can't feed you.'

But nothing fed her like being with Enid. Peggy remembers a

long day walking. Walking for miles along the coast to Shoreham. They lay in the long grass on the river bank, where the river broadened and poured into the sea.

Four bare feet smeared with pewter mud and Margaret can feel the pulse of Enid's heart in her chest. Above them, a mackerel sky is lit with gold and they should go, they should surely head for home. The water is lapping, tidal, turning…

Peggy is jolted into the present by a shout from next door. Her sweet tea is tepid and only half drunk. She pushes it away, gets up and heads to the telephone for the faded, blue address book where she can touch Enid's name. She flicks to W and there it is, Wilkinson, Enid, an address in Essex and a faint full-stop. That's where Enid Gallowglass is hiding, under someone else's name on this fragile sheet of paper, thin as tissue, bold as brass.

Above the address, there are four previous entries, each crossed through as life moved her on. Her husband, Richard, is a hearty town planner. Their boys, Keith and Jonathan, inked in and now gone. Peggy knows nothing more than the facts of her life, added to Christmas cards over the years. She's nobody real. But she's still there in Peggy's mind. She's a pure, glowing memory and Peggy strokes the name as tears fill her eyes.

Mr Gallowglass is raising his hand to wave goodbye as the uniformed men lift him into the ambulance. Margaret waves back but turns quickly to Enid, standing motionless at her side.

'But if he's in the sanatorium, what will you do, Enid? If he dies will you move away? Will you have to go?'

Enid gasps and Margaret knows that she's a monster, that this too-much love is monstrous. Enid turns away and walks into her house.

They'd gone back to Brixton – to an aunt and a spare bedroom. It was the sensible choice. It was the only way. Peggy remembers standing at the station, the platform edge an abyss, as they said their goodbyes.

Enid, her mum and three battered suitcases, small beside the London train. Margaret is balling her damp, slimy handkerchief, frantically, into her shaking hand as Enid gnaws her lower lip. She shifts from foot to foot, clearly desperate to be gone.

'I'll write. I'll write. You don't need to cry, Margaret.'

And then they were gone and there was nothing but pain. Blank days stretched out in front of her. There was no-one to tell. There was no-one to ask how long this feeling would go on, if she would ever want to laugh again.

There's a boiled egg on her plate and she's dipping a crust of cold toast in its congealing yolk. Mum is talking, saying something about the weather, while Dad packs his pipe with tobacco. In her sleep last night, something burst from between her thighs... something she can't name. Unbidden and shameful, a terrifying sweetness. Enid brought it. Just the dream of Enid brought it and now what? Now how can she live? What can she do?

Letters came that were worse than no letters, each one landing on the mat like a slap to her face.

Dear Margaret, I hope that this line finds you well. I went to the flicks with Bert Simpson again. Mum sends her best and Dad is no worse...

It was a tidy re-making of Margaret and Enid. A re-writing of love into just insipid pals. Peggy takes the remains of her tea and throws it into the sink, watches as it puddles in the rim of the plug. She's surprised by her anger, the bite and the roar of it, that makes her pause for a moment, then slam the mug down.

What will there be for Little Gold? What will life bring her? Who will it take away? She pictures the blonde head, the up-turned face and guileless eyes. Such eyes won't keep her safe in this world.

The anger fades to weariness and Peggy sighs, rubs her knuckles against her breastbone and lets out a bubbling cough. What can she know of the future? This is Little Gold's time. A different world.

She returns to the telephone table and fetches her Basildon Bond. Folding the newspaper, she puts it aside and writes her address and the unlikely date. How can it be 1982? The wet nib of the pen hangs over the paper and she finds there's only one thing she really wants to write.

Dear Enid. Dear Enid. My dear, dear Enid.
I think this might be a different world.

Peggy screws the lid back onto her fountain pen and returns the writing pad to its drawer.

CHAPTER TWENTY

On the first morning of the holidays, Little Gold is hesitating at the top of the steps down to the beach. The tide is at its lowest point and she can't help but gasp at the vast, mirrored expanse of wet sand in front of them. Malcy's away, jogging down the steps already, calling over his shoulder.

'Come on!'

They always go to the left of the Palace Pier, at least two beaches, that's Mum's rule since they were small.

It's filthy right by the pier and there's too many trippers.

But Malcy's heading right, past the row of tatty trampolines sunk into the pebbles and down onto the beach there. She has no choice but to follow him.

'Malc! Malc!'

The trampoline man's looking at her and she stops shouting, keeps her eyes averted as she runs past him. Being down the beach without Mum isn't something they've ever done before and they mustn't get in trouble.

Malcy's stopped on the shingle bank, thrown down his plastic bag, and he's crouching, undoing his trainers. As she approaches, she watches the breeze lifting his hair and rippling the blue of his t-shirt like a ship's sail.

'Malc! Why've you come down here?'

He falls back on his bum, tossing his trainers down the bank and starting to fire pebbles at them as soon as they land.

'This is where Kev comes.'

'So, he could've come along to our beach.'

Malcy scores a direct hit, a small grey pebble smacking the toe of his trainer with a hollow tock.

'Yay!'

She's irritated at his readiness to abandon what they do, like their way is inferior to Kev's, like Mum never told them anything. But it's too late. Malcy won't move now. He's settled there, raining down a swift volley of missiles on his poor trainers.

'I'm gonna swim, Malc. You coming in?'

'Nah! Gonna wait for Kev.'

She slips out of her jeans and t-shirt and kicks off her own trainers, tucking her odd socks inside them so the wind won't whip them away. Then, arms crossed over her chest, she picks her way carefully across the pebbles.

The exposed legs of the Palace Pier are covered in wet seaweed and crusty barnacles; its ugly nudity on display. It's not bothered though, it looks as confident as ever, reaching out from the land across the shining expanse and into the waves. She steps from a large, rocking pebble onto the cool sand, Brighton's low-tide secret, and starts to run towards the criss-crossing streamers of the tiny waves. She feels like she's been waiting years for today, for the first beach day of the holidays and, even if the sun keeps disappearing behind the bubbling clouds, even if Mum isn't here, even if they're going to meet Kev and Malcy will probably ignore her all day, she's going to enjoy it. They've got a Sunblest bag of honey sandwiches and a bottle of watered squash. They don't have to go home for hours.

The wet sand streams with rivulets that trickle from the pebbles and, here and there, soft, bubbling jets liquefy the surface and suck at her toes. As she arrives in the tiniest waves, she kicks at them, sending arcs of spray into the sunlight, flinching at their cold return. It's best to get in quick and she runs into the water, feeling the strange heaviness as it reaches her thighs, until she's forced to drag her legs on, flinching as the waves lap up around her hips and wrap her body in an icy burn.

'One, two, three, four, FIVE!'

Little Gold ducks into the water, kicking hard, fighting the urge to leap out, to run from the cold, back onto the beach. She can swim a ragged breaststroke and she bobs along, her head aloft, panting at the chill. It won't be this cold for long. If she can just stand this bit, it will get easier and, as long as the sun stays out, it'll actually feel good.

The ruffled tip of an approaching wave splashes her face and rainbow droplets dangle from her eyelashes. She blinks them away, licks her lips and tastes the salt.

Just keep swimming, LG.

'Kev!'

She looks inland to see Malcy leaping from the pebbles and running diagonally across the beach, sliding and staggering on the steep shingle banks. Coming down the steps from the prom is Kev and, behind him, his mum and dad. Little Gold feels her glorious day slip away. She turns in the water, motoring her small feet into the bottomless cold, realising she's out of her depth and not caring, just wanting to swim on forever and not to see the beach with Kev's horrible parents on it. She's been stupid. She should've realised they'd come. Why wouldn't they? They've come in their big silver car from their massive house with a cool box and a windbreak and folding chairs. Even now they'll be spreading it all out, making a kingdom, and Malcy will be crouched there beside them with his tatty Co-op bag.

She swims as close to the pier as she dares, remembering Mum's warnings about sharp metal hidden in the water, about weeds that might shackle her to its rusty leg forever, then she turns again and heads back. She's tiring now, her legs juddering and her chest tight with effort, but the cold is barely noticeable, instead there's a feeling of clarity, a washed-clean feeling that she can see exactly what's here. She swims inland until she's certain she's in her depth and puts her feet down. If she bends her legs a little she can stand here with her shoulders under, catching her breath, rocking in the water, her arms wide and sculling at the surface.

She was right about the kingdom. Roy is hammering a windbreak into the pebbles with a mallet, adjusting it around Kev's mum, who's already stretched out on a sun lounger, oiling her legs. Malcy and Kev have their heads bowed over a large black bag of what looks like sports stuff – a cricket bat and a football are visible at its gaping mouth.

She can't stay in the sea forever. She looks up and down the beach, just a few families are dotted across the pebbles. It's early still and Malcy might want to stay until five, six even. Maybe they'll stay until Roy offers them a lift home in the silver car. The silver car brings an unwelcome image of the seatbelt, his hair-splattered knuckles on her chest.

The day has transformed into something to endure and she has hours to get through. For now, though, she can just swim. She turns back to the horizon but as she kicks into an oncoming wave, a sharp cramp bites at her left foot. It's a ferocious pain, impossible to ignore, and she has no choice but to hobble inland.

Why didn't she bring her towel to the edge of the pebbles? Why? If she'd thought ahead she'd have known the wetness of her swimming costume would make it worse. She ducks her eyes down to her chest. The blatant lumps are puckering the costume right where the seam of the blue top part meets the red of the bottom. She notices with horror that there's a hair too, sneaking out at the leg, clearly visible on her thigh. She tries to shove it back in with her finger, panicking at the thought that someone looking at her right now, someone on the beach, would see her touching herself there.

Once the water reaches just her ankles, she turns and looks out to sea, taking the opportunity to glance down again at her body. Thankful that the hair at least has disappeared, she wraps her arms around her chest and, head down, starts her slow progress up the beach.

'Hello, young lady!'

He's stopped hammering at the windbreak and he's standing with his hands on his hips watching her approach.

'Kay, this lovely young lady is Malcolm's sister.'

Little Gold is almost at her bag. She grabs the protruding corner of her towel, tugs and it unrolls in the air, sending her knickers flying across the pebbles towards Kay's sun lounger. She ignores them, concentrates instead on wrapping the towel around her.

'Hello, sweetheart! That looked like a chilly swim.'

Her voice is as oiled as her long legs. It rolls with what Mum calls 'put-on posh' and Little Gold's conscious of the Brighton twang in her own vowels as she replies.

'Hello. It was okay as long as I kept moving.'

'Well, you won't catch me in there. I haven't been in the sea since Tunisia last year.'

She smiles, flashing large white teeth, and lays her arms down the sides of the lounger. Her nail varnish is turquoise, the exact colour of her bikini, and each nail is filed to a perfect point. She closes her eyes.

Little Gold crouches on the pebbles, wrapped in her towel, feeling the trickle of sea water from the hair between her legs, dripping down steadily onto the stones. It feels like betrayal, like her body will do all it can to humiliate her. She notices a small piece of green sea-glass, pitted frosty-white, lying next to her trainer and, letting go of the towel with just one hand, she picks it up and finds that Kay has opened her eyes again and is watching her.

'Give yourself a rub-down, sweetheart, and I'll put some oil on your shoulders.'

'S'okay, thanks. I never burn.'

'Right! Boys, let's get this cricket going then!'

Roy has stripped off his polo shirt and shorts and is standing there in nothing but flip flops and a tiny pair of trunks like David Wilkie off the telly. She's startled by the bulge there, terrified that he'll see her noticing, but it's Kay who catches her eye, holds it and, smiling again, tugs at the bow on the halter neck of her bikini top and lets it fall into her lap. The scrap of fabric lies on her smooth thighs and she scoops it away like a fallen songbird, down onto the pebbles.

Her breasts are full and tanned a rich bronze and Little Gold can do nothing but stare, conscious of the rising heat in her face.

'Hey, LG, you playing?'

Malcy's voice breaks the spell. She turns to him in confusion, shocked at his apparent failure to notice the naked woman next to them both. Has he seen her do this before?

'Oh, no, she doesn't want to play with you lads, do you, sweetheart? Stay and chat with me.'

'No. Yeah, I'd like to play…'

She can't sit here with Kay like that.

She drops her towel and pulls her t-shirt over her head as Kay exclaims,

'Oh! Don't soak your t-shirt!'

'It's fine.'

Little Gold stands, pulling down the t-shirt so it skirts her hips, as the boys start sprinting down to the sand. Kay's treacly voice pours over her bowed head.

'Aw! Are you shy? You don't have to be shy with us, does she, Roy?'

'Of course not, lovely girl like you.'

Little Gold curls her shoulders. She glances at Kay and then Roy – the devil and the deep blue sea – before crouching again to tie her laces, her chilly fingers thick and clumsy.

Roy heads off down the slope, calling back to her.

'Come on then, Little Miss Women's Lib, let's see what you're made of.'

Kay chuckles and closes her eyes.

Roy's nearly at the sand now, the bright sun striking the corrugated surface of his dark hair.

'Okay, lads, prepare to be out for a duck!'

She follows him towards the boys who are standing, reflected in the glassy sand. Malcy barely reaches Kev's shoulder. His blonde hair is badly in need of a cut, blowing across his face and annoying him. His skinny shins are a mass of bruises, every colour from deep purple to yellow.

Kev looks like he's made of different stuff to her brother. He has Roy's broad shoulders, albeit in a smaller size, and sturdy limbs.

Roy stands next to Malcy and turns to her.

'Right then, young lady. Going to be our fielder?'

She nods because there's no choice, of course, and Roy explains that they have to touch the ball to a line of pebbles that marks the wicket to get the boys out when they're running. He'll judge if someone's bowled. It's a crude, rubbish version of the game, for a place so unsuited to playing it that she wonders why they are even trying. Malcy would always rather play football, she knows that, and he hasn't even swum yet.

But her brother takes his place at the flinty wicket with his cricket bat braced and ready. The wind catches his hair again and he thrusts it, angrily, off his face.

Roy is wandering down the beach as if he's no idea they're

poised and waiting behind him. Eventually he turns and, taking long, loping strides, sends a slow, curving ball towards Malcy. Malcy hits it, straight and long down the beach and the boys start to run. Little Gold runs too, her trainers slapping the wet sand and her heart thumping. She picks up the white tennis ball from a shallow puddle and spins round. It's too far, there's no way she can throw that far, and into the strong cross-shore wind. Roy is standing with his hands on his hips, like Beach Action Man, and she's filled with a sudden fury. She sprints along and, with a jerk that wrenches her right shoulder and almost flings her down onto the sand, she throws the ball at him. He reaches casually to his left and plucks it from the air.

'Right. This one…'

This time, as the ball leaves Roy's hand, it's caught by the wind and is blown wide but Malcy swipes wildly to his left and makes contact. It arcs into the air and falls fast, with an audible plop, into the water. Roy kicks off his flip flops and runs in after it, dropping into a half-dive and powering out to where the ball is bobbing like a gull on the rocking surface. He plucks it from the wave and throws it towards her. The sodden tennis ball falls fast, coming straight at her out of the blue and white sky and she flinches, steps back and lets it land on the sand. By the time she reaches the wicket, Kev is there, panting and laughing.

'No chance, LG!'

Cocky bastard. Rich and cocky, in his stupid gleaming Spurs shirt, bringing his horrible parents to ruin her beach day.

Roy arrives, running his hand back across his wet hair. Little Gold watches the droplets of water taking crooked paths down his chest, speeding through the forest there. He coughs into a curled fist and then shouts to her brother, standing at the opposite pebble wicket.

'Nice shot, Malcolm, nice shot!'

Then he turns to her.

'Good try, young lady. You need to be a bit quicker on those little legs.'

His eyes slide from her face down her torso and settle on her bare thighs. She can feel his stare like something sticky on her skin. Malcy's voice is over-excited, high and shrieky.

'Come on, Kev, let's see if you can get it so far out your Dad drowns!'

The eyes peel up from her legs and something clouds their blueness for a second. The wind buffets her with a thumping gust and she shudders, rubbing at her goose-pimpled arms. Roy turns away, muttering,

'We'll see about that, we'll see about that.'

Kev is squinting towards his dad as Roy delivers a much faster ball. It hurtles towards him. He lifts the bat defensively against its pace and the ball ricochets up from the edge and smacks into his cheekbone. He screams, drops the bat and turns away, his hand coming up to his eye.

Roy is laughing as he jogs towards his son, who's crouched down now, both hands over his face. Little Gold and Malcy go over too and she catches the tail end of Roy's words.

'...make a fuss!'

Roy hauls Kev to his feet and then pulls his hands down from his face. Kev's crying, his cheeks wet and shining snot snaking over his top lip. There's a purple-pink welt on his cheekbone that's swelling fast, the surface of it grazed and slightly bloody.

'You're alright there, son. No need for the drama.'

Kev's trying to cover his face again and she sees Roy's strong hands tighten on his wrists. The muscles in the man's arms tense, overpowering him so that Kev has no choice but to stand, snotty and exposed, crying and sore. Little Gold looks away. If she can't cover him then the least she can do is not look. She wishes she hadn't been resenting him – imagines somehow that this is her fault. Roy's voice is calm.

'I said, stop it, Kevin.'

The sun has disappeared behind a thick bank of clouds tinged dark on the undersides as if they're carrying rain. Little Gold is thoroughly chilled, shivering in her wet costume and damp t-shirt. More than anything, she wants to just pull on the rest of her clothes and go home, even in her wet costume, even without Malcy.

She turns her head away from the scene but is scared to move her feet, afraid of attracting Roy's attention and becoming the target of his rising anger.

'He's alright, isn't he, Malcolm?'

She glances across at Malcy. He's frowning slightly, his eyes darting nervously from his friend's damaged face to the man holding his wrists. He says nothing. Roy speaks again.

'Isn't he?'

Malcy's reply is swift, fearful but still, somehow, apologetic.

'Yeah.'

'Your friend can see you're okay, Kevin, so you can stop now. No-one's impressed with this display.'

She hears the strangled hiccup of Kev doing his best to swallow a sob. Then there's another and, after a few moments more, there's just occasional sniffs. Roy whispers,

'That's better... that's better...'

Still his hands are tight around Kev's wrists and his eyes are locked on his face as he murmurs the words over and over. There's a single trickle of red from the edge of the graze, like a bloody tear, and Roy wipes it away with a broad thumb, pressing harder than he should on the delicate flesh. Kev winces and another sob escapes.

Roy speaks again to Malcy, without looking at him.

'He's making a ridiculous fuss, isn't he, Malcolm?'

Malcy doesn't reply. He's shivering too, clenching and unclenching his hands, their fingernails pale blue.

'Isn't he?'

Roy's voice leaps up several decibels between the two words and all the children jump. Malcy's body convulses a second time though, and a third, as he replies, falling over his words.

'Yes. Yes he is.'

Malcy's panic is complete. She's scared for a moment that he'll run, scared that, if he does, Roy will simply reach out a powerful arm and catch him. In her mind's eye, Malcy is squirming in Roy's grasp already, his breath starting to tighten and haze into a wheeze. Does he have his inhaler?

Suddenly, and without another word, Roy lets go of Kev, turns and strides up the beach towards Kay and away from them all, as if they hold no further interest. The children follow him in silence, Malcy carrying the bat and the sopping tennis ball.

Roy is yanking the windbreak from the stones and Kay opens her eyes and starts to tie a sarong around her body.

'What's happened now, then?'

'Well, you'd better ask Kevin, darling. He seems to be determined to act like a girl over nothing.'

Kev is facing away from his mother, looking down at the pebbles. She takes his arm and turns him around to face her. Then she tuts, her head on one side, considering him with slight disapproval as if he's broken a plate.

'Well, that's just a graze, isn't it, Roy?'

'It is. But it seems our son would rather make a fool of himself in front of Malcolm and his sister than be a man about it. So we're going home.'

Malcy slides the bat and ball into the bag of sports equipment, stepping quickly away as Roy snatches it up and thrusts it at Kev.

'You carry this. And take your mother's lounger.'

Kay is arranging her beach bag on her shoulder. She slides on a pair of sunglasses and then smiles at Little Gold and Malcy.

'You kids come and see us soon, eh?'

Little Gold isn't expecting the turquoise-tipped fingers that cup her cheek and she flinches.

'No need to look so anxious, sweetheart.'

She nods at Malcy and drops a slow wink.

'And I'll look forward to seeing you, handsome.'

Roy's already halfway to the steps, Kev struggling behind him with the bag and the folded sun lounger. Kay picks her way through the pebbles on white sling-back sandals and ascends the steps with a sashay.

Little Gold rubs her face with a cold hand. Her head is pounding and she's starving suddenly. As she roots in her bag for the sandwiches, she's startled by Malcy's sudden shout.

''Bye! 'Bye, Kev! 'Bye, Roy! 'Bye, Kay! 'Bye!'

It's like he's scared he might never see them again. She tugs at his t-shirt.

'Shuddup, you div. Get the squash out, yeah?'

CHAPTER TWENTY-ONE

'I had no chance to say anything, just smiled and took my change!'

She watches the dance of Vi's mobile mouth. Her confidence, joy in her own ready wit, is one of the things that Peggy loves most and here it is still, never seeming to fade. Vi's fingers roll the stem of her glass and Peggy pours more of the rather good wine.

Taking Vi's empty plate, she stacks it under her own and carries them both to the sink.

'I haven't made pudding.'

'Well that's a poor bloody show! I suppose we'll just have to finish this off.'

She tops up their glasses more, right to the rim.

'And there's Cognac for later, so that'll be okay.'

Vi's brought both wine and brandy as well as some flowers, an extravagant bunch bursting out of the vase. She twists the stem of an open lily and presses her face to the bloom, sniffing with indecent ardour.

'You were always a bad influence, Violet Collins.'

'Oh, yes. You were a good girl before I came along.'

Peggy's standing at the sink, rolling her shirt sleeves and turning on the tap. Vi shouts to make herself heard above the flow.

'Leave that, for God's sake! I'll do it in the morning. Come back and have a fag with me.'

She pats the chair beside her own. They light up, heads over the same trembling flame, and Vi takes Peggy's hand.

'And what have you been up to of late? Still enjoying your retired-lady life?'

Peggy curls her fingers into Vi's, squeezes her palm and lets go.

'Oh, I am, indeed. I can't see that changing! I've been having a real sort out.'

'I thought you'd had a go at the garden. And someone's weeded the front room shelves. That was surely never Peggy Baxter, getting rid of books?'

'It's all long overdue, isn't it? I've got the time and...' She lifts her cigarette to her lips, inhales, exhales, '... and I've got a helper too.'

Vi's head jerks up from the table, where her fingertip's teasing a pile of spilled salt.

'You're never seeing someone, are you, you old goat?'

Peggy can't help but enjoy the moment, Vi's slight irritation that there could be someone else. No, she's meant to be alone here, sorry and solitary, coloured forever with heartbreak's sepia wash.

'I am seeing, every now and then, a very lovely new friend. She lives a few doors along the road.'

Vi struggles, a slight scowl puckering her eyebrows, but she manages to quell the pique and offer up a smile.

'Well, how exciting! Tell all! How old is she?'

'Twelve. Nearly thirteen, I believe.'

Vi glares like a gorgon and shoves Peggy's upper arm.

'You rotter, Peg Baxter, you know you had me all agog.'

Peggy flicks her ash, chuckles, and takes a sip of wine.

'Ha! Well that doesn't take much, does it?'

Shifting in her chair, she tugs her shirt free from the waistband of her trousers.

'Let's go in the other room and flop.'

Vi switches on the lamp, sits at one end of the settee and waits for Peggy to settle at the other.

'You know, that's almost bigger news than if you actually were seeing a woman. How do you come to have a child helping? It's not some scheme for the elderly, I don't suppose...'

'No it bloody isn't! She's a nice kid. I like having her here. Single mother with three children, she's the youngest. I get the feeling things are quite a struggle, not easy anyway, at home.'

'Yes, well that's life with children, isn't it? As I think you've always known.'

Her words are clipped and cold and Peggy knows she's nudged the pain. Like a body under ice she sees it slide through Vi's dark eyes. She's brought them out onto this perilous surface by mentioning Little Gold and all she can do now is hope the surface holds. Vi's silent for a moment but, in the end, curiosity wins out.

'And she comes here then? She comes to help? Alone? Just you and a child?'

'Only for an hour or two.'

'But you've met the mother, yes?'

'I've nodded to her once or twice. She's rather over-stretched. The dad walked out, apparently, so I think she's got a job…'

'But the child has her permission, to be spending time with you?'

'Vi, I don't think it's a problem, love. As I said, she's over-stretched and…'

'Struggling to cope, you mean?'

'Oh, oh, I'm not… I couldn't say. I haven't been to the house so…'

Vi's evident anxiety seems somehow out of place. When she's here, when it's Peggy and Little Gold, there's no need for all this fear.

Peggy lapses into silence, waiting for her mind to clear. Is she struggling to cope, the mum? It's true that Little Gold is grubby round the edges, eager, always, for some food. But children do get hungry and who is she to judge? Perhaps she should knock on the door, make sure things are okay. But the thought of that, of explaining herself, makes her shudder and reach for her wine.

'Well, I suppose you know what you're doing, Peg. I don't have to tell you to be careful, do I? I've never known a more cautious woman than you.'

Peggy's picturing the day in the loft, watching Little Gold's typewriter eyes devouring that old newsletter. Vi would be surprised at just how little caution she's exercising. But that's enough sharing for tonight.

The silence beats on though, for several moments more, and her courage surges back. Sometimes you have to push yourself, Peg Baxter, sometimes things should be said.

Vi's feet are curled up, close beside her, and Peggy reaches out. She cups the stockinged toes and squeezes, catches Vi's elusive eye.

'It's funny but I've come to love her visits. When she comes there's more fresh air. I suppose it's youth, that promise of tomorrow. I never thought I'd feel this way.'

She's gone too far and the ice has broken. She watches Vi slip through, into the clear blue water of regret. Her beautiful, regular features are a mask as she rocks her wine glass gently in her lap. Peggy waits, not regretting the words she's said but sickened by their destructive power.

Finally, Vi knocks back her wine and puts the glass down on the floor. Rearranging herself on the narrow sofa, she takes Peggy's hand and lets out a sigh.

'Here's the thing, Peg Baxter, the baby fantasy was just that. There was never going to be a child and some part of me always knew.'

Peggy nods and holds her nerve, though she's longing for Vi to stop.

'I was too old, it was all too hard and my body was just letting go. Letting go of the thing that it hadn't done. Does that make any sense to you? It was just a moment of crisis, Peg. Darkness and confusion, you know?'

She nods again and tightens her grip on the fringe of the cushion by her side.

'But what caused me to go, what drove me away, was the barrier between us. You locked me out. You held me apart. And I realised that you always do.'

This time the nod is a tremulous dip of her weary, weary head.

'I so needed you to let me in. Let me in more than you did. And I realised that need was oppressive for you. There were things you wouldn't share and I didn't respect that. I couldn't pull back. I was always battering through.'

Peggy doesn't trust herself to speak. The weight in her chest is a stone. A stone made of liquid, topped up to the brim, borne carefully inside her ribs.

They sit in silence and Peggy runs her eyes over the thinned-out shelves. There she is, the bones of what matters to her, the precious books and people in frames. Maybe she could have been braver, but then... She turns her face to Vi.

'Well, would you like to meet her? Would you like to meet the child?'

'What, your little friend? I'd be honoured to. Did you tell me her name?'

'Her name is Little Gold.'

'I beg your pardon?'

'That's her name, well her nickname. She doesn't like her real name, too feminine for her taste.'

'Ah, I see...'

'See what?'

'Oh, you know.'

Vi chuckles and pats her leg.

'I'm quite squiffy after all that wine. Fancy a cup of tea?'

Peggy watches as she stands and stretches, her head thrown back and arms wide.

'Well, you know what I'd really like to do, Vi? Regardless of squiffiness and all the rest... Would you like to go to bed?'

'Peggy Baxter, are you propositioning me?'

She wishes she could trust her body but these days it's hard to be sure. Better to make no promises, to be honest about where they are.

'I don't expect so, sweetheart. But will you come up anyway?'

They walk, hand in hand, through the house they once shared without turning on the lights. Finally, in the bedroom, Peggy takes Vi in her arms. She breathes into the slender, scented neck, softened and creped with age.

'God, it's good to hold you, old thing. It's been far too long.'

As her clothes fall away, Peggy shudders with cold and Vi beckons her under the sheet. Peggy catches, in the dim light, the fear in Vi's eyes and, quickly, she draws her close. The lips on her shoulder, the urgent whisper, flutter against her skin.

'What's happening, darling? What's going on? Tell me, tell me, please.'

Outside the open curtains, the gathering dusk becomes night and passing cars sweep the darkened room with sudden beams of light. There's the hum of their mingled voices in the warmth of their cocoon and when, at last, Vi starts to cry, Peggy rocks her in her arms.

The birds begin and the light surges up in the left of the bay window. Still Peggy holds Vi as she trembles in sleep and her body leaps with the occasional echo of a sob.

CHAPTER TWENTY-TWO

The kitchen windows are completely steamed up. From her perch, Little Gold can see the ghost of Mum going backward and forward between the cooker and the sink, her fuzzy outline giving no hint of the dirt and disorder of her un-misted self. It's nice. It might almost be a year ago – her in the tree waiting for Mum to open the back door and call her in for tea. Sausage and mash, the *Generation Game*, it would all have unfolded with a calm predictability as Mum ironed the sheets for the Sunday change.

She doesn't know what it means that Mum's got up today, wordlessly washed enough plates and pans for tea, peeled and chopped potatoes – silent, distracted but persistent.

She glances down the row of gardens, following the flitting of a blackbird from privet to wall, to privet again. Peggy Baxter's back bedroom window is open a few inches and she tries to magic the old lady to it – pictures her heaving up the stiff sash and leaning out, calling her name, waving.

'Little Gold!'

Mum is leaning out the back door and looking up at the tree, shading her eyes against the sun.

'Coming!'

She drops onto the grass and walks slowly down the steps.

Ali's sitting at the end of the table, her red Woollies overall gaping to reveal her No Cruise Missiles t-shirt. She's looking suspiciously at the dollop of mash Mum has just deposited on her plate.

'Little Gold, can you go and get your brother?'

Just at that moment, Malcy bursts through the front door, his football under his arm, soaked in sweat.

'Ah, no need…'

She's making a huge effort. Little Gold can see the will it's taking for Mum to serve the food, to provide the lumps of mash, blackened sausages, and small, watchful smiles for each of them. She's draining herself to do this and there must be a reason. Something must have prised her out of bed, compelled her to make a meal for the first time in weeks.

'Here we are then.'

She spears a sausage with a trembling fork and Little Gold looks away. Ali's spreading and scoring her heap of mash into a thin chessboard as Malcy scoops and swallows, barely pausing to chew.

'Slow down, Malcolm, you'll give yourself a tummy ache.'

It's strange, Little Gold thinks, how she can come back to life like this, like that Bible bloke that Jesus raised from the dead, and be so concerned about possible tummy ache in a boy she's barely seen for days on end.

Malcy slows slightly, catches Little Gold's eye and looks immediately away. He's hardly spoken to her since the day with Kev's family on the beach. She thinks back to the bus ride home with him and her final, irritated response to his constant needling.

No, I don't bloody think they're cool, Malc. He's a bloody bully and she gives me the creeps, okay?

And Malc had said she was a prat and immature and that he hadn't even wanted her there in the first place.

She sweeps a circle of sausage through a sticky patch of ketchup, scraped from the dregs of the bottle, and tries not to care about it. She and Malc don't row, though, and she misses him. Mum lays her cutlery down carefully and, resting her elbows on the table, folds her hands as if she's going to pray.

'I need to tell you all something about your dad.'

'Oh, fuck that!'

Ali shoves her chair back from the table and stands up.

'Wait! Just wait a minute. It won't take a minute but I've promised I'll tell you so please stay.'

Mum's voice is pathetic and Little Gold's relieved when Ali seems to hear that too, and sits, slowly back down, a look of shame on her face.

Malcy's got a wide streak of dried mud across his forehead and it cracks as he frowns, raining a tiny shower of grit onto his mash.

'What? What is it, Mum? Is he okay?'

'Yes, yes, he's fine. He wanted me to tell you that he's sorry he hasn't been in touch but things have been difficult.'

'Ha!'

'Ali, please, just let me tell you. His job with the duplicator firm didn't work out and apparently they've had to move from the flat they were renting.'

Little Gold thinks about the golden eagle keeping watch over the scrap of paper in her bird book, over Dad's block capitals. It's not worth anything after all.

'They've been staying in a B&B for a while but now Sally's brother's offered your dad a job in his car hire firm…'

Mum's voice is so almost like it used to be. It's like she's listened to a recording of how she used to talk and learned to do it, like an impersonator, like Janet Brown doing Mrs Thatcher. It's worse than the heavy, robot voice because it's so close to the Mum she remembers, like being shown a reflection in a mirror and yet knowing that if she reaches out, real Mum won't be there.

'… in Aberdeen.'

The Mum impersonation is sitting, staring at her plate, shoulders rounded and white face passive.

'Well, it makes no difference where that bastard goes really, does it? He's made it clear he doesn't give a shit what's happening to us and I don't really get why he bothered to tell us at all. Did he say if he was actually going to come up with any money, Mum?'

Mum waves her hand in front of her face as if Ali's words are flies buzzing around her head.

'Because we're totally buggered here if he doesn't, aren't we? How many months are we behind on the mortgage now? And we're on red bills with the gas and the phone. And if I wasn't buying food with my wages, we wouldn't actually have food in the cupboards either, would we?'

Mum doesn't reply and Ali goes on, she's on a mission now, going in for the kill.

'You can't just deliver his bloody message Mum and leave it at that! You can't wake up for a day, tell us he's pissing off to the back end of nowhere and then go back to your bed with a bottle and new packet of pills! I'm going to go, Mum. I'm going to go in the autumn, no matter what happens, I'm going and these two can't look after themselves!'

She's standing now, leaning over the table, shouting into Mum's blank face. Little Gold can see the bones of her skull, the dark dips of her temples and the hollows around her eyes.

Mum lifts her hands in front of her face, palms turned out, to block the flow of words.

'I...'

But she can't respond to this. It's taken all she had to put on the show for an hour, to cook the food and say what she'd promised she'd say.

'And if you're imagining that he'll come back, if you're still fantasising that the bastard ever loved you at all, you're wrong. You're wrong about all of it and you always bloody were...'

Ali's voice is wavering up and up, onto the trembling edge of tears. Little Gold can't stand it and she shouts over her sister's words, hoping she might still manage to calm things, to make a space for the questions circling in her head.

'Ali, stop it! There's no point shouting at Mum, it's not her fault.'

But Ali spins round to face her, just redirecting her fury with renewed vigour.

'Oh, for Christ's sake, LG, do you not understand? If she doesn't pull herself together, she'll lose this house! She clearly can't count on him for a fucking penny and she needs to make a plan, work out how she's going to support you two. Because I won't be here, you know?'

Ali's exhausted herself at last and she sinks back into her chair. The questions fade in Little Gold's mind. All that seems to matter now is what Ali just said, that she will go, that it will soon be just her and Malcy, alone with Mum. She looks at her brother.

He isn't making a noise, that's the most frightening thing when she thinks back to it later. Malcy has always been a loud crier, the one of them most likely to sob, to let his pain be heard, but when Little Gold looks at his face, she sees that it's twisted, his open jaw juddering and tears streaming from his eyes, but he isn't making a sound. When had he learned to do that?

'Malc?'

And that's enough to send him running from the room and up the stairs to their bedroom. The crash of the door into the frame makes the house shake. Little Gold looks at Mum, still a white-faced shop dummy, and Ali, her lollipop head twisted on the stick of her body. She pushes back her own chair and runs after him.

She shoves the door open with her shoulder and there he is on his bed. He's face-down, sobbing into the pillow, with his arms bent back and folded around his head. She perches on the edge of the mattress.

'Malc! Malcy, it's okay. It'll be okay.'

She doesn't know why she's saying that. It's rubbish. He rolls over, dragging a hand across his streaming nose.

'It isn't okay! He never even bloody writes, LG. He hasn't even phoned to talk about us staying in Division One!'

Little Gold blinks. He really thinks that? He thinks that Dad should have phoned to talk about the Albion? She can't find a reply.

'And I thought he might, you know, he might come down and see us now it's the summer an' all that and we might go, we might go to the…'

He's crying too hard to go on and she sits down beside him and puts an awkward arm around his shoulders.

'Look, Malc, look, how about we write to him? Both of us, both of us could write to him. I was going to before but I didn't. But we could do it now. We could get his address off Mum and send him a letter, yeah?'

She can hear Mum in her own voice. Somehow, by some spell, she's overtaken him in age and, as she looks at his tear-wrecked face, his blotchy neck, she's knows he's a child in a way she just isn't anymore. It's not a welcome feeling but there's no point running away from it so she sits there, patting him and muttering the sort of soothing words Mum used to.

'S'okay, Malcy. S'okay. I'm here…'

Slowly, his crying quietens, until there's just trembling and sniffs. She pats his shoulder again and then gently withdraws her arm.

He rubs his pink eyes and croaks,

'Were you really gonna write, LG?'

'Yeah, I put his address in my bird book to keep it safe but it's no good now. Still, we can ask Mum for the new address. I'll do it. I'll ask her and I'll see if Ali wants to join in with the letter. It can be from all three of us and we'll ask him to come down, yeah?'

Malcy nods without speaking and she wonders if she's pretending, if she actually has any faith that Dad will come, no matter how good the letter. It's a strange sensation, watching herself perform for Malcy. But even if it's fake, she still wants to try, wants to lead them in this brave mission to make things better. Somebody has to.

Ali's music, David Bowie shouting about Five Years, is coming through the wall from next door. Now's the moment, while she feels so courageous. She pats him again and stands.

'I'll ask Ali now. Wish me luck!'

She grins at him and he manages a weak smile in response.

The door's ajar and she wonders why, wonders if maybe Ali is expecting her. It might be a good sign. Still, she hesitates before knocking lightly and leaning into the room.

'Hiya.'

'Hi.'

'Can I come in?'

'If you want.'

Little Gold steps inside. Ali's lying on her back on her bed, staring at the ceiling. It's fiercely tidy – the floor clear and all the clothes put away in her drawers. Her college work is organised on the shelves above her desk – a row of red ring-binders have subject names in thick black capitals on their spines. She fixes her eyes on HISTORY 1 as she speaks.

'Ali, we're going to write to him, me and Malcy. We're going to write to Dad and ask him to come.'

David Bowie's singing about love. She doesn't get these words, they don't make any sense –

Love descends on those defenceless, idiot love will spark the fusion…

His taunting, cat-like voice goes on and on and it's all nonsense. She looks over at the spinning record and wants to slap the arm away, make him shut up so Ali will hear her.

But maybe Ali's heard her anyway. She levers her bony body from the bed and, crossing the clear expanse of carpet, opens her desk drawer. Maybe she's getting paper, ready to start the letter. Is it really this easy?

But Ali returns with a yellow Kodak envelope of photographs in her left hand and a pair of scissors in her right. Then she settles cross-legged on her bed, her back ramrod straight and the cords of her neck stretched taut. She tips the envelope and the coloured prints fan across her duvet.

Little Gold looks at her scattered family – Mum, Dad, Malcy, Ali, her. Ali lifts a photograph of all of them posing by the Needles lighthouse and starts to cut. David Bowie yowls the first line of a new song,

I'm an alligator…

'No!'

Little Gold grabs her wrist but Ali jerks it away, holds the scissors in front of her face and speaks to Little Gold through the open mouth of the blades.

'Don't you touch me, LG, if you don't want to get hurt.'

As she watches (as David Bowie Freaks Out in a Moonage Daydream, oh yeah) her sister edges the blades between her parents. She trims around the top of Malcy's head, where he's leaning back on Dad, until Dad falls away and he's leaning on nothing but thin air. Dad has abandoned his hand, weirdly pink, on the shoulder of Mum's blue anorak and on the other side of Mum, Ali and Little Gold are standing, unaware of the butchery.

'Don't do that, Ali. Please.'

Her sister doesn't look up from her work. Her face is concealed by the curtains of her hair, her skeletal hands twisting the print between the gaping blades.

'I'll do what I like with my own photos thanks, LG. You can help if you want.'

She reaches for the next photo on the pile. It's one of Dad and Malcy pulling faces by the cable car down the cliff, pretending they're scared. Again Dad drops onto the bed and Malcy's standing alone, the cliff falling away behind him and the beach far below. This is too hard to watch and it isn't going to stop.

Little Gold leaves the room, closing the door behind her to

keep the music in. She's not brave any more. She's not some magic-spell person with the power to lead them all through this forest. She's just herself and now she's aching with the raw images of Ali slicing through the photographs like a surgeon amputating Dad.

She walks back into their dusty bedroom, drenched in the warm evening sun, to find that Malcy's gone. It's a relief.

Standing at the window, she picks him out from among the boys in the park. He's in goal again, falling too slowly to stop a crappy left-footed attempt by Wayne Whittaker. The celebrations involve Wayne's knuckles grating on Malcy's head. Her brother's flailing his skinny arms to get free and, when he does, he's smiling his weak smile.

She watches for a few moments more before turning away. The boys chase, shove and shout, seemingly endlessly motivated to get the ball, to keep it in play and to strive for a goal. It seems to matter so much more than it should and she remembers Malcy's devastation that Dad hadn't got in touch about the Albion.

Little Gold sits down on her bed and considers the footballers lined up in their little sticky frames across the front of Malcy's drawer – they seem to be assuring her that, yes, it's all terribly important. But she can't feel it. She looks at Ian Rush, his arms folded across his chest, his direct gaze brimming with confidence.

'It's just a bloody game, you know?'

There's the toot of a horn outside and Little Gold returns to the window. At the far edge of the park, beyond the heavy branches of an elm, a silver car is drawing up at the kerb. As she watches, Kev and Roy emerge from the dancing green leaves and Malcy abandons his post to run towards them.

CHAPTER TWENTY-THREE

Little Gold wakes to the phone and Malcy's cursing, skidding descent of the stairs to answer it.

'502-689! Hello!'

She sits up. Her watch is still on her wrist, twisted so that the face is on the inside. It's midday. They stayed up really late, her and Malc, watching a horror film called *Demon Seed* about a woman getting a baby by a robot thing. It had been horrible, the kid born all covered in shiny scales that had peeled off to reveal actual skin underneath. They hadn't got to bed 'til after two.

'Yeah! Yeah, 'course I can. Yeah, that's brilliant. Yeah, ten minutes.'

He thunders back up to their room and starts to hurl stuff about.

'Seen my trunks?'

'Who was that?'

'Kev! I'm going over to his house. They're having a party thing again and Roy's gonna set up a massive paddling pool by their flat roof so we jump in.'

It sounds very unlikely. How deep is this paddling pool meant to be? And who has parents that let them jump off roofs?

'Yeah, and Kay's doing burgers and potato salad and they've bought a SodaStream now.'

Little Gold's mind sends her vivid images that collide incongruously – a plate piled with creamy, solid chunks of potato and Kay's bronzed breasts – and she looks down at the floor.

'What are the people like, their friends? Are there lots of kids?'

Malcy's found his trunks, bunched inside a towel on the floor by the chest of drawers. They're crusty as coral and he's shaking them roughly as he replies.

'Last time there was just me, Kev and this kid called Peter.'

She remembers the overheard conversation when she was in the park. A kid from a children's home, Kev had said, and it had stuck in her head. One of her favourite books has a girl in it who escapes from an orphanage with her friends and lives on a canal boat disguised as a boy.

'Is he nice?'

'Yeah. He's a bit quiet at first.'

Malcy's shaking the towel too, sniffing it suspiciously before evidently deciding it'll do and shoving it into a plastic bag with the trunks. He's still in the clothes he wore yesterday and he hasn't washed at all but he's clearly not going to bother getting changed.

'Is he someone's, um, foster kid or something?'

'He comes with Keith. What's it to you, anyway, LG, I thought you didn't like Kev's family.'

He's not going to let it go then and she can't deny it. She doesn't like Roy and Kay. How could anyone like them? Still, she finds she's full of questions.

'Is it a party with music and stuff? Who are the other people?'

There's a toot from the street and Malcy leaps up.

'See ya later, LG.'

Little Gold flops back in her bed. At least they're proper friends again, her and Malcy, and he's gone off happy anyway.

The sky's a blank white sheet, not the sort of day for lying on a sun lounger. And there's Kay's body in her mind again, sparking a feeling that's slippery and fierce, and suddenly she wants to find that magazine. Now's her chance to have a proper look.

Malcy's mattress buckles and folds as she lifts the corner, revealing the lattice of metal that makes the base of the bedframe. There's no sign of the magazine and she wonders if it's slipped through into the mess of stuff underneath. On her belly in the fluff she roots through annuals, clothes, the flattened box of the Cluedo spraying out its cards. She turns one over and it's Miss Scarlett – a glamorous head on a little cone of red body, as creepy, suddenly, as the horror film child from the night before.

She wriggles back out of the space, no longer wanting to see the magazine and aware of the hollow burn of hunger.

Ali's bedroom door is standing ajar and she's not inside. Everything looks as ordered as ever, with no indication of the hacking of the photographs that she witnessed just yesterday.

Little Gold opens Mum's door gently. There's the whistling sigh of sleep coming from the darkness and she lets the door close again, sliding her hand carefully from the handle. Then she paces down the stairs and into the quiet kitchen.

In the fridge there's just an empty box of cheese triangles, a bowl with a heap of ancient beans, their juice congealed like amber, and the slimy end of a cucumber. She yanks down the iced-up door of the freezer compartment and there's nothing but the tray for making ice cubes. Two of the gaps in it are plugged with grey and the rest are empty. She upends the tray over the kitchen counter and gives it a whack, catching the cubes as they skitter away.

With a cube in each cheek, she roots through the cupboards. The ice is numbing her face, trickling its melt onto her tongue. She can feel the cold basting her empty insides and, for a minute, she considers just going to the Co-op and asking for a loaf. But she knows she won't.

At the back of the cupboard, far back behind the rolled bag of flour and a packet of pearl barley, her hand finds a tin. The cracker tin. Inside there are four stale cream crackers and a butter puff and she sits on the floor, the tin open between her splayed legs, her back against the cupboard door, and munches through them. She saves the butter puff 'til last and it's as she's posting the last quarter into her mouth that she spots Shaw outside, washing his paws on the top of the trellis between their yard and next door.

She opens the back door and he glances at her and stalks away, off towards Peggy Baxter's house. Little Gold runs up the back steps to the garden and climbs the tree, watching the cat as he leaps the intervening walls and hedges and settles on Peggy's lawn.

The air is heavy and close, the slab of white sky threatening above her. It's going to storm. The heat is drawing out sweat and yet there's no sunshine, not a glint, not a hint that the sun is there at all. Somewhere, behind that big house down in Surrenden Road, Malcy's running and laughing, shoving Kev into the water, chasing the shy boy from the children's home. Then he'll eat a big plate of food, heaped with potato salad and a juicy burger. Her stomach, barely appeased by the crackers, growls loudly.

Roy's probably pouring drinks for the grown-ups, Cinzano, like on the adverts. She pictures him handing a glass to Kay, can see the black hair on the backs of his fingers, imagines his voice.

Here we are…

And then she can feel his fingers on her chest in the car, his eyes on her bare legs as the wind blew across the beach.

Young lady…

Little Gold hunches, curls around her body, conscious of its weight, its shape, the chafe of her nipples on her t-shirt. She feels like climbing right out of it, leaving it here on the branch like a set of unwanted clothes.

She stands up. If she can't leave her body then perhaps climbing will free her from the images flashing in her mind – the wet tennis ball in her hand, Kev's damaged face, Kay's bare breasts, Roy blocking out the sun. She clambers up through the swaying branches, wedging her trainer into cracks, hauling herself higher, until she's conscious of the danger, the perilous sway, and the fact that above her is just sky, just sky forever.

Crouching in the top crook, she finds there's a hairy caterpillar on the rough bark beside her. Her heart knocking at her chest, she lets go with one hand and scoops it into a leaf, addressing her words to its waggling head.

'Hey, brave little caterpillar, what are you then, eh?'

The caterpillar lifts its upper body as if it's challenging her to a fight. Mysterious creature, a terracotta stripe running down its hairy back, its eyes painted on like face-paint. If it can survive the birds and make it into a cocoon it will be something quite different when it emerges. She nudges it gently back onto the branch and gazes out across the line of small gardens.

Peggy Baxter appears, coming up her back steps, talking over her shoulder to a woman behind her. They sit together on the grass, the visitor smoothing her skirt over her knees and plucking a buttercup from the grass. The murmur of their voices drifts through the air, peppered with occasional chuckles from Peggy Baxter and Little Gold realises they don't know she's there.

The visitor rubs Peggy's shoulder, firm and tender all at once and Little Gold is transfixed. She's never seen that before, never seen old ladies touch beyond a peck on the cheek or the linking of arms. The touch goes on, the confident press of her palm on the old lady's body and then the visitor leans close, speaks something right into Peggy Baxter's ear, making her laugh. It's one of her sea lion barks but it transforms into something else. It takes flight and wraps around Little Gold's tree.

A sudden gust of wind rocks her perch and Little Gold drops a foot onto a lower branch to steady herself. Peggy Baxter's head jerks up.

'Little Gold! Come and meet my friend, Vi.'

She waves.

'Okay!'

Little Gold scrambles down the tree and runs through the house, leaving the back door ajar but slamming the front one behind her.

*

Vi drinks her tea without any milk in it. Little Gold has never seen anyone do that. It looks like quite a different drink, something dark and mysterious. She also insists on,

'A proper cup and saucer please, Peg Baxter, and not one of your grotty mugs.'

Her hair is the colour of dark steel, bobbed in a sharp line to her neck. Her shirt's a shining emerald, her skirt navy blue and across her chest is a necklace of silver rectangles that lie flat against the green. She reminds Little Gold of a picture of Queen Cleopatra – her almond eyes sliding sideways as she blows lightly on her tea.

'So, you're Peg's helper in the grand sort out, are you?'

Her voice is crisp, as sharp as her bob, more precise and slightly posher than Little Gold is expecting. It feels like a challenge to be met and she finds there's surprising confidence in her reply.

'Yes. You used to live with Peggy Baxter, didn't you?'

'I did indeed. I lived here for thirteen years and then I went to live in Bath.'

Little Gold takes a swig of her own tea, with lots of milk and two sugars and in one of Peggy Baxter's blue mugs rather than a fiddly cup and saucer. She lifts her Bourbon to dunk it but wonders if that's rubbish manners and so just holds it still as she replies.

'I've been to Bath once.'

'And did you like it?'

'Yes. I liked the baths. I like Roman things.'

As Little Gold chews a mouthful of un-dunked biscuit, fat rain drops splatter across the window. Peggy holds out her cigarette packet towards Vi and nods at the speckled pane.

'Here we go! I said to Vi we'd be having a storm today.'

The window beads quickly with drops that start to stream down the glass as Peggy strikes her lighter. She offers the flame to Vi, who crosses her legs and blows a long stream of smoke out of pursed lips. Her lips are painted a dark red and Little Gold looks at the ring of colour she leaves on the cigarette stub. She feels Peggy's eyes on her and looks away.

'Got you out of that tree just in time, eh?'

'Yeah.'

Vi rolls her cigarette gently around the edge of the ashtray. Peggy Baxter has a wide selection of ashtrays and this one is Little Gold's favourite. It's the shape of a silver crown for a tiny king and she imagines him sitting there between them all in his ash-filled crown and regal robes as they flick their cigs at his head.

'Only one thing for it…'

Vi seems to be addressing no-one, or both of them, Little Gold's not sure.

'Where's the Scrabble then, Peg?'

Peggy narrows her eyes as she replies,

'I know your game. Beat me as usual, eh? It's in the middle bedroom. Little Gold, would you do the honours and fetch it? It's on the bookshelves. That is, if you like Scrabble?'

Little Gold takes the stairs two at a time and finds herself facing wide shelves mostly lined with books. But on the bottom shelf there are a few games – the Scrabble, something called Halma and a thick slab of wood dotted with tiny holes for pegs. They're the games of another time, olden days' games. She picks up the wooden board and runs her fingers over the holes. It feels like a mystery she'll never solve.

Scrabble's one of her favourite games but she can usually beat Malcy so he doesn't like to play it. He prefers Monopoly, in which her anxious dithering about whether to save or spend is usually her downfall. She runs back downstairs and deposits the game between the old ladies, noticing Vi loose Peggy's fingers from her palm under the table. Vi peels open the box.

'Pull up a chair, Little Golden One, and let me show you how a Scrabble Mistress operates.'

No-one has ever done that with her name. She considers this sharp, smart old lady, clicking the tiles into her rack. She hardly seems old at all but the battered board, the wooden racks, the tape holding the corner of the box rigid, they betray the vintage.

As they play, the rain continues to fall steadily in the fat, decisive drops of a summer storm. The light falters and Little Gold finds herself on her feet, flicking the switch of the standard lamp without being asked.

They don't talk. Everyone is concentrating and there's just the totting of scores, the tick and slide of the tiles. When the game's over, Vi has triumphed by more than twenty points. Little Gold has come last but not by a shameful margin. Peggy laughs, tossing the biro down onto the pad with its columns of numbers.

'You see, Little Gold? She always does that to me. There I am, building up my glorious six letter words and she slips ahead with judicious use of S's and cunning placing of the occasional X.'

'There is only one X, Peg, which, if you paid more attention to tactics, you'd have noticed years ago.'

Little Gold watches them, teasing, jabbing with their words, close like sisters. But not.

'More tea!'

Peggy slaps her hands onto her corduroy thighs and rises to her feet. There's a sway, a tight circling of her torso over the table, as if they're on a ship. Vi is beside her in an instant, cupping her elbow to guide her back into her seat.

'I'll make it, Peg. And I think she needs a couple of Bourbons after being so soundly thrashed by me, eh, Little Gold? Come and give me a hand.'

Vi gathers the cups and Little Gold follows her into the kitchen, leaving Peggy Baxter leaning back in her chair in the bay window, taking a cigarette from her packet.

'Peg has the odd dizzy turn these days. You might have noticed. It's fine. She just needs to sit down if one comes on. Okay?'

Little Gold nods and then feels the swell of an approaching tummy gurgle. It rumbles out in an unmistakable bubble of sound.

'Blimey, girl! I think we'd better do you a sandwich, eh?'

Her mouth is already watering at the thought.

'Thanks, yes.'

'You make the tea, eh?'

It means using a pot and spooning in loose leaves but she's watched Peggy Baxter enough times and it's satisfying, the sequence of ordered things in the clean kitchen. She bats away an ugly image of the kitchen at home.

Vi slices cheddar and spreads butter thickly on two slices of a crusty loaf. She adds two Bourbon biscuits to the edge of the plate and hands it to Little Gold.

'Can you manage that and your tea?'

'Yes. Thank you.'

Peggy Baxter's looking better. She drinks a glass of water that Vi offers and then points over to the bookshelf.

'Little Gold dusted you and Bumpkin the other day, Vi.'

Little Gold's tearing at the crusty bread with her teeth, doing her best not to drop crumbs. She looks up at the photograph. That woman is beautiful, beautiful enough to kiss. The clarity of the thought startles her and the plate on her knees tips sideways. She snatches at the plummeting sandwich.

'Aha, yes, me and Bumpkin, both sleek and dark and rather gorgeous, weren't we, Peg?'

'Ha! And didn't you both know it?'

Bumpkin must be dead. That's what happens with pets but she wants to know, suddenly, where he is.

'What happened to Bumpkin? Is he, um…'

Peggy Baxter takes a swig of her tea.

'He lived to ten and then managed to get run over by a milk float, of all things. Not the sharpest knife in the drawer, that cat.'

'We buried him under the lavender in the front garden, Little Gold.'

Vi's pointing out the window to where the sodden bush is dripping over the front wall onto the pavement below. Sometimes she's pulled off a bit of that lavender, to roll the flower between her fingers and feel it crumble away, releasing its scent. All the time, Bumpkin was underneath.

'I think,' says Peggy, 'that being popped under a bush is a jolly sensible and straightforward solution to the whole business.'

'I'll bear that in mind, Peg. Next to Bumpkin, or perhaps over in the park?'

They laugh again and she wonders, can't imagine, what it must be like to be that old, for life to be behind you and death so close in front. She licks her finger and sweeps it around the plate, gathering the flakes of crust, and lifts her eyes to find them both looking at her. The clock chimes six.

'I think I'd better be getting home now.'

Vi takes her to the front door. The rain is still lashing down. She hesitates for a second, imagining home – the lights off, the dripping tap and the empty fridge.

'Want to borrow a brolly?'

'No, I'll just run. It'll be fine.'

As she's about to step out onto the path, Vi places a hand on her arm.

'Are you free tomorrow, Little Golden One? I'm going to take Peg on a jaunt up to Devil's Dyke if the weather's anything like. I think the forecast's good, believe it or not.'

There's a rush of joy that she's sure is visible and she doesn't care.

'Yeah! Definitely! That'd be great.'

'Do you need to check with your Mum?'

'Oh, yeah, but I'm sure she'll say yes and I'd love to come. Thanks.'

Vi squeezes her arm lightly.

'Lovely. Ten o'clock in the morning, then, unless we hear otherwise?'

She sprints along the pavement, water leaping up from her slapping trainers. Tomorrow, tomorrow she can see them again and go to Devil's Dyke, the top of the world. She turns her key and bursts into the house, panting.

'Hello?'

There's no reply and in the kitchen she finds a note propped against the kettle.

Came home but you were both out. I'm going round Gemma's and might stay over. I'll get some food in tomorrow if Mum signs the Family Allowance book. If she gets up then make her do it. Ali.

It doesn't look like Malcy's home and she thinks of him for the first time all afternoon. It can't have worked out with the paddling pool in this weather. What's he been doing all day?

Leaving the empty kitchen, she wanders upstairs. Mum's bedroom door looks just as she left it earlier but surely she can't still be asleep? Little Gold turns the handle.

'Mum?'

Her whisper's soft, exploratory, hoping to provoke some small reassurance that everything's okay without drawing Mum from the room. But there's no reply at all, not a sound, so she leans a little further in and tries again.

'Mum?'

As the smell hits her, Little Gold reels back. It's a cocktail of vile odours but dominating them all is vomit.

'Mum!'

She gropes for the light switch. Mum is on her side in the bed, her duvet pulled up around her face. She takes a tentative step towards her.

'Mum!'

Reaching out, she shakes Mum's shoulder but there's no response. She heaves, her fingers digging into the soft, putty-like flesh of her upper arm as she tugs her to and fro.

'Mum, wake up!'

The sick's on her bottom sheet – a thin, yellow streak of it that stinks out of all proportion to its substance. But then she realises that the moisture has mostly sunk through to the mattress, marooning the few creamy clumps on the surface. Mum grunts.

'Mum! Mum, you've been sick!'

Her eyes flicker open.

'S'alright, A'son.'

'Mum, you've got to get up and get clean.'

Mum rolls on the bed, her face rocking closer and closer to the sick, oblivious.

'Mum!'

Little Gold takes hold of her wrist and heaves. All her strength lifts her torso no more than three or four inches and then she has to let go. Mum flops back onto the bed.

She takes the glass from the bedside table and rinses it in the bathroom, re-filling it with cold water to the brim.

'Mum! Here's water for you.'

Should she throw it over her?

'S'aright, A'son.'

She's not bloody Alison. Alison isn't here. Malcy isn't here. Dad isn't here. She smacks the water down next to Mum.

'Water! Here!'

She turns away and walks down the landing into her bedroom to wait for Malcy's return.

Little Gold sits on her bed without turning on the light. The rain isn't going to stop. The sky is slipping from grey to indigo and car headlights are spangling the street, sweeping across the wet trunks of the trees.

She waits as the darkness deepens and the wind rises, thumping the window. Finally she can stand it no longer and she steps back out onto the landing.

The lightbulb's gone and she picks her way through the darkness, past the glow of Mum's room, vibrating now with deep snores, and down the stairs to the kitchen.

The address book is tucked in beside the phone. As she turns the pages, past names she dredges up from years before, people who used to be Mum's friends, great aunties from Crawley and Guildford, she digs in her mind, trying to draw out Kev's surname.

Just as she's thinking it might not be there, that, perhaps, she's just going to have to go round there, the entry leaps from the page.

Roy and Kay Mansfield (Kevin)
14 Surrenden Road
502-479

It's Mum's writing. She imagines it on shopping lists, letters to school saying she was off sick, or on the form last year for the trip to Fishbourne Roman Palace. That had been such a brilliant day. But the tightening in her chest is getting dangerous and she mustn't be crying on the phone, so she lifts the receiver, ready to dial.

She's expecting the hum of the dialling tone, her finger already in the circle marked 5, but there's nothing but blank silence. Nothing. She presses the buttons on top, jiggling them up and down like they do in old films to make the operator appear. Nothing happens. The phone's dead. She traces the cable to the box on the wall but it all looks normal. Then she flips the phone over and looks at the underneath. There's just the blank, slate-grey plastic looking sealed and impenetrable.

When had they last had a call? Just this morning, when Kev rang. She remembers the ringing dragging her from sleep, Malcy's excited voice floating up from the kitchen.

And now it's stopped being a phone. Now it's just a lump of plastic. At some point this afternoon, when her back was turned, it transformed, became this useless thing. Anger flares and she wants to throw it. She weighs it in her hand and lets herself imagine the crack of it against the wall, the ripping of the wire from the back. But the scrape of a key in the lock makes her just drop it and run towards the front door.

As the door swings open, she sees his silhouette against the orange street-light, speckled with the endless rain.

'Malcy! Where've you…'

Another silhouette blends into Malcy's and then there's Roy's voice.

'Hello!'

Little Gold reaches the switch just inside the door and the hall is bathed in light. Roy blinks.

'Ah, it's you. Is your mum about?'

They're ducked into the porch, Roy's hand on Malcy's shoulder.

'She's having an early night. She's got a headache.'

'Ah, right, well I'm just delivering him back. We were watching a film and it got rather late. I think there's something wrong with your phone. He did try to ring.'

He gives Malcy a shove. It's gentle but it's there, a shove that propels him over the threshold.

'Goodbye then, young man. See you soon, I'm sure.'

He pauses to turn up his collar and fixes Little Gold with a steady eye.

'You know you're welcome too, don't you? Next time.'

She nods and closes the door as he jogs down the steps, his car key dangling from his hand.

Malcy flings his bag down onto the floor.

'What's wrong with the bloody phone, LG? Have you left it off the hook?'

'I don't know. It's not work…'

'It *is* off the bloody hook! Look!'

The phone is hanging from the table where she dropped it, the receiver lying on the floor and the cable running taut to the box on the wall.

'No. It's dead, Malc! Listen!'

Malcy scoops up the phone, puts the receiver to his ear and then slams it back into the cradle.

'Bloody thing!'

'Malc, you need to help me. Mum's been sick in her bed and I can't get her up.'

His roar startles her.

'Aaargh! I don't WANT to get her up. She's so fucking useless!'

He slams the phone receiver back into the cradle again and again until she yanks it from his hand.

'We have to try, Malc. We can't just leave her!'

'Why not? What bloody use is she when she *is* awake? We live in a shit-hole these days because of her. She's like a fucking zombie.'

They hear Mum's bedroom door close and, after a minute, the flush of the loo and the whine of the hot tap. Little Gold hisses,

'What if she heard you?'

'I don't care.'

He crumples into a kitchen chair, his head hanging.

'I don't care.'

She looks at the wash of grime on the back of his neck and can see that below it, reaching up from under his t-shirt, there's the purple-red of a fresh bruise with four clear fingermarks at its crest.

CHAPTER TWENTY-FOUR

Little Gold's wiping her palms on her shorts as she waits for a reply to her knock. It's hot already, the heat pouring back after the drenching rain, and the day smells clean and rich. She'd stopped alongside the lavender bush and pushed her face into its depths, still damp from the night before, inhaled the mixture of flower and earth and wondered how long it took for bones to become part of it all. The thought is still circling, flickering in her mind like something intimate and precious.

'Good morning, good morning!'

Vi flings the door wide, letting the light stream down the hall behind her.

'Come on through to the kitchen, I'm just packing up a picnic.'

The back door's standing open and Peggy's sitting at the kitchen table with a cup of coffee and a newspaper folded to reveal a partially completed crossword. Little Gold sits down beside her.

'She'll bring enough to feed an army, Little Gold, she always does. How are you? Did you sleep well?'

'Yeah, thanks.'

She thinks about the night, about opening her eyes in the darkness to the sound of Malcy crying – a new cry, high and keening but muffled by his pillow. She'd stood beside him, barefoot, long enough to get chilled in the night air but he'd never turned over and not spoken a word. Now she's left him lying on the settee watching telly and guilt squirms in her stomach.

Vi's voice brings her back to the kitchen.

'Some of us, Peg, have healthy appetites and see no reason why they shouldn't be indulged.'

Peggy Baxter leans over, takes a slim, purple cushion from an empty chair beside her and throws it, by one corner, sending it spinning in the air to hit Vi in the side of the head.

'Oi! That's got butter on it now, you great child, you!'

And she does look like a child for a moment, her eyes a mixture of dare you and don't care.

'I'd sacrifice all my cushions for the joy of seeing your hair disrupted, Vi. And well you know it.'

Vi takes the cushion to the sink and blots away the butter with a yellow j-cloth, tutting at the dark patch on the fabric. Then she lays it back on the chair, turning it so that the sun will dry it off.

The sandwiches are a teetering stack before she's finished and she presses a broad knife through the tower, creating triangles fat with lettuce and ham.

'These are ham, lettuce and tomato. How does that sound?'

'Lovely. Thank you.'

'Good. You see, Peg? Some people have excellent manners. If you pay attention you might learn something.'

Peggy laughs and then gets up and helps Vi make a thermos of tea and pack everything into a tatty woven basket. They move around each other, close and swift as the starlings in a murmuration, each in her own space, not talking. Finally, Peggy rinses the cloth in hot water again and wipes down the counter. Little Gold watches steam from the cloth rising into the sunny air. Vi pats her shoulder as she passes.

'Now, just give me a minute while I make myself presentable and we can be off.'

She bustles down the hall and pads upstairs as Peggy sits down again in the chair next to Little Gold. She's slightly breathless.

'At least five minutes. She'll be titivating herself for at least that long.'

Little Gold giggles, the sound bursting out of her like a sneeze.

'It *is* rather a good word, isn't it?'

The old lady winks, takes a cigarette from her packet and flicks her lighter. The tip of the cigarette glows orange and the grey ash lengthens each time she inhales. She smokes like she really means it, not in the rather off-hand way that Vi does. At last she flicks the cigarette – the length of ash broken into the dish of dark specks and discarded stubs.

'I'd better stoke up now because Her Ladyship doesn't like it if I smoke while she drives, which is pure jealousy because she can't manage both at once. Never could.'

'Did she have a motorbike like you?'

'No. Rode pillion with me. That was when we first met. She rode pillion with Magsy too, when she had a bike for a bit.'

How would it be to speed along on a motorbike and have someone behind you, holding on, trusting you? How far could you go like that? Vi's coming back down the stairs. She calls to them.

'Come on then, you two.'

She's put on a brighter red lipstick and her hair's perfect again. She's got changed too, into dark slacks and a blouse the colour of bluebells.

'I think we've picked a cracker of a day. Have you seen that sky?'

Outside there are two high white clouds, piled up like ice cream mountains in the blue.

Vi's car turns out to be a khaki-green Renault 4, hunched on the opposite kerb like a square-nosed beetle. As she unlocks it and flings open the doors, there's a gust of hot air from inside, thick with the smell of sun-warmed plastic. Little Gold starts to climb in but Peggy catches her arm.

'Hang on there! Vi, picnic rug from the boot, I think, or Little Gold will burn her legs on that seat.'

'Oh, blimey, yes! They get like molten lava. Don't want you stuck in there forever!'

Vi spreads a hairy, navy check blanket across the back seat and Little Gold settles in for the ride.

'Here we go then! Hold on to your hats.'

The car eases out onto the road and Little Gold watches her street flicking by. There's a steady stream of air from Vi's open window, rushing into her face.

'Let me know if that window's too much and I'll shut it.'

'No! I like it!'

The car ploughs up the steep hill to find the long road to

Devil's Dyke, lined with detached houses and then fields, falling away on one side to the sparkling sea. Unsought, there's a memory suddenly of an open-top bus ride, all of them together and Dad beside her for once.

Her peaked cap's caught by the breeze, whipped from her head in an instant and lost forever and Dad's arm is round her shoulders. There's the scratch of his bristly chin against her neck as he speaks into her ear to drown out the wind.

'That cap's been taken by a bunny in the field. She's the coolest rabbit in Sussex now.'

Still she'd cried. She'd cried into the Olbas smell of his big, cotton hanky.

They pull into the car park and there's the whole world suddenly. It's a map of patchwork fields, dark nubs of woodland and worms of roads with tiny cars crawling along them. Little Gold catches her breath. If you could ever fly, it would be from here.

Peggy and Vi stand on either side of her and she feels Peggy's hand on her back.

'Lovely, eh? That's called the Weald, that great flat bit, you know? It means wood in Old English. All that used to be woodland.'

And Little Gold sees it that way, greens of every shade, ruched over and over on itself and from inside, deep inside it, fingers of smoke winding into the air from woodcutters' cottages and the houses of witches.

'Right then. Base camp over there, I think.'

Vi spreads the rug from the car and unpacks the basket. Peggy was right, there's too much food, and after three sandwiches and a piece of pork pie, Little Gold's full.

'Have a plum, though. Go on, they don't take up any room and they're beautifully ripe.'

The plum is green gold, sweet and perfect and she finds she's eaten two without thinking. Finally, she can manage nothing more and she notices, for the first time, the families dotted around them. There's the odd grandparent here and there, plonked in folding chairs, but nobody like Peggy Baxter or Vi, lying on the rug, smoking and laughing and throwing plum stones away into the long grass.

Peggy lies down flat on her back, her arms folded behind her head and her crinkled eyes closed. Little Gold watches as Vi tugs the blanket and folds it over her. Then she reaches into her handbag and offers Little Gold the car keys.

'Have a look in the boot. There's something that might amuse you while we old 'uns have a rest.'

It's a kite. The sort of kite that illustrates the letter K in an alphabet book – a red and blue diamond made of stretched cotton over a light wood frame. It's another of their olden-days' things, stored away somewhere, waiting for today. She locks the boot again and runs back to the blanket, dropping the keys next to Vi, who's sitting with her back very straight, her arms around her knees, staring out across the weald.

'Thanks! I'll try it.'

It's not easy on her own but she thinks it through, props the kite against a hummock of grass, nose up to the sky, and unspools some of the string. Then, jerking the string taut, she starts to run down the hill, skidding through the silvery strands of the long grass, feeling the pull of the kite behind her and then, finally, a new sensation as it's caught by the breeze and lifted into the sky. She turns, letting out more string from the wooden spindle. The power of the tugs, the jerks of the kite in the air, are surprisingly powerful and she finds she can yank back, making it jump and leap, seemingly with no danger of it falling. Somehow, though, it finds an unsupported space suddenly and starts to fall, reaching a critical point from which it has no option but to tumble downward to the ground.

Again she sets it up and runs and again it is caught, dancing in the air. And as she stands looking up she becomes aware of someone close beside her. It's Peggy Baxter, shielding her eyes against the sun. Little Gold holds out the spindle of string.

'Do you want a go?'

'Do you know, I will.'

The heavy, loose-skinned hand cups her own for a second and then Little Gold is standing with her arms dangling, watching Peggy Baxter's upturned face and the kite, high above them both.

'I used to be able to do this, I think…'

The old lady swirls her hand in the air and Little Gold watches as the kite twists, falters and nose-dives into the grass just beyond a wire fence that cuts across the steep slope in front of them. Peggy throws up her hands and laughs one of her barking laughs.

'Ah, well, nothing ventured, nothing gained. Think you can get it back for us?'

'Yeah, I'm sure I can.'

Little Gold runs down to the fence, the spindle in her hand, the loose string looping and writhing in the grass at her feet and then slithering after her.

'Watch out for barbed wire, Little Gold!'

But there isn't any barbed wire and she scrambles easily under the gap at the bottom of the fence, posts the kite over the top and wanders back to the rug winding the string. Peggy Baxter's sitting down again, panting slightly and grinning.

'Ah, well done! You're a hero.'

Vi opens her handbag and takes out her purse. It's a red leather pouch, secured with a tight gold clasp.

'Fancy a Ninety-Nine?'

'Ooh, yes please!'

'Get me one too and an Orange Maid for Peg.'

The van's parked at the edge of the car park and as she stands in the queue, Little Gold looks back at the others. They're both laughing again and she wonders what it is that makes them laugh quite so much, that makes them so happy.

'Yes, young man?'

The ice cream lady's leaning down from the window, her bust propped across her forearm, clearly annoyed that her customer's not paying attention. Little Gold drops into her huskiest voice and squares her shoulders.

'Two Ninety-Nines and an Orange Maid please.'

The white ice cream curls from the nozzle of the machine, spiralling into the cones, and the lady jams in the flakes. Holding both the cones in one of her large hands, she bends into the freezer for the lolly and slaps it onto the counter.

'That'll be 75 pence, please.'

Little Gold hands over the fluttering note and shoves the lolly into the pocket of her shorts, to leave her hands free for the cones. As she pockets the change and reaches up to take the ice creams, she feels the lady's eyes sweep across her chest. Never mind, she's away now and nothing will be said. She walks carefully back to the rug, her eyes pinned to the cones as their swirls soften and start to trickle.

'Well done! Well done!'

Vi takes a cone from her left hand and Little Gold pulls out the lolly for Peggy Baxter.

'Well handled, Little Gold. You're a resourceful woman with useful pockets.'

She smiles as she sits cross-legged on the rug and concentrates on a swift drip-tidying exercise, catching a trickle of white as it crosses her knuckles and then nibbling at the soft edge of the dampened cone. She's got a game-plan – eat half the white tower, then the flake, then push the rest of the ice cream down the cone with her tongue as she goes. It's what she and Malcy always do. The thought of Malcy flutters in her cold belly and she realises they haven't had an ice cream together this whole summer.

She's startled back to the rug by Vi issuing a long, low cat purr from her throat.

'Mmmm. Ambrosia!'

She's even more astonished when Peggy Baxter, her tongue swept around her Orange Maid, makes the same noise back.

'Mmmm. Nectar.'

And then they laugh again, on and on, giggling like kids and Vi has to fish in her handbag for a tissue to dab her eyes. Little Gold stares at them, forgetting her ice cream for a moment. Peggy Baxter takes a bite of her lolly and smiles.

'Don't pay any attention to us, Little Gold, we're a couple of dotty old ladies together.'

CHAPTER TWENTY-FIVE

Ali's bought two packets of rubber gloves, J-Cloths, a big bottle of Dettol and some Fairy Liquid. They're lined up on the kitchen table like a selection of rubbish raffle prizes. Little Gold knows that she and Malcy are the lucky winners, turfed out of their beds at eight o'clock for the presentation.

'Okay, so here's the deal, right? You two do all the washing, and I mean *all* of it. You sort out what you've got buried in that tip of a bedroom. Clean the kitchen – washing up and all the surfaces and wash the floor. In return I'll bring in *Smash Hits* and some pick 'n' mix, okay?'

Malcy speaks through his yawn.

'Can you get blackcurran' chews?'

Ali ignores him. She's pulling on her overall, scraping with her fingernail at a flake of something that's crusted over the embroidered letters of Woolworths.

'And there's bread, okay? You can have toast and sandwiches. Don't go mad though 'cos it needs to last a bit.'

She splits and yanks her ponytail to tighten it and Little Gold watches the rubber band twist and tear at her hair.

'Just do it properly and, if Mum gets up, ask her to look at some of the post, okay?'

Ali's picked up all the envelopes from the floor behind the front door, thrown away the free newspapers and leaflets about church jumbles and window cleaners, and arranged the rest in a stack on the table. Little Gold has been watching the slick spreading across the patterned carpet for weeks, flipping the envelopes to check for Dad's writing and seeing instead the red ink peeping around the edges of the milky windows, the dark capitals of FINAL DEMAND.

'Reckon we should try to get her up though, Ali?'

There's evidence in the kitchen that she was up in the night, a plate with a smeared mixture of Daddies' sauce and egg yolk, abandoned, inexplicably, on the back door step.

'No. Just concentrate on the cleaning and I'll see you after work.'

Malcy's biting the cuticle of his thumb, his hair tousled and his eyes filmy. Little Gold realises she mustn't let him go back to bed or she'll end up stuck with the whole job.

As the door slams, Malcy sinks down onto one of the round-backed chairs, hoicking his bare feet up and curling there, his thumb now slipped into his mouth. He's washed-out, his lips pale and dark smudges under his eyes. When did he start sucking his thumb again? Her heart sinks at the thought of the park boys finding out.

'Come on, Malc. Let's make toast and then get on with it.'

His reply's muffled, his lips moving round the wet thumb. She can see his teeth locked into place on its pink, battered skin.

'Let's go back to bed, I'm bloody knackered, LG.'

'No. No, look, come on. If we just get on with it then it won't take that long. And if we don't then she'll go ballistic.'

He doesn't reply but curls tighter and closes his eyes. His toenails are black and the soles of his feet rimed in grit from the floor.

'I'll do us some toast. Come on, Malc. Please.'

He speaks around his thumb again, without opening his eyes.

'Make toas' then.'

She arranges four slices of bread on the grill like the panes of a window. Under the mesh of the rack there's a thick layer of white grease and she longs, suddenly, for the saltiness, the bubbling fat on the sheened surface of bacon. There hasn't been bacon for ages. The marg tub is suspiciously light and when she peels back the lid it's almost empty but there's half a jar of red jam and she spreads it thick over the golden slices.

'Here ya go, Malc! Come on!'

She shoves his arm and he jumps awake with a fear-filled cry that startles her.

'Sorry…'

He's embarrassed, avoiding her eyes as he shifts in the chair and reaches out for a slice of toast. They eat quickly, without talking, and when the toast's gone, Malcy gets himself a mug of water.

'At Kev's you can have what you want now they've got a SodaStream. Lemonade, cola, Irn-Bru…'

He gulps again. She looks around the room, wondering how to start.

'Yeah?'

'Yeah, and if you want some you can just go in the kitchen and get it. You don't have to ask or anything. And the same with snacks. They have actual Dairy Milk bars in the cupboard just for whenever you want. How good is that?'

'Mmm…'

They're just going to have to get started.

'If I go round and collect up all the dirty clothes and get the first load on, will you have a go at the washing up then, Malc?'

''Spose. But we could watch telly for a bit couldn't we? It's not gonna take all day and she's not back 'til nearly six.'

He's edging the mug into the only available space on the surface beside the sink, nudging it along, causing the crockery stack to shift worryingly.

'No! No, I think we're just gonna have to get started Malc. Then you can get over the park later.'

Little Gold's eyes flick around the room. The dirty pans have overwhelmed the hob and are stacked on the floor next to the back door. The floor itself is tacky with every step and littered with screwed-up tissues, the papery peel of onions and a dense scurf of crumbs around the edge. The doors of the lower cupboards are streaked with long drips of dark liquid, the weeping of tea bags on their way from mug to bin.

And it stinks wildly today. There's a sweet, rotten stench pouring out of the jammed mouth of the swing bin. It means that, underneath the crest of crumpled bread packets and newspaper, something particularly pungent is festering away. Little Gold looks under the sink and there's a black bin bag. It would be best to sort it out now, before they do anything else, just so they don't have to stand the smell. But already she's getting used to it. Whatever's in there is going to unleash its full, oozing, stomach-flipping horror if they get it out and she decides to go and get the laundry first.

Mum's door is ajar and she leans in, waiting for her eyes to adjust to the dark.

'What are you doing?'

Her voice is clear, properly awake and not drunk.

'Oh, Mum, I just came to see if you had any washing. I'm putting a load on.'

'Oh.'

It's an entirely neutral response, not an invitation to come in and not an order to go away. She hesitates and Mum shifts on the bed, turning onto her side and saying nothing more. Little Gold edges into the room, the laundry basket wedged on her skinny hip.

She crouches and picks at clothes on the floor. There's a pile like the shed skin of a snake. She lifts the tangle of tights and knickers by one toe then scoops up the rest and backs out of the room, dragging the basket behind her.

Ali's laundry is all in her hamper in the corner of her room and Little Gold stops in there for a minute, looking at the clear, clean expanse of carpet. The room belongs in a different house altogether. Under the desk there's a new set of bathroom scales she must've got with her staff discount at Woolies. Where her revision timetable used to be stuck on the wall, there's now a page ripped from a magazine.

Slim for Summer! Know your calories and you're halfway to that bikini he will love! Apple (small) – 80. One tablespoon cottage cheese – 110. One slice bread – 100.

Ali's added other foods underneath the printed list, scrawled on in her own spidery writing – one digestive biscuit, ten twiglets, other things she loves.

Her and Malcy's room has become impossible. Not only has the carpet disappeared completely, but the door's stuck half-open. She yanks at the comic and the swirly purple towel that have bound into a wedge right up by the hinge. When they finally give she falls back into the sea of stuff.

She harvests the clothes quickly, chucking socks, t-shirts

and pants out onto the landing where they bury the already-full basket.

It's the speed that causes the accident. The glass of water on Malcy's bedside table's been there weeks, getting progressively obscured by the piling up of annuals and other junk and she barely registers that she's knocked it over until she feels the cold water dripping down onto her sock-clad foot.

'Ah, shit! Bloody hell, Malcy.'

She starts to hurl annuals onto the bed, dabbing ineffectually at the soaked clutter on the table with a t-shirt.

'Shit, shit shit.'

And then there it is, lying flat underneath the last annual, soaked and stuck to the surface like a lick and stick transfer. But it's not that, it's a twenty pound note.

She stops blotting at the water and nudges at the corner of the note with her index finger. The very tip lifts from the moisture and she starts to peel it away.

'Hey! That's mine.'

His shoulder cannons into her upper arm and she falls sideways, losing her footing and staggering across to her own bed.

'Jesus, Malc!'

He's scrabbling at the money in a panic.

'Careful! You'll rip it. Peel it off carefully an' it'll be okay.'

'What the pissing piss have you done to my money? What were you doing poking about in my stuff?'

'I wasn't 'poking about'. I was getting the washing and I just knocked over that glass.'

'Yeah, well, you shouldn't be getting in my stuff. You're always poking about in my stuff. You should mind your own business.'

'Oi! I was just getting your stinky bloody socks and pants! It's not my fault if you leave water on your side! Anyway, where'd you get it?'

'It's none of your bloody business where I got it! It's mine!'

'What, twenty quid? You just happen to have twenty quid?'

'What if I do?'

He's leaning forward, shouting now, his eyes wild and bulging.

'Well, where'd you get it?'

'It's none of your bloody, bloody business, you nosy little shit.'

She's still holding the damp t-shirt, screwed up in her right hand, and she hurls it at his distorted face, watching, as if in slow-motion, as he registers the impact, sweeps it away and roars in fury.

'Aaargh! You little shit, you little shitting shit!'

And she's running down the landing, scattering the clothes, feeling them tug and pull around her ankles, and, just behind her, trembling the air, there's Malcy's swiping hand.

She turns at the bottom of the stairs, her own hands up to protect her face.

'Sorry, Malc! Sorry, sorry, I just…'

He gets one cuff around her left ear and then his hands fall to his sides and they stand panting, looking into the mirror of each other's shocked faces. She tries again.

'Sorry, I…'

Malcy just shakes his head in response and looks away. He's leaning against the wall and she thinks she can hear the faint, high strand of his wheeze underneath the panting.

Please, no.

After a few minutes he speaks, directing his words to the skirting board.

'Roy gave it to me.'

She knew. She knew he was going to say that.

'Why?'

Is that his wheeze? Is that his wheeze starting or just her imagination? There's a shaft of sunlight illuminating the top of his head, the arced strands of his blonde hair and the wall behind. She doesn't look into his eyes, even when he lifts them from the floor and goes on.

'You don't get it, LG. They're loaded. I don't just mean they've got enough like we did when Dad was here, I mean they're properly, properly loaded.'

'So?'

'So, I dunno. It's…'

There's no wheeze. There's no wheeze and he's okay. She can feel tears rolling from her chest though, barrelling in tightness up her throat.

'Need a wee!'

She runs up the stairs and into the bathroom, slamming the door and sliding the bolt. As she rests her head on the wood panel, she lets the tears brim and spill, brim and spill again, and she wipes her nose with the back of her hand. The image of the sodden note, of Malcy's twisted face, replays on her eyelids. And then she's sure, sickeningly sure, that the other thing she found in their room, the dirty magazine, Roy gave him that too.

*

Little Gold's lying on the settee, half-watching a black and white film about a girl who rides a horse in the Grand National. She wants to watch it, wants to know what's going to happen to this girl who won't keep her braces in and loves the big, black horse. But, still, her mind slides from it into anxious circles, throwing in images and words she fights to push away.

The kitchen's better than it was and outside the clothes line is heavy with wet washing but she wishes they hadn't scrubbed the floor with Dettol. As she watched it swirl in the hot water, turning it cloudy and releasing its distinctive medicinal tang, she realised that it would just make everything smell like they had something to hide. Like Ali behind the closed bathroom door.

'Hello?'

It's a man's voice. A man is walking into the house and calling out to announce his arrival. She sits and spins round, joy surging up.

'The door was open.'

Roy's standing in the front room doorway, leaning against its frame, his car keys in his hand. The joy curdles in her stomach and she stands.

'Hello.'

'Hello, young lady. You on your own?'

'No, Mum's… Mum's upstairs.'

He nods.

'Right. And Malcolm?'

'He's just over the park, I think. I can show you.'

'I think I know my way to the park.'

He's smirking, spinning the car keys on his finger, looking into her face until she feels the blush start to seep up her neck.

'Smells like a hospital in here. Somebody ill?'

'Mum's just been cleaning.'

'Right.'

Still he stares and she locks her eyes onto the empty grate, the scorched-out back of the fireplace. It's black and hard and she'll just wait. Finally, he speaks again.

'Well, I'll go over and tell Malcolm this myself but the invitation's for you too. Tomorrow's Kay's birthday and a couple of friends over at Henfield have a pool. We'll be heading over just before eleven and we can pick you up on the way. You'll need swimming gear, obviously.'

Little Gold can hear the swoosh of her own blood. He's crossing the room towards her now and then he stops, close to her right side, and suddenly bends his knees, dropping so that his head is alongside her own.

'What's so fascinating in that fireplace then, eh?'

There's the smell of coffee on his breath and she feels its hot gust against her cheek.

'Eleven, okay?'

She nods and he chuckles as he stands up again and leaves the room. She watches from the window as his charcoal-grey back retreats down the path and his head bobs away down the steps.

Her knees are trembling, feather-light and uncontrollable and she sits down heavily on the settee. The girl, Velvet, has dressed up in the silks and jodhpurs of a jockey and she's going to ride her horse in the Grand National. All the way through the film she's wanted to do it really, of course she has. He's called The Pie. They're going to win, because it's a film and that's what happens in films. As he leaps and the hooves thunder, all the fear comes tumbling out of Little Gold, her teeth chattering, her fingers locked tight around her knees.

*

She's lying in the tree, cowled in Malcy's burgundy hooded top, its softness framing the pale evening sky. Stretched across the ridge of the roof and dotted across the aerial there are starlings, black as crows against the light.

'LG!'

Malcy's calling from the back yard.

'LG! Ali's home! Pick 'n' mix!'

She doesn't have to go. She doesn't have to go indoors now or to the party tomorrow. She never has to leave this tree. What will they do? They can't drag her down. For now, for now at least, she can just climb higher – into the spindly branches. She can live like a boy in *Brendon Chase*, escaped into the woods, dressed in furs, calling to his brothers like an owl in the night.

'LG! Come on!'

Malcy leans out the back door.

'She's brought blackcurrant chews and those mint creams you like!'

Little Gold climbs down and crosses the damp evening grass, feeling it chill and moisten her socks. The starlings peel away into the sky as she plods down the steps.

Ali's sitting at the end of the table and Malcy's got two of the tiny silver bowls, the sort they used to have trifle in at Christmas, and he's sharing out the sweets, dipping into the bag.

'One for you, one for me, one for you, two for me…'

Little Gold looks at the mounting wrappers and paintbox colours, filling the bowls.

'Well done for getting it sorted out in here, LG. Malcy says you're both invited to a party tomorrow?'

'Yeah.'

'That's nice.'

CHAPTER TWENTY-SIX

Peggy turns the round brass handle and is relieved to find that the door swings open. Halfway down the long hill she'd realised that it was Wednesday and that the clock-mender would close at lunchtime. She's breathless from hurrying and a gentle wave of dizziness sweeps over her as she steps into the tiny space. The counter is unattended but the shop is packed with scores of glassy faces arranged on shelves. Several grandfather clocks, and some huge disc that must surely have come from a station or a town hall, are crowded onto the faded carpet. Peggy stands in the small patch of remaining floor space and calls out.

'Hello?'

A man steps through a heavy curtain that screens the doorway into the back. He's accompanied by smells of cooking – something rich and meaty in gravy and the comforting hum of overcooked greens. He blinks, owlish and unhurried.

'Good afternoon.'

He looks as a clock-mender should, she thinks – bottle specs and his grey pullover a little threadbare at the elbows. She wonders how many years he's been here, in his nest of timepieces.

Reaching into her bag, she brings out the small, wooden clock.

'I wondered if you could service this for me? It's keeping pretty lousy time these days.'

He takes the clock in knowing hands and pulls off the circular brass plate on the back. After a cursory look inside, he reaches for a pad of carbons and a biro.

'Yes. I can probably see to this by next week. Name?'

'Baxter. Thank you. It's worth the work then?'

The man writes something in a scrawling hand, along with her name, tears out the top copy of the page and hands it to Peggy before he replies.

'Perfectly good clock.'

A fellow of few words.

'If I call back next Wednesday then?'

He nods.

'Do you need a deposit or…'

He shakes his head.

Suddenly, the tiny shop whirrs all around her and she's bathed in the overlapping peels and chimes of one o'clock, announced in a hundred different voices. Time to go.

Peggy glances back at the shop as she walks away. It's the anxiety of leaving a loved one in hospital and she mutters to herself.

'Bloody fool, Peg Baxter. It's a clock.'

But this clock, this personified timekeeper, has been a companion from childhood. Humpy Clock, whose tick punctuated a thousand Sunday afternoons as she lay on her bed with Bible Stories for the Young, or made, and made again, the jigsaw of Glamis Castle. He stood on their chest of drawers, across the narrow landing, beating out the safe, predictable moments. Wound weekly by her father. Polished by her mother.

Lifted under her arms to the chest of drawers, her little shoes bump on the chipped veneer.

'Hold it carefully now.'

'Humpy Clock. Him's Humpy Clock and him eats tick tocks.'

Does she really remember it, or just the re-telling, years later by her laughing mother?

'You were such a fanciful child.'

She tries to peel apart the tone of the telling. What rang with mockery was lined with other emotions, wasn't it? Affection, perhaps? But fear, certainly. Fear of little Margaret and her fanciful nature.

Dad, young and still willowy, holding her round the middle as she sits there, Humpy Clock filling her hands. She looks down and squeaks, seeing, suddenly, the drop to the floor.

'Don't be scared. Daddy won't drop you.'

Peggy stops on a garden wall for a cig and lets her breathing slow. There's no bus to help with the long hill home and she can't face it yet. What she needs is somewhere close at hand where she can sit and gather her strength. Somewhere to just be for half an hour, where no-one will notice her.

In these residential streets, with their quiet front lawns, she feels horribly exposed, but just to her left is a station, Preston Park, the penultimate on the Brighton line. It's a commuter stop, heavy with suited traffic at either end of the day but likely to be deserted now, in this hot, lunchtime lull.

The entrance to the platforms is through a low tunnel. It's painted with glossy cream paint that reflects the light from lozenge-shaped lamps set into the brickwork of the roof. She steps inside and is enveloped in the cool subterranean air.

The deserted space and her echoing footsteps create a sense that she's walked out of time. As she paces, slowly, up the steps to the ticket office, she's not quite sure what she will find. The man in rolled shirtsleeves, sitting in the ticket booth, reading his *Daily Mirror*, might belong anywhere in the last forty years or even to some time in the future.

'Do I need a platform ticket?'

'No, love, you're okay.'

He waves his hand at the open doorway as if granting her access to the whole world, and, as she expected, she's quite alone here to take her pick of the empty benches.

A blackbird is serenading her from nodding trees up the track to the North and she takes the bench closest, shaded by a canopy, and lets her eyes close. She can hear just the lusty singing of the bird, the swish of wind through leaves and, in the distance, the roar of the cars on the London Road, somehow reassuring.

The cars anchor her here, in the present day and she reflects on this modern plague. It seems there are more and more every year, lining the kerbs, chasing each other's tails. In her childhood a car was a rare event, attracting a gaggle of kids.

She could tell Little Gold about that, how a car was a thrill in her day. And then Little Gold would turn astonished eyes and maybe then she'd say,

Was a car really something special then?

And on and on they'd talk.

There's something direct in her, that's the thing, an attentive, direct air. It makes Peggy certain that what she says is being filed, stored inside and that the child won't ever forget. But that's probably wishful thinking. That's probably fantasy and vanity. She mutters to herself,

'How do you know she'll remember a word of it? You don't know any such thing.'

The dizziness is back again and she grips the edge of the bench. The world turns and tilts and slowly settles and the blackbird flies from the tree. She mumbles a reply to herself, feeling more gentle now.

'Well, I think I'll just have faith in that.'

Suddenly the rails start to sing. The gleaming silver tracks are ringing in anticipation of the arrival of a train. Peggy opens her eyes. The face of the train appears down the track, larger and larger and finally lengthening into its full self as it rattles alongside her. Heads pop from lowered windows and hands reach through for the door handles on the outside. A single green training shoe is dangled from an open door, gliding the length of the platform on an invisible skateboard. Some impatient lad. A boy with somewhere to get to.

The train stops and the green-footed person leaps down from the carriage. It's a girl with a bouncing, red ponytail and blue jeans tight on slender thighs. Peggy laughs at herself, at her own assumptions.

Half a dozen other passengers climb down from the train, singly or in pairs, slamming the doors behind them. The last is a young mother with a baby on her hip, a folded pushchair in her other hand and a bag swinging on her fragile shoulder. The guard, far down the platform, his whistle raised to his lips, clearly has no intention of helping and Peggy gets to her feet.

The mother's fighting with the pushchair, butting it up against the train. The baby, impassive and silent, is swaying across her braced arm.

'Can I give you a hand?'

She's startled but relieved and turns to Peggy with a smile.

'Can you just take him for a minute?'

She's holding the baby out to her and Peggy has no choice but to take the child.

He is such bounty – rounded and placid, his eyes a chocolate brown. He regards her, for a moment, with the solemnity of a very old man. Then he turns to locate his mother, who's assembling the pushchair as the train pulls away.

Peggy cradles him close against her body. He's an older baby than she has ever held, with a comforting solidity in his arms and legs and a little, barrel chest. His lips are open, pale pink and moist and there's a warm shush of air from inside, soft and damp on Peggy's neck. He blinks his steady eyes.

'Thanks, thanks so much. I was worried I'd get taken on to Brighton. Can you just hang on to him for a minute while I get this sorted out?'

The flimsy pushchair, just a low-slung strip of shiny, deckchair stripes, looks wholly inadequate for this precious creature, but the mother wants him back. Peggy loosens her grip and watches as she clips him into place.

'Off we go then, Joshy! Thanks again.'

And then they're gone, away down the steps at a worrying, racketing pace and Peggy needs to sit down again. She has one more cig. It's far too hot still, hotter perhaps than it was when she took refuge here, and the hill is a looming impossible thing.

She thinks of Vi and her car. She's somewhere on the M4 now, probably going much too fast. She'd have brought the clock down if Peggy had asked her. But she didn't and now here she is.

The chap from the ticket office sets off to water the tubs of flowers. His heavy can bounces off his shins as he walks and water sloshes onto his shoes. He drenches the tub of petunias next to Peggy and wipes his wet hand on his shirt.

'You alright, love? Waiting for the 13.51?'

Peggy swallows her pride and it hurts going down.

'Actually, no. I need a taxi. I don't suppose I'll find one at the rank outside. Would you be able to telephone for me, from your office, do you think?'

And that's all it takes to identify her as an old lady in difficulty. Peggy has to be firm, force herself to be grateful for the cracked mug of water, the shoulder to lean on and his presence on the steps. He places her hand on the rail in the tunnel as the taxi toots from the street.

'You'll be alright from here then, love?'

'Yes, thanks. You've been very kind.'

In the car, Peggy lays her head against the seat, embarrassed as the impossible hill is devoured by the car in less than five minutes and they draw up alongside her house. She gives the driver an extravagant tip and brushes off his offer to see her to the door. As the taxi pulls away, she turns to her front steps and, slowly, very slowly now, she starts to climb.

*

When Peggy wakes, she finds she's fully dressed and the room is bursting with evening light. The button is open on her twill trousers and the cuffs ridden up round her shins. Shaw leaps onto the bed beside her, rubbing his head against her knuckles, starting up his wet purr of request.

'Alright then, Mister, is it tea time then?'

But there's no Humpy Clock. The silence is eerie, unsettling her as she twists the watch on her wrist.

'Let's see where we are then. Golly, half past eight and nothing in your bowl. What must you think of my negligence? Let's get you sorted out.'

She strokes him and rises, slowly, from the bed, following his padding paws down the stairs and into the kitchen, where she switches on the light.

'Whiskas!'

She forks out the end of the tin into his shallow bowl and watches as he thrusts his muzzle into the pallid meat. There's the sound of his sticky chewing and lapping at what gets smeared and she turns away to the kettle, sickened by the noise.

She can't stomach a meal but makes a cup of tea and carries it down the hall along with a lit cigarette. Sitting in the glow of the standard lamp she looks out at the park.

The house without Vi has an ache this time. Rather more of an ache than it's had for years. She peers out into the darkness, wishing the child would come. But it's late, it's far too late for that and she grinds out her fag with a twist. She's lonely now, after so much unaccustomed company and there's no point in denying it's hard.

'You're too old to deceive yourself, woman.'

She's wracked by a shudder, flushes hot and then cold.

'And you've got a bloody temperature. Tablets, hot water bottle, bed.'

Lying in bed, Peggy feels her pulse fluttering in her neck. It's racketing, slightly fast with fever and she touches the trembling skin. It's moist under her fingers, damp and warm, as if the baby is breathing there still.

She pictures his placid face. She feels his weight in her arms again and the press of him against her chest. But when she looks now at the little face, she finds that it's transformed. The brown-eyed baby has disappeared and she's holding a golden child.

CHAPTER TWENTY-SEVEN

'This way.'

Roy leads them up a winding path through the poplar trees. The lawn around them is immaculate, the green as dense as a carpet with not a single daisy or dandelion, as if it's been hoovered clean and brushed with a hairbrush to this perfection.

The wind ruffles the trees, making the speckled shadows dance on the path ahead of her, and Little Gold fights the urge to run. There's something so possible about it – the lawn rolling away to a low fence, an unmetalled road and beyond that woodland. She pictures her feet on the struts of the fence, pounding over the flint-dotted track and sprinting through the trees, beechnuts cracking. And then she'd find the river, the river Adur that she knows runs down to the sea at Shoreham. Shoreham has a station with trains home. It's all so possible. If she lived in a book she'd do it, like Margaret Thursday escaping the orphanage and running away with her friends. But she's not leading anyone, she's following. A little lamb trotting up the garden path.

Still she hangs back though, watching Kay's teetering progress ahead of her. The woman's long foot slips to the side of her towering white sling-back and she flings out a spindly arm to stop herself falling. It's like walking on stilts. A man's voice makes Little Gold lift her eyes.

'Roy!'

He's coming around the side of the house, wearing a sailor's cap with a large gold anchor above the peak. For a moment she wonders if it's fancy dress, so complete is the sailor costume.

His white deck shoes are blinding on the emerald grass as he approaches.

'Doug!'

The two men shake hands, Doug slapping Roy on the shoulder. Doug has a pendulous belly hanging over the waistband of navy shorts and long socks turned back underneath fat, hairy knees. The knees are little more than dimpling in legs that appear to be just tapering thighs ending in his small, sparkling feet. He's a pig, up on its hind trotters, dressed up in clothes.

'Roy! Kevin! And Mrs Mansfield, Birthday Girl! Ravishing as ever.'

He takes her hand and presses his broad mouth to the back of it, sweeping the sailor cap from his head. As he leans forward, Little Gold notices the thinness of the greying hair on the crown and the scorched, speckled skin of his scalp peeping through.

'Come on round…'

He's still talking as he turns away and she strains to hear what he's saying, catching just snatches,

'Done us proud… in the pool already…'

Behind the house there's a wide patio with a swimming pool sunk into the middle. At each corner, where there are steps, the silver arcs of handrails wink in the sunlight reflected from the water. There's someone there in the bright blueness but she can't make them out with the sun in her eyes. Doug's pointing to the people dotted around the pool and down on the lawn beyond the patio.

'Don and his good lady wife, Elaine.'

The couple are seated in deckchairs in a patch of shade cast by the side wing of the house.

'Keith and Terry over on the lawn there, and that's Peter in the pool.'

The two men are on sun loungers, one with his back to Little Gold. They're deep in conversation but, at the mention of their names, both look round and Roy lifts a hand and nods to them. Doug turns back to the patio.

'And there's my Jackie with the birthday feast.'

Jackie's holding a plate in one hand, piled high with some sort of pastries that Little Gold doesn't recognise. She waves with her other hand, bending just the tips of her fingers up and down. She's wearing some sort of wrap-around dress and as she leans to lower the plate onto a far corner of the table, the blue fabric parts and one long, brown leg emerges.

Roy strides over and kisses her cheek, squeezing her bare upper arm and saying something quietly in her ear. Little Gold's aware, suddenly, of Doug close beside her, kissing and squeezing Kay in a similar fashion and then turning to Kev.

'So, lads, I think it's ladies first in the changing room, eh? Or you can just get stripped off down by the trees.'

Kev and Malcy run down the lawn and disappear into the cover of horse chestnut trees at its end. Little Gold is left with Kay, who picks up her bag and follows Doug towards a door standing ajar at the back of the house.

Inside there's a sort of mini changing room, with a tiled floor and slatted wooden benches. In the corner of the room there's a cubicle made of pine strips. Little Gold thinks it might be a sauna.

'Right, ladies, I'll leave you to it. There's an en-suite just through the bedroom if you need it.'

He gestures at the door at the end of the changing room, which is standing open, revealing a pink bedroom beyond.

'Have you got everything you need, darling?'

Kay's unpacking her fat, floral bag, shaking out a fine cerise wrap and laying it along the bench.

'Yeah, thanks.'

Little Gold's had the forethought to wear her costume under her clothes, of course, so all that's necessary is to take off her trainers and slip out of her shorts. She does that quickly and stands beside the door, facing away from Kay, who's stripping off behind her.

'You just enjoy yourself here, sweetheart. Everyone's ever so friendly and you just help yourself to whatever you'd like to eat.'

'Thank you.'

'And Peter's a sweet boy, so don't be worried about that.'

She isn't worried about Peter. At this moment she isn't worried about anything more than being in here with Kay. As if reading her mind, Kay tuts and says,

'Oh, give me a hand with this, sweetheart.'

Little Gold turns back slowly to face her. She's bare-breasted, dangling the white string of her bikini top from her long fingers – the cups the shape of two scallop shells, trimmed with gold piping.

'If I sit here, can you just tie it for me?'

Kay perches on the bench, her slender, amber thighs pressed together, and arranges the bikini top on her breasts. Little Gold tries to focus solely on the wooden slats of the seating, her heart thumping in her throat. But her eyes are darting across Kay's body, startled by the expanse of flesh and glimpses of her firm, dark nipples.

'It's just fiddly with my hair.'

She scoops the mass of auburn curls with her forearm, revealing the pale nape of her neck. With her other hand she grasps the two strings. Little Gold takes them from her and ties a half-knot, unsure of an appropriate level of tension, scared of catching a stray hair.

'Oh, aren't you a careful little thing? You can pull a bit tighter.'

She tightens the half-knot and makes a fumbling bow.

'Perfect. Now then, you take off that t-shirt.'

Little Gold feels her heartbeat leap up her throat and she coughs.

'It's okay, I just have to be a bit careful with the sun.'

Kay's laugh deepens the flush sweeping from Little Gold's neck to her scalp.

'Oh, I thought you said you never burned? Sweetheart, there's no need to be shy here. If you're really worried about the sun, I've got the answer right here.'

She rummages in her bag and brings out a bottle of dark brown oil with an orange lid which she spins with fingers tipped today by pale pink nails.

'Just take off that t-shirt and I'll do your shoulders.'

There's no choice but to comply and Little Gold curls her toes on the tiled floor as she lifts the t-shirt over her head. The backs of her fingers are icy as they brush across her warm torso, clad in nothing now but the sheen of her swimming costume, tight as a second skin. Outside, one of the men laughs. Kay's voice is quiet, close to her ear.

'That's it.'

And then there's a palm on the back of her neck, long fingers reaching underneath her costume, pressing on her spine. Kay tugs the straps over her shoulders and Little Gold starts, jerks away, making a sound that's almost a word. A sound that's almost no.

'Nnn.'

But the hand returns with murmurs that are low, intense, more intrusive even than the pressing fingers. Little Gold can't speak or move the rigid limbs of her invaded body and so she leaves it, slips up to the crack of a high, frosted window and then through it, and into the top branch of the swaying poplar outside. Tiny and fast. A pied-wagtail, maybe.

'There we are. There we are then. Don't want you burning, do we. How about those little legs?'

The oiled hand tightens on her shoulder and she feels the dig of the pink talons into her skin as her body is turned. Kay lets go for a moment, bastes her palm in the dark oil again and reaches down to Little Gold's thigh.

From outside there's a shriek and then Kev's voice, loud and over-excited.

'Hey! Malcy, look at this!'

His voice seems to break into Kay's trance and her hand falls away.

'Off you go and play with the boys then.'

She's screwing the cap back onto the bottle, her eyes averted, as Little Gold flits back into herself, steps away and reaches for the door handle.

The light outside is painfully bright and she looks down at the pale paving slabs, blinking. A cascade of water rains down across her feet as Kev smacks into the pool.

He surfaces and swims confidently to the side.

'Good one, Kev!'

Malcy shouts from the far end of the patio. He backs away a couple more steps to increase his run-up and then hurtles across the paving slabs and leaps, his body thrown into angles, his hair a white halo. For an instant he's held there above the pool and then the water swallows him. Little Gold's breath is shallow and her knees feel soft, weak and unreliable. More than anything she's aware of her exposed body, the tightness of the swimming costume across her chest, the biting of the piping around the top of each thigh. She's desperate to cover herself but her towel is back in the changing room from which Kay is yet to emerge.

Peter's still in the pool, tight against the side where he was when she first arrived. Little Gold slips in opposite him, gasping at the cold but thankful, immensely thankful, for the feeling of coverage, the sense that she's become nothing more than a head. But her breathing is still ragged and fast and she longs for warm water, soap, a cloth to scrub away the sensation of Kay's oiled hands on her skin.

Peter's clinging to a silver bar running around the edge of the pool, just under the lip of concrete. Little Gold bobs a couple of times and then swims a shaky breaststroke towards him, her head out of the water. At the other end of the pool, Malcy and Kev are having a splashing battle.

'Hello.'

She can just reach the bottom with the tips of her toes but she treads water as she speaks, feeling somehow less foolish if she's moving. He doesn't reply, in fact he turns his head and looks away, down the long lawn towards the men on the loungers.

'I'm Little Gold.'

His reply is quiet, spoken to the garden, but she hears it.

'Peter.'

'I'm Malcy's sister.'

He nods and she realises he's shivering, his lips dancing slightly as his teeth chatter. She looks again at his hand gripping the bar. He's still looking down the garden at the men and she looks too.

They've turned their loungers to face the pool and they're sipping something the colour of blood oranges out of sparkling glasses. Malcy's clambered out again and he takes another mighty leap in, sending water cascading down around her and Peter. Peter shakes his head wildly like a wet dog on the beach, but silver droplets have settled on his afro.

One of the men, Keith or Terry, she doesn't know which is which, puts down his glass and claps. He's wearing heavy gold rings on nearly every finger.

'Bravo!'

Little Gold watches as he rises from the lounger and strolls towards the pool. He plucks a shimmering red plastic ball from a net on the patio and tosses it into the water.

'There you go, boys!'

Kev grabs the bobbing ball and throws it to Malcy, who struggles to catch it as it arcs over his head. But he does and then he hurls it, spinning, down the length of the pool towards Peter.

'Pete!'

The ball falls short and there's a fine, hard spray of water directly into his face. He screws his eyes tight but drips cling to his long eyelashes and he doesn't wipe them away, just tugs himself tighter to the edge, his eyes still closed. Little Gold senses the chattering pulse of his fear. He's hating it. He's hating it in the pool and yet he doesn't get out.

The man comes closer, leans over the edge and nudges the ball towards Peter with his gold-weighted fingers.

'Throw it back then.'

For a moment she thinks he's going to ignore the voice, his eyes stay closed and he doesn't move. But the seconds pass and it's clear the man is waiting. There's the slosh and slap of the blue water against the side of the pool, the murmur of conversation from across the patio, and the man clears his throat.

Peter's eyes flutter open and he reaches out with one hand, trying to scoop up the ball into the cradle of his palm, while still gripping tightly to the silver bar.

'No! You're going to have to use both hands!'

The man nudges the ball a little away from him and Peter makes a small noise of panic before suddenly letting go and lurching out, scrabbling in the water, gasping and struggling to catch hold of it.

'Hahaha! Come on boy, make a bit of effort!'

Peter's foot slides on the bottom of the pool and the water laps over his face as he grunts in panic, his fingers flicking the ball, sending it spinning further away from him and towards Little Gold. She reaches out, grabs and hurls it, in one fluid movement, towards her brother.

'Malc!'

Peter scrabbles back to the side and catches hold of the bar, panting and coughing, his eyes closed again. The man's voice is as oily as Kay's fingers. It flows over her as he fixes her with hard eyes.

'Oh, got a little tomboy, have we?'

Peter's coughing, Kev and Malcy's shouting and the man's words are chopped together in a syncopated ensemble, but his eyes, fixed on hers, are transmitting a message of cold hatred. She catches just part of what he's saying to her.

'... don't worry... one or two here who'll cure you of that...'

He straightens abruptly and strolls back towards his lounger, leaving her treading water. His words are repeating in her head, heavy with threat and so odd and inappropriate from a stranger that she's starting to doubt them immediately. She must have misheard and he said something else, surely? The other man, stretched out with his arms behind his head, shouts across the lawn to his approaching companion.

'I told you they're no good in the water!'

'Other talents though, Terry! Other talents!'

Peter's stopped coughing and he shoots a venomous look at Little Gold before climbing out of the pool and running across the patio towards the other boys. She hears Malcy calling to him.

'Come on, let's play football down the end.'

Little Gold swims, as hard as she can, backwards and forwards across the width of the pool, choking back tears. She's completely wrong here and yet Malcy's acting like he's quite at home, larking about, somehow oblivious. Is he happy? How can he be? She imagines her watch, pushed down at the bottom of her plastic bag in the changing room, pictures its face and wills the hands to spin, fast, to swallow the afternoon and send them both home.

At the corner of the pool, where Peter had been, she stops, panting. The two men have turned their loungers away to watch the boys play football and, beside the table, all the other adults are standing in a loose circle, smoking and drinking. Doug has his fat arm draped around Kay's bare shoulders. Roy says something and there are nods all round. No-one is looking at her. This is her moment to get out, to get to the changing room and back into her clothes.

In the dim room, Kay's bag is lying open, the tanning oil is nestled against a bright pink purse, wide as a slab of meat and trimmed in gold like her bikini. For a second she pictures her fingers sliding the zip, taking one or two of the notes she's sure would be inside. It's not something she's ever considered before. She's never stolen anything, not a penny chew or a pencil, nothing. Then why, she thinks, as she wraps herself, swiftly, in her tatty towel, why is she thinking about it now? She knows she won't do it. Of course she won't do it but she wants to, wants to hurt someone here, somehow.

But right now the most urgent thing is to get dressed and the room doesn't feel secure. She can't see a way to lock the door that leads to the garden and she stands shivering for a moment, her mind spinning with panic. Her eye falls on the boxed-in corner of the room that must be a sauna and, gathering up her plastic bag and trainers, she steps lightly across the room, trying to stick to the cracks between the tiles so she won't leave a trail of footprints.

Inside it's pitch black and it smells richly of pine and something else, something strange and acrid she doesn't recognise. She doesn't dare to reach for the cord that might be a light switch, fearful of activating some control that will cause the place to heat up, to give out light and noise and advertise her presence. Instead she pulls the door to, leaving just a crack for a finger of light and, in the strange twilight, she strips off her sticky costume. She towels her shaking body quickly, registering the goose pimples, the uncontrollable tremor in her legs and arms, but not daring to slow down and rub in some warmth. Instead she yanks at her t-shirt, feeling a creak in the strained stitches of the side seam as she pulls it over her damp skin. Her knickers roll into a tight sausage of fabric and she fumbles with numb fingers to straighten them. Once safely clad in shorts as well, she puts an eye to the crack in the door. She's about to step out when the changing room floods with sunlight and Roy's voice fills the air.

'I *told* him not today so he's got no business complaining.'

Little Gold takes a step back into the darkness. She hears Doug reply.

'Well, if you're sure.'

'I am. That's why I made it clear. I need to take it steady.'

'Look, I understand completely, Roy. I think Keith just forgets we're not all in the same position as him. You're clearly doing wonders with the boy.'

'Hmm.'

They're standing so close to the sauna that she can hear the squeak of Doug's deck shoe on the tiled floor as he turns.

'Not that the boy's my main interest, of course.'

'And that's got to go slower still, Doug. Slower still, you understand? It's early days there.'

'Are you sure about that? Kay seems quite close to her already. You two aren't just keeping that one for yourselves, I don't suppose?'

Little Gold's startled by a grunt, the noise of a tussle and thud as something heavy hits the wall of the sauna. Then Roy's voice, through gritted teeth, snakes between the wooden panels and into her hiding place.

'Look, you fat bastard, I've sourced these ones and I'm the one who says how they're to be handled. I'm the one taking all the risk here and so, until I say, there's going to be nothing in that direction. Nothing.'

Doug's voice is a flurry of high, scared appeasement delivered in little more than a whisper.

'Alright! Alright! I'm not arguing, Roy. I'm not arguing there. Now, do you want to see the prints they brought from Croydon?'

'Of course. Birthday treat for Kay if they're any good.'

'Oh, you wait 'til you see them. Jesus, Roy, the best. Really, the best.'

Little Gold hears the thrusting noise of the door into the bedroom scraping across the thick pile carpet and realises they've gone into the house.

She approaches the crack again and presses one eye to the thin column of light. She can see across the pink bedroom, to where Roy and Doug are standing together beside a white, scrolled dressing table. Doug hands Roy a large envelope from the top drawer.

'I can't tell you how pleased I am with these ones, Roy. I haven't seen this sort of quality in the country. They match the best I've had from Nils.'

Roy is flicking through the sheets he's taken from the envelope. They're something thicker than paper. Little Gold sees a blur of colour from one and realises they're photographs.

'Yes. Yes, these are good. I'll take these.'

'Good. I'm glad you like them. And I'll tell Keith you're happy to take the boy up for a shoot in the next couple of weeks then?'

Roy has taken something from his pocket – a roll of notes secured with a clip. He peels off purple twenties, one after another, and presses them into Doug's outstretched, hammy hand. Little Gold leans her head against the pine slats of the sauna door as a wave of sickness swells in her belly, picturing the twenty pound note on Malcy's bedside table, soaked in spilled water, stuck there in the grime of their room. He'd have peeled it off like that, put it in Malcy's palm.

'I'll be in touch. You tell them that. I won't be rushed.'

She looks through the crack again and Doug's pushing the notes into the pocket of his shorts.

'Okay, okay! But even I can understand their impatience there. Like a little Oliver Twist, isn't he? And it's not like you haven't got him started.'

Roy doesn't reply, just licks the flap of the envelope and runs his thumb along it, pressing it closed.

'And she's just exactly where I like them, Roy. Right on the cusp. I'd be honoured if you and Kay would share when the time's right.'

Roy spins around and heads back into the changing room and Little Gold steps away from the door again, feeling her heart smack at her chest wall like a kick. For a second she's sure that somehow he knows she's here, that he's going to wrench open the door of the sauna and pull her out. But he strides past and she hears him going back out into the garden without another word. Doug calls after him,

'Tell Jackie I'll be out in a tick if she wants to do the cake! Just going to the kitchen for smokes.'

Little Gold finds herself moving without thought, opening the sauna door and stepping out into the changing room. Her body seems to have a plan and she realises she's trying to get to Malcy, now, as quickly as she can, with no thought beyond that. But she can't ignore the stinging burn of a full bladder. She's going to have to use the toilet, so she hurries through the bedroom into the en-suite beyond.

She shoots home the small bolt with trembling fingers as she feels the first trickle of hot pee on her thigh and, yanking down her shorts and knickers, staggers onto the toilet. It's a high toilet, her tiptoes barely reaching the floor and she teeters there, whispering to herself as the hot flood of urine pours from her body.

Get outside and get to Malcy. Get outside and get to Malcy.

The pink bathroom has golden dolphins, nose to nose, on the ring that holds the hand towel, adorning the top of the mirror and even one forming the door handle. She doesn't stop to wash her hands but quickly snaps the bolt, twists the dolphin handle and steps out into the bedroom.

Doug's standing at the dressing table, his sailor cap clasped in two fat hands, looking at himself sideways in the mirror. He turns, startled.

'Oh, hello! Where did you spring from?'

And she runs, runs the half-dozen steps it takes her to get to the changing room, the half dozen more to reach the patio and then on, past the adults at the table, past the two sun loungers where Keith and Terry are draped, and straight into the middle of the boys' match.

'I'll play. Can I play? You and me, Malc, against Kev and Peter.'

''Spose so. Kev? Pete? Yeah?'

Malcy rubs at his neck with his palm. The chlorine in the pool has irritated his eczema. She thinks about the burn of it, wants to pull his hand away, drag him from the game and shout 'run'. But instead she runs towards Kev and makes a weak attempt to tackle him.

As she kicks and chases, Little Gold tries not to look up from her feet, the beautiful lawn being scraped and scarred by their trainers as they chase the ball. But as they play on she feels the adults closing in around the match, catches the closer scent of cigarettes and the rise and fall of their laughter. Finally, Kev sends the ball straight through the trees with a wild shot and, as he runs to fetch it, there's a pause in play. Little Gold stands as close to

Malcy as she can get, feeling the heat radiating from his bare arm, and looks up at the adults standing around them, leaning on tree trunks, sipping drinks and watching. There's the tinkle of Jackie's bracelets as she reaches across to brush a wasp from Roy's shoulder. The sun's behind them now and their shadows – the draped women, the low bulk of Doug, the broad shoulders of Roy and the two long sun loungers occupied by Keith and Terry, stretch across the sunny grass like the silhouettes of monsters.

Roy swigs down the last of his drink.

'I think it's time we did the cake and hit the road now, Doug. I don't want to get tangled in traffic on the way back into town.'

CHAPTER TWENTY-EIGHT

Peggy is considering the ham she's put aside for her tea – baby pink with a rainbow sheen and a thick strip of yellowy fat. She peels a slice from the greaseproof paper and drops it down for Shaw. It drapes over his bowl in a loose fold. She returns the other slice to the fridge.

Her temperature's down and whatever it's been that's so floored her the last few days is ebbing at last. She feels properly awake and not dizzy at all, but still it's hard to eat. In the end she settles on soup, a tin of tomato, which she stirs, meditatively, on the hob.

It's a pleasing pool, red-orange, in the dip of her earthenware bowl but still she needs a distraction to get her to actually eat it. She stands in the bay of the front room window, spooning up the soup, dimly aware of the salt and sweet but looking for the child.

It's getting harder to bump into her now she's not going out as much and there's a sudden stab of jealousy that somewhere, someone else is with her Little Gold.

Shaw regards her from the armchair and she imagines his feline tone, silken and superior, as he stretches and leaps to the floor.

She is not your Little Gold, old woman, any more than I am your Shaw.

'Oh, get on with you, you cantankerous cat. Go and eat my ham.'

The cat stalks away and she returns her attention to the window. The days have been scorching and glorious, the child has probably been to the beach. Up on the Downs again, perhaps, flying a different kite. Her mind returns to Devil's Dyke, the wind whipping the child's blonde hair. And now? Now she's with her family and you've got soup to eat.

She abandons the bowl and brings her face closer to the pane. Beside the darkening shrubbery at the corner of the park, a middle-aged man leaps out of his car, rather hastily parked. It took her years to realise that the public conveniences there weren't blessed with so many weak bladders, that the draw was something else. She remembers Vern leaning across her dinner table to jab at Dick's plump arm.

'If you don't cheer up, you gloomy old queen, I'll pop over the road and find myself some entertainment…'

Peggy shudders at the thought of the stinking trough, the grubby floor and vandalised stalls. Entertainment, really? Is it that? Or some deeper need? There's a certain simplicity in it and that she understands. And who's to say what she would have done if she'd lived her life as a man?

Wakeful, restless, she paces around the room, stopping in front of the bookshelf and scanning the remaining spines. *Love on the Dole*, first edition, bought at work in '38. Staff discount but still an extravagance, a sentimental whim. Mr Gallowglass had recommended it, just before he went away and when she'd seen it there it had seemed like a message from the times she missed so much. And it had been an excellent story – real people who made mistakes. She'd devoured it in her lunch hours and offered it to Lenny when he arrived.

Lenny Rennolds, the new lad, standing, two hands hanging, mystified by the urn. His hair is white-blonde, his acne-scalded face a livid pink. He's a panicking slab of coconut ice, ladling tea into the pot.

'How many is it? Do you know?'

He twitches the tea-leaves across the worktop and Margaret sweeps them into her palm.

'Five. Pour two straight away and let the rest brew.'

They'd sent him down to make the tea because that was the junior's job. His arrival had meant her promotion in the informal pecking order of the shop. Margaret was good at the tea-making, good at the lot and she was a hard act to follow. If the pain of losing Enid had taught her anything, it was that work could blot out a churning mind. So she'd spent the previous nine months specialising in tea, in being quick on errands and accurate in change. A job in a bookshop was a blessing, as her parents never tired of telling her, and she had a duty to make the best of it.

But Lenny wasn't destined for greatness. His days were all disaster and muff. Whether it was a smashed box full of bottles of Indian ink or an unfortunate tone at the desk, somehow he took every chance there was to be caught looking idle or dim. Margaret watched with a sense of unfurling despair as his little boat was holed and doomed in the first couple of weeks. It would take a miracle to keep him in the job.

Still, though, she'd liked him, lent him this book, though he'd returned it un-read. Why would you borrow a book and do that? Why say yes to a lend but not want to read it? For the first time ever she wonders if it was the word love. Perhaps he'd thought it was some sort of message, that slippery, dynamite word. Such a tricky word, so easy to misread, so easy to misunderstand. Perhaps he'd imagined, from that inconsequential moment, that she'd loved him.

Laying the book in her lap for a moment, she rubs at her cramping hands. Working them loose from the grip of the cold, she tugs a rug over her knees. How strange to realise, suddenly, what the book might have meant to Lenny. As beasts that can grasp the complexities of science, it's odd that we forget how much perspective alters truth, she thinks. Back then, all the other shop staff had been ancient, and she and Lenny young adults. From here, in her waning sixty-third year, all the characters are young – she and Lenny almost children and the rest just muddling through middle-age. She remembers lunch times with the boy, their laughter blowing like a gale through the muted sighs and stifled tuts of their elders. She sees his attentive eyes.

Giggling together on the back step, licking marg from their fingertips, Lenny whispers to do her.

'Did you see him, Margaret? I really thought I'd die! When his dentures fell on the post scales I couldn't look at you.'

He offers a white paper bag of toffees. A shy boy – sweet, kind, always trying to reach her.

'I don't like to, Len. I never have any to pay you back.'

'That doesn't matter, Margaret, I bought them for us both.'

Peggy lays her palm on the cover of the book, imagining his

hand has left an imprint there. They weren't courting. Mum and Dad had said she was too young for that. If she'd asked for their permission it would have been denied. But she hadn't said a word that day, just told them she'd be late, told them it was stock-taking and headed from work straight down to the pier. Margaret and Lenny Rennolds holding hands on the prom.

She shivers, rubs her arms and slides the book back on the shelf. The wind's got up. It whistles in the chimney like a ghost.

Go up to bed, Peg Baxter, before you get too tired.

But even as she says the words, she knows that she won't move. Instead she grits her teeth against the first, strong, wave of pain.

She hadn't been expecting it. She'd thought maybe a kiss. She'd wanted the experiment. Because now there was no Enid. There was no Enid and there must be something.

'Let's go down on the pebbles, Margaret.'

The wind is hard off the sea, whipping her face and stinging her eyes. They water. Her vision is blurred in brine and his fingers, cold and thick, are bound in hers. She's startled by his sudden, sticky mouth. There's a sweet slick of barley sugar on his ardent, pushing tongue but she feels no burst of electricity. There are no lights, no sherbert fizz, not the delicious rightness that she felt with Enid. There is just the wet and warm of it. It's a faint, dim pleasure. At one remove. Nothing quite connects.

There was time to stop, if she'd wanted to stop, his fumbling, ignorant hands. His clueless pursuit of her body's prize was a hesitant, clumsy dance. But in her silent compliance, she'd been praying for something to wake. That living thing she'd known with Enid. That whole, sweet part of herself. She'd tried to force it alive, gripping his shoulders, crushing her lips against his. And still it had felt distant, unlikely, like something happening to someone else.

The pebbles tumble and shift on the shingle bank and she's surprised at the weight of his skinny frame. His blind fingers poke at her stocking tops and all the time there's his barley-sugar breath.

'Someone might see us.'

'Sh, sh, they won't.'

The lights of the pier are smeared on the dark sky and she closes her eyes. It's a knife-sharp dart of pain and for a moment she's glad of it. She's glad to feel something real, something intense, but quickly it dissipates and then there's just the shame. His weight, his thrusting weight, is a laying on and on of shame. Margaret lets it happen. Margaret waits for it to end. She's shaking as he walks her home. Her body trembles and her teeth are locked as he pecks her cheek on the corner of her street. She can feel the mess and chill in her underwear. There's a wash of fear across his eyes.

Peggy drops her face into her palms and hears his voice in her ear, barely broken, stammering with nerves.

'Th-thank you, Margaret. You're a smashing girl.'

And when she looks up he's there. Lenny Rennolds is reflected in the window pane. A sweet boy. Just a sweet, clumsy, hungry boy. Beyond him is an old woman she struggles to recognise.

CHAPTER TWENTY-NINE

The envelope is lying next to a steaming mug of tea. Every few moments, Ali picks it up, runs her finger over the gummed flap and then places it back on the table. Little Gold yawns and rubs her eyes.

'Go on, A…'

'Sh!'

Ali picks up the envelope again and then repeats the caress, this time slipping the tip of her index finger under the corner of the flap before putting it down again. The heavy footfalls on the stairs startle them both and Mum comes into the kitchen in her dressing gown.

'Morning, girls.'

Her voice croaks and then breaks open like a sealed jar so that the word 'girls' comes out too loud. She reins it back to a more even tone.

'Your brother not up for the big event?'

As she crosses the kitchen to the kettle, Little Gold notices that she's washed her face and the hair at her temples and across her forehead is still damp.

Ali gives no indication of having heard Mum at all, just picks up the envelope again and, this time, holds it on the flat palm of her left hand as if inviting it to fly away. The strangest thing is that it's addressed in her own handwriting, handed in at college ready-written and stamped before her last exam, so that it looks for all the world as if Ali from the past is sending her the vital news of her future.

'Shall I get him up, Mum?'

'Yes, pop up and wake him, Little…'

But it's too late, the tear, the crumple of the thin paper drawn from the envelope and Ali's gasp are one noise. There's a moment in which she just stares and then she speaks.

'I did it. I've done it. BBB. I can go.'

'Oh, love, I'm so, so glad for you.'

Mum strides across the kitchen and she descends on Ali with open arms. Ali allows the hug for a second before extricating herself from the tangle of dressing gown and gently pushing Mum away.

'Yeah, well, it's not that big a deal, eh?'

'It is, it is and I'm so proud of you!'

Little Gold looks at her mum and her sister, separated now by six inches of space. Ali's still staring at the sheet of paper marked with her fate. Mum reaches out as if she's going to stroke the dipped head but then she lets her hand fall back to her side.

'Can I tell Malcy, Ali?'

'Yeah. Yeah, if you like.'

Little Gold gallops up the stairs. She's buzzing with the infectious excitement of it, glowing slightly with the pride of association. Her sister's clever and she's going to university. For the first time since the pool party, there's something else centre-stage of her mind. If Ali can do it then so can she, find a way out of the house, move on.

She yanks open the door and bursts into their bedroom.

'Malc! Ali got her grades, she's go…'

He's up already, sitting on the edge of his bed, his duvet covering his legs. There's a flurry of coloured paper as he thrusts something under his pillow.

'Jesus, LG! Knock, yeah?'

'Sorry! Just thought you'd want to know.'

His body is angled away from her. He doesn't turn, doesn't reply, and she backs awkwardly out of the room.

'I'll just… Do you want a cup of tea?'

'Yeah. I'll be down.'

It's gone, the moment of hope. She pictures Malcy's fumbling hands as he hid the magazine. It's the tentacle of a slimy beast, right inside their home. As she plods downstairs, the threadbare carpet fades and she sees instead the surface of the pool. She sees the water lapping over Peter's face and his struggling, thrashing limbs.

You're clearly doing wonders with the boy…

Little Gold pauses, breathes and waits for the images to fade before going back into the kitchen.

Mum's wiping the kitchen table with a damp cloth and Ali's still sitting in her place, holding the piece of paper with two hands as if she's scared it'll evaporate. Little Gold sits down opposite her.

'You got work, Ali?'

'Not 'til one but I'm going to go down to Gemma's and see how everyone did.'

Mum makes a valiant attempt to scoop the crumb-laden cloth into her hand but she's shaking wildly and there's a gritty cascade back onto the table top.

'Oh, I thought I might make us all some breakfast.'

'I've gotta go, Mum. I can't call my friends to see how they did without a phone, can I?'

Ali slips on her denim jacket and waves a hasty goodbye.

'See you both later.'

She's smiling as she closes the front door.

Mum's frozen, staring at the empty front hall and Little Gold touches her arm.

'I'd like breakfast, Mum, and Malcy would. He's just coming down.'

'Yes, let's get some toast on for you two then.'

The shaking reminds Little Gold of the man who used to run the greengrocer up the road. In the end he couldn't shepherd half a dozen Golden Delicious into a paper bag without them ending up rolling about on the floor and he had to sit at the till. His wife did all the serving then and he just nodded and smiled. He's gone now.

'Right then!'

The fluttering, jerking knife is smearing marg over pale toast. Mum cuts the slices diagonally and shouts up the stairs to Malcy.

'Malcy! Come on! Breakfast!'

Little Gold tears into her first slice, chewing fast, biting and shoving the corner in. Something inside is urging her to eat, to get properly full up and then, it seems to be saying, then she'll be able to work out what to do. What she wants most of all is to go to see Peggy Baxter again but she's afraid that the simmering anxiety, the horrible images, will follow her there. She doesn't want them to invade Peggy's house. Maybe, just maybe, she can find the words to talk to Mum.

Mum places three mugs in the centre of the table and lowers herself with a sigh.

'How about that, then? Ali off to university!'

There's a nasty tang on her breath and Little Gold turns her head away slightly to avoid the gusts of stink.

'Mmm.'

She's started on her second slice and still no Malcy but then she hears the loo flush and his feet pounding down the stairs. There's a loud knock at the front door.

'I'll get it!'

As the door swings open, Little Gold leans sideways in her chair. There are two men on the doorstep, both wearing suits and ties. They're not old like Clive, in fact one of them doesn't look much older than Ali. He's got bleached hair slicked back with too much gel and a few spots on his forehead. The older man unzips a black pouch and pulls out a sheet of paper.

'Good morning. Can I speak to Mrs Arnold please?'

'Yeah, hang on.'

Malcy turns away from the door and, in that instant, the younger man's foot starts to cross the threshold. It's hovering over the door mat when Mum's voice cuts the air, full-throated and loud as she leaps from her chair and plummets down the hall.

'Shut the door! Shut the door, Malcy!'

She careers into Malcy's back. There's a tumbling thud as the door is closed and the foot shoved back outside.

Malcy staggers away, gawping at Mum, who's leaning on the door. Her back is against the patterned glass as the letterbox opens wide.

'Mrs Arnold! Mrs Arnold, we just need a word!'

Little Gold can see the moving lips beyond the flap as though the door has learned to talk. And then they're replaced with a pair of dark eyes that peer straight down the hall into hers.

The letterbox flaps shut and the man outside stands up and starts to thump on the door. She can see the pink fuzz of his beating fist clarifying into skin as it smacks against the glass.

'Mrs Arnold! This isn't going to go away, Mrs Arnold! You need to open the door!'

Mum's flapping her hands at Malcy to usher him back down the hall. She shuts the kitchen door behind them and leans there like she thinks her puny body is some defence. Little Gold can hear the man's voice still, clearer, as if he's shouting through the letterbox again.

'Our clients aren't prepared to let this matter lie, Mrs Arnold. The County Court Judgment entitles…'

'Eat your toast, Malcolm.'

Mum's gesturing at Malcy's plate. Malcy sits down and bites into his toast, chewing like a robot as Mum talks on, over the top of the man's blaring voice.

'Now, I think we'll have baked potatoes tonight because that's one of Ali's things, isn't it? And maybe you could make her a nice card, Little Gold, with one of your lovely drawings…'

There's a sort of flurry of thumps now, like the man might actually break his way in, and Little Gold takes a step towards Mum.

'Mum! Why don't you open the door and talk to them? I don't think they're going to go away.'

As if to prove her a liar, there's sudden silence from the hall. Then the squeal and thud of the letterbox and nothing more.

'Mum, who…'

Mum holds up a hand to silence her and then opens the door a crack. The hallway is tranquil, sun on the wall, swimming dust in the air and a bright, white envelope on the mat.

'Mum…'

Once again Mum holds up her hand and Little Gold bites her lower lip, struggling to hold onto the burst of words in her throat.

'I don't need a lot of questions. You just don't open the door. You do not open the door to them, do you understand?'

Little Gold nods.

'Malcolm? Did you hear me? You don't open the door to them.'

Malcy nods, still chewing his unappealing toast. His face is impassive as he swallows and takes another bite.

Mum goes to the baking cupboard and takes down a half bottle of whiskey that has somehow materialised there. She sloshes some into her tea mug and takes a swift swig. Slipping the bottle into her dressing gown pocket she heads back up the stairs, calling over the banister to them.

'Remember, family tea time. Be nice to your sister, she's worked hard.'

Little Gold watches Malcy push his plate across the table with a shove. It rocks like a ship on a heavy sea, scattering dry crusts. She's not going to talk about what just happened and she knows that he won't either. But the other thing is rumbling up, pushing words into her mouth.

'What you doing today, Malc?'

'Town.'

He wedges his knees against the table edge and tilts back his chair, his head lolling and hair hanging down. His pyjama trousers are far too short, displaying bony ankles and pale feet.

'You going to spend that money?'

He shrugs.

'Malc, you know Roy and Kay?'

'Yeah.'

'You know you don't, you don't have to go to their parties and stuff, yeah?'

Malcy's head jerks up.

'What are you on about, you div? Why shouldn't I go to their parties? Just 'cos you've got something against them. I don't even know why you came to that pool party, anyway. Kev's not your friend, is he? I don't know why you came and hung around there if you don't like them. What is it, do you fancy Kev or something?'

Malcy's words are streaming fast from his lips, like he's been waiting to say them, like he had that line about Kev all ready to use. He thinks it'll shut her up, knows it'll embarrass her, but Little Gold swallows it down and goes on.

'It's just, I think they're a bit weird. Those blokes that bring Peter along, they're not nice, you know?'

'They're not *nice*, you know?'

Malcy mimics her in a high, prissy voice and then starts again with the stream of anger and accusation.

'You're just jealous 'cos I've got a friend who's loaded and got nice stuff and invites me to cool places. And they only bloody invite you along 'cos you haven't got any friends and they feel sorry for you. An' if you think Kev bloody fancies you then you've got to be joking, bloody joking 'cos he wouldn't look twice at you an' you're a bloody kid, you are, acting all high and mighty when you haven't even got a clue…'

'Ah, shut up, Malcy! Just bloody shut up a minute and listen to me!'

'No! Why should I listen to you when you just want to slag off my mate?'

'I'm not! I haven't got anything against Kev…'

'No, too right you haven't! You just bloody fancy him and…'

'For Christ's sake, Malcy, I don't bloody fancy Kev, alright? Stop and listen to me for a minute…'

'What so you can say a whole lot of shit about them when you don't even know…'

'I DO know! I do know about them. They're creepy, Malc. I know you think it's all cool but I know what…'

Malcy stands up, shoving his chair away so hard that it falls onto its back like a shot soldier. She's struck by a sudden vivid flash of memory, of playing cowboys with Malc in the kitchen one day when they were little, of his leaping onto a chair and going over with it, his forehead catching the corner of the table and the instant rising of a purple welt, split and bleeding. He leans into her face, shouting.

'Just shut up! Shut up! Shut up!'

And suddenly she hasn't got any more words. Suddenly she realises that there's no way on from here without saying things she just can't say. Malcy's blush is total, his whole face livid with it, and she realises it's not fury, not genuine fury, that's making him shout. He's using this angry performance to cover his embarrassment and he's doing his best to bluster her into silence before something unsayable gets said.

They look into each other's faces for just a moment more and then Malcy turns and stamps from the room. Little Gold watches his retreating back, the tangle of blonde hair, the too short legs and arms of his old green pyjamas. Something tips inside her, like watching Malcy falling off the chair when they were little. She can feel the approaching ground flying up to meet him and there's nothing she can do.

CHAPTER THIRTY

From where she's sitting in the window, Peggy can see the blonde head. It's bobbing at the foot of her steps as if Little Gold can't make up her mind. It's a moment for a plea to that non-existent deity.

Please.

And then there she is, Little Gold, standing on the path with some flowers. Peggy plucks a hand from the soft, soapy water and knocks gently on the window. The child doesn't look decided, still, and she doesn't want her to disappear. She waves and smiles, then mouths through the glass.

'Hang on!'

Little Gold smiles back. Drying her hands on the tea towel, Peggy hurries to the front door.

'Hello! Good to see you, come on in.'

There's a blast of hot, dry air. Peggy steps back to get out of the heat and beckons Little Gold inside.

'I brought you these.'

She's brandishing a fat handful of sweet peas, stems trailing, clearly stolen goods. Her face is pinched, pale and shy, with a streak of dirt on her cheek. But, like a longed for gift, she's pure perfection and Peggy's mind offers up thanks.

Thank you. Thank you for bringing her.

'Ah, they're glorious! How kind! I think we'd better get them a drink pronto though, eh? I don't want them to flag before bedtime.'

She takes the flowers from the sticky hand and lifts them to her face. Light as tissue, bright pink, soft lilac, trailing their sugar through the air.

In the kitchen, trickling water into a vase, Peggy's acutely aware of the gaze, the solemn young eyes taking her in, and she does her best not to shake.

'Why are you washing-up in the front room?'

'Ha! It is a bit odd, isn't it? I wanted the sunshine and I'm washing all my glass birds and boxing them up safe.'

'Safe from what?'

'Do you want to help me?'

The child nods and follows her lead as Peggy heads back to the living room, carrying the vase. Light is pouring through the west-facing pane of the gleaming bay window and Shaw's stretched on the carpet, his belly to the sun.

'He's like some sort of feline sundial, that cat. He just moves across the room as the day goes on.'

Little Gold crouches and strokes the cat. Shaw arches his back in appreciation of the ruffling hand in his fur. Peggy watches the attention being lavished on the cat and wonders if Little Gold has any pets. There's so much she doesn't know. At last the child stands, wiping her palm on the seat of mucky, towelling shorts.

'Right then, sit you down and marvel! These, Little Gold, are very precious to me. These are my tiny pieces of freedom. Have a look.'

Little Gold handles each one in turn, running her fingers over faceted wings and pinching slender beaks.

'Are they all real birds?'

It's not the question she was expecting and, for a moment, Peggy doesn't know what to say. It's as if Little Gold's asking her for magic, for a storybook world where the birds come alive. But she's not, of course, she's asking about species.

'Ah, well, I think some of them are more a suggestion than an accurate copy of a bird. And there's definitely something going on with scale.'

She holds up the peacock and the robin side by side and Little Gold laughs. It's a relief to see her smile. She's solemn today, preoccupied with something.

'And I think this is more a generic owl than any particular sort. It's probably my favourite of them all, I think. Now then, can you dry? Especially careful though, eh?'

Little Gold nods and Peggy dips the owl into the foam. She moves it through the water and then places it in the child's palm. For a moment, she wonders about cleanliness, but it's too late to mention that now, and she watches a linen-covered finger sweeping the concave eyes. Then the child stands the owl on her palm and looks into its face.

There's something, something on her mind, and Peggy tries to decode the stare. But it's blank, no clues, no starting point. Perhaps it's best just to talk.

'Did you like my Vi then, Little Gold?'

Little Gold gives a sage nod.

'She is a fine woman but I'll warn you now, a devil of a poker player.'

Little Gold's face remains expressionless as she waits for the next glass bird. This one's a wren, the fragile tail like a piece of spun sugar.

'You been up to anything nice since I saw you last?'

She passes the dripping bird to the child, who cups it in her palm and presses her thumb to the point of the beak – a triangle, needle-sharp.

'What's this one?'

'That's a wren, a little Jenny wren. Mind how you go with the tail.'

'Do their tails really stick up like this? Like a pencil on their bum?'

Peggy barks a laugh as she washes the next bird.

'Yes, though I've never heard it put like that.'

'I think I saw one the other day, under a bush in the park. Very small and brown, smaller than a sparrow.'

'Yes, I expect that was a wren.'

Little Gold stands the wren next to the owl. Suddenly it's a mutant giant or the impressive owl has shrunk.

'So, *have* you been having a nice time, Little Gold?'

It's like pulling the child's teeth.

'Me and Malcy... Malcy and I went to a party with some friends.'

'That's nice. Was it a birthday party?'

'Yes.'

'And how old was the birthday boy or girl?'

'I don't know. She's grown up. She's Kev's mum. He's one of Malcy's friends.'

'Ah. A sort of family friend?'

'Sort of.'

Little Gold rearranges the cluster of birds, lining them up in ranks. That's that it seems, nothing more to say, so Peggy reaches down to the floor.

'Now, we're going to get these wrapped in tissue and I've bought this packet new. There's nothing more depressing than crumpled tissue paper so my birds are getting crispy, clean sheets.'

They work together to wrap them and nestle them into a box. Several times Peggy senses a word, poised on Little Gold's lips, but on each occasion it stays unspoken, as the box fills with the mummified birds.

The tissue swaddles but they can feel the different shapes within. And Peggy watches as Little Gold arranges and rearranges again. The fanning spread of the peacock's tail covers the nestling wren. Legs and beaks, tails and heads are fitted like pieces of a jigsaw. Finally, she takes the owl, a rectangular, solid form, and slides it into the central space, before folding the box-flaps closed.

'Owl in the middle?'

'Yeah... He's the strongest one.'

Peggy rips sticky tape with her teeth and passes the strips to Little Gold. She watches the child pressing, smoothing them into place, reaching for another and another piece, until Peggy stops.

'That's enough.'

She lifts the box onto the shelf.

'Where'd you get all your birds, Peggy Baxter?'

'From a gift shop down in the Lanes. Years ago now, right back in the forties. I got every one in the range.'

'Did you get them for birthdays and Christmases?'

'Oh, no. I bought them myself. They weren't hugely expensive, they're not quality things but they pleased me. That was enough.'

She smiles at Little Gold's earnest face but there's no smile in return.

'The owl I got with my first pay packet from Vokins, when I started in payroll there. My shoes needed reheeling, I remember, and I was on my way to the cobbler when I spotted him. I stood and looked in the window for ages and finally decided I would. I had grotty shoes for another month but I got my crystal owl.'

She glances at the box.

'My little pieces of freedom, they are. My own money. My own choice.'

Little Gold nods. Her words are so quiet that Peggy barely catches them. It's as if she might be talking to herself.

'They're very lovely.'

'Yes. They are. I've always thought so.'

For a moment she considers touching the child but there's something keeping her away. Like a scent in the air or a low, repelling hum, Little Gold is sending a signal. Don't touch. Hands off. Keep your distance.

'Now, I've ventured into new biscuit territory. Will you be brave and try something called a Taxi? I haven't risked it yet. But, if you will then I might give it a go.'

In the kitchen, Peggy makes the tea. Shaw's followed them and he's twisting round her ankles as she moves between counter, fridge and sink. A sudden slip to one side almost sends her reeling and she catches hold of the cooker to steady herself.

'I swear this cat wants to murder me sometimes. Don't you, Machiavellian Beast?'

Little Gold says nothing but crouches low and holds out her hand toward Shaw. Palm down, offering her knuckles, he butts and nuzzles with his large, black head.

'You're honoured. Shall we sit out the front for a bit? I think it's cooler than it was and the air's good for my bones.'

In fact it's the last thing she wants to do, but Peggy wonders if the air might loosen the child's tongue. Sometimes it's easier to talk outdoors, with the broad, empty sky to swallow your words.

Little Gold sits cross-legged on the path, cradling her mug of tea. A lone hollyhock has seeded itself in the gap beside the wall and it towers over her, nodding gently in the breeze. Peggy perches on the wall beside it and taps it with an outstretched finger.

'Isn't that ridiculous? Vi said it looked like a flag pole. Must be four foot tall!'

'Has Vi gone back to Bath?

'Yes. She had to get back to work.'

Little Gold's teasing a ladybird with a dry, brown leaf, putting the huge obstacle in its way over and over again. It tires of the challenge, lifts its wings and hums off across the garden. The biscuit, the Taxi, has disappeared already, the crumpled wrapper lying beside her grubby knee. Peggy holds out her own.

'Don't fancy this at the moment. I think you'd better eat it for me, it'll only melt.'

'Thanks.'

Little Gold sets about the biscuit immediately, taking swift bites, barely pausing to chew. There's something in the sight of her, small, dirty, chewing hard and fast, that takes Peggy back to the war. She pictures a child, bombed out from London, wolfing GI chocolate on the station concourse.

Shouts, a chorus of jeers, drift across from the park and Peggy glances over the road where there's a familiar blonde head in goal.

'Is that your brother over there being goalie?'

Little Gold doesn't look up.

'Yes.'

Peggy lights a second cig and Shaw slinks through the open front door, flopping down next to the child, looking for a bit more love. His long fur is lacquered immediately with grit but he's oblivious to that, rolling ecstatically as she strokes him, over and over, with her small, firm hand.

'It seems you're a cat person then, eh?'

'I do like them. But Malcy's allergic. Allergic to cats and dust.'

'Oh, that's a shame.'

'He wheezes.'

'Ah.'

'At night sometimes.'

'That must be frightening for him.'

'I just have to help him find his inhaler then he's always fine...'

There's a splatter of angry words from the park, emerging from a chorus of disdain.

'You fucking poofy spaz! A fucking spastic girl could have saved that.'

Peggy cranes her neck to look towards the source of the voice and then down at Little Gold, who gives no indication of having heard a word. She keeps her head bowed and strokes on. But the voice hasn't finished yet.

'Yeah, that's it, you go home to your mummy!'

Suddenly, Little Gold stands, startling the cat onto his paws and away across the path. She's dusting off her hands on her shorts as she turns her face to Peggy.

'I think I'd better be going now.'

Peggy tries to hold her gaze. She can't tell if the sadness in the air is her own or the child's and it's impossible not to say, not to ask.

'Little Gold, is everything okay? You're a bit quiet today.'

'Sorry.'

'No, I don't mean you've done anything wrong, I just wondered if things were alright.'

'Yeah! Yeah, everything's fine.'

The forced jollity is sickening. It's the first time, she thinks, that the child has lied to her – flat, outright lying to her face as if she really believes Peggy won't know she's being deceived. It's that, the naivety, that makes Peggy want to weep, even more than the fact that she feels she must pretend. That she thinks she can just gloss her face and Peggy won't know is a reminder of quite how young she is, no matter how sharp. And suddenly, the grubby face with its watchful eyes, the tense silence between them, seem to be singing out a word in Peggy's head.

Vulnerable.

'Shall I stroll home with you? I could do with a bit of a walk.'

Little Gold says nothing, just stares across to the park.

'I've been thinking I should pop in and say hello to your mum. I wondered if she might have any use for the small sideboard in my loft. I don't know if you noticed it when we were up there… It's a nice piece of furniture, but I haven't got anywhere for it to go.'

Still Little Gold says nothing. She's craning her neck now, to peer along the road.

'Little Gold? Shall I just come home with you now and have a quick word with your mum?'

'She's not in. She's gone to town for curtain hooks.'

Curtain hooks are such a perfect lie, just the sort of fiddly thing she might not find at Fiveways. Peggy opens her mouth again but, without accusing her of lying, is there any way to push this? A startling burst of nausea demands her attention. She needs to get indoors, to her bathroom and her bed.

'Well, another day then.'

Peggy rises and takes a couple of steadying breaths.

'See you soon, I hope.'

'Yeah, see you soon, Peggy Baxter.'

There it is again, the veneer of light-heartedness, as the child turns and runs down the steps. Peggy watches her jump the last two and then she's gone. But she's left an intense grinding, a twisting of anxiety in Peggy's chest that she can't ignore. There is no escaping it. She will have to go to the house, unannounced, uninvited, no matter how uncomfortable. She will have to find the strength – and soon. But as Peggy steps from the light into the darkness of her front hall her mouth floods with the saliva that heralds vomit and all she can think about is her bed and sleep.

CHAPTER THIRTY-ONE

Malcy's in the bathroom. She can hear the tap running and, underneath that, occasional sobs. She sits on the top stair, weighing up the value of knocking on the door given their argument this morning. He'd gone straight over the park afterwards and she'd gone to Peggy Baxter's and now she's not sure if they're even talking.

She swallows a rush of fury, pushing up from her chest, anger that she's here, sitting on the stair when maybe she could've stayed with Peggy Baxter, played Scrabble and stroked Shaw for the rest of the afternoon. A sudden thud from the bathroom makes her jump and she stands up. The noise comes again and again and the fourth time it's followed by Malcy's voice.

'Aaargh! Fuck it!'

There's a heavier thud and something falls against the bathroom door.

'Malc!'

He doesn't reply, there's just a series of grunts and thumps inside the room and then quiet.

'Malcy!'

The tap's still running in there, a high-pitched whine and occasional gurgle from the plughole.

'Malc!'

The door opens and there he is, his hair damp with sweat and his pink eyes small and buried in a face flushed and swollen from crying. The side of the bath, the pale yellow panel that matches the suite, has a ragged hole in it. It's dark inside – a thick blackness. Malcy's panting, his shoulders hunched and fists clenched lightly like a boxer waiting for his opponent to get up from the canvas.

Little Gold takes a step backwards, nervous in spite of herself. His leg is cut, only a small gash, just under his knee, but blood's running down his shin in three thin streams. She stares at them rolling across his scuffed shin, over a grey bruise and into the grubby white of his thick football sock. The panting has a wheeze in it, that definite meshed sound as he inhales. Suddenly he's not a threatening boy kicking in the side of the bath, he's Malcy and he's wheezing.

'You're wheezing. Where's your inhaler?'

He shrugs, dropping his shoulders, no longer ready for the fight to recommence. He leans back against the towel rail, wheezing louder. She thinks about the level of chaos in their room and realises it's just not going to be findable without a clue at least.

'When did you last have it?'

He's slid down onto the floor opposite the damaged bath now and the drips of blood have smeared across his lower leg. The cut's gaping slightly.

'Took it to the pool party. Co-op bag.'

The bag's behind their bedroom door, in the top strata of mess still, so she finds it quickly and tips it onto the floor. The scent of the pool and a sprinkling of dried grass accompany the scrunched towel and she feels a heady wave of fear along with a flash of memory again – Doug, paunched and ruddy, reflected in the bedroom mirror.

Back in the bathroom, Malcy takes the inhaler and she turns away, looking out the open window at the sky, not wanting to look at his bloody leg or the ragged damage to the bath. After a few minutes the wheezing quietens and Malcy gets up and finally turns off the tap that's been pouring into the sink the whole time.

'Thanks, LG.'

'S'okay.'

He leans over his cut leg now, prodding it with an index finger. Little Gold considers the toilet roll on the holder but it's the last one, a precious and dwindling resource, so instead she yanks the towel from the rail and, after running it under the hot tap, hands it to her brother.

'Wipe it clean in case there's bits in it.'

He dabs at his leg, making messy red prints of blood around the cut, but giving no sign that it hurts. After a couple more dabs he chucks the bloodied towel into the bath.

'It's okay.'

'We might have a plaster, hang on.'

In the bathroom cabinet there's a battered packet of assorted Elastoplasts, the ones they say are waterproof but really just go slimy when they're wet. There are two inside, one of the tiny round ones she can't imagine a wound for, and the largest square one. She holds it out to him.

'That'll do, yeah?'

'Nah, it doesn't need something that big!'

'Well it's that or nothing.'

'It'll be fine.'

'Malc, cover it up. Ali'll be home soon and we've got to have tea and all that. It's better if they don't see it, isn't it?'

'But what about that?'

Malcy nods his head towards the broken panel. Little Gold shakes out the towel that's lying in the bath, folds it so that the bloody section's hidden and hangs it over the edge so that it covers the ragged, black hole entirely.

There's the rattle of a key in the front door and Ali's voice.

'Hello?'

Little Gold goes out onto the landing and looks down at her sister.

'Hiya! You had a good day?'

'Yeah, thanks, LG. Gemma got what she needs for Bristol so she's chuffed. Martin and Dave too. I'm just gonna have a bath and then I'm going back down Gemma's for the evening and staying over.'

She hangs her bag and overall on a peg in the hall and starts to walk up the stairs. Little Gold looks from her sister to her brother. Malcy's eyes are wide with panic and before he can slip out of the bathroom, Ali's in the doorway.

'Oh, hello, didn't know you were here. What's going on?'

Little Gold steps between Ali and the bath.

'He just had a wheeze. He's fine now though.'

'Oh. Well, that's good. You got enough in your inhaler, Malc?'

He nods.

'Okay, well, if you don't mind then, I want a bath.'

Ali's holding the door wide, expecting them both to leave. But it's hopeless, she'll have to move the towel. Little Gold grasps the corner of the damp fabric and pulls it from the edge of the bath.

'We had a bit of an accident too.'

She steps to one side, giving her sister an unimpeded view of the broken bath panel.

'Bloody hell! What did you do?'

'It was an accident, Ali, we were just mucking about and it got kicked.'

Ali sighs, crouches to look at the hole in the panel and snaps at them.

'Well, that's bloody lovely, isn't it? How wonderfully helpful and mature of you both to smash up something else in the house. Has she seen it?'

Little Gold shakes her head.

'She's been asleep.'

Ali sighs again.

'Yeah? Well, I'm not bloody telling her for you. I'm going to have a bath and then go out. Feed yourselves, okay? I think there's still some stuff in.'

She chivvies them from the room and slams the door. Little Gold looks at Malcy but he won't meet her eye.

'Malc…'

She feels the words deserting her again, everything she wants to say, might say, might ask him, just slips out of her open mouth unsaid and, for the second time that day, she's looking at Malcy wordlessly.

'I'm going back over the park.'

He clomps down the stairs and she watches him go, the little cylinder of his inhaler wedged in the pocket of his shorts, his blonde hair bouncing on his collar. He's going back to the torture in the park because it's better than being here with her and her dangerous mouth. As the door closes, Little Gold buckles, exhausted and wrecked with self-pity, she runs into her room and lying face down on her bed, she cries herself to sleep.

CHAPTER THIRTY-TWO

The following afternoon, Little Gold's reading in the tree. The words of the letter, three sides of Mum's writing pad, are the most carefully chosen she has ever put on paper and she allows herself a moment of pride. The first time they did letter writing at school, Miss Hawkhurst said that the point of a letter was to say what needed to be said and she's held that in her head with every sentence. She's told him that there's no money, that Mum can't manage to get up properly, that Ali will be going away and that Malcy's sad. She signs it at the bottom, 'yours sincerely' because it's not a business letter and she thinks she has been sincere. If sincere means honest, which she thinks it does.

The words of the courtroom oath pop into her head.

The truth, the whole truth and nothing but the truth.

It's the whole truth that she's not sure about. Because the whole truth would have the other thing in, the other reason why she knows they need his help. And still she hasn't found a way to put that into words, not even in the private space of her mind.

But it's not a bad letter and she folds the sheets, slides them into the envelope and licks the sticky strip to seal the flap. She writes his name on the front and puts it in the pocket of Malcy's hooded top. He doesn't seem to mind her wearing it and she's become very attached to the softness of the hood, the sense that she's sheltered.

The next bit's probably going to be harder still, getting the address to send it to, and she rubs an inky index finger across her wrinkled brow. She'll have to ask, and at the right moment too.

But for the next five minutes, Little Gold lies back in the

tree and watches clouds. There's a succession of soft peaks, her favourite sort, that drift over the roof as she lies there. She lets her eyes close and can see them still as patches of light on the dark.

Malcy's in the park again, accepting his place as goalie. She's keeping away because he clearly doesn't want her around – ignoring her pointedly – and she can't find an excuse to lurk at the edges of the match when she plainly has no reason to be there.

Little Gold opens her eyes. Shaw's sitting on Peggy Baxter's garden wall washing his paws. A car backfires somewhere down the road and he darts into the house. She imagines him settled on a cushion while Peggy Baxter sits reading in a chair. It would be quiet there, still and safe. But it's too much to turn up every day. She knows it is.

Mum's bedroom curtains twitch and open and there she is at the window, shoving up the stiff sash. She pauses for a moment, her pale face still and unreadable, and then turns and disappears from sight. This might be the moment. She climbs reluctantly from the tree and drops onto the grass. The envelope crackles in her pocket as she jogs down the steps.

Mum's sitting in the front room in her dressing gown, watching *South Today*. Little Gold stops in the doorway. She could go again; she hasn't been seen. She could climb back up the tree and not do this. She rocks on the balls of her feet. Stay? Go? Stay? Finally, Mum turns her head and fixes her with a vacant stare.

'Oh, hello! I thought you were Ali home.'

'No, she isn't in yet.'

'Mus' be bad buses. I'll do us something in a mo.'

Mum tucks her dressing gown closer around her body and yawns. The *South Today* man's talking about a fundraising drive in a place called Havant, which seems appropriate. Little Gold edges into the room and sits down on the carpet. Words are dancing in her head.

Mum, can I have Dad's address? Has Dad sent his address yet, Mum? Mum, can I write a letter to Dad?

A fat, black fly lands on her hand. She shakes it off and it crawls away over the rug. It's circling a lump of something thick, clotted in the strands. It takes her a minute to recall what it is but eventually she does – yes, Malcy trod on a fish finger last week.

He never tried to clean it up. They'd both stood and stared and not known where to start. It couldn't be wiped, it couldn't be swept, and the idea that they'd have to pick it out, to tease it out by hand, it simply hadn't occurred to them. But she can see it now. It's going to be the only way.

'Mum…'

There's the sound of a key in the door and Ali appears, drops her bag and flops into a chair.

'Hi, Ali!'

'Hello, LG.'

Her red overall reaches halfway down her shins and her legs, sticking out of the bottom, are like thin white saplings when the bark's stripped away. There were some in the park last year. They had to bind them with wire to keep the dogs off.

Ali kicks off her shoes and rubs at her feet with mottled hands.

'Is Malcy in, LG?'

A phlegmy gurgle rolls up and out of Mum. Her mouth's dropped open and her left arm's dangling over the edge of the settee. Little Gold raises her voice to be heard above the next snore.

'Still over the park.'

'Uh huh.'

Ali leans back and yawns. Little Gold wonders if it's contagious, if she's going to drop off too. Everything feels treacly now, slow and impossible to shift. A wave of frustration makes her slap her hands on her thighs. She leaps up and turns to her sister.

'Shall I put us some soup on, Ali?'

'Blimey! You're lively. Yeah, soup'd be good.'

Soup's okay for Ali; vegetable is best. Nothing creamy though. Little Gold's fingers scramble into the dark recess of the cupboard and close around something, a small tin of minestrone. It'll have to do. It won't stretch to Malcy but he can sort himself out later. Maybe there's still an egg or something.

Little Gold jams the opener into the tin and manages to get it half-way round. She prises up the lid with a fork and the soup splutters out into the pan. It's a thin orange liquid with soft chunks of carrot, potato and white worms of pasta. As she heats it on the gas, a spitting ring of bubbles forms. She watches as it froths and rises, rolling up the pan, and snatches it from the heat, just in time.

'Ali!'

'Coming!'

Afterwards, Little Gold isn't sure if she imagined the noise of Ali's head on the banister. It was too loud, startling, comical, a 'clonk' to be the real noise of someone's head on wood, but she knows her memory of the fall is accurate. Ali rounded the corner from the living room and seemed to just fold up, the hinge of her knees giving way and her body falling mostly straight down, veering a tiny bit to one side though. Just enough for her head to make contact with the thick curled end of the banister. It was what Little Gold had always imagined fainting would look like.

Running down the hall, expecting to see closed eyes, she's shocked at Ali's upturned gaze.

'Ali!'

'It's alright. I just went a bit dizzy for a minute. I'm okay.'

There's a lump on her head the size of a meatball, seeming to swell as Little Gold watches it. Her sister explores it with tentative fingertips and Little Gold winces.

'Ugh, that feels pretty horrible.'

She looks at her fingers, presumably checking for blood.

'It's okay. It's not bleeding, Ali. It just looks like when a little kid goes over on the concrete in the park.'

'Right.'

Ali rolls onto her side and slowly lifts her body into a sitting position, leaning back against the banisters.

'Blimey! Must've overheated or something.'

'Hang on, I'll get you some water.'

She sips the water, cupping her forehead gently in one of her pale hands, avoiding the swelling lump. The skin between her thumb and index finger is taut and thin, like plastic stretched across her all-too-prominent bones.

'It gets really hot at work and I was on the back till all afternoon.'

'Yeah? Yeah, it must get really hot.'

'I'm okay, LG. Just stay close while I get up though, eh? Just in case.'

Little Gold hovers at her sister's side, unsure whether or not to touch her, to try to support her fragile frame. In spite of the fact that she's mostly bones, and surely weighs nothing, she's a good five inches taller and probably capable of knocking them both down if she collapses again. But this is no time for cowardice.

'Lean on me. Put your arm round my shoulder. I'm really strong. I won't drop you.'

There's nothing in the leaning though, no weight to brace against, she's barely there at all.

Safely deposited in one of the round-backed kitchen chairs she looks like a toddler stowed in a highchair and Little Gold relaxes slightly. The lump seems to have settled on its chosen size and Ali shows no sign of further dizziness. Still, people shouldn't just faint, not teenagers. And if she can do it walking down their hallway then she could do it in the street, in the road, under the wheels of a lorry…

Stop. Stop panicking.

'Ali, do you think you need to go to hospital and get it checked?'

From the front room, Mum's snoring ratchets up a few decibels, like she's joining in the conversation the only way she can. Little Gold remembers a time when she got kicked in the head by someone on a swing in the park and Mum shone a torch in her eyes to check for concussion. Maybe she should be doing that? Ali shuts her eyes and replies, quiet but firm and not sounding in the least like someone who might be fuzzy in the head.

'No! No, it's not a big deal. I just got dizzy. I do sometimes when I'm on.'

'Oh.'

Little Gold considers the bowls sitting on the counter. The soup will undoubtedly be tepid now, and there's an unappealing filmy sheen over the surface of the liquid. But it's something.

'Think you should have your soup?'

'Yeah. Yeah, I probably should.'

Little Gold tries to slow down her eating and make it as quiet as she can. Malcy's eating noises disgust Ali to the point where she often claims it's impossible for her to take another bite. So, sliding the spoon through her lips, steady and slow, she swallows mouthfuls of soup almost without chewing. It *is* cold and too salty.

Ali dabs at her spoon, imbibing the orange liquor like a hummingbird. Then she draws its silver tip around the bowl in convoluted loops, avoiding solid matter as much as possible.

'You supposed to be in work tomorrow?'

'Yeah. Yeah, but I'll be fine, LG.'

After a couple more spoons of soup, she pushes the bowl away and sips water instead.

'Ali, where will you live at university?'

'In halls.'

'Is that just a bedroom?'

'Sort of study-bedroom. You get a desk and chair.'

'And you'll get a grant to live on?'

'Yeah, that's right. I got Mum to do all the forms so I know that's gone through okay.'

She's got it all worked out, how she's going to survive when she leaves them here. Little Gold bites her lip to hold the thought inside.

And will there be someone to pick you up when you keel over in the corridor?

'Want tea, LG?'

'Yeah, thanks.'

Ali pushes back her chair and walks over to the kettle. Malcy's left the marg out and she tuts as she puts it back in the fridge. Pacing the kitchen, fetching the cloth to wipe the counter, making the tea, she's like a glove puppet, like Mr Punch with a papier-mâché head and her overall just an empty drape of fabric. Little Gold longs for Mum to rise up from her snoring heap and scoop Ali into her arms, scoop them both close and tell them how it's all okay. How it's all going to be okay. Ali glances over from where she's dunking their tea bags.

'Hey! You alright, LG?'

'Yeah. I'm just a bit... I'll miss you.'

'I'll miss you too but I'll be back at Christmas, you know?'

'I know.'

She thinks about Ali's angry words of the other day.

She'll lose this house...

Does she really believe they'll be here, just getting by somehow?

'And you'll have Malc.'

'Yeah. He's not… I don't think he's really that happy though, Ali.'

Ali plonks her tea on the table.

'Malc? He's okay, LG. You know what he's like. You just have to make sure he's got his inhalers and stuff, don't you? And try not to trash anything else in the house.'

She thinks about the ragged hole in the bath panel, the blackness inside.

'Yeah. I think he really misses Dad though.'

Little Gold imagines she can hear the slam of Ali's mind, like the noise of the big prison door in the opening titles of *Porridge*, the turning of heavy keys in locks. She's blown it with just the mention of his name.

'I'm going to have a bath. Then I'm going down Gemma's again.'

In the front room, David Bellamy's been shrunk down like Mrs Pepperpot to do a Backyard Safari. Little Gold likes him, his fuzzy voice and endless enthusiasm for the natural world. He's there in his shorts and shirt, pretending to be scared of a giant earwig.

Mum doesn't smell too bad so she snuggles in, curling around her back and feeling the useless, unaddressed envelope crackle in her pocket.

The soup's lying in her stomach – acidic, bloating and empty at the same time and Little Gold realises her head's pounding. There's pain thrumming behind her eye socket and she wants comfort. She wants Disprin dissolved in squash, the purple blanket, a bucket in case she's sick and Mum's cool hand on her cheek.

Like a calf butting for milk, she nudges at the hard, wrapped sharpness of Mum's shoulder blade with her forehead, allowing herself a quiet moan, the whine of a small child.

'Mu-um…'

'Wha…!'

She jerks awake, her shoulder blade cracking against Little Gold's nestling cheek.

'Sorry, Mum, sorry! It's just me.'

'Oh…'

In an instant she's asleep again, drawn back into the lubricated depths without another word.

Little Gold turns away, curls instead into the crook of the settee, as the credits roll on and the voice announces that now it's time for *Medical Express*.

This week, six willing guinea pigs have been trying out diets…

She prises herself from the sofa, switches off the telly and wanders up to her room.

It's getting late. Malcy should have been home ages ago so she goes to the window to look across to the park. There's still a very meagre match underway. Two boys on each side, sprinting across the balding grass and taking shots at open goals marked by saplings and sweatshirts. There's Malcy, getting the ball for a minute and haring off. He shoots for the goal and the ball goes wide, hitting the tarmac of the path and beginning a speedy descent down the steep slope. He trots after it, slipping out of sight behind bushes and benches.

In his absence, the match loses another player and she thinks that's probably it for the night. They won't bother going on with three and Malc will come home. And no matter what mood he's in, no matter what, she wants him here, all of them here and safe. A few minutes pass and he doesn't reappear. The remaining two boys pluck their sweatshirts from the grass and start to wander away, up the road towards Fiveways.

Still she waits, craning her neck to see further down the path towards the clock tower, willing his blonde head to appear. And then there he is, Malcy walking up the slope with his football under his arm. But he's not alone. He's talking to someone beside him, someone partially obscured by the bend in the path. And then the path straightens and she realises it's Kev.

There's a shout and both boys turn their heads to where Roy's standing beside the silver car, one hand raised in a wave. The back door of the car's open, gaping, ready for Malcy to step inside and Little Gold turns from her bedroom window and runs. The pain in her head's acute, violent, accompanied suddenly by flashes of purple-white brightness that dart in from the side of her vision. But she keeps going, takes a chance on the road, rounds the corner by the toilets and is just in time to see the taillights of the car as it turns at the bottom of the park. In the back window she catches a glimpse of Malcy's yellow hair. Little Gold pants, feels the cramping heave inside her and vomits into the privet bush.

CHAPTER THIRTY-THREE

She wakes. The pain's stopped. Her head's light, far too light, like something stuffed with feathers and air and the relief is instant and overwhelming. And then she remembers. The skin of her face is crusted with dried tears and snot and she remembers crying and then nothing more. That sleep came and took her is evident but astonishing and she wonders if it was the headache, closing her down for a while.

His tangled bed's empty and the orange glow of the streetlight's falling over the exposed bottom sheet, its crumpled terrain of valleys and hills. Where is he?

She listens to a car whooshing down the hill. He might have gone to Kev's for a film. He might be staying over and that's all, just watching a film, just sitting on a sofa and watching a film and falling asleep on a camping mat on Kev's bedroom floor. That's all. That's all. But her teeth start to chatter and she tugs her duvet tight to her chin, over her fully clothed body.

It's quiet outside, the quiet of very late, and when the car draws up, she knows it's him. There are footsteps on the path, the turn of a key in their front door and someone closing it carefully, carefully so it doesn't slam. He stumbles on the stairs and she hears the latch of the bathroom door.

She waits but he doesn't come out. Minutes stretch, soft as chewed toffee, gluey, sticky moments she struggles to endure until finally she climbs quietly from under the covers and peers down the darkened landing. The glass panel above the bathroom door's yellow with light. She takes a tentative step towards it, then another and another, until she's standing outside the door, her ears pricked for the slightest noise in the room. It's silent, so she grips the handle and twists. There's no resistance and the door swings open.

'Malc?'

Her whisper echoes in the empty space. He's vanished. For a moment she wonders if she imagined the noises of his return but no, he was here – there's a harsh smell, a mixture of outdoors and alcohol, and dark pee in the toilet bowl with no accompanying paper. He must have gone back downstairs. She's about to turn away when something in the basin catches her eye, something wet and crumpled in shallow water that wasn't there earlier. She takes a step closer and peers in.

It's a pair of Malcy's pants. White pants with navy piping around the hems. Floating in the water with them there's a bar of Shield soap, marbled bright turquoise. He was trying to wash them, probably trying to wash them out like she does her clothes. Her fingers reach to take the soap from the water and then she jerks her hand away. There's blood. Malcy's pants are bloody – a patch of bright red, slightly darker around its rim, big as a 50p piece, with smears stretching out across the cotton.

She backs away from the wash basin, backs towards the door, pulling the cord to make the room dark, to make them disappear. But they are still there, lying there in the darkness like some puffed, sodden sea creature lying dead on the slab in the fishmongers.

There's a noise from downstairs and she looks over the banisters to see Malcy leaving the house again. He doesn't close the door but leaves it ajar. She paces slowly down the stairs, tugs on her trainers and follows him out of the house.

She'd been hoping he might just be on the front path, or sitting on the garden wall maybe, though God knows why. But he's already at the bottom of the steps and jogging towards the road and suddenly she's certain she must stop him. The blood in the sink, the damage done, feels suddenly like the herald of something worse and she realises why. Malcy wouldn't have left those pants there, left that awful mess right there in the sink, unless he wasn't coming back to it. And then there's nothing too awful to imagine and nothing she can't do to stop it.

'Malcy!'

He turns his head, looks straight at her and runs, runs across the road and into the blackness of the park. She sprints after him, is about to cross the road too, when her courage fails and she gulps down a sob.

'Malcy!'

It comes out choked, too quiet, useless. She turns and looks around but there's no-one in the deserted street. And then her eye falls on Peggy Baxter's house and the dim light in its front window.

She takes the steps two at a time and once she's on the front path she can see her, Peggy Baxter, standing at the window in the soft glow of her standard lamp. She's wearing a grey dressing gown and cradling a mug in her hands.

Jumping the garden wall, Little Gold knocks on the window, pressing her face close. Peggy's cry of shock is sharp enough to penetrate the glass and she sloshes tea from her mug over her cuff. But she looks into Little Gold's eyes, puts down her mug and, in a second, is opening the front door. She steps out onto the path.

'Little Gold! What is it? What's wrong?'

Little Gold swallows, catching the sob as it competes with her words.

'It's Malcy. He's not okay. He's gone to the park in the dark, I...'

'Come on, we need to get your mother.'

Peggy grasps her hand and leads her along the path and down the steps. She's breathing hard, swaying slightly with each step down, but holding tight, firm, checking Little Gold's galloping progress. As they reach the pavement though, Little Gold wrenches her hand away.

'No! We have to go after him. Now! I don't think he's safe. Right now. Please.'

And Peggy nods and holds out her hand, once again, for Little Gold to take in hers.

The park in the dark is a swish of black on blue, a panting animal in the night. Little Gold grips the cooling hand in hers, tugging Peggy across the grass and now it's the old lady's turn to resist.

'No! Stay on the path. If I fall over we're in a whole lot more trouble. We go down to the bottom and up the other side and if we don't find him we to go back to your house. Okay?'

'Yes, yes, but come on…'

Halfway down the path, the silhouette of the clock tower looming beside them, they hear the clash of metal on metal – the gate of the playground swinging closed behind someone. Like a bell sounding. An alarm. And Little Gold feels another moment of tipping, a terrible tipping of Malcy away from her.

She lets go of the hand in hers and sprints, blind, into the darkness.

'He's at the swings! Catch me up.'

'Wait!'

But she doesn't stop. She registers the muttered curse behind her but she presses on into the black with her hands in front, striking the fence and feeling her way along the hoops of cold metal to the gate.

He's just movement on the top of the climbing frame – his dark shape shifting against the dusty orange of the street-lamp sky. The dip and rise of his blonde head is the only thing that makes her sure that it is him. It is her Malcy up there and she runs on.

'Malcy!'

Suddenly there's a void under her right foot and she falls heavily forward. As she hits the ground there's the jolt of teeth on tongue and blood mixed with sand in her mouth. Spitting, pressing her palms to the damp sand, she heaves herself forward and plunges on into the darkness.

Malcy is leaning from the side of the climbing frame and she sees him there, stretching out into the space in the middle with one hand and one foot, like an acrobat waiting for applause. And then he lets go.

He doesn't fall. Malcy doesn't fall, instead there's a jerk and then he's writhing, twisting in the air, hanging from the top of the climbing frame.

'Peggy Baxter! Peggy Baxter!'

Little Gold grabs at the kicking limbs and Malcy's trainer catches her chin, sending her staggering backwards. But then there's Peggy, real and solid, enfolding Malcy's legs in her arms and lifting him, cradling him as she speaks through gritted teeth.

'Get help! Now! Get help!'

Little Gold leaps the fence and just a few more strides away there's a row of houses. Hammering on the nearest door, she doesn't wait for a reply but tramples through a flower bed, over a low wall and beats on the next. As she presses door bells and thumps with her stinging palm, she shouts,

'Help! Help! We need help, please!'

As she progresses from house to house, upstairs rooms illuminate like a chain of lights running along the pier. Front doors swing open and people pour out, surrounding her.

'My brother, on the climbing frame. Peggy Baxter's holding him up but he's hanging there, my…'

There's the urgency of men's deep voices and heavy feet running across the road. A woman curls an arm around Little Gold's shoulders and the night spirals away for a minute. Far off in another place, people's words are flying in the dark like bats swooping around her head but she can't speak.

'Ambulance.'

'Police.'

'Shock.'

'Know his mother.'

'Up the hill.'

'167, I think.'

'Take him inside.'

'Think it's a girl.'

And then the night spins close again and sparks her limbs to run. She must get back. Pushing and dodging, she slips from the women's hands and crosses into the park, jumps the fence and runs in the shadow of the tall privet hedge, back towards the climbing frame.

The women's voices are ringing in her wake.

'Dave! He's run off! The kid's run off! Alan! Alan! Dave! Have you got him?'

She stalks, close to the climbing frame, ducking low. Underneath the tall structure the men are huddled in a circle. Sliding between two pyjama-clad backs she finds herself in the centre, alongside Malcy, lying on his side on the concrete, rasping wetly. There's a jumper under his head and a thick, towelling dressing gown covering him but the men are standing back, murmuring like a chorus of monks in their nightclothes, not touching.

'It's okay, son. You're alright.'

'Malc! Malcy!'

She drops to her knees, grabbing his shoulders, making the covered body shake.

'Hey! Hey, careful now!'

A vast paw grabs her shoulder and yanks her away. She scrambles back to his side but this time lays just a gentle palm on his chest, listening to the grain of his breathing, the awful, obstructed noise and, underneath it, the high whine of his wheeze. She grabs at his shoulders again.

'Sit him up! Sit him up! Malcy has to sit up when he wheezes! He needs his inhaler! He needs…'

And then she's lifted in arms so vast and thick that her struggling and kicking makes no difference at all. Placed on her feet on the grass, outside the circle, she's simply held there, static and contained, shouting snatches of fury at the backs of the men.

'He needs his inhaler! Let me… It's his wheeze! He needs…'

Pulses of blue light transform the playground as an ambulance draws up in the street and then there are torches bobbing and sweeping towards them until finally they settle on Malcy, holding him in a pool of light as an ambulance man crouches over him. Above the tableau, dangling from the highest cross-bar of the climbing frame, ragged and torn, ripped through by one of these huge-pawed men, there's the twist of Malcy's old dressing gown cord.

She stops struggling and the hands loose their grip. Reaching out, she taps at the jacket of an ambulance man. He doesn't turn and she taps on, on and on, her teeth chattering as she speaks.

''Scuse me, 'scuse me, M…Malcy… g…ge…gets…wheezy. He…He…has an…in…inhaler.'

The chattering teeth get worse and worse and she can't form words now. A voice cuts through the murmuring of the men, loud and clear, and the ambulance man turns towards it.

'The child is trying to tell you that her brother is asthmatic. Have you got that?'

Little Gold turns her head too, picks out the shape of Peggy Baxter on the bench just inside the gate. Something is draped around her shoulders. She lifts her arms wide and Little Gold runs into them, into the wide wings of the blanket. Peggy holds tight and whispers into her hair.

'I've got you. I've got you, Little Gold.'

CHAPTER THIRTY-FOUR

The window in the room is frosted, revealing nothing but blurred patches of colour as people walk down the grey street outside. The air feels used, as if it's been in and out of a thousand pairs of lungs, and something in the room has been washed down with bleach not very long ago.

Mum coughs, a wet little burst into a tissue, and then scrapes her chair a bit closer to the table. The policewoman who showed them in returns carrying two white plastic cups. She makes a laboured entrance into the room, struggling to hold the door open with her shoulder, a cup in each hand and a clipboard wedged underneath her arm.

'Here we are then.'

Mum's cup has tea that's almost as orange as the squash in hers. The policewoman sits down opposite them and smiles. Little Gold looks away and takes a sip of the squash. It's very strong, thick and sticky, like a melted sweet rather than a drink. The police lady reaches across the table and pats Mum's arm.

'Now, as I said, we don't think there's any need for this to be a terribly formal business or to take long, because we've got your son's statement and that of Mr Mansfield, as well as your own and your elder daughter's. And Miss Baxter, of course.'

She picks up a clipboard and pen and turns to Little Gold, who looks steadfastly away. The shadow of a seagull crosses the top corner of the silver window.

'So, you understand, sweetheart? You don't need to be worried about anything. I know it's all been a horrid, frightening time but all we want you to do now is answer a couple of questions.'

Her voice is as syrupy as the squash and lilting, cajoling, as if Little Gold's five years old.

'On that day, the day your brother had his accident in the park, did you spend any time in the park too?'

'No.'

'Right, so you didn't go for a run around or to play on the swings or anything? Not at any point that day?'

'No. I stayed home in the garden.'

The policewoman pauses and writes something in blue biro on the printed form attached to the clipboard. Her handwriting's fat and blobby and Little Gold looks away again, willing the window to clear, to show her the sky. The strip light flickers above them.

'And you had tea with your sister, your brother didn't come home, that right?'

'Yes.'

'And Mummy was having a lie down because she had a bad headache.'

Mum shifts in her chair.

'Yes.'

'And then, later in the night, you woke up when your brother came home, and went outside and followed him to the park with Miss Baxter, yes?'

'Yes.'

'Right, and we know what happened then so there's no need for us to talk about that.'

Little Gold grips the seat of her chair, the plastic rim biting into her fingers. The policewoman's writing again and Mum takes a sip of tea with a hand shaking so violently that a splash lands on the table like a teardrop.

'Right. I don't think we have any more to ask you, sweetheart. You've been a very good girl and very brave and there's nothing to worry about now.'

Little Gold blinks and there's Malcy suddenly, lying on his side on the floor in the corner of the grubby room, just as he did underneath the climbing frame. She sees the pool of torchlight and the ripped cord dangling above him. And then there's the sound of her own voice as if the words are speaking themselves, flowing out of her, setting their own pitch and tone. Dull and loud they fall out onto the table.

'Roy took him in his car.'

The policewoman looks up from the clipboard.

'Yes. That's right. We know about that. Your brother went to his friend's house for tea.'

'He took him in his car, I saw him.'

'You saw your brother go? So you did go over to the park?'

'No, I… Not during the day. But I saw out the window and I ran after.'

'You saw your brother leaving from the window? And then you went to the park? So that wasn't quite true that you didn't go to the park all day, was it?'

She's frowning, the nib of her biro hovering over the paper.

'Only just for a minute, when I saw him go. I ran after…'

The words are drying up. Little Gold closes her mouth.

'I see.'

The syrupy voice dies and the policewoman's tone is clipped and irritated as she goes on.

'Now, this is very important. I need you to be very clear. Do you understand?'

She nods.

'Did you see any men around the toilets in the park when you went there?'

Little Gold can feel Mum tensing beside her, coughing again. She unclasps her handbag and takes out a new tissue, spitting daintily into it before balling it in her palm. Little Gold struggles to form words.

'I saw Roy taking Malcy in his car.'

'Yes, we know about that. Your brother went to the Mansfields' house for tea and then, later on, Mr Mansfield dropped him home.'

'No. He took Malcy. *He* took Malcy. He…'

The syrupy tone's back as the policewoman puts down the clipboard for a moment and tilts her head to one side.

'Now then…now then…'

She drips and coos her words, reaching out for Little Gold's hand. When no hand is forthcoming she pats the table instead.

'It's alright. It's alright. There's no need to get upset. I know it's all been very frightening and…'

She stops speaking and glances at Mum, who gives a small nod.

'And, perhaps, it might be easier to understand if I try to explain a little bit…'

Little Gold freezes, sits rigid, and tries to send her mind out into the white sky. She's determined that even the sealed window, the low ceiling with its buzzing strip light, won't stop her. But the voice intrudes, snakes around her ankle, pulls her back down and locks her into the plastic chair, forcing its way into her consciousness.

'After Mr Mansfield dropped off your brother that night, something bad happened. Your brother did a very silly thing.'

There's a scrape and rustle as Mum shifts her chair.

'He went back across the road and close to those toilets there. You know those toilets in the park?'

Little Gold makes no response.

'There was a bad man there, at the toilets in the park, and he hurt your brother. He hurt him…'

She takes a deep breath.

'Well, I think, perhaps, you know where he hurt your brother, don't you?'

Little Gold blinks and this time it's the pants, the pants crumpled and bloody in the sink and she rubs her eyes, rubs them hard, sending bursts of light across her eyelids.

'It's alright. There's no need for us to talk about that any more. We just…'

Her treacly voice wavers and Little Gold finally realises it's a sticky cover over her fear. The policewoman's scared. Mum blows her nose and Little Gold can feel the tremble of her shoulders, so close beside her own. Mum's crying gently, sniffling and gasping.

She has to get out. She must get out of here.

Little Gold takes a deep breath and throws back her head, looks straight up at the polystyrene tiles on the ceiling as if she could break through them with her gaze. Then she looks into the wide rabbit-eyes of the policewoman, seeking another way out.

'Can I go home now?'

'Yes, of course you can, sweetheart.'

Their three chairs scrape on the floor as they stand. Mum's tea and her squash, with the single splash between them, sit barely touched on the table. The policewoman hands her the biro and the clipboard.

'All you need to do is sign your name on that line there.'

Little Gold forms the letters of the name that isn't hers, that she thinks will never be hers, and passes the clipboard back to the policewoman.

'Lovely. And, if you can add yours here, just to confirm you were present.'

Mum signs the paper too, picks up her handbag from the floor and the policewoman holds the door open for them.

'So, of course, we'll let you know, should there be…'

Mum nods and ushers Little Gold ahead of her down the corridor of blank, closed doors. A heavy-set policeman, wearing a peaked cap, steps out of one, laughing with someone inside the room.

'That's what I said… Oh, excuse me.'

He stands aside as they pass and Little Gold can feel his eyes on her, all the way to the end of the corridor, across the lobby and out into the street.

CHAPTER THIRTY-FIVE

She stops at the high desk just inside the ward where a nurse is sitting with her head bowed over a sheet of paper. After a few minutes she realises that she hasn't been seen.

'Um, excuse me.'

The jerk of the nurse's head makes her jump and she takes a step back but a warm smile breaks across the broad, brown face before her.

'Oh, I'm sorry, darlin' I didn't spot you there! Who you come to see then?'

'Peggy Baxter.'

'Ah, so you're the Little Gold we all heard so much about then, eh?'

'Yes.'

'Well, she'll be pleased to see ya. Las' bed on the left, darlin'.'

Little Gold digs her fingers into the moist paper around the stems of the chrysanthemums in her hand. The last bed's hidden by a curve of royal blue curtain that reaches almost to the floor.

She walks slowly down the row of beds, the shop display of old ladies – all broken but some more than others. There are beds with family crowded around, some without. One of the occupants is fast asleep with her mouth open, showing pink, sea-shell gums and darkness inside. There are black bruises on her skinny, crepe paper arms, and beside her bed, dangling from the frame, there's a plastic pouch fat with pale yellow liquid. Little Gold doesn't want to understand what that might be, but she does.

She pauses at the curtain, her fingertips resting lightly on its hem. If you know, you know someone's dying, do you say so? Do you? She draws back the fabric because she has to. Because her trainers are showing underneath and Peggy Baxter can probably see that she's there.

'Hello, Little Gold!'

She's yellow but she's still Peggy Baxter – the grey dressing gown, the white cloud of hair. The blue-sky eyes. They stand for a moment just looking at each other and then Peggy pats the bed.

'Climb up here.'

Little Gold hoists herself onto the hospital bed and looks down at her swinging trainers. It'd be a long way to fall.

'I thank you for those chrysanthemums, Little Gold, slightly battered as they are.'

The drooping bronze flowers lie on the bed between them, looking defeated.

'Sorry. I think it was a bit hot for them on the bus.'

'I'm sure it was. And for you too, no doubt.'

So this is what they'll do, just talk like they don't know. Just talk about things like it's not true, like, maybe, they're not even in the hospital at all. Little Gold feels the first flutter of tears and she's not sure if they're from relief or disappointment at this stage-managed interaction.

Peggy Baxter pushes the wrapped flowers onto the bedside table and grabs at the plastic jug of water there.

'Have some of my water.'

Little Gold jumps down and lifts the jug with two hands.

'I can do it.'

She pours a beaker full and drinks it down.

'Now one for me, if you please.'

There's something soothing in the pouring of more water into that same beaker and the placing of it in Peggy Baxter's outstretched hands. She takes a sip, winks, and returns the cup.

'Enough's as good as a feast. Come on back up here.'

She climbs onto the vertiginous bed and inches closer to Peggy. The bed is covered with a white cellular blanket, its little hexagons measuring the distance between them and when there are just three little cells separating their two hands, Peggy reaches across and closes the gap, enfolding Little Gold's small hand with her large one. She squeezes.

'Little Gold, I want to tell you something.'

The shadows under her eyes are the darkest thunderclouds now. It can't be long until the storm.

'You were right that night to come and get me.'

Little Gold says nothing and Peggy goes on.

'If we'd gone back to get your mum it might've been too late for Malcy. And I think you should remember that. When it was a moment for knowing what to do, you did know.'

No-one has said that to her. In all the words, and there have been plenty, about being brave, no-one has said that she was right. And no-one has said that about Malcy either, that it might easily have been too late, and the weight of wondering, wondering and not saying, is lifted from her shoulders. For a moment she sees him – slack, cold, soaked in dew – and then the picture bursts and is gone.

'We were a team, Little Gold. We were a top team that night.'

She reaches for the beaker and Little Gold stretches across to place it in her hand. She watches as Peggy gulps – her neck so thin now that each swallow is like a great fish leaping in her throat. Little Gold replaces the beaker on the locker beside the bed and Peggy takes her hand again.

'You know, what happened to your brother was a terrible thing.'

Little Gold searches the face, the heavy jaw, the pale lips left slightly open and finally the pale, sky-rim eyes that seem to be saying, 'Here I am Little Gold, here I still am.'.

'Malcy said it was a man in the toilets in the park.'

'Yes, that's what the policewoman said to me when she came.'

The eyes hold her still as Peggy speaks again.

'And is that what happened, Little Gold?'

The words are heavy, each one a pebble. They are stacked in her throat, in a tower stretching from her lungs to her tongue, immovable. So she thinks each one, sends it with her mind.

It was Kev's dad. They took us, me and Malcy, to this party and I saw. They had photographs. They took Malcy in their car. Malcy screams at night, when he's asleep. Mum says he'll be okay. I don't believe her.

Then she lies down, in the narrow strip of bed alongside Peggy Baxter's swaddled legs.

The sounds of the ward, the words of other people's lives, float through the gap in the curtain.

'Show Grandma again, Stephen!'

'And if I've told her once…'

'I'll bring it in on Tuesday.'

This is her life too. This is Peggy Baxter's life still, just, and they are here together.

'Do you love Vi, Peggy Baxter?'

'Yes. I have always loved Vi.'

'And that's not dirty.'

It isn't a question because she knows. She's seen it. But she wants to be sure. Needs to be sure.

'Love isn't dirty, Little Gold. Loving people isn't dirty.'

'It doesn't make you dirty?'

Peggy Baxter cups her cheek and leans close to her ear, like the day in the Co-op, a hundred years ago when no-one was bleeding and no-one was dying and no-one was screaming in the night.

'No. Not ever. Not ever.'

'And not wrong?'

'Not wrong.'

The curtain sweeps back and there's Vi holding a bottle of Lucozade in one hand and a packet of cigarettes in the other. She's smiling like someone on stage for a curtain call, as if she might sweep into a bow. But she narrows her eyes at Peggy.

'Ah, I see you have no need of my comforting presence, Peg!'

Little Gold sits up and takes in the shine of her – the peacock blue blouse, the soft sand of her crumpled trousers, the sweep of her lashes, heavy with mascara. Peggy Baxter lets out her sea lion laugh.

'Ha! Vi, you silly old coot! Get me into a wheelchair and down to that smoking room, pronto. And, Little Gold, take some money from her and go and get yourself the best ice lolly they offer in that shop downstairs.'

She doesn't run because it's not allowed but Little Gold strides to the lift and then along the corridors to the shop. She buys a pineapple Mivvi, rides back up to the correct floor and then follows the signs to the smoking room.

They're alone. Vi has parked Peggy Baxter by the window and opened it as far as it will go, which isn't very far. But, this high up, it's allowing in a steady stream of air and Vi and Peggy are seated in two high-backed chairs, turned towards the window for the view. The coils of their cigarette smoke are binding like rope above them and outside there's the sea, reaching away to the white light of the horizon. The coastline curves off to the stacks of the power station at Shoreham and, below them, the town moves, beetling with people and life. Little Gold sits in a third chair, eating her ice lolly and watching the sun sink. Close by, hanging and wheeling in the air, just outside the window, are scores of herring gulls.

CHAPTER THIRTY-SIX

Mum is buttoning her corduroy jacket as she talks.

'So, I'll be back in about an hour. An hour, okay?'

Little Gold's doodling a vine around the edge of the free newspaper. She starts to add birds – beaks and tails peeping out from behind leaves and stems.

'Yes.'

'And you and Malcy just stay here and don't answer the door or the phone, okay?'

She's brushed her hair over-enthusiastically and it's swept up into a steep wave above her forehead. But she's clean and smart enough and Little Gold imagines bank managers must be used to people being a bit nervous. Mum leans towards the kitchen window, where she's reflected faintly, and applies a sweep of bronze lipstick. She rolls her lips together and spins round.

'What do you reckon?'

'Yeah, fine.'

Mum strokes Little Gold's hair as she passes her chair and leans in to kiss the top of her head. She's shaking, there's Extra Strong Mint on her breath, but still Little Gold can feel the kiss lingering, the warm press of it on her scalp, even as Mum closes the front door behind her.

It's the first time they've been alone, she and Malcy. As the days have passed, Little Gold's sat alongside him, for hours, watching any rubbish on telly. Ali's brought cream soda home from work and they've played Monopoly together, gulping down the fizz and sweetness and bankrupting each other. But always there's been Mum, woken as if from the lifting of a spell, or Ali, watchful over the top of a paperback. And he's said nothing.

At bedtime Mum reads to them, chapters of Wilbur Smith like when they were little, then props the door open and leaves the landing light on. He turns his back and she hasn't dared to send a word out across the open space between them.

And when he wakes her in the night with the screams, there's still no words but Mum's, cutting through his mangled cries.

'Malcy, you're alright. He's okay, Little Gold. You go back to sleep.'

Now she can hear him upstairs in their room – the pad of his footsteps overhead, the squeak and slam of a drawer. She climbs the stairs slowly, each step both an obligation and a compulsion. Because they have to go on from here. Somehow they have to go on.

Malcy's standing beside his bed. Awakened, Mum has cleared the floor in their room, hoovered and dusted and changed their sheets and, in the centre of Malcy's clean duvet, there's a jumble of colour. She steps closer, picking out the component parts of the small heap. There's Malcy's football sticker album on top, underneath it the flash of a bare breast on shiny paper, an envelope, thick cream, addressed in looped handwriting, and money. There are at least two twenties and a tenner.

He doesn't try to hide any of it. Instead he steps to one side, as if displaying the things there for her comment.

Little Gold finds she has only one question, the question she's been holding for weeks now.

'Have they been in touch?'

He nods, picks the envelope from the litter of objects and holds it out to her. Little Gold lifts the thick flap and slides out what's inside. It's a large card, raised silver lettering over the cartoon drawing of an elephant with a bandage wrapped round its trunk. She opens it and reads.

Dear Malcy, Get Well Soon! Here's hoping you're soon on the mend. We're so sorry not to see you before we go but Roy's new job in Dubai starts next week and there's so much to do before then! Kevin sends you all the best. With best wishes for the future, Kay, Roy and Kev XXX

Little Gold reads it through again. It's extravagant handwriting – fat, flowing letters and the kisses looped in a chain.

'They're going away?'

'Gone. Sent that last week.'

She gestures at the things on his bed.

'What are you…?'

'Having a bonfire. Help me?'

Malcy fetches the old galvanised bucket from the back yard and Little Gold brings the matches from beside the cooker. The garden's overgrown, the grass reaching to the middle of their shins now, and Malcy beds the bucket into the waxy greenness, rocking it slightly to make sure it's on stable ground. Little Gold glances up.

'We need to be careful of the tree.'

'It's okay, we'll keep the flames low.'

But Little Gold makes him wait while she returns to the kitchen, digs out a jug from the back of the cupboard and fills it to the brim with cold water. As she carries it up the steps it sloshes and splatters the toes of her trainers. She settles it alongside the bucket.

'Just in case, yeah?'

They shred the free newspaper to get the flames going and then Little Gold sits back, waiting for Malcy to start on the rest. He begins with the sticker album and she can't stifle her gasp as he wrenches the pages from the stapled centre. The faces of the footballers curl and blacken in the orange flames.

'Did Kev get his finished?'

It's a ridiculous thing to be asking him but he turns a calm face to her. There's something in his face now, some lengthening of his features that makes him look older. She knows it can't really have happened in just these few weeks.

'Neither of us did.'

He pokes another page into the fire.

'Malc, did Kev…'

He picks up the corner of the flaming page and twists it, pressing it deeper into the bucket.

'Kev was my friend.'

She remembers Kev and Malcy joking around in the park,

tapping on the window of the silver car as Jake the puppy ran riot inside.

'What about Jake? Have they taken him with them, or what?'

Malcy shrugs.

He holds out the porn magazine to her as if it were just a copy of *Smash Hits*.

'Rip this up for me?'

It looks different in the sunlight, less of a thing, and she tears the cover off.

'I didn't say anything to the policewoman.'

Malcy doesn't reply to that but jerks his head in a tight nod. He's taking the torn images of nudity from her, feeding page after page into the bucket and concentrating on his task, working systematically until the whole thing's done. The fire's giving off real heat now, shimmering the air and scorching one side of Little Gold's face.

She watches his bent head, his eyes blinking from the billowing smoke. He's wearing a navy blue polo shirt, the collar turned up around his throat, but when he turns to face her she can see the darkened ring of skin still.

He holds the first note to the licking flame and it bursts with fire, gone in a moment. He offers one to her and Little Gold feels a fierce spike of adrenaline as the money burns. It's the best feeling she's had in months – the strongest, wildest feeling of power – and she wishes they had a pile as big as a haystack to burn.

She hands him the envelope and Malcy slides the card from it again, running his fingertip over the embossed letters. He looks up and into her eyes and Little Gold meets the darting, anxious gaze.

'I thought they liked me.'

'I know.'

The crumpled envelope burns well, the heavy, cream paper curling into a blackened rose, but the card keeps going out. The small rolling flame at the rim smoulders and dies over and over again. Malcy strikes match after match, cursing through gritted teeth,

'Fuck it! Pissing thing!'

They'll run out of matches if he goes on so she lays a hand on his arm.

'Stop, Malc. Just wait a minute. I know what we need. Just hang on.'

In the cupboard under the sink there's a bottle of white spirit. They need this, this and something else to support the fire, to be kindling. Malcy's hooded top, her top now, is on the peg in the hall. It's still there, the letter she never sent, the words that don't mean anything now, so she takes it from the pocket, ripping it in half as she walks back up the steps to the garden.

The acrid smell of the white spirit tightens something behind her eyes. She won't let him pour it. She twists the paper and dips just a corner into the clear liquid then screws the lid on.

As she tucks the letter down into the bucket, she glances at Malcy. Dad's name is visible, the inked blue letters and the empty space underneath.

'Wait while I move this bottle well away. I saw a thing on telly and it might ignite.'

She takes the white spirit over to the steps and returns to her brother, kneeling close beside him.

It needs one match, just one match and the letter to Dad is a mass of fire. Malcy tucks the card in alongside it and the stroking flames beat and beat at its surface, flickering green over the silver letters. Flecks of black are flying up from the bucket now, flitting through the air like insects. Little Gold watches them dancing against the white sky.

'Malc, if they ever get in touch again… If they ever write to you or anything…'

Malcy tosses a match into the fire and it fizzes into flame.

'I'll burn it.'

She takes the box from his hands. If they use the last one then Mum'll want to know why. Then she hands him the jug of water.

'Douse it.'

There's a hiss as the last flames are drowned. Little Gold steps away through the grass, glancing back at her brother still crouching alongside the blackened bucket.

'We need to have baths, Malc. We must smell of smoke. You go first. I'll run it.'

She picks up the white spirit and paces down the steps into the yard.

CHAPTER THIRTY-SEVEN

Peggy is longing for her home, for her clock, her books, the quiet. This forest of brushed nylon is exhausting in its noises of anguish. Over and again, the inhabitants moan at the pain under their lace-trimmed nighties. They cough and cry out, confused and lost, down the length of the hospital ward. She and Vi have lapsed into silence now, beaten down by the lack of hope.

'You'd better go, Vi. It's past visiting time and you don't want to get locked in.'

She grins and winks in a vain attempt to bring them back to themselves, to be Peggy and Vi and not just two old girls under this medical thumb. But the pain just mocks, with a knock and a grind, and she can't hold back a gasp. Vi's eyebrows knot and she bustles around the bed.

'Let me just do your pillows before I head off. Do you want me to get the nurse?'

'No, the tablets will work in a minute Vi and I'll be out like a light.'

Vi leans her forward, her hand so familiar and warm between Peggy's shoulder blades. For a moment her courage fails and she longs to simply plead.

Take me home. Take me home, Vi. Let me go back home.

But once Vi has plumped and straightened the pillows, she's regained control of herself.

'I'll be in in the morning then, love. You'll be alright? Nothing more you need?'

'I'm dandy, sweetheart. You must go now. Go and get some

sleep. Make sure you eat too. You must have a meal. There's a tin of mince in the…'

'I'll look after myself. Don't you worry about me. You try to get some sleep. And promise me you'll call a nurse if it gets too hard again?'

Peggy nods and Vi kisses her cheek. She waves from the door and is gone.

The pills are starting to work now and she can feel the velvet drips of sleep overcoming her body, making her eyelids dip. They open, dip, open again and the light in the ward has dimmed.

Her radio's gone. In its place there's a book, thick and dark with gold letters on the spine. Dangling from the pages, a thin ribbon is marking a verse. She knows, without looking, what it will be.

For you, Lord, are good, and ready to forgive; and plenteous in mercy to all them that call on you.

It isn't really there, of course. It's something slid out of time. It's a thing of dream and, yet, somehow, she knows she is awake.

She must speak out loud to break the spell and make it disappear. But Peggy finds she can't lift her tongue – the drug has weighted it. Her limbs have the same immovable heft and she feels herself slipping down. Dumb and paralysed she's dragged down and down, into this waking dream.

Margaret now, deep in the cold, cold winter of '38, in a bed, in a row of other girls, voiceless and contained.

Closely packed bedsteads stretch down to the window, the foot of each frame is an arc of moonlight. Something is running, like a finger of liquid, trickling down the inside of her thigh. It's not from her bladder, it's not pee but the waters, the breaking. Her time has come. Her bare feet slap on the lino as she waddles, bunching her nightdress between her legs.

The clutch of the first pain makes her gasp. She hadn't known what it would be but it is this, this tightening inside her. She waits for the woman to rise from her bed, watching as she ties back her hair, speaking into the mirror of a dressing table. The pain ebbs away.

'You can make yourself useful and strip those sheets.'

Alone in the laundry, resting her forehead against the wall as the next pain comes, Margaret's breath mists the tiles. This time it's a fierce grip. It lifts the great drum of her belly.

The third pain comes in the corridor and they usher her, swiftly, into a whitewashed room.

Again and again it happens but it's a hesitant, reluctant opening. The women's hands come to her belly and inside her too.

'It needs to turn.'

Day becomes night becomes day becomes night.

'She still at it? Come on young lady!'

Their laughter is like a spray of shingle flung up on the prom from a high-tide wave. Then a dizzying pause, a moment of nothing, followed by sudden sickness, a violent retching of yellow bile.

The new feeling is a demand, a command from her body, bringing fresh energy. It's an order to expel. The vast, descending force of it is swift. The burning rip of the crowning head makes her scream and then a woman holds it aloft – red and steaming.

There's sticky blood in the pale hair. A gummed hole is open, crying heat and injury into the icy night. Margaret holds her in shaking arms, breathing into her petal ear.

'No!'

Peggy is lucid again – her own voice ringing as she struggles to sit up in the hospital bed.

'You're alright now. You're alright, Peggy.'

Slowly the ward becomes what it is. The dark humps in the beds are elderly women. Her radio is back where the phantom Bible lay.

She considers her hands – slack-skinned, liver-spotted, corded and notched with thick, soft veins. Old woman. Old woman. She rests her palms on the blanket over her knees and wills them to remember the fragile silk and hardness of the tiny head. The warmth, the slightly conical shape, the pulsing dip of empty skin. She holds up the small body and presses her mouth to the soft flannelette of the chest. There, in her lips, she feels the fluttering wing beats of the heart.

Peggy inhales, as deeply as she can, into her broken lungs. She conjures her baby from a gauze of memory and lets the pictures come.

Six weeks. There had been six weeks to know her and endless floors to mop. Prayers in church but no miracle granted. The moments together were rare, too rare.

But in those moments, sometimes the baby's eyes would swim and fix, mapping the contours of Margaret's face like a terrain she needed to learn. The pink protrusion of exploring tongue would taste the air between them. And then she would be lifted from Margaret's arms and swaddled again tight in the cot alongside the others.

Margaret bled, heavy and fast, with occasional, sickening clots. They made her eat liver and never stop scrubbing – steps, clothes, her soul.

Her breasts swelled and burned, pouring in rushes that felt like hot, sweet sin. Like the other rushes that she knew made her wicked. Patches of shame bloomed on her overall as her body leaked and drained.

Slowly, slowly it died away. Margaret shrank and closed. She closed tight.

There had been a day, just a single day, in the whole of those six weeks, when she'd allowed herself to imagine stepping into the street. She had pictured the beasts of London buses, roaring next to the kerb, the men in suits and ties, the women with headscarves and shopping baskets and her baby's shawl billowing in the wind. She knew there was a bus to Victoria. She knew there was a train to Brighton. And she knew, with her baby in her arms, that she had no home there. There was no point in imagining so she didn't do it again.

When the day came, she went into the office. Behind the frosted panes of the door, she signed in blue ink. Her name was smudged by the side of her shaking hand and they made her do it again.

Mum is waiting on the bench in the passage. She's wearing her green felt hat on her bowed head and twisting something soft in her hands.

'I've brought your scarf. It's bitter out there.'

Outside the bus window, the streets are littered with prams and Margaret closes her eyes. The world is too loud. On the station concourse, a swirling mass of people, Mum breaks a bar of Dairy Milk in two.

'Just have a bite, it'll keep your strength up.'

She misses her step as they board the train and ladders her stocking. The pain in her shin feels like relief. Margaret clings to the slow burn of the graze, relishing every second that it pulses.

'Don't sit with your back to the engine, Margaret.'

Outside, bare trees are dark on a heavy sky tinged almost yellow.

'It's looking like snow. That'll be the first this winter…'

They cross the Ouse Valley Viaduct. The train rocks and chunters. You left her there you left her there you left her there…

The jaundiced sky darkens to dusk and Mum speaks again. Her words are barely audible, spoken to the grimy carriage floor.

'Your father will be pleased to see you. We'll never mention this again.'

Peggy slides a finger under the waistband of her pyjamas and strokes the soft skin there. Low-down, beside her jutting hip bone, is a small silver space. Skin that buckled and broke where it wrapped her baby, skin that was never the same again. She knows that, when it's exposed to sunlight, it glows like a knife blade. It is the only mark.

CHAPTER THIRTY-EIGHT

The vaulted glass roof of the station is as high as a great church and the concourse is flooded with light. As Ali lifts her rucksack and struggles into it, a pigeon takes off from a white-crusted protrusion at the top of the nearest pillar, dislodging a gentle scatter of guano and small, downy feathers into the air.

Little Gold watches as Mum flits around Ali, tugging her jacket straight, untangling her ponytail from the strap of the rucksack. Her sister waits, accepting the flurry of attention without objection. She reminds Little Gold of a horse she saw once on telly, being shod by a blacksmith. There's the same air that she can tolerate this only because she knows that in a few minutes more she'll be off. Finally, Mum steps away from her.

'You've got those stamps I bought you, yes?'

'Yes.'

'Because I know it's expensive to call. I won't be expecting you to ring every five minutes.'

That's a good job, Little Gold thinks, given that the phone's still cut off. She sees the same thought pass through Ali's mind and her sister grins at her.

'You'll write to me, won't you, LG?'

'Yeah, 'course I will.'

Malcy's standing slightly apart from them, shuffling from foot to foot. He's often anxious outdoors now and the crowd on the concourse is thickening in advance of the Victoria train. Ali reaches into the Co-op bag that's holding her jumper and book and brings out two parcels wrapped in crumpled yellow tissue paper.

'Right, I got you these anyway.'

She hands Malcy his parcel first and he rips open the paper. It's a new Albion scarf, one of the white, silky ones printed with a seagull and with fine, soft tassels. He holds it draped across his palms and looks up at her.

'Thank you, Ali. It's great.'

'S'okay. It's the one you wanted, yeah?'

'Yeah. It's brilliant.'

'And this is for you.'

It's a notebook with a rainbow on the cover and thick, plain pages inside. There's a pen with it too, a proper cartridge pen like Ali's. Little Gold can imagine how it will feel to use, how the ink will flow. It's the best pen she's ever had. It's the notebook she knows she would have chosen from all the ones in the shop.

'Thank you, Ali. They're really lovely.'

She steps towards her sister. Hesitantly, and not without difficulty because of the large rucksack, they hug.

Malcy's looped the scarf around his neck in loose circles. Little Gold can see him from the corner of her eye but she can't bring herself to look properly. Instead she turns back to Ali, who's raising her hand to her brother.

''Bye then, Malc.'

''Bye.'

Mum's bustling again.

'You've got your ticket somewhere safe, haven't you? They'll check, and the railcard too. If you get to London late then don't rush on the tube, will you? You need to go carefully with that rucksack on.'

Ali's had enough. She squeezes Mum in a swift hug and then she turns, holds out her ticket for the gateman to see, and walks onto the platform. The Victoria train stretches away, carriage after carriage, the end disappearing from sight round the slight bend in the tracks. They watch as Ali walks alongside it, her stick-like frame dominated by the size of her pack. Little Gold finds that she's not worried, suddenly not worried at all about Ali, though she can't say why. She slips the pen into her jeans' pocket.

As they pick their way out through the surging crowd, she tries to look at Malcy in front of her. The scarf is loose enough that it could almost be the cowl neck of a jumper and she decides she'll make herself look straight at him, with it on, as soon as they get out onto the pavement. But as they pass the flower stall, Malcy suddenly yanks at the scarf with his right hand, pulling it off, and shooting swift glances from side to side. Then he breaks into a chaotic and pointless run, smacking into people around him, tripping, stumbling over feet and cases. Mum reaches for him but it's too late.

'Malcolm!'

Little Gold touches Mum's arm as she steps swiftly past her.

'It's okay, I'll get him.'

She darts from side to side, littering her progress with nods and apologies.

'Excuse me, sorry, 'scuse me.'

Malcy's never far ahead and she finds him quickly, across the road from the station entrance up a steep little street, leaning on the green tiles of a pub wall.

He's got his eyes closed and he's breathing deeply. The scarf's trailing from the pocket of his bomber jacket and Little Gold reaches out to tuck it in, to lift the soft tassels from the gritty pavement.

'You're okay, Malc. You're okay.'

Mum's waiting on the corner, watching them from a distance, and Little Gold knows this is up to her. Malcy's opened his eyes but he's keeping his gaze averted. She waits for a few moments until she's sure he isn't about to run again and then she speaks.

'Come on, let's tell Mum to get the bus and we'll walk. We can go up and over the Dials and then go the long way home, through Preston Park, yeah?'

For a minute she thinks he might not reply but when he does it's more words than she's expecting.

'Yeah. I'd like that, LG. Let's do that.'

'Okay. Well, hang on a minute. I'll tell Mum.'

As she jogs down the road to where Mum's standing with her shopping bag between her feet, she's aware that she means that. She'll tell Mum. She won't ask Mum. That won't be how it goes now.

'Mum, we're gonna walk, me and Malc, up and over and home through Preston Park. Can you take my notebook and pen?'

'Oh. Oh, well, if you want to dear. That's probably good for Malcy to get some fresh air. But you be careful on the roads, won't you?'

'Yes. And, Mum, you're just going to get some bits in Fine Fayre, just some bread and milk and then veg at the market, yeah?'

'That's right dear, then the 26 up the hill.'

It's as close as she can get to saying,

And not drink. You're not buying drink.

It would be better to go with her, to watch what she put in the basket, but she can't be everywhere and Malcy's waiting for her.

'See you later.'

The route they take is far from direct, heading West first, to the Seven Dials, where roads stretch out into Brighton and Hove. They follow Dyke Road and walk along talking, reminiscing about the times when they were small and they used to come up this way with Dad and Grandad. Malcy's voice is definitely deeper now – it's come out of the rasp, the huskiness caused by the damage, as something transformed. He stops for a moment, clearly ready to say something difficult and she waits for the words to come.

'Mum said she couldn't even tell him, you know?'

'Dad?'

'Yeah. He's done a real disappearing act on us, hasn't he?'

She thinks about the letter she wrote and about watching it burn.

'Yeah.'

They sit for a minute on a bench outside a small museum. Malcy nods at the burgundy and gold painted sign.

Booth Bird Museum

'He brought us here once, didn't he? D'ya wanna go in? It's free, I think.'

Little Gold looks at the stone steps, the broad double door. She remembers the museum well – the glass cases stretching from floor to ceiling, labelled with black and gold lacquered signs that name the inhabitants. Inside them, every type of bird you could imagine, from puffins to golden eagles, clutches of songbirds and tall waders, nightingales and barn owls. All of them glass-eyed and the air tangy with something, something they use to keep the death at bay.

'Nah. Let's go on. We can go down The Steepest Hill in The World. Then we can go through Preston Park. There might be matches on.'

Malcy laughs at her using the silly name, what they used to call The Drove, the road that will drop them down into the valley where Preston Park is spread out across several acres.

It's Saturday afternoon, so men will be playing football there. They're not professionals, of course they're not, but they have kits and seem to take it pretty seriously, doing all the roaring and thundering about. They don't do so much of the name-calling though, the poof and spaz. And there's no playground like in their park.

'Okay then. Steepest Hill and then Preston Park. I've got 15p so we could get a Panda Pop at the café if you want. Split it.'

'Cherry?'

'No way. Orange.'

As Malcy stands, the scarf slips from his pocket onto the bench and she picks it up.

'Here, Malc. You don't wanna lose this.'

Little Gold forces herself to watch as he winds the smooth, white scarf around his neck. It's just a scarf.

CHAPTER THIRTY-NINE

Out

'Don't go too far, Margaret!' Dad
against the sky.
Ripple around her ankles banded light
and dark with shadow. Suck
and suck of wet sand softening.
Barrel organ music.
Trickle and leap of tiny breakers rushing
around her toes.

In

'Put him in here!'
Green crab between her fingers, dropped
in a jar of sunlight and brine.
Bob of her hair, iridescent, moving, stroking
the skin at the nape of her neck.
'I love you, Enid.'
'Don't say that.'

Out

Railway lines. Strips of silver.
Toes of shoes on the platform edge.
Liquid sky pouring over the glass roof,
streaming and blurring,
her gaze down the tracks.
Shrinking, shrinking
away to nothing,
the vanishing
tail of a
leaving
train.

In

Pebbles grinding on her spine.
Beyond his face the navy sky, the inky sea
all shush and shush
as the strings of light run
the length of the pier.

Out

Heavy bolt and knuckles to her belly
grinding and praying the red blood out.
Wipe again. Crackle of paper,
resolutely white.

In

Table in the back room, chenille fringe,
Mum's best tablecloth.
'A man. He bought me cherry brandy.'
'Get her out of my sight.'
Slut.

Out

Monkey-tight grip. Twisting,
twisting to free her ink-stained finger.
Pearl glass panels in the dark green door.
A woman, indistinct, bending.

In

'Call me Peggy.'
Lips on a cigarette.
A shrouded, clouded moon. The town
blacked-out below her. Waiting
for the dawn.

Out

Pen nib over a column of figures. A call
on the office phone.
A gull-screech.
The crematorium.
Daffodils in sodden beds.
Mum tilts the urn. Dad whipped away
across the muddy grass.

In

The taste of gin on urgent lips. Stockings
on the back of a chair. A gas-fire hiss.
The arch of her back. Anonymous,
broken cry.

Out

Vern beside a dew pond, mirror-
still and flecked with grass.
Shirt-sleeves rolled, pale skin
pinking, flicking his ash
and tossing the butt. Beyond
him the scut of a white-tailed rabbit
disappears into the gorse.

In

'You're beautiful. You are, you
are…' fingertips on her scalp.
Warm pennies dropped.
appreciation,
revelation,
love.

Out

Vi holding a pottery handle, sheered
from the body of the squat teapot.
'What have you done, woman!'
Laughter transforming,
rocking her back-lit frame.

In

A warmth on her lap, a length of sleeping,
thrumming weight of cat. A book
in her hand. No dialogue.

Out

Lifting, bearing
the body of the boy.
Her voice through gritted teeth.
'Do not let this child go. Do not.
Do not let him go.'

In

Flint garden walls, green paper pennies
falling from the elms.
Brighton rolling away to the sparkle.
Little Gold.
Riding her bike along the pavement, shimmering,
calling out.
'Hello, Peggy Baxter!'
She's ever-closer, close enough
to touch.

Out

Peggy opens her eyes. At the end of the ward a nurse is sitting in a pool of lamplight. The pool widens, darkness receding in its path. The light rolls on through the night-time hospital, gulping down the rows of beds. It floods the deserted operating theatres and the empty waiting rooms. Finally, it pours through Peggy's open eyes and bursts the walls of her mind. All that remains is ripple and glow.

CHAPTER FORTY

The tree's in blossom. Little Gold, undoing the zip of her school skirt, can see the bright white burst of it out of her bedroom window. One of the best things about inheriting Ali's room is that she can see her tree every time she glances out. She keeps her eyes on its swaying canopy now, as she slips out of her blouse, trying not to register the gleam of the bra underneath. It takes only a moment to get her jeans and sweatshirt on, and her new baseball boots that Ali bought for her, and then she scampers down the stairs, through the kitchen and out the back door.

As she braces her curled foot against the trunk, hauls with her arms, she feels the crust of the school day falling away and, settled in her branch, she can breathe again.

The people living in Peggy Baxter's house have a dog, some sort of Jack Russell thing that runs in tight circles around the back lawn. It's scuffed the grass away to nothing and sometimes Little Gold imagines she can hear the tight thoughts in its head.

Gotta go, gotta go, gotta go

It's doing it now, skirting the top of the steps by a margin that makes her feel sick, that makes her imagine it in the air, yelping, twisting as it falls.

She shuts her eyes and pictures Shaw on the lawn instead, rolling over for her to stroke his dense, silken belly. And then she sees his green eyes, his broad, watchful face peeping through the bars of the wicker cat basket as Vi lifted him into her car.

'I can't guarantee he'll write, Little Gold. Cats are very unreliable. But I shall.'

And Vi does write, in a slanted, flowing script full of

exclamation marks and dashes. And every letter ends with the same sentences.

And how are you Little Golden One? Write and tell Vi all about it.

Sometimes, when she's lying on her bed composing a reply, Little Gold is certain Peggy Baxter is behind her, just over her left shoulder, reading. It's second-best to visiting her in the churchyard and perhaps, in the end, it'll be better even than that.

There's the sea lion laugh in her mind and the voice.

'Ha! That's it, get yourself swayed by a pretty face and a bit of charm and leave old Peggy down the road on her own.'

She replies aloud, because why shouldn't she? Up here there's no-one else to mind, except the blackbird that's watching her from the back fence.

'You know I'll never do that.'

'So I should hope.'

That you can continue to talk to dead people and not actually be mad, that's been a shock. That dead people seem to reply is somehow less surprising. And the gap, the fact that the gap won't ever close, that's just something you have to carry. And she does.

The woman from Peggy Baxter's house calls the dog and it pulls up short next to the flowerbed, turns and plunges down the steps. She hears the slam of the back door and tries not to mind about how rough they seem to be with everything, how little care they're taking of the house. Peggy Baxter's house. Her house.

That letter had come a few days after the funeral and, for a moment, Little Gold had wondered if it was a thank you note, as if Peggy Baxter had dropped her a line to thank her for attending at the crematorium on the hill, on that windy day. Of course, it wasn't. It came in an A4 envelope with a thick sheaf of typed pages, headed with a sequence of surnames in block letters and the addition, *Solicitors and Notaries*.

Dear Little Gold,

My solicitor, Mr Lemkin, will have contacted you to explain that you are the chief beneficiary of my will. Apart from some special things for Vi and my friends, everything I have to leave I am leaving to you. I don't have lots of money in the bank but I have my house and you must sell it.

It would be very sensible to help your mum sort out any debts or other financial worries she might have. Certainly you should spend any money you need to be secure living in your house. But then put the rest away. Put it away and carry on growing up. I won't say a word about how you should do that, except to say I have every faith that you will do it well and you will be a fine person always.

I am so very glad I was able to meet you and have you as my friend.

With love,

Peggy Baxter

P.S. I'm afraid I did have to use your official name, as it were, for the legal side of things. But please be assured that I know who you really are.

And so the house, empty of Peggy Baxter's things, echoey and marked with ghost picture frames, had been handed into the care of an Estate Agent from Fiveways and, in just a few weeks, had been sold.

Always a popular area but on the up, I think. Ideal family home.

And there they are, the noisy family with the Jack Russell and curly-haired boys who play cricket. They must have the kitchen window open because she can hear one of the boys.

'Hey! Mark, you idiot…'

Movement from below makes Little Gold glance down into the yard. Malcy's on his way up the steps, still in his uniform, the sleeves of his jumper yanked down over his hands in the way he's taken to doing.

He stops below the tree and looks up at her.

'Mum says tea soon.'

'Okay.'

He pulls himself up just enough for them to be face-to-face, his forearm braced along the sitting branch, his hand still hidden up the sleeve, giving him an inefficient paw-like grip.

'You're jammy, still fitting up here.'

His shoulders have broadened into a bony coat hanger and he twists them sideways to lock himself in place.

'I know. Don't 'spose I will forever though.'

'I dunno. Women can be pretty small. Mum is.'

Little Gold considers Mum up the tree. It's true, she probably would fit.

Malcy slithers down and stands there, his head bowed, white petals lying in his hair.

'Sorry, Malc.'

'Doesn't matter, div.'

When he looks up she can see it for a moment, a dark line like ink rising from within the pale skin of his throat. She blinks and it disappears. It happens less and less. Maybe one day she'll stop seeing it altogether. But the night screaming, the way Malcy shreds the skin around his finger nails with his constant, burrowing teeth, that just seems to go on and no-one can stop it.

'You coming in for tea then?'

There's something she needs to do first.

'In a minute, yeah?'

'Okay.'

He walks down the steps, brushing the pale blossom from his black school uniform.

Little Gold reaches into her jeans pocket and slowly extracts a small parcel. As she unwraps it from the crumpled white tissue, the thing inside gleams.

Vi brought them the day after the funeral, her crisp voice drifting upstairs on a wave of her perfume.

'I need to see her in person because these are a special delivery. She said they had to come by hand. And she gave me the job of courier.'

Little Gold weighs the bird in her palm. It's the dip-eyed owl, his pupils tiny black beads in his crystal face. Nothing about him is real – he's got squared-off claws and a head too large for his body. He's just a suggestion really, a hint of what an owl might be, in all its majesty and mystery. It isn't even night-time, it's barely dusk, as she lifts the owl, held carefully between forefinger and thumb.

'There we are.'

Peggy Baxter replies.

'Ah, my tiny pieces of freedom.'

'Yes.'

And Little Gold holds the glass owl steady against the sky, its body filled with gloaming and possibility. She hopes it might know, almost, how it feels to really fly.

ACKNOWLEDGEMENTS

Many thanks to my editor, Lauren Parsons, and all the team at Legend Press. Finding a home for *Little Gold* is the fulfilment of a dream.

I would not have got close to that dream had it not been for the input of my dedicated agent, Veronique Baxter. She saw promise in *Little Gold* when the book was just a sketch of its final form and never let me lose sight of the goal of publication.

Thanks to Kerry Hudson, who tutored me at an Arvon course in 2014. As well as being an inspiration as a writer, she set up the Womentoring Project that put me in touch with my mentor, Catherine Hall. Catherine encouraged me to believe in the quality of my work and to seek representation. Having validation from such talented women pushed me on and I'm grateful.

My writing group – Nikki, Lisa, Suzanna, Sandi, Deb and Lucy – kept me going with love, criticism, wine and crisps. Sharing each other's successes has been a real joy and I know Eira would be pleased for us all.

I appreciate the lively creative community of Brighton and Hove that makes our city a place of such verve and fizz. I've had opportunities to learn, share, read and perform with a lot of inspiring folk.

I am lucky to have a wide and wonderful circle of friends. I would be lost without them. To all those who helped me with this project, from reading drafts to promising to buy the book one day, I say a heartfelt thanks.

I have my dear Buffaloes to thank for keeping my head above

water many a time and for supporting without judgement. May t
and Tunnocks always see us through.

Thank you to my family – Mum and Jenn, Dad and Gi
my brothers, Jon and Biff, and their families. To the out-law
cousins, nephews and nieces, and all in the tribe who ever ask
how the book was coming along, thank you.

Pearl and Leo, thank you for being your brilliant selves. Bei
a mum to such determined and imaginative individuals feeds n
mind and heart in many ways. And you make me laugh. Than
for growing up now and giving me the time to write.

Thanks, most of all, to Dani for being Dani. This book, a
much else besides, would not exist without her wisdom, courag
integrity and warm heart.